SMUGGLER QUEEN

BOOK FOUR OF
CHIMERA COMPANY

Tim C. Taylor

Theogony Books
Coinjock, NC

Chris Kennedy/Theogony Books
1097 Waterlily Rd.
Coinjock, NC 27923
http://chriskennedypublishing.com/

Publisher's Note: This is a work of fiction. Names, characters, places, and incidents are a product of the author's imagination. Locales and public names are sometimes used for atmospheric purposes. Any resemblance to actual people, living or dead, or to businesses, companies, events, institutions, or locales is completely coincidental.

Cover art and design by Vincent Sammy.

Ordering Information:
Quantity sales. Special discounts are available on quantity purchases by corporations, associations, and others. For details, contact the "Special Sales Department" at the address above.

Smuggler Queen/Tim C. Taylor -- 1st ed.
ISBN: 978-1648551673

Chapter One:
Lily Hjon

Hundra-7

L ily satisfied herself that her gauntlets and boots would hold her fast against the contours of the ice cliff and that her center of gravity was safely over her footholds. Only then did she allow herself a few moments of rest.

How far had she climbed?

Halfway?

She glanced behind her, hoping to see *Ghost Shark* standing on the leveled ground of the shore of the methane lake.

But she couldn't. Her suit was rated for hostile environments, and the bulky helmet wouldn't let her head turn that far. Maybe its designers regarded that as a feature, not a flaw. What you couldn't see couldn't terrorize you.

She should be able to set up a rear camera view in her HUD, but until she trained the suit's rudimentary intelligence to learn her voice, it was far too irritating to use.

She tightened her grip further—though her fingers dug no deeper because the water-ice of the cliff was hard as granite at this temperature—and twisted her torso so she could look down to the cliff's base.

The rocky ground was littered with dirty water-ice boulders that shimmered and blurred. This was the effect of the petrochemical smog. It reduced the visual spectrum to a narrow band running all the way from rusty water to stale nicotine.

Despite the smeared visuals, she confidently judged she had ascended about 250 feet.

That was good. She'd made it a little better than halfway.

But when she looked up, she felt a kick of worry. The cliff had been so sharply defined when they had looked up from the valley floor. From her ledge, the summit was hidden in the smog. The cliff appeared to go on forever. Worse, her climbing companion had disappeared too.

"Activate comms! Captain, I have lost eyes on you. What's your status, over?"

"*Activating cooling system.*"

"No, you stupid suit. Cancel cooling!"

"*Warning! Ambient temperature is 108 Kelvin.*"

"I know. It's as cold as the Second Hell. Cancel cooling system!"

"*Comm system not active. Warning! Ambient temperature is 108 Kelvin. Danger of death.*"

Lily took a moment to calm herself. 108 Kelvin. That was around -160 Celsius. They were numbers on scales named after long dead Earth people—men, most likely—that represented a sweltering heat in comparison with the vacuum of deep space she was more used to. There was a crucial difference. Space was a perfect insulator, which meant the environmental controls spent more time preventing you from boiling in your suit than keeping you warm. But here on Hundra-7, the atmosphere was soupy thick. And that meant you could lose heat all too quickly.

Her cheeks burned with cold, and her fingers were numbing. Not good 250 feet up a cliff face.

She wasn't supposed to be here at all. Sybutu had trained in the suit until the captain had asked her to take his place, just before leaving the ship.

Lily puffed out her chest and tried to emulate the clipped growl of the Legion sergeant.

"Cancel cooling system!"

"*Cooling system canceled.*"

A gentle warmth blew over her face. Heat spread through her gauntlets.

She was still enjoying it when her helmet beeped.

"Everything all right, Hjon?" enquired a cheerful voice.

"Just taking a breather, sir."

"While I understand the temptation to stop and take vacation snaps of the strange worlds we visit, you should resist the urge until *after* we finish the job."

"Roger that, sir," she replied through gritted teeth. She raised one hand, dislodging a cloud of the powdery hydrocarbon snow that coated the ice cliff, before closing her grip around a higher handhold.

"And less of the *sir*, Lily. I don't want my team to sound too military."

"Don't think Sergeant Sybutu has received that memo yet, Captain." She pushed up the cliff, not pausing for breath this time. She was determined to catch up with the space mountain goat of a captain.

"Would it help if I throw rope down to you?"

Yes, it would, she thought. "Not necessary," was what she said.

She was making rapid progress now. The cliff was steep, but there were plenty of routes that weren't sheer vertical faces and overhangs. Confidence mattered, she decided. Fitz had it in this situation. She didn't. Not yet.

Soon, he emerged from the dirty clouds. He dangled one-handed from an overhanging ledge and was observing her progress.

She slowed, just for a moment, and tried to firm her thoughts about this man so they would stay still and make sense.

This was an inhospitable environment. An unrepaired suit breach would kill them long before they could get back to the ship. And yet, the annoying show off was dangling off a cliff. Then there was the way he'd drugged his jacks back on Eiylah-Bremah to put them where he wanted while he went off on an interstellar tangent. That should have left Sybutu and his men wanting to slit Fitz's throat, and yet, they hadn't.

There was something special about him. It was very difficult to dislike Captain Fitz, no matter how much you wanted to.

Perhaps the environment suit was protecting her from his aura because she didn't trust him now.

One last scramble, and she'd be with him. She reached for the next handhold.

She half felt, half heard her foothold ledge snap. Then she was dropping three hundred feet to the valley floor below.

Momentarily, she was confused by the slowness with which she fell in the 0.37g. She swung both hands forward, fingers outstretched, and rammed them into the cliff face.

They slid on the greasy petrochemical snow…and came away. Now, she was not only falling but tumbling backward!

She tucked her lower legs behind her as best she could in the cumbersome suit and activated the thruster pack control panel beneath her left wrist. It wasn't voice-activated. In fact, it used the same interface she was familiar with from a regular spacesuit.

When the puff of reaction gas buoyed her up, she directed it to nudge her onto the cliff. She reached out and gently slid down the sooty ice until her toes found a narrow ledge, and she was once more secure.

She prayed silently, not really sure to whom she was directing her prayers. Not the Immortal Empress of the Legion cult, that was for sure.

Her eyes closed as she waited for her heart to cease pounding. *Don't say a word, Captain.* She wasn't in the mood for one of Fitz's quips.

But his reply wasn't spoken. When she looked up, a rope was dangling just above her head.

"It's secure," Fitz told her. He had disappeared in the smoke once more. "Trust me."

Sweat ran down into Lily's eyes. She blinked it away, but that only stung, and there was no way to wipe it clear.

Doesn't look like I have a choice, she mused and reached for the rope.

* * *

Lily cursed the captain as she used the rope to pull herself up. The higher she climbed, though, the more she redirected her curses toward Lord Khallini. They were on Hundra-7 to give him the same information about the buried mystery ship they'd used to get Nyluga-Ree off their backs. The Hundra system was uninhabited, so she wondered why they couldn't have tight-beamed the data from orbit. Even if you accepted the need to deliver the data in person, *Ghost Shark* could have deposited them closer to the coordinates Khallini called home, but the sorcerer had made them park a ways out and come to him on foot.

On this, at least, Lily couldn't fault the captain, because Lord Khallini was the kind of person who didn't need to explain himself. When she pulled herself to the summit, her grumbling faded.

The view from the top was astonishing.

It was also daunting.

She'd reached a dirty-yellow ice plateau. It gently descended to dunes that rose like enormous toffee embankments from a sea of oily rust flakes. Compared with Earth (a planet no one had set foot on for thousands of years, but was still the yardstick for most measurements), the gravitational pull trying to flatten the dunes was weak, allowing them to rise hundreds of feet into the smog. Prevailing winds blew them so they ran transverse to the route she and Fitz needed to take. Without a detour of a hundred klicks or more, the only way ahead was over the top, and she could see at least three rows of dunes.

Beyond them, something glinted in the distance. She hoped it was the methane river they'd seen as they descended in the ship, but it was difficult to tell in the haze.

For the first time, Lily began to wonder whether she could make it that far.

"I admit," said Fitz, "I didn't think the dunes looked like much of an obstacle when I saw them from *Ghost Shark*. But now that I see them in the flesh…" He drew a sharp breath.

"That sounds about right," Lily said with a chuckle. "With our luck, 'in the flesh' won't be a figure of speech. Those dunes will be living organisms. Woman-eating carnivores we'll sink into and be slowly digested over weeks."

"Oh, dear. I hadn't considered that."

Shit! Fitz sounded genuinely scared.

"You mean like the badlands of Psonex-43?" he asked. "Except the rock trolls of that benighted place keep their victims paralyzed, but alive, for decades. Meanwhile, their half-mineral, half-organic offspring grow within their victims' flesh."

"You're kidding, right?"

"Am I? These dunes won't hurt you, Hjon. Catkins got me the readout on the way down. They are this world's equivalent of snow dunes. Amino acids, ammonia, propane, adenine, esters, and lipids galore—a frozen primordial soup passed through a grinder. They won't hurt you. Not unless you feel a sudden urge to emulate Bronze and take up smoking."

Lily strode down the long slope toward the first dune. "Quit yacking and suck it up. I've had my share of pointless physical training, and I bet you have too, boss."

"In my youth, perhaps." Fitz bounded forward to catch up. He kept pace, a companionable distance to one side.

They walked the first klick in silence. Even in his heavy-duty environment suit, Fitz radiated cheerfulness. What was it about him? When she wasn't paying attention, she'd started to like him for no reason she could explain. She began to wonder whether she was being drugged or whether she was caught in a subtle form of mind control. Maybe likeability was his special mutant power?

As her explanations became more outlandish, the sound of her breathing and the deep churning rumble of the suit's life-support systems grew louder.

The walk was easy. Gravity was low, the hydrocarbon snow was a shallow covering over hard ice, and although the suit didn't have muscle amplification, its energy return system was highly efficient.

"Why am I here, Captain?" Immediately, she felt relief at having broken the silence.

"Because no one could wish for a finer companion, Hjon."

Lily found herself laughing at the teasing in Fitz's bullshit. "No, really. Sybutu is the senior Marine. He was supposed to come with you until you changed your mind at the last moment. Zavage has his…mind-reading tentacle lumps. Bronze is a spy who knows more than he's letting on. I think we all know the same could be said for Enthree, and Colonel Lantosh left to wage her own secret war. That leaves just me and Darant. I have the tattoo. He has the goat. So why me?"

"The decision was not last moment."

"Well, no one told…Oh, I get it. It's a stupid test. Get me off balance and see how I perform."

"The way you put it, I sound like some kind of monster." Fitz cleared his throat. "My apologies, Hjon. Sybutu gave me a stern talking to about my having to earn trust. More than once. I have much to learn too."

"That's very true, but you haven't explained why you picked me."

"We need to retrieve Vetch from Nyluga-Ree's sweaty clutches. And we shall succeed. What then? Sergeant Osu Sybutu and Sergeant Vetch Arunsen. Compare and contrast as potential leaders of my Marine contingent."

Lily found herself chuckling again. How did Fitz put her at such ease? "They're twins. Mirror images. Sybutu is a ramrod straight jack with a buzz cut, dark skin, and Legion to the core. Vetch is the palest human I've ever known who wasn't ill. He's irreverent and defiant, and his beard is bejeweled. For the past two years, coaching him to be the best NCO in the Militia has been my side project. Sybutu is Vetch's Legion equivalent, without my mentoring. They're two rounds from the same clip. Everyone can see it but them. In fact, they're *too* similar. They will butt heads with each other no matter who's in charge. They can't help it. Making them joint squad leaders would be even worse. Which means…"

Lily halted. She could feel her boots sink into the smog snow.

It felt like a bad omen when the skies chose that moment to drop fat blobs of methane rain, which carved streaks through the smog and splattered against her faceplate.

"You see my problem," Fitz said.

"I'm not commanding anything. I'm Trooper Lily Hjon, and that's how it's going to be."

"Face it, Hjon, you were hung out to dry by the Militia and publicly humiliated for the encouragement of others. After the events on Eiylah-Bremah, I think we can say that, among our many other problems, you and the other Raven Company survivors are considered traitors and deserters. I expect the jacks are too."

"The thought has crossed my mind. I can't ever go back."

"To the Militia, no. As for coming in from the outlaw cold, that's a different matter. You've seen bad people thrive because they cover their tracks by pulling strings. Well, good people can do it too…if they have the right friends."

"You mean Lord Khallini?"

"Possibly. I haven't pasted it all together yet. However, we've joined up with people who believe they have the power to seize control of the entire Federation. They will protect their assets. That includes you. I believe you were a fine officer once, Hjon. I want you as my Marine commander. Think about it."

"If I say no?"

"I believe it will be time for Hubert the Goat to show the galaxy what he can do."

* * *

"It's easy to let the universe grind us down," said Fitz. "Which is why she provides wonders like this for those who search for them. It's beautiful."

"Copy that." Lily's whisper was swallowed by the waterfall's roar.

Having crossed the soot dunes, they'd followed the methane river upstream to this majestic spectacle. The scale, the power, the sheer physical presence of the phenomenon was humbling, but what made it so special in her eyes was the purity of its color.

After a landscape entirely constructed from sludgy yellows and sticky browns, the methane shed its impurities as it tumbled the hundreds of feet to the pool below, transforming into a delicate powder blue. Even the rain had stopped to allow the view to be enjoyed in all its wonder.

Moored nearby was a simple raft with a pair of outboard motors. At its banks, the methane river had lost its color purity. The edges of the raft were coated in what looked like foaming beer crusted with dark yeast flakes.

"I guess the raft's for us," said Lily. "But how do we get into Khallini's base?"

"I expect we're supposed to figure it out as we go. Don't worry. That's my specialty."

They boarded the raft, and Fitz steered it toward the center of the waterfall. The sheets of methane pummeled them with ever-increasing ferocity, making visibility difficult.

At the point where Lily calculated the raft should have been at the fiercest heart of the waterfall, the pounding ceased. She was drenched in methane—barely blue pools of the liquid almost covered the floor of the raft—and the noise was still deafening, but they were in a clear channel the waterfall would not touch.

"Told you so." Fitz sounded cheerful. "Three of my favorite words."

"Force field?" she speculated.

"Sorcery," Fitz replied. "Or so I've heard."

They moored at a jetty on the far side of the methane waterfall and were met by a droid floating in the air. It was a messy composite of small modules, each uniquely shaped. The machine was about a meter across.

"What is your name, droid?" Lily asked, hoping to get on the machine's good side.

"My name is Andrus. I don't appreciate the term droid. I find it demeaning."

"If you're not a droid," she said, "what are you?"

"I have explained. I am an Andrus. I am *the* Andrus. I'm as alive as you are, unidentified human and Captain Fitzwilliam. The only difference between you and me is that I converse with my creator every day."

"What makes you think I don't?" Fitz asked.

Andrus zipped in front of the captain. "What makes you think I care? Hand over the goods, Fitzwilliam."

"The goods?" Fitz laughed. "Here you are." He presented a data chip.

Andrus puffed gas over it, waved it in front of a variety of sensors that emerged from its casing, and then inserted it in a port.

"The contents are acceptable," Andrus announced. "Follow me through the showers. Can't have all those hydrocarbons exploding when we get inside. Once you've scrubbed up, I shall lead you to the Creator."

* * *

"You were supposed to come alone, Fitzwilliam. That's one of the reasons your landing field is a short trek away."

"I decided I needed a friend," said Fitz. "You can be quite a scary fellow."

The old man shot a look at Lily. Saw right through to her soul.

She took a step back on the painted wooden floor, gasping for breath. She'd just been pistol whipped mentally. Or psychically. Maybe spiritually? She didn't know what had happened, but she surely didn't like it.

The experience was too similar to the last time she'd encountered Khallini, back on that bloody mess of an operation on Lose-Viborg. The sorcerer had paralyzed her that time. She'd gotten away lightly compared with the jacks trying to kill him.

"Lily Hjon. You wore pigtails last time we met." Khallini licked his cracked lips as he considered her with a leer. She'd had men leer over her before plenty of times, but this was worse. He wasn't seeing her as a woman. Not even as a human being. He studied her the way a taxidermist might consider where to place a new find within his collection. The jerk gave her serious creeps.

"As an adolescent," he rasped, "you wished for a career as a historian, but your father wouldn't hear of it. Isn't it better to make history than to catch distorted echoes of what has already transpired? That's what your father told you. Do you agree with him now?"

"I was angry with him at the time," she replied, determined not to show the shock she was feeling inside that he knew her secrets. "But I don't do regrets. Can't afford them. So, yeah, I prefer to make history rather than read about it. Just like Dad said I would."

Khallini tapped the floor with his brass-topped cane, the perfect acoustics of the room amplifying the sound. The Receiving Room, Andrus had called it before departing for *less demeaning duties*. In its vaulted roof and shiny mounted knickknacks that were probably priceless, there was a precision to the room's opulence that was not reflected in its owner.

On Lose-Viborg, Khallini had looked the part of an aristo with wealth enough to own entire worlds and every person upon them. Here, he was dressed in a belted smock. Wisps of dark hair sprouted from his liver-spotted head and tumbled halfway down his back.

He was a crinkled gnome caught in his palatial lair. Only his polished cane suggested wealth and power.

Khallini turned to Fitz. "Congratulations, Captain. You surround yourself with interesting people." He gave Lily a small bow. "Hjon is acceptable as your guest."

That was *enough!* This wizard had plunged inside her mind as if he owned her. Lily's blood finally boiled over. "I'm glad I'm acceptable, *old man.*"

Fitz sputtered, "Please, Lily. Show respect."

Khallini laughed. "Respect is for the respectable, Captain, and I was never that. Always an outsider. Never wanted except when I was needed."

"My apologies, my lord," said Fitz.

"My lord? I reject that title too. I was never an aristocrat. It is merely a label that has some modest value but has bored me for some time." He turned to Lily with a twinkle in his rheumy, old eyes. "Your captain, though…he is a genuine aristocrat. At least in the sense that when the Exiles first came here, they briefly flirted with feudalistic titles. In those days, they were intellectually stunted children, having to learn for themselves the treacherous contours of political liberty. With nothing to build upon, they designed what they thought were new systems of governance, criminal justice, education, economics, and hierarchy. Though in their ignorance, they mostly copied their past and repeated the mistakes of their forebears. Did you learn that in your history classes, Hjon?"

"That's not the consensus."

"I don't care about *consensus*. I care only for facts. The Exiles made many mistakes in the early years, and you would do well to remember that. The dead-end flirtation with neo-feudalism was the least of their errors."

"There are aristocrats today," Lily pointed out.

"True. An upper-class elite self-appointed itself. It always does in one form or another."

Fitz joined in. "As with the Outer Corellian Commerce Guild, sir."

"You mean the smugglers. I have arranged payment, Fitzwilliam. You will have the funds to pay any remaining debts to Nyluga-Ree. The financial ones, anyway."

Fitz sighed. "If only it were that simple."

"I am aware that Ree still has a hold over you. She has a member of your team as a hostage. But I can free this person for you."

"For a price," Fitz accused.

"Naturally. Before I reclaim your hostage, there is something I need Nyluga-Ree to see. I fear that if I were to compel her, she would resist and be killed. Therefore you will kidnap her and bring her to a specified location."

Fitz laughed. "Wait…are you serious?"

"I find that when you've lived as long as I have, Captain Fitzwilliam, it is difficult to be other than serious. Seeing the playfulness that is so evident in you is bittersweet for me. It is a skill of the mind that, once lost, I don't believe can ever be relearned. I've heard every joke, every wry observation on life, and no matter how excellent the rendition, I've seen it done better. It is good that humans have such short lives, because otherwise you would realize what a sham it is when you tell yourselves that you are all unique individuals. I see clearly that you are the echoes of those who went before you. As your descendants will echo you, and their descendants them. And someone or something will eventually come along from this uncaring universe and wipe you all out. Only then will the echoes cease."

"You profess a tragic philosophy, my lord."

"And yet an inevitable one. I also find it difficult to laugh because I find it difficult to care about you. Surrounded in my abode with my AI companions, I don't need anyone else for my own contentment. However, that leaves me disconnected from regular people, and I now need to reconnect. I need to care. That is why I commissioned you to take me in person to Rho-Torkis. And why I wanted to see you here in the flesh."

"Is it working?" asked Lily. "Because, let me tell you, I've had better *chinwags*."

"Perhaps a little." The old man gave her another piercing look, and she felt as if a corpse's gnarled fingernails were scratching at her soul. "I know it can be done. In fact, it was one of your friends, Hjon, who tried to smash my head with an oversized war hammer. The situation was so beautifully ludicrous that I spared his life. Later the same day, I thought back on the incident and laughed for the first time in centuries."

"His name is Vetch Arunsen," said Lily. "He is the crewmate Nyluga-Ree took hostage."

A look of surprise came over the old man. Lily could almost hear the desiccated skin crack as it stretched into near-forgotten contours. "Careful, Captain," he rasped. "Your people are beginning to intrigue me."

"May I ask one question before we depart, Lord Khallini?"

"One? I perceive several burning in your mind. Very well, but only one. Choose carefully."

"If you find it so difficult to care about mere mortals, why are you interested in capturing the Nyluga? Why do you care about her?"

Nice one! Lily had been wondering the same thing.

"Come now, Captain. Isn't it obvious? Why should I care about anyone other than my AI companions? You can answer that yourself."

Lily sensed that behind his dark glasses, Fitz was stumped by this response. So was she. Regular people were just bugs to this ancient freak. Why *would* he care?

Fitz clicked his fingers. "Of course! The only person you care about is yourself. The only reason you need Ree—the reason you invited me here—is because you need us. And you need us because you're afraid."

Was there the barest nod from the old man? "Very well done, Captain."

Khallini transitioned from warmed-up corpse to deadly threat in a nanosecond. He snatched out his right hand and dragged Lily out of her body. With his left, he reached out toward Fitz, yelling at him, "The knowledge that something out there in the galaxy scares me should paralyze you with terror."

Lily was experiencing all this from a distance, her mind floating outside her static body. It was like being evicted from your home and watching from the street outside as it was put on the market. Literally *watching.*

Gods, her mobile tattoo was looking good!

This stupid, random thought shook some sense into her. And since she was out of the fight, outgunned by Khallini's sorcery, she stopped thinking about her own nightmare and concentrated on Fitz's.

Use your fancy hand cannon, she willed him. *Blow the creep's warty head off.*

"Get out of my skragging mind!" Fitz screamed. He fought against an invisible resistance to push his arm down toward his thigh holster, but he was losing that battle. Fitz was about six feet away from Khallini's clawed hand, the tendons and veins standing out from the captain's neck like steel cords. She felt sure they would snap because she knew Fitz well enough to know he would never give in.

Come on you stubborn bastard. Fight him!

Cut off from her body, Lily could only think the words, but Khallini shot her a penetrating look, and she knew he had heard her. By Orion's Balls, *he could read her sodding mind!*

"Your captain refuses to divulge the information I wish to take from his head," he told her. "I can extract it anyway, but I don't wish to break him. After all, he is currently an important contractor of mine. Whereas you—" he squeezed the hand aimed at Lily, thrusting her back into her body, simultaneously choking her, "—you are mere *decoration.*"

The roaring in Lily's ears drowned out her pitiful gasps. She clutched at her throat, trying to prize away the invisible hands clawing at her windpipe. But there was nothing there! Was he screwing with her mind? Was she imagining being choked?

He raised his hand, and Lily felt herself lifted off the wooden floor. Her toes brushed the wood.

It was real all right! She pulled frantically at the invisible force at her neck, but she tired quickly.

The world was falling away.

Colors were fading to gray.

Fitz drew his hand cannon.

"Don't threaten me!" Khallini roared at him. "I will hear your mind instructing your finger to squeeze the trigger, and I will kill you before the message is received."

"I call bullshit. Release Hjon."

"When you lay down your weapon and let me into your mind. Then I will release your friend. You are no threat to me."

"I've started counting down in my head," Fitz told him. "When I get to zero, we'll find out who's telling the truth, punk."

"Punk!" Khallini snorted. "How strangely words echo and distort through the ages. Very well. I doubt you could do as you say, but perhaps you are right. It is, in any case, a more satisfying challenge to influence people the old-fashioned way."

The vise around Lily's throat vanished. She collapsed to the floor, pulling heaving breaths into her lungs.

"Yeah," Fitz told Khallini. "Go old school, you wizened old skragg. Get what you want through memos and subliminal messages hidden in videos of cute animals in zero-g. Same as the rest of us." He thumbed a control on the grip of his F-Cannon, activating a whirring noise that could as easily be chambering a round as readying a spell in his weird alien handgun.

With his barrel trained on Khallini's head, Fitz advanced a step toward the sorcerer, leaning heavily into the movement as if he were heading into a hurricane. "We need to be clear on just one thing, my lord. Don't *ever* mess with my people!"

Khallini laughed. It began as a snigger but built into a full-strength chuckle. His laughter poured out like a stagnant stream that had been dammed for centuries and desperately needed to be drained because something trapped inside had putrefied.

Fitz sidestepped to Lily's position. "You okay?" he asked, without taking his aim from Khallini, whose laughter had not yet abated. *Crazy old creep.*

She rubbed her neck, but she felt no pain there. "I've survived worse. I don't fancy Khallini's chances, though, when I get my hands on him. Did he really call me *decoration?*"

"I intended no offense, Hjon," said Khallini. "I merely meant that you are nothing more than background detail. Whether you live or die is of no consequence to the galaxy."

"Yeah," said Lily. "Cause none of that would be offensive."

"I told you I intended no offense. I did not say I cared whether you felt offended. Hjon, Fitzwilliam, I withdraw all threats. Neither of you has anything to fear from me at this time. If I were going to kill you, you would be hearing these words from the afterlife." He stared at Fitz's F-Cannon.

The captain didn't lower his weapon.

Far from being worried by this, Khallini smiled with what looked like intense satisfaction, but who could tell? The old man was insane.

As if to confirm Lily's opinion of him, Khallini went on to say, "My boy, please remove your dark glasses."

Fitz lifted his shades and narrowed his purple eyes at the sorcerer.

Khallini's mouth formed an 'o.' "Incredible! You're so much like your mother."

"My what? Don't tell me you're my wicked great uncle or something."

"Amazing." Khallini closed his eyes. "I can hear her in your voice." He took a deep breath through his nostrils, as if scenting the air for the first time in eons. "Get out," he whispered insistently, though not angrily. "I have given you your orders and your lives. I shall transmit further data to your ship. You have bested me, and very few can say that. Now take what you have won and go!"

Keeping Khallini covered, Fitz helped Lily to her feet. Together, they backed out of the receiving room.

Outside, Andrus was waiting for them.

"Congratulations on your continued existence," said the flying ball of modules. "Your outer garments await in the boot and pressure suit room. I took the liberty of cleaning them. Outside *and* in."

The AI resembled a mishappen metal blackberry yet, somehow, it gave the impression of wrinkling its nose at these uncouth visitors.

"Don't get to meet real people much, do you?" Fitz asked it as he assessed Lily's neck for injuries.

"*Real?* A more accurate term for you people is *ephemeral*. And you needn't waste my time by examining your colleague's neck. Her windpipe was folded from within."

"Andrus is right," Lily said as they followed the AI along the tiled passage. "Khallini almost choked me unconscious, but I don't feel any bruising coming on. Not that it lets the creep off the hook."

Fitz nodded that he understood and proceeded in silence. That wasn't like him, but then that line from Khallini about knowing his mother was pretty deep.

It left room for Lily to try a little quippery of her own. "Let me tell you something I don't think you've realized yet, robot," she said as they passed through a blast door and out into a section of the complex that had the functional look of a starship deck, unlike the palatial inner chambers.

Andrus sighed. Lily had never heard a mechanoid do that before. "I know it's difficult for someone of your limited intellect to keep up, but I am an AI, not a robot."

"Whatever, metal head. You're smart, though. Smarter than me. Right?"

"Indubitably."

"Then you've already worked out that we'll be back soon. Your boss needs us, which means this is the beginning of a long and intimate relationship, Andrus. Think on that."

Lily enjoyed the sight of the floating android shuddering with revulsion. It was her first win since stepping off *Ghost Shark,* and boy did it taste good!

* * *

"Khallini didn't literally know your mother. Did he?"

Fitz gave nothing away. He squatted in front of Lily as she steered the raft downriver from the methane waterfall.

She left him to his silence in which he was processing Khallini's weird insinuation. It sounded too bizarre to take seriously, but it was clearly troubling him.

"Ma had a reputation in her youth," he volunteered once they'd moored on the bank. "She was unconventional. Double-crossing too."

They walked down the methane riverbank toward the rendezvous they'd arranged with *Ghost Shark*, but Fitz would say no more on the topic.

By the time they'd climbed the ladder into the luxury yacht and boosted for orbit, the captain was back to his usual irrepressible humor, telling tales of how the two of them had engaged Khallini in a battle of wills against dark sorcery—a version in which he had the decency to promote Lily into a far more active participant than she'd been at the time.

He acted as if he'd forgotten the memories he'd stirred in Khallini.

But Lily knew better.

For the first time since she'd met him, she sensed that Fitz felt lost.

* * * * *

Chapter Two:
Green Fish

Abandoned Research Station, Orbiting Omicron-San

When the many races of the Exiles arrived in the Perseus Arm, three thousand years previously, the Zhoogenes immediately singled out the humans and labelled them extremists.

They weren't wrong.

More than the other Exiled races, humans supplied the main drive to seek out truths in the realms of science, political ideology, religion, and so much more that took root in the earliest colonies of the Far Reach Federation. That was despite the Exiles having to overcome many existential crises. Even in this largely uninhabited sector of the galaxy, establishing new communities in a hostile universe was hard. Once the first rash of crises was over, the truth-seeking impulse grew ever stronger.

New orthodoxies formed, only to be torn down by revisionist uprisings that replaced the old assumptions with new doctrines and dogma. They, in turn, would fall to the criticism of the future.

It wasn't that the existing Perseid civilizations lacked these drives. Just that none were so extreme as humans.

Initially, the nonhuman Exiles defended their human allies. Without the humans and their monomaniacal obsessions, none of them would have escaped the Orion Spur. Over many centuries, they slowly came round to the Zhoogene way of thinking. It wasn't that humans were evil people, as such, just that they could be, well…a little hard to handle sometimes.

The quartet of long-abandoned research facilities orbiting the poison world of Omicron-San exemplified many aspects of this human extremism.

In the last millennium, a radical political movement had burst onto the scene. Its well-received populist slogans had left it bloated with funds and supporters, but it lacked the ideological underpinnings to know what it should be radical about.

A faction of this group had looked into Earth's past and found the answer in socialism. They argued that the reason no society had ever freed itself from poverty and the curse of labor exploitation was because they had always lacked freely available, unlimited, and portable power generation. Infinite power for all; that had always been the missing pre-requisite for the socialist dream.

The solution was to be the quantum bias generator.

This was the scientific breakthrough that would deliver the social transformation of the galaxy.

In great secrecy—to ensure only they could control the bias generator's development and rollout—the organization channeled their funds into four research stations orbiting the third planet in the Omicron system. In size, composition, and the star it orbited, Omicron-San was nearly identical to Earth. But this world had taken a different path, becoming a hellish nightmare, lashed by the hurricane storms that raged in its sulfuric acid clouds.

The work would be dangerous, but the researchers were convinced they were on the cusp of a new future. The project team at

Omicron-San would be revered for thousands of years to come. Everyone knew it. They spoke of little else.

Yet dangers abounded.

Each orbital consisted of a central cylinder that spun about its axis. Four gravity modules connected to the central hub by kilometer-long tethers. These four orbitals were widely dispersed around the planet in case of catastrophe.

Station Gamma exploded when first powering up. But the survivors persevered, clawing their way along the path that would take quantum bias from theoretical concept to practical reality.

Two years into the project, a factional coup devastated the parent movement.

The scheduled Omicron resupply ships never set off.

The technicians all starved to death.

Omicron-San was an unwanted world in a dead system, but rumors that something had taken place there spread, grew, and eventually convinced a wave of salvage rats to investigate.

Valuable salvage was stripped quickly. Reaction mass, fuel pellets, conventional power generators, and medical gear went first. Data cores were stripped, though selling them was more difficult, and they were soon lost.

Salvage teams had a poor reputation, but they weren't savages. The corpses of the technicians were fired at the planet below, and a few solemn worlds spoken, commending the souls of whoever the hell they'd been.

After the salvage rats left, no one visited the silent orbitals of Omicron-San for over a thousand years. Automated systems kept the three surviving stations spinning through the vacuum at a constant 67 seconds per revolution. Year after year. Century after century.

Then a political historian researched the ancient movement and speculated on what the mysterious project could have been that so much money was sunk into it. His speculations were way off the mark, but others dug deeper until they came up with logs of numerous support missions sent to Omicron-San. They drew the connections.

And now, salvage rats had returned.

"Orion's tits! I think I found it."

Still holding the laser cutter, Green Fish backflipped in excitement. She landed perfectly, which wasn't difficult in the minimal-gee.

"Cut that out," Sinofar snapped on principle, but she sounded as delighted as Green Fish. That was the way Sinofar was—tough as old space boots one instant, borderline indulgent the next—ever since the day and night she'd spent in her cabin with Bronze on the journey to Eiylah-Bremah.

Green Fish decided not to push her luck by pointing out to Sinofar that 'cutting that out' was exactly what she had been doing.

From the outside, Green Fish could see Sinofar's HUD light up with a drawing of the quantum bias field generator they'd been sent to acquire. It resembled a perforated exhaust pipe bent at one end into a J-shape.

Sinofar thrust her head inside the hole Green Fish had cut through the hexagonal equipment bank. "That's our baby," she said. "Good work."

The praise made Green Fish radiate with joy, which was embarrassing.

Join the Militia and…strip dark tech from abandoned space stations. When she'd been forced into the Militia, she'd thought it would be a career of riot control, intimidation, and protecting the privileged. If she'd known how it would turn out, maybe she'd have signed up willingly.

After a few moments work with a micro-plasma torch, Sinofar yanked the field generator out and held it aloft.

Green Fish figured the chance of this junk pipe changing anything other than their credit balances was about zero point fuck all.

But it was fun to imagine this compartment at the height of its operational use a dozen centuries ago.

At the center of the hexagonal base, she'd cut into a ring that had once held something now long gone. Three devices that resembled particle cannons were suspended overhead, aimed at this missing element. They were three-meter-long tubes that terminated with lenses like a camera. In place of a gun breech, each cannon had a box peppered with data ports and plugged into fat power cables that draped onto the deck, their power source liberated a millennium ago.

Back in its day, this room must have been electrified with hope. To believe you were part of something huge, something wonderful— very few people had that privilege.

"We've got company," Zan Fey commed. "I see two humanoids. I'm exiting the main cylinder for Grav Unit 3, and they are in pursuit. They appear unarmed. Get out here and show them the error of their ways."

"Roger that," Sinofar acknowledged.

"Shouldn't we have told the boss we've got the prize?" asked Green Fish.

"Our priority in these situations is to eliminate all opposition. Until then, everything else is a distraction. Activate your blaster and watch my six. We shall proceed to Grav Unit 3."

Hard-as-boots Sinofar was back in the saddle. Green Fish took a moment to spray sticky threads on the prize and attach it to the back of her suit. Then she hurried after the senior crewman.

* * * * *

Chapter Three:
Tavistock Fitzwilliam

•

***Ghost Shark*, Jump Space**

Fitz had taken *Ghost Shark* out to four times the planetary radius above Hundra-7 before forming a rift tunnel and jumping through. *Phantom* had jumped at 1.1 in a pinch. Most private traffic jumped between 2 and 3. He told his crew he was jumping so far out from the gravity well because he was still testing out the luxury yacht they'd tactically acquired from Eiylah-Bremah's late dictator. But the real reason had nothing to do with safety. Fitz needed to clear his head.

That damned space wizard they'd left behind on the planet had Fitz buzzing with a whole new set of worries. And he wasn't about to admit to his crew or Khallini how troubled he was.

Capture Nyluga-Ree!

The idea was preposterous.

He could rescue his mislaid Viking without the assistance of that smock-clad, old prune.

But then there was the money…

Khallini had paid a fortune for the information Fitz had delivered on the ancient ship dug out of Rho-Torkis. The deal was even sweeter because Fitz had already won a reprieve from Nyluga-Ree by giving her the same intel.

When they'd discussed the fee for kidnapping the Nyluga, Fitz had asked for three times the credits he'd just been paid. Khallini had agreed without hesitation, which showed what chump change this was to the sorcerer. Not to Fitz, though.

With that amount, maybe they could hide out the coming troubles. He could even start paying his crew a salary, an awkward topic he couldn't put off forever.

He took the thumb-sized communication device from his jacket and gave it a click. Just a simple on then off.

Somewhere out there in the galaxy, a twinned device would register that simple communication.

Click! I'm still here.

That was all it meant. But it meant a lot.

His own device clicked back. Instantly, his fears about Khallini and Nyluga-Ree melted away to a level he could forget.

It was a tiny sound, something you would ignore as the honest noise of a working starship unless you were listening for it.

Izza was out there. In this moment. Connected to him via the little boxes in their hands.

They clicked to each other most days, leaving it at that.

He hoped she was thinking of him now because she was all he could think of.

What was she doing? Where?

She could be walking down one of *Phantom's* passageways, eating with the crew, or trying to teach Lynx some manners. He closed his eyes and pictured her. Whatever she was doing, in his mind's eye, she was doing it naked. And it was strenuous activity that bathed her in a sweat sheen that dripped over lush contours. Azhanti! They'd been apart for too long.

He shifted the device to voice mode, praying she was able and willing to respond in kind.

"Busy?" he asked when the voice comm mode indicator lit up.

"Very. But you got two mikes."

"Okay." His desire for her was a drug. He always needed more, so he held the device in front of him and switched to video mode.

She did the same. A holographic view of his wife's face projected in front of him. She was inside a helmet. He couldn't see where she was, just her face. And she looked troubled.

"Are you in space?" he asked.

"Yes. Salvage operation on an abandoned research orbital. Turned out it wasn't as abandoned as advertised. I'm okay for the moment. Verlys will sort things out."

Fitz wasn't so sure. Izza's breathing sounded heavy to him, but the sound from inside a helmet was always intimate.

"Was there something in particular you wanted to talk about?" she asked.

"Lord Khallini paid up for the data you unearthed. He also mentioned he knew my mother."

"Your mother? You must have misunderstood."

Fitz shook his head. He'd replayed that conversation too many times to have gotten it wrong. "His words were: 'You remind me of your mother.'"

"Have you heard from her? From Mama Zi'Alfu?"

"No."

Fitz grimaced. Ma was a noxious topic he liked to keep buried deep beneath the surface of his mind. "Izza, would you be so kind as to pay a visit to your mother-in-law? I want to understand the connection. Khallini wouldn't have mentioned it lightly, and my instinct says it's important, however nonsensical it appears at the moment."

Her beautiful eyes rolled low to look at something below her. Her face pinched with worry, but she fixed her gaze back on the camera's focus spot. "You and your damned *instincts*. If there's one thing I've learned, the more annoying they are, the more accurate they'll be. Your gift of foresight is far stronger than you admit to yourself, Tavistock."

Fitz adopted a wounded expression. Izza didn't want to visit his mother, but he knew she would do it anyway.

Suddenly, Izza gasped in shock. Fear tightened her face. "Bylzak! I'm being shot at."

"I'll go. Be safe." Fitz reached for the device to switch it off.

"Not yet. You're my human rogue, Fitzy. Tell me you haven't forgotten."

"You own my heart, my lady. Forever. You know that."

"I do, but I still need to hear it. I'll be in touch. Stay alive, Tavistock. I have plans for you. Out."

* * * * *

Chapter Four:
Izza Zan Fey

Abandoned Research Station, Orbiting Omicron-San

I zza fired two bolts at the pursuers climbing the tether after her.

She missed.

Aiming was difficult on the disk she was riding up to Grav Unit 3. That it worked at all was surprising, but the ride was jerky to say the least. She hit the red button to bring it to a stop. Then she undid the strap around her chest and knelt on the platform, cupping her blaster's grip in both gauntleted hands. She hated gunfights in gloves, but this was the life she'd chosen. With knees pushed up against the platform's rim, she leaned out with her blaster ready.

They were waiting for her. And there were three of them now!

The vacuum lit with brilliant flashes as blaster fire headed her way.

She managed to squeeze off just one shot before a bolt slammed into the platform's base. The shock kicked through her, and she pivoted on her knees and fell forward. Still taking fire, she rammed her toes into the rim and used them to pull herself back behind the cover of the disk.

She hit the stud to reactivate the platform's motion while comming her team. "Our new friends are playing dirty. Shoot on sight."

"Copy that," Sinofar replied. "We'll get to you, boss. But we're having to fight our way out."

"Dammit." Izza allowed herself a few seconds of cursing. She'd let herself get distracted, and Sinofar hadn't been her usual paranoid self lately. She should never have listened to Fitz when he suggested they split up.

No matter. Next time, they would do better.

Sparks flew from the motor that moved the platform along the tether. Although the platform was still wobbling and jerking, she realized it was no longer advancing up the line to the grav unit.

More bolts slammed into the metal beneath her feet, warping the material with their intense heat. One more bolt, and it would be her internal organs that were melting. She cued an evasive maneuver program in the thrust pack wrapped around her chest and readied to spring off the disk.

"Here comes backup," announced Fregg, who had remained on *Phantom* with Lynx.

Izza's first instinct was to order Fregg to keep back, knowing that with her inept flying, *Phantom's* logistics manager was as likely to ram the central cylinder as do anything halfway useful.

Another bolt hit the disk from below, blowing off the front half and shattering it into dozen pieces. *This is getting desperate…*

"Hit 'em, Fregg," she said.

Phantom was a hot spark streaming across the star field just above the haze of Omicron-San's atmosphere. The spark grew quickly. Too quickly.

"You're coming in too fast," she whispered.

Brilliant green dashes lanced out of the spacecraft's nose and the turrets on the upper and lower hull. The barrage crossed the gap too fast for the eye to track and lashed the vicinity of the space station with blaster cannon fire.

None of the bolts she saw came within ten klicks of the target, but her enemies didn't know that Justiana Fregg couldn't hit a battleship at ten paces.

Izza took her chance and jumped.

Her finger was by the stud to activate the thruster pack, but what she saw at the central cylinder stayed her hand.

Of the three space-suited figures who'd fired at her, one was either a floating corpse from her earlier shot or was making a good attempt at playing dead. The other two were in an altercation. One was trying to get back in the cylinder and the other was trying to stop them.

Another burst of *Phantom's* cannon fire lit the area.

This time, Fregg hit something. One of the other gravity units exploded in a fireball.

A part of Izza's mind noted that there must've been combustibles in that unit, and that implied valuable salvage the earlier scavengers had missed. Maybe there was more she could claim for herself?

But there was another part that said she had to stay alive to face the daunting prospect of meeting her mother-in-law. The two rival scavengers were looking in horror at the destruction. Izza took careful aim at the one who hadn't wanted to retreat inside the central cylinder and put three bolts through them.

The other scavenger fled inside before Izza could shoot them.

She twisted around to bring *Phantom* into view. The familiar shape of the animal horn KM conduits brought a smile to her face. "Well done, Fregg. I think you just—"

Fregg let loose another burst of cannon fire.

One of the bolts came straight for her.

In less than a second, the bolt had flown past, missing her by inches. The shock of what had almost happened hit her body a few seconds later. It hit hard.

She was shaking inside her suit when *Phantom* shot past. Her suit diaper would earn its keep today.

"Fregg, ceasefire," she squeaked.

Phantom streaked past.

"Fregg to the captain. Are you alright? You sound weird."

Izza's slow rotation brought Grav Unit 3 into view. She'd been headed there before the trouble kicked off but, now, more scavengers were emerging from it. All carried blaster rifles.

"It's not over yet," she told her team. She hit the thrust pack stud and initiated evasive maneuvers.

* * * * *

Chapter Five:
Green Fish

Green Fish loosed the last of her bolts at the hatch and bounded away across the hydroponics compartment to a new position.

"Green Fish, swapping charge packs." She announced her status without thinking, just as Sergeant Arunsen had taught her, forgetting she wasn't in the Militia now.

She swapped packs without looking, keeping her attention on the hatch in the overhead. Through that open hatch was the central passage tube that ran along the axis of the cylinder.

Her task was to keep the scavengers bottled up in that central tube. Meanwhile, Sinofar would enter the tube via another compartment and flank them.

Excitement and fear tingled inside her, fizzing up her guts. The scavengers were there but were keeping out of sight.

Were they stacking up to assault through the hatch? Perhaps some of them were keeping her busy while the rest of them out-flanked her?

Her gaze switched to the door by the curved deck through which she and Sinofar had entered. Would they come through there?

She looked up again at the overhead hatch.

Orion's arse! She screamed and jumped.

She wasn't jumping anywhere in particular, just anywhere but here.

While her attention had been elsewhere, two scavengers had dropped through the hatch, feet first, firing at her.

The room was filling with splintered glass from the capillary tubes that led from the plant troughs up to the overhead feed tubes.

The cylinder was airless. If it had been pressurized, she would have been crapping herself at the ferocity of the attack. Without any sound, she hadn't even noticed.

The combination of spin, low-gee, and Coriolis forces was confusing. Her return fire missed.

Her random leap had landed her on one of the empty plant troughs. She bunched her knees and pushed off higher.

It was like a deadly aerial ballet. Except without the air. She was jumping higher as the pair of scavengers descended.

Shit. Shit. Shit!

She winced as she shot one in the gut as they passed each other in the middle of the compartment. There was no way the other scavenger could miss her.

She tensed up inside her suit, waiting for the killing shot, though she still took aim at the second scavenger who…*didn't fire.*

Something was sticking out of the inside of the scavenger's elbow joints. Daggers.

She fired anyway, blowing the back of the helmet out in a geyser of blood. As she reached the apogee of her leap and began to drop back down, she covered the overhead hatch and saw a figure standing there wearing one of the suits they'd found in *Ghost Shark.*

Sinofar gave her a thumbs up. "This is Sinofar. Central tube is clear. Green Fish, retrieve my lucky daggers and join me at the exit to Grav Unit 3. Sorry for the delay, boss. We're on our way."

* * *

"**D**itch the cutter," ordered Sinofar.

Green Fish looked guiltily at the heavy laser cutter in her hands. Its weight felt comforting, which was why she'd grabbed it from the deck of the hydroponics room. "Might come in handy," she replied. "Besides, I've brought it this far."

They were stacked up behind a closed hatch. On the far side was the staging area with access to the tether the boss had used to escape.

Sinofar turned and glared through her faceplate at the junior crewman behind her. "It's a 22-megawatt laser. That's a lot of power, but its focus point varies between one and ten centimeters. It's not a weapon. Ditch it!"

Green Fish dropped the cutter and drew her hand blaster. Sinofar gave a silent countdown with her fingers and then opened the hatch.

"Get some!" yelled the Pryxian as she sprayed the room with her Z'Lox "Slammer." The shallow drum strapped to Sinofar's back slowly rotated, delivering a constant stream of ammunition to the five rotating barrels of her minigun.

She leaned forward into the recoil that had to be pummeling her like a thousand mailed fists.

Sinofar could lift objects that beggared belief, but she wasn't entirely immune to the laws of physics. She only managed a short burst before the Slammer's barrels lifted high, and the recoil pushed her off the deck and into a backward jump.

By then, Green Fish was already charging through into the compartment, edging to the left to give Sinofar a clear fire zone.

She was too late. The only scavenger in the room had already been shredded into a red mist that was sluggishly falling onto the deck.

Green Fish took a moment to check for more hostiles, but there were none in view. No concealment to hide them, either. "Clear!"

She pushed on to the open exterior hatch and took in the scene outside the central cylinder. A taut cable only a few inches thick stretched through space and connected to the grav unit a kilometer away, spinning it around to give it pseudo gravity like that on an Earthlike planet's surface. Two-thirds of the way toward the grav unit, the boss was using a thruster pack to zip around while sending blaster fire toward the module's open hatch.

The return fire was far fiercer.

The boss had been matching the orbital's rotation. Now, she abandoned that and drifted up and out of Green Fish's field of view. She'd rotate back into the enemy's field of fire in just over a minute

They had to do something. Fast.

Green Fish raised her hand blaster but thought better of it. Her bolts would carry that far but hitting a target a klick away was impossible.

"Out of the way!" yelled Sinofar.

Green Fish shifted aside to let Sinofar set up with the long-barreled blaster rifle. The Pryxian had shouldered the Slammer, a weapon too heavy for Green Fish to lift.

Next time, I'll bring the binocs, she told herself because she felt helpless. The faceplate of her spacesuit lacked magnification capability. All she could see of the distant grav unit was a white smear.

Four of these grav units had been tethered to the central cylinder she was on, though one had just been destroyed. The central hub rotated once every sixty-seven seconds.

As the planet below gently rotated into view, displaying its sickly yellow and green atmosphere, Grav Unit 3 slid down the star field and revealed two incoming scavenger ships.

"I see two ships inbound," Green Fish reported. An idea hit her, and she set a timer running. "Sinofar, keep their heads down in Grav Unit 3." She hurried back inside the central cylinder. "Fregg, where are you?"

"I've flipped about," Fregg replied, "but I'm still headed in the wrong direction. Shall I open fire?"

"No!" cried Green Fish and Zan Fey simultaneously.

"Whatever you're doing, Green Fish," said the boss, "make it snappy. This thrust pack is the only thing keeping me alive, and it's almost out of fuel."

"Can you hold on for…" Green Fish checked the timer and made a quick mental calculation. "Forty-three seconds?"

"I'll try," said the boss. "But no longer. What's your plan, Greenie?"

"Have you heard the tale of David and Goliath?"

"Can't say I have. Yes! Good shooting, Sinofar. They're retreating inside the grav unit. Oh…shit. Those scavenger ships are almost here. I am heading back to the hub. Who was David and what did he do with Goliath?"

Green Fish was hurrying along the deck of the hub, the heavy cutter back in her hands, and her breathing loud in her helmet. "Allow me to demonstrate, boss."

She returned to the tether point and was relieved to see the cable moving away from the boss. The system of cylinder tethers and grav units rotated onward, and Zan Fey appeared to rise overhead.

With each rotation taking sixty-seven seconds, that left Green Fish about twenty seconds to cut the tether.

Sinofar finally grasped the plan and got the hell out of the way.

Green Fish set to work, slicing the cutter's beam through the cable.

It cut through easily.

Which was bad. Cutting the cable too soon was as much of a disaster as too late.

Her timer said she had eight seconds remaining.

The uncut section began to fray.

Green Fish ignored it.

"I'm on my way," Fregg told them.

Six seconds…

"Keep it steady, *Phantom*," said the boss. "If this works, park as close as you dare, and we will come to you. Do not overshoot!"

The cutter jerked in Green Fish's hands as she finished slicing through the cable.

The severed end gave a deadly flick, but it was already moving safely away from Green Fish and the hub.

Blaster fire and destruction had come to the floating mausoleums that had once housed a secret dream to transform the galaxy. Until the team from *Phantom* had arrived, its rotational mechanics had continued serenely as they had for a dozen centuries. A fact that made

Green Fish suspect the station couldn't be as dead as it appeared. Not if it had remained stable all that time.

Every sixty-seven seconds, the world of Omicron-San would rotate into view, dazzling observers on the station with its vivid planetshine. Then it would slide out of sight, though its light still reflected off the facing sides of the gravity units.

That ancient motion had been disturbed when Fregg shot up Grav Unit 2. Now it was shattered.

The central cylinder wobbled beneath Green Fish's feet, sending pulses out from the two grav units still connected.

Grav Unit 3 flew away at a surprising speed. More important to Green Fish than the velocity was its trajectory.

It was aimed directly at the two scavenger ships.

She watched, barely daring to breathe. She unashamedly wanted to see what would happen when a space station module slammed into a space vehicle filled with people trying to kill her.

They panicked. That was what happened. The two ships veered away and opened their throttles.

On the grav unit she'd converted into a slingshot missile, scavengers were crawling onto the hull. From the way they were gesticulating, she guessed they were arguing whether it was best to abandon the module or stick with it. They couldn't agree. Half of them jumped, which made little difference to their velocity, but would gradually separate them from the module.

Phantom returned to Green Fish's field of view.

And then vanished as the cylinder rotated it out of view again.

When it slid back a minute later, Fregg was shooting at the nearest of the scavenger ships. Her aim hadn't improved, and was no match for the scavenger ships trying to cut through *Phantom's* cockpit with turret lasers.

Phantom's shields were easily up to the task, flashing briefly as they absorbed the energy attack. The KM horns glowed with lilac fire as they safely radiated the energy out into the Klein-Manifold Region.

The scavenger ships were outclassed, and they knew it. They veered away to retrieve their fellows who had been cast adrift and then stayed just outside *Phantom's* effective weapons range. They were wrong, of course. *Phantom* had a lot more firepower to dish out than the nose-mounted blasters Fregg had used.

Phantom parked near the hub. Her crew thrusted over to her, taking turns imparting momentum to the boss, who had finally run out of fuel.

* * *

"D o we skragg them?" Green Fish asked once they were aboard and helmets had been removed. "They *did* fire first."

"Negative," Zan Fey replied. "None of this was personal. Just business. Always best to keep it that way if you can, kid."

The other crew had stations to go to. Green Fish didn't. At a loss and still buzzing with the adrenaline rush, she followed Zan Fey onto the flight deck. "But they fired first!"

The boss hesitated. She seemed torn inside. "They did," she said angrily.

"No one messes with *Phantom's* crew," said Green Fish. "The sector should know that. And those scavengers might not have seen our ship before, but they have now."

"That's a very good point." Zan Fey turned and placed a hand on Green Fish's shoulder. She seemed impressed. "Let's see what we can do about that."

Zan Fey took her seat and gestured for Green Fish to join her in the copilot position.

Green Fish looked at the small seat dubiously. Her butt was big in a space suit. Before she could say anything, the seat expanded until it was the perfect fit. *Still got a lot to learn.*

The boss removed her gloves and stretched out a long green finger to flick on the intercom. "Captain to all hands, get ready to look out the portholes and observe some tactical showing off."

The crew acknowledged their readiness in their various ways.

"Strapped in and sick bag ready."

"C'mon, Cap'n. Show your moves."

"Is this really necessary? I have some reading to do."

The tension left Zan Fey, and a sly grin slid into place as she unleashed the awesome potential of *Phantom's* engines. They crossed the gap to the scavenger ships at a speed that must have had the skraggs testing the limits of their suits' body waste management systems.

"Verlys," she said. "It's time for your target practice. See if you can take out those lasers."

"Roger that," Sinofar roared from the ventral turret.

The flight deck filled with whoops of joy. Zan Fey was in her element, sending *Phantom* swooping like a space bird around the hapless scavengers. Green Fish enjoyed the flying display from her copilot seat, her eyes glued to the stunning view through the cockpit window.

Only when *Phantom* turned the tightest of her loops did she feel a slight pull of g-forces.

"Can I have a go in the other turret?" she begged.

"Next time." Zan Fey laughed. "Sinofar will be done before you get there."

Phantom darted close to the scavenger ships, holding station for a second or so for Sinofar to lock on and shoot out the enemy lasers.

The surviving enemy weapons accurately returned fire.

It made no difference. *Phantom's* captain always had the shields angled the right way to meet the attacks, using the KM horns to disperse the energy to upper dimensions.

Zan Fey pulled the ship through a final series of loops just for the hell of it and then opened the throttles to race for the outer system.

There was nothing Green Fish could imagine wanting more than to be Izza Zan Fey.

She was sublime.

"Arse!" The boss face palmed. "Five Hells!"

"What is it?"

"The quantum bias generator. Someone please tell me we *did* retrieve the damned thing."

Green Fish stood and turned her back to the boss. "J-shaped tube. Is it still on my back?"

"Azhanti's Grace!" Zan Fey removed it and clamped it safely to the bulkhead attachment point. "If we ever meet up again with Fitz, never tell him what a hash we made of our first job without him."

"Everyone has teething problems," said Green Fish, sitting back in the copilot seat. "Even the girls' team. We just need to learn and get slicker for next time. We like having Fitz and the others around, but we don't need them."

Zan Fey gave her a peculiar look Green Fish couldn't interpret. "Girls' team?" she asked after a few moments. "Are you forgetting Catkins?"

"Nope." Green Fish grinned.

Zan Fey's eyes flashed with color as she chuckled. "Girls' team. I can run with that. First, we need to get to safety. Then we celebrate."

She pushed forward the drive activator, forming a jump tunnel in front of the ship's nose.

Phantom fell through.

* * * * *

Chapter Six:
Izza Zan Fey

Phantom, **Orbiting Omicron-Schoertchi**

Glass of Florinette beer in hand, Izza left the others, minus Catkins, partying in the mess room. The engineer was on watch, snuggling happily with a case of his disgusting herbal firewater in his engineering space. He was also monitoring the recharging jump drives as they orbited one of the Omicron system's outer gas balls.

The science station they'd salvaged the bias generator from was only 82 light minutes away in the inner system, but Omicron was such a nowhere place, they might as well be in deep space.

The memory of *actually* being marooned in deep space brought her feet to a halt. That episode still had too many gaps. Holes that Fitz had been unwilling to fill to her satisfaction.

"I'll get the truth out of him in good time," she told herself and headed for the privacy of her quarters.

On the way, she passed *Phantom's* lounge. It was an opulent space, unchanged since Nyluga-Ree had used it. For some reason, the crew preferred to socialize in the cramped space of the mess room or the engineering eyrie. Perhaps, when they reunited with their missing Marines, that would change.

The corner of her mouth lifted. She'd partied in that lounge. Hard. Those had been good times.

She dwelt a moment in the past and then completed her walk to her quarters. She locked the door and activated the comm link to Fitz.

She thumbed the mode selector switch to video.

At the heart of the device was a lattice of material that was quantum entangled with a twin at Fitz's end. Her science classes at school had taught her that faster-than-light information transfer between entangled particles was impossible. And yet the device worked.

She had asked the Nyluga about this inconsistency once. The Guild boss had responded with the smug pout that meant she was relishing secret knowledge she wasn't about to divulge. All she had told Izza was that these rare and expensive devices were not entangled with qubits but with *ch-bits*.

Whatever they were, once a ch-bit had been used up, it was gone forever. They had no replacements.

A video signal consumed ch-bits much faster than voice, so she thumbed the device back to voice mode and clicked.

Fitz responded immediately. "Are you safe?"

Poor human man. He sounded exhausted with worry.

"We're perfectly safe. Other than, you know…Nyluga-Ree ordering my capture and this Andromeda Corruption business. Aside from his cryptic comment about your mother, how was your meeting with Khallini?"

Fitz sucked in a breath. Never a good sign. "Exotic. Bizarre. Profitable. I think he's lived alone for a very long time. Keeps himself sane by building pet AIs to keep him company. He was delighted with the location data of the buried ship you left for me at that desert temple. That was an epic location for a drop, my dear. Well done. In fact, we found that data for Khallini far quicker than I expected."

Her eyebrows shot up. "*We* found it?"

"Yes, *we*. I graciously allowed you to throw me off my own ship like unwanted ballast. And that freed you to get your data while eyes were on me."

Izza laughed. "Let's see. You're admitting that the more light-years between us, the more I can achieve. And I don't need to split the proceeds with you. Tell me again why I should have you back."

"Because your green heart doesn't beat properly when we're apart."

She answered with a noncommittal grunt. He was right, of course, but he would be insufferable if she admitted it. "Perhaps this deep cover idea did work. And it has been fun running girls-only operations—"

"What about Catkins?"

"What about him? Anyway, like I said, it's been fun—some of it—but it won't work forever. Let's call it a win and reunite."

"Let's not be hasty." Fitz sounded extremely defensive.

"Tavistock, if you were about to say we should continue with this separation to *keep me safe*, then think very carefully before you open your stupid mouth."

"Perish the thought, my lady. I accept I may have been in a panic back on JSHC when I initiated the deep cover protocol. And I might have contributed toward the slight miscommunication episode that led to the whole ballast-dumping thing."

"Episode? Fucking debacle, more like."

"You have such a way with words."

"One of us has to."

"Izza, our supply of entangled bits is finite. So, in the interest of moving on, let us assume we may insert a list of my numerous inadequacies here. However, deep cover has succeeded. My instinct was proved correct. Does anyone suspect the truth at your end?"

"Green Fish worked it out almost immediately. I blame the Kur-lei's influence. By the way, she recovered from her wounds enough to help at our last salvage job. She saved our butts. Sinofar knows our secret too, but only from overhearing Green Fish. Lynx has been acting ever more peculiar of late, but who can tell what that means?"

"You need to hold our secret a little longer."

"Or maybe I don't. I tell you, we need to kill this deep cover business while we're ahead."

"There is one thing I must ask you to do before we finish this charade."

"I know." She groaned. "Visit your mother."

"Well…yes. Speaking of which." Fitz sent across an image he'd taken of Khallini in his lair. "Okay, two more things," he said. "This other one might be *unsafe*."

"Spit it out, human."

"There's a princess needs rescuing."

She laughed. "Just like the good old days before we picked up a crew."

"I use the term loosely and irreverently. The princess is Vetch, who has become the unwilling guest of Nyluga-Ree. I want you to free him from her palace."

"Oh. Is that all?"

"No. I also want you to fail."

"Are you going to tell me why?"

"It's best that you don't know."

"Keeping me in the dark. How did that work out for you last time?"

"Dumped on a beach to be shot at by angry Marines." There was a long pause at Fitz's end. "I do think it's best that you don't know, but I foresee that you'll persuade me to tell anyway. So, I'll save ch-bits and come out with it. It's like this, my love. I had a very interesting chat with Lord Khallini."

"Is that why our outer shell of accounts has been credited eighty million?"

"I see you've begun to discover the transactions. There should be nine more like that, although the transaction updates will be carried by data couriers. We won't know for sure for a few weeks, but I trust Khallini to pay up."

"Eight. Hundred. Million." She purred. Noisily.

Large sums of money had the same powerful effect on her that her pheromones had on humans. It wasn't the goods and services money bought that particularly interested her, although *Phantom's* consumables and maintenance did cost eye-watering amounts. It was the thrill of winning so copiously that was making it hard for her to speak.

Eight hundred million credits. For most people in the Federation, that was a thousand lifetimes of earnings. She and Fitz were playing in the big leagues now. And they were winning!

"That's payment for the location data," Fitz said, "plus a third upfront for me—for *us*, because you'll help with distraction, of course—to borrow Nyluga-Ree for a while."

Izza rattled her tongue against the roof of her mouth. To abscond with Ree...that was a *very* high stakes game.

"Ree adores you," said Fitz. "You're like a favored niece. It's not without danger, I admit, but I don't think she'll hurt you. Not permanently."

"You've committed us to this insanity," she snapped. "To kidnap the Nyluga? You should have consulted with me first."

"Your words wound me. The sorcerer paid a third up front just so we would think seriously about it. We could still take the money and run. Maybe run so far that Kanha Wei, Khallini, and Ree can all suck on our rift space trail and never find us again."

Izza knew she should hold her tongue. But the words were too electrifying. She had to speak them. "How much, Fitzy? What's the balance if we pull off this craziness?"

"Another eight hundred mil."

Izza shuddered with a powerful mix of delight and horror.

Fitz's breathing was ragged with excitement too. "One point six billion," he whispered, ruthlessly pressing against her weakness. "You aren't seriously thinking of turning that down?"

"No."

"So, we're going to kidnap Nyluga-Ree?"

"Yes."

They enjoyed a few moments of silent contemplation. "We both know we'll take the job," said Fitz. "I just wanted to discuss it first. But it's the closest to a suicide mission we've ever taken on, so I'll ask once more. Should we go ahead?"

"Yesss." Her lungs seemed to be overflowing with hot air. "Fitzy," she gasped, "tell me again how much Khallini's paying us."

"One point six billion credits."

"Oh, yesss." Her body tingled in ways that were sweet torture with Fitz's touch being light-years distant.

"I need you here," she said, her voice husky with need.

"I know." His words came sticky as molasses.

She swallowed hard and licked her upper lip. She began picturing each member of her crew in turn, transporting them from the mess room to her quarters and dressing them in more interesting ways. Or *un*dressing them. Who could best satisfy her buzzing? Green Fish was fresh and pretty...

No! Crew was family. They must forever be off limits. Bylzak! Her season was approaching fast, and if they didn't resolve this soon, Fitz wasn't going to be with her when it happened.

But she *could* bring him a little closer.

"Tell me again about the money, Fitzy," she breathed. No longer caring about the skragging bandwidth, she thumbed the comm selector to video mode.

* * * * *

Chapter Seven:
Izza Zan Fey

Phantom, **Orbiting Omicron-Schoertchi**

"Here's the plan," said Izza. She scanned the faces in the mess room. They looked drained and half drunk. All except Catkins, who was on the flight deck listening in over the intercom, and Hubert the basten goat, who was happily munching something he probably shouldn't underneath the table.

A mellow crew. Fitz once told her the best time to hit them with bad news was when they were relaxed.

Or was it the worst time? If she got him back, she would take notes in case she had to throw him out again.

"Thanks to our success in acquiring the package—"

Sinofar gave a hearty cheer and held the quantum bias generator high in one hand while squeezing Green Fish's shoulder so hard it made her new best buddy wince.

"Our next stop is to deliver that fine antique to our client on Flux City. Officially, *Phantom* is a marked vessel, and its crew is to be seized on sight by the Guild. But they only know me and Sinofar, so we'll borrow another ship for the handover, and send in our B Team."

Fregg rolled her eyes, but the other member of the B Team wasn't taking it as well.

"Your labelling is divisive," Catkins scolded. "Captain Fitzwilliam was never so rude."

"Yeah, he was," said Fregg. "You just liked him better. The boss is only joking."

Green Fish got to her feet. "Catkins, you and Fregg are both Guild members too. You might not have been on Flux City recently, but you may be recognized. I think we should deploy Team C. Me. I've never set foot on Flux City. No one knows who I am."

A thousand objections went through Izza's head. The human had done well back in the inner system, but she was reluctant to send her on a solo mission in such a dangerous environment.

Dangerous it might be, but venturing into Flux City was the calm before the storm compared to what she'd cooked up with Fitz.

And beyond that…the galaxy seemed to be on a one-way trip to the crazy zone.

Everyone here had to up their game, and, deep in their bones, they all needed to know they could rely on each other to do so. The very fact that Izza had doubted Green Fish was all the reason she needed to send the girl.

"All right, Team C." Izza forced a grin. "You get the job."

Green Fish smiled back, deep dimples forming in her cheeks. *She looked so young!*

Sinofar gave the girl a comradely slap on the back, which made her cry out in pain.

"My bad," said the Pryxian. "I forgot you had a barbed ritual spear sticking out of that spot."

They gave Green Fish a moment or two to recover. Then she said, "When I've made the exchange, and I'm back with the money, you'll need to celebrate properly. I'll snag us takeouts. What are y'all having?"

"I like this human girl," said Catkins, a little too loudly. "Give her a year or two, and she'll make a better skipper than you, Captain Zan Fey."

Izza laughed at that with the others. Everyone was laughing, she noticed, except Green Fish herself. She sensed the girl was imagining herself in the captain's seat, and not for the first time.

Young she might be, but she was ambitious. Nothing wrong with that, but she needed to be watched.

And I need to tell my crew the mission Fitz and I agreed on.

Izza hadn't the heart. The crew was happy. They were bonding with their newest member, and that was important too. There would be plenty of time to tell them about Vetch and Nyluga-Ree later.

* * *

Phantom Flight Deck, Jump Space

"Treat it as a learning lesson," Izza told the most junior member of her crew later after Green Fish returned from Flux City and had given her report. "Even without Fitz around to throw his customary chaos bomb into the works, the best plans can fall apart. The important thing is that you adapted and completed the mission."

Izza narrowed her eyes. Green Fish was sitting in the copilot's seat. *Her* seat. The girl had nearly died making the exchange on Flux City *and* had nearly lost the quantum bias generator. Nearly. But she'd won in the end and seemed untroubled by the close call.

"You did well, though. All the others are waiting for you in the lounge to give you a proper welcome. Congratulations. You've proven that you deserve to be a part of my crew."

Doubt clouded Green Fish's eyes. "Am I actually part of the crew? I mean, what happens when...?"

The girl saw Izza's glare and shut up. The two of them in the flight deck knew the split with Fitz was temporary, but it was not something to speak of. Ever.

"Sorry," whispered Green Fish.

Izza felt a glimmer of satisfaction at seeing the young human stumble. After a few seconds, she felt guilty and moved to wrap things up. "Was there anything else to report about Flux City before we go celebrate?"

"Yeah." Green Fish sucked in her lip. "The client sends her compliments and says that once things are smoothed out with Nyluga-Ree, she…ahh…wants you to come back."

"Why? Does she have another job for us?" Izza asked innocently, picking up on the hesitation.

The client had been the Guildswoman, Pyruula, and she had flirted hard enough with Izza the last time they had been on Flux City that it was obvious what the lungwoman wanted. It seemed their little Green Fish had an amusing weak spot.

"Not exactly another job," the girl said, blood flushing her cheeks.

"Well, spit it out then. It's vital that you tell me exactly what she said. Word for word."

"Pyruula said she wants you to visit her when the season is upon you and you're in full bloom. She wants to rub her—I think she means her neck fins—through your head blossom. And then she…"

"Yes? What then?" Izza couldn't hold it in anymore. She collapsed into laughter.

"Oh, you can go to hell, boss. If you want to hear the fish woman's sex talk, you can ask her yourself. All I'll say is that the scenarios she planned were extremely detailed. She's obviously spent a lot of time thinking about what she'd like to do with you. And stop teasing me. It's not fair."

"Very few things are, Green Fish. Seriously, you gotta lighten up. The Smugglers Guild is filled with randy-as-fuck animals. And I refuse to butcher my body by taking hormone suppressants. Which means we're all going to have to deal with me coming into season soon. If you can't even say the word sex without heating up like a supernova, that's gonna make you stick out. I can't be having that."

A tear rolled down the girl's cheek.

"What the hell is this?" Izza asked, furious. So, the child was missing her Kurlei boyfriend. Izza was missing her husband, and *she* didn't cry about it. "Stop that. Now!"

Green Fish didn't. Tears became sobs.

"You and your damned human exceptionalism. Wait…" Izza wondered if she'd misread the situation. "Humans reach sexual maturity a lot later than Zhoogenes. Is this…this weakness because you're inexperienced with physical intimacy?"

"I've only done it once." The human's crying subsided, and she chanced a smile. "The boy I took a fancy to had his DNA corrupted. He still recognized me at the end, just before he rammed a spike through my chest."

"*Meatbolt.* Green Fish, I'm so sorry."

"Yeah?" She glared, defiant. "Then act like it."

Izza watched her storm off the flight deck. Damn. She'd meant to praise the girl. Normally, she left it to Fitz to screw up managing the crew. He was welcome to that job when he got back. Maybe he could understand Green Fish. He was the right species, after all.

Humans! Life would be so much simpler without them. And what a sorry galaxy that would be.

* * *

Phantom Lounge, Rift Space

I zza waited a few minutes for Green Fish to calm down and then joined the others in the lounge.

True to her word, Green Fish had brought back gifts from Flux City. There were cured meats, brandies, and sweets suitable for a variety of gut enzymes. There was fragrant synth-coffee too, and she'd given Catkins gaming dice carved from the polished skulls of small lizards. Izza thought the vegetarian Gliesan would be revolted, but he was gushing his thanks.

Helping herself to some of the brandy, Izza raised her tumbler and toasted the new recruit. "To Green Fish! Welcome to the crew."

The others echoed the toast. Even Lynx. It was all smiles and laughter, the awkwardness of the flight deck forgotten.

"Thank you," said Green Fish. "Everything is possible when the girls do it for themselves."

She winked at Izza, but before anyone could ask why, Catkins snapped, "That makes no sense. I am not a female, and gender holds no meaning for Lynx. Well, except when Captain Fitzwilliam ordered Lynx to cease using that _alluring femme fatale persona_ as he called it."

Sinofar loomed menacingly over the engineer, muscles bulging. "I agree with Green Fish. I enjoy men whenever I can—" she paused as if remembering a recent event, "—but we shall do better without them. You will have to be an honorary female, Catkins. There's nothing else to be done about it."

Catkins didn't look enamored with the idea, but he held his peace. Sinofar often had that effect on people.

"Yes," said Izza. "Speaking of which, our next job is to rescue a princess."

"Already, I love this," said Sinofar. "Rescuing princesses is a classic mission objective."

"The individual in question," said Izza, "is bearded and heavily tattooed."

"Sounds intriguing," said Sinofar. "I like her already."

"Yes, about that…" Izza threw up her hands. "Oh, hell, I don't know how to keep spinning an amusing line like that irritating human who used to share my quarters." Izza nodded at Green Fish. "It's your old sergeant, Vetch Arunsen."

"Why?" asked Fregg. "I thought we had split from the old captain's group."

"Don't worry," said Izza. "It's just Arunsen. There's no Fitz. None of the others are involved."

"I say we pick him up," said Sinofar. "I enjoyed his beard. It was very manly."

Fregg shook her head at her Pryxian friend. "I can't figure you out sometimes, Verlys. So, boss, who's holding Arunsen?"

"Details later," said Izza quickly. "Celebration now."

Fregg looked at her suspiciously. "What aren't you telling us?"

Izza put down her drink. The lounge went quiet. "We're stopping off en route at Elder Sun. I have someone I need to see there. I can't think of anything beyond that."

"The Elder Sun system," Catkins mused. "Isn't that where…?" He drew in a sharp breath and wrapped his wings about him.

When it came to reading the room, Catkins was mostly blind. But even he remembered who lived at Elder Sun.

"What?" Green Fish didn't act like a wannabee starship captain now. "Catkins, what's so important about Elder Sun?"

The Gliesan pulled his wings tighter around him. "I don't know," he mumbled.

"Let him be," said Izza. "It's where my mother-in-law lives. I need to see her."

The celebration wound on for a while, but the mention of Mama Zi'Alfu sucked the life out of it, and the crew couldn't wait to sneak away to reconvene somewhere safer. Either the mess room or Catkins' eyrie.

Izza let them go, chewing over how easy she had found it to skirt around awkward details. Just the same as Fitz, though without his charm.

When her crew eventually learned who was holding Vetch, they wouldn't be so cheerful. As to how she was going to explain the need to fail convincingly without any of them getting killed…she decided that was the kind of detail best left alone for as long as possible. Preferably until after the events played out.

She wanted to muse on that in private, but one person hadn't deserted the lounge.

"Why are you still here?" she demanded of Green Fish. "You want to pry into my personal affairs now? You want to know about Fitz's mother?"

Green Fish folded her arms. "No. Although, if you need to tell me, I've a listening ear and all the time you need. It's obvious your relationship is complicated. That's not really what's on my mind."

"Spill your thoughts, Green."

"I've been thinking about Omicron. The salvage mission on the science station. We got lucky that day. The mission could have gone to merdeville because Fregg flies this ship like a blind woman wearing rocket skates."

Izza shrugged. "Fregg does her best."

"That's fair. Until her best isn't good enough, and we all die. Here's a better idea, Captain. Teach me to fly the *Phantom*."

"What?" Izza took a deep breath. "Have you any flight experience?"

"On game sims, yeah."

Izza snorted. "Flying starships is nothing like playing a sim, you simpleminded clown-human."

Green Fish looked unimpressed.

Izza realized she was pulling her ear lobe, a nervous habit she had when she was lying. *Damn! Thought I'd killed off that tell.*

The problem was that flying a starship was *exactly* like the sims. The maneuvering and weapons fire parts anyway.

"So, you played spaceflight sims. What are you saying? That you beat your mom once?"

"On my homeworld of Taractacus Alpha, I was consistently ranked in the Top 100 for SysDef Patrol 4, out of 30 million active players."

"You're a gamer girl. Good for you, but sims don't give you the feel of a real vessel under your feet. Flying *Phantom* is like a partnership. The ones and zeros of a game don't convey the intimacy of partnering with a ship like her."

"I agree. I've also clocked over four hundred hours flying gliders in real life."

For some reason, Izza didn't want to be impressed. But she was. "That's proper flying. Girl, you've got the wrong name. They should have called you Flying Fish. We'll speak about this, I promise. I can't think about such things now. We're two days out from Elder Sun. Before I can face Fitz's mother, I plan to sail to the Seven Suns on good brandy and sober up just in time to dock. This place is dead. No wonder we don't use it. Let's grab some bottles and join the others."

* * * * *

Chapter Eight:
Izza Zan Fey

*P*hantom fell through the skein of reality into the Elder Sun system.

Fitz liked to say, at these moments, that he felt the universe popping with excitement as it welcomed him back into its more civilized dimensions.

Zhoogene eyes saw more clearly than humans', and hers perceived more keenly than most.

To her, the sight through the cockpit window as they left the rift tunnel was like passing through a flight path ladder of raging star stuff. Except this wasn't an artificial view generated by a HUD. The fiery exit tunnel was really there, just meters away.

A loud hiccup escaped her lips, punctuating the final moment of emergence.

Izza's body always did this. It was embarrassing, but it was what it was.

"Are you okay, boss?" asked the young human from the copilot seat.

Izza glared at Green Fish and her idiotic grin. "Report!"

The girl lost her smartass attitude and studied the console displays with the same seriousness she had shown during Izza's coaching sessions.

71

"Klein-Manifold horns actively tunneling. Force keels biting. Emergence position within tolerance. No collision hazards. No hostile threat. Green across the board."

From the pilot's position, Izza confirmed her new apprentice's assessment. "I concur," she told her. "Inform the crew."

The girl's grin came back as she flicked on the intercom. "All hands, emergence from J-space has been successful. The jump went without a hiccup. Well…" She winked at her boss. "Except for the captain, of course. ETA at Kryzabik is…"

Izza flicked across the course plan she'd just worked out.

"We will be docking at *Alsace-14,* an orbital around Kryzabik, in fifteen minutes," said Green Fish. "Last one at the bar buys the drinks. That is all."

* * *

In the end, Izza made the call to her mother-in-law from the flight deck. It was more formal than doing so from her quarters. More businesslike. The downside was that Fitz's absence loomed even more heavily here.

If he had tapped her on her shoulder and yelled, "Surprise!", she wouldn't have been surprised at all. The sense of him was so strong, he almost had a physical presence.

The holo-comm registered a successful connection, and Izza's heart stopped beating. She waited for someone to answer.

Most likely, that person would be Creyoh Zi'Alfu.

Zi'Alfu was just an old human woman, she told herself. Fitz had to have had a mother at some point, and it just so happened it was this woman.

No matter how much Izza told herself she did not require the woman's approval, the knowledge that Mrs. Zi'Alfu despised her daughter-in-law cut deeply.

The holo flickered for a moment and then she was there. Arms folded and a look of defiance on her face, it was Creyoh Zi'Alfu.

"You!" Zi'Alfu's purple eyes widened in shock. Her arms dropped to her sides.

"Good day, Mrs. Zi'Alfu."

"Why are *you* here?"

"I was in the system and wanted to drop in and see you."

"You were always a weak liar."

"I just want to see you for a private chat. On a…" Under her skin, the hydraulic bands around her chest tightened so much she could barely speak. "Family matter," she squeaked.

"Make it snappy, Izza. You caught me heading out on vacation."

"No problem," she replied, relieved not to be meeting the woman in her own territory. "Tell me where you're going, and I'll meet you there."

"Well, you see…" A distant look slid over Zi'Alfu's features. The same expression Fitz had when he was spinning a yarn. "When I say *vacation*, I mean go anywhere but here fast, or the bad people will get me."

"Are they really bad, Mrs. Zi'Alfu? Or did you do something first to make them angry?"

"There may have been a misunderstanding," the old woman admitted with a grin. "And they *are* angry. Are you in orbit, dear?"

"Yes. We're docked at *Alsace-14*. How should I contact you?"

"You shouldn't. I'll find you." She sighed. "I'll be lying low for a while, so call me." She rolled her eyes. "I'll be traveling as Creyoh Fitzwilliam."

Izza laughed. Mama Zi'Alfu hated the family name Fitz had dreamed up.

"How is he?" asked the woman, her features suddenly aging. "I don't see him on your flight deck."

"He's not aboard."

"I figured that much. He might not think much of his poor old mother, but he has the decency to speak for himself." She sighed. "So, you two are going through a rough patch. It's to be expected, I suppose. My advice to you, Zan Fey, is to divorce him. Get yourself a nice green man."

Izza felt the hydraulic bands around her abdomen harden more firmly than ever. Mother-in-law always had this effect on her. "See you on *Alsace-14*," she gasped and cut the link.

* * *

Thirty-six hours later, the last of *Phantom's* crew began to return from the orbital, weary, pale, shaking a little, but happy.

Izza was not amused. There had been no word from her mother-in-law and no reply to her comm pings.

"You have command," she told Sinofar, who looked the least wasted of the group. "I need to go find someone."

"Good luck, I think," Sinofar called out as Izza stormed off the ship, "I hope you don't find her."

Izza growled but didn't answer. Sinofar was probably right. Izza had never met Fitz's father, but she was damned sure all his bad impulses had been inherited from his mother.

* * *

The data broker's premises were extremely spartan. Bare, metal bulkheads and a high grip plas-steel lattice floor. Izza passed through the final security arch into a compartment housing twenty-eight identical booths secured behind shielded doors.

It looked like a high security lavatory block.

She pushed through one of the doors marked with a green 'vacant' glyph, half expecting to see a toilet on the other side. But it was a narrow space divided in half by a security screen. A Transgoan sat on the far side, a particularly sullen example of the squat, three-legged species.

Izza sat on the stool on her side of the barrier. "I wish to trace someone. Two days ago, they were planetside. They were supposed to meet me here on the station but never showed."

"One hundred and fifty credit fee. Fifty credits payable in advance. The rest on successful completion."

In front of her, she could see the Transgoan's mouth moving, but its voice came from the air behind her, which was unnerving.

She placed her Guild token against the screen.

Seemingly bored by this development, the Transgoan drew a transparent disk the same size as Izza's token and aligned it against hers on the other side of the screen. Izza felt her disk vibrate in her hand, and saw bars appear on the data broker's. They stabilized in the same pattern of pixelated stalactites and stalagmites as those on her own token.

"I accept your status, Guild member," said the broker. "No initial fee. Fifty credits on completion. What can you tell me about the target?"

"Her name is Creyoh Zi'Alfu, though she may be traveling under Creyoh Fitzwilliam. Resident of Otizen in Kadeja Province. Age 92 years, though she's had rejuvenation. Her eyes are...purple."

"Ah, yes. The *mutant*. Creyoh Zi'Alfu should present us with no problems. I'll be a few moments. You can wait here if you like, or if you prefer to give me your contact details—"

"She's not a mutant," Izza insisted. "Her eyes are purple. That's all."

"Yes, but surely..." The broker stopped. It wasn't uninterested now. If anything, it looked worried. Slowly, it raised its gaze to meet Izza's, swallowing hard when it saw the unique eye coloring of its new client. "My apologies, Del-Saisha Zan Fey. I misspoke."

"When Creyoh Zi'Alfu's son was aged just nineteen standard," Izza told the broker, "she stole his first starship, his pride and joy, and emptied his credit account while she was at it. She is not a good person, but she is a human with purple eyes. Not a mutant."

"Again, my apologies, ma'am."

Izza sat back and let the broker do its job.

The alien jerked suddenly. "Found her."

From the way the Transgoan's thin lips trembled, this wasn't good.

"I regret," said the broker, "the price I must charge has risen to accommodate a risk surcharge. It now stands at 350 credits."

"And for a Guildswoman?"

"That is with your discount. Full price is now 2000."

Izza pressed her forehead against the security screen and looked threatening, although she very much doubted she had the firepower to get to the person on the other side. "I'm not paying that," she said quietly.

The broker sighed. It looked highly relieved.

"Apologies for the inconvenience, ma'am. I'm sorry we couldn't do business."

"Why is it so damned expensive?"

"Because aiding you could be seen as an aggressive move by people our organization does not wish to cross."

Izza brandished her token once more. "I understand. And I hope *you* understand that not charging a fair rate would have the same effect with me. I am also somebody you do not wish to cross."

Transgoans didn't go pale when they were worried. Their flesh hardened. Izza enjoyed watching this one's skin transform from Slern-like smoothness into rough bark. "The security in this booth is significant," it stated.

Izza rested her head on her steepled fingers and whispered, "I wasn't thinking of killing you *here*."

She enjoyed watching beads of sweat on the broker's craggy face coalesce into rivulets of fear. But she decided this danger surcharge was not a battle she wanted to fight. "Very well then," she said. "I shall pay your fee." She made the transfer. "Now tell me where that damned woman is!"

"She is at the Orion Nights Club, an entertainment venue on Sector Four, Level VIII."

"That doesn't make sense. Why would she be there?"

"The club is owned by one of the two primary crime gangs on the station, led by Miss Kilrine. The trail I'm following indicates your target has been either at the club or locations associated with Kilrine since shortly after arriving on the station the day before yesterday. Creyoh Zi'Alfu has been developing a certain notoriety in the Elder Sun system. You might call her toxic. I suspect that Miss Kilrine has found a way to leverage that toxicity. Perhaps she's enjoying her company while she negotiates with Zi'Alfu's enemies the price of her return to the planet. There are vested interests who don't wish her to die quietly. They wish her end to be that of a reviled monster, not someone who could be held up as a martyr."

"Who wants her dead planetside?"

"That would require me to charge for a new query."

Izza casually drew her blaster pistol and blew over the barrel. "*Alsace 14* is a big orbital, my friend. That means there are many places to hide and to observe." She leaned forward and smiled. "And to *ambush*."

The broker swallowed hard. "What I meant to say is that, although it's a new query, I would be honored to answer your question as a personal favor without charge. The truth is that many people want Creyoh Zi'Alfu dead. Most of them because they're conditioned to hate her. But if you want to point the finger at a single entity most likely to be behind all this, it would be Gliar-G Mining Corporation. She's been a shard in their flesh for years."

"Because she stole something valuable of theirs?"

The alien's head blew up to twice its normal size, a Transgoan expression of surprise. "No, ma'am. Because she's eaten into their profits. Kryzabik is a mining world, and your target is a violent environmental extremist."

* * *

Orion Nights Club, *Alsace-14* Station

Izza hesitated at the edge of the dance floor, giving her sensitive ears time to numb to the pounding music.

The Orion Nights club catered to Zhoogenes, though, and the noise levels weren't as insane as those at human-only venues.

She moved into the throng of dancers.

The bass from the banging anti-didj beats rumbled through Izza's legs and goosed her organs with fat, yet dexterous, fingers.

She liked it.

Enough to let a sway come to her narrow hips.

To humans, rhythmically grinding hips were a sexy turn on, but on the Zhoogene frame, the movement looked as jerky as a cheap animation. Hot Zhoogene dance moves came from the shoulders, not the hips, but Izza was part human so she could almost pull it off. Besides, she didn't care.

Which was...*strange*. Normally, she would. Bylzak! What were they putting in the air?

Puffs of colored clouds swept the dance floor at random intervals. They carried the oiliness of herbal essences, blended with tangy stims that tickled her tongue.

She pushed through the dance melee, bumping off revelers as she went. A few of them gave her startled looks, but their expressions transformed into beams of joy or...breathless lust. Hot damn! She looked again and realized the clientele was overwhelmingly human. Given the looks she was getting, the owners must be pumping Zhoogene sex pheromones into the air.

Suddenly, a few feet in front of her, a hexagonal section of dance floor rose in the smoky air. One unlucky dancer fell off, though she was caught by the fun goers below. The remainder showed off their best dance moves six feet in the air. A matching hexagonal column of red light lanced down from the ceiling, encasing the dancers. Their silhouettes could be seen within, slowly shrinking and rising from the hexagonal base, until they were no more than a pulsing ball.

They seemed happy, though.

Neat optical illusion.

Still infected with the beat, Izza dodged around the hexagon and made for the tables on the far side, reasoning that even with her mother-in-law's rejuve, a 92-year-old would spend most of her time off her feet.

She located Zi'Alfu at a table by the back wall, which glowed with ultraviolet hexagonal patterns human eyes couldn't see.

Watching over Zi'Alfu were two human men in white tank tops stretched tightly over impressive muscles. They were being very obvious about the sling-holstered handguns above their hips.

Izza crossed to a nearby table at which a mixed-species crowd of friends were in heated conversation. She hovered on the edge of the group, implying to any onlookers that she was a part of it.

From here she observed the area. Zi'Alfu seemed bemused at being at a club where the average age was less than a quarter of hers. Clothed in an old ship suit bearing the half-hidden black disk logo of Elder Sun Transport, she was chatting with a human man dressed in a tailored, high collar suit, with an excess of gold and jewels on show. Izza knew nothing of local fashions, but even to her eyes, his appearance spoke of wealth.

What she couldn't explain was the man's tight-lipped look of resentment. He looked like he'd been dealt a monstrously bad hand but had no option but to play it. Not the boss of this setup, then.

Zi'Alfu and the rich guy were surrounded by three individuals equally spaced around the table at a surprisingly large distance from it: about three meters. Two of them were the armed men with ripped torsos she'd already noted, but now Izza realized there was a third. She was a Zhoogene female who was flaunting a red fishnet halter top and a long chiffon skirt that changed colors in time to the beat. Izza's eyebrows shot up when one of those 'colors' turned out to be transparent and revealed that the Zhoogene hadn't troubled herself with undergarments.

Like Izza, the girl allowed her body to express its nature, rather than bind herself with the hormone suppressants many Zhoogenes took. That much was obvious from the proto-blossoms peppering the girl's head. They meant she was nearly in season, just a few weeks ahead of Izza's own cycle. Perhaps that explained her raunchy look.

Or maybe she was just a beautiful young woman out having fun at a club. It had been a long time since Izza had been to a place like this. Much too long.

"What do you think?" asked one of the human males from the table she was using as cover.

She swallowed. And wrenched her attention away from the hot girl. Doing so wasn't easy. "Whaaa?" she slurred.

"About Uffdel. I think he'd have to be nuts to go through with it."

Izza glanced back at the girl. The Zhoogene was staring right back at her, lips open seductively.

"I think Uffdel's right," she told the guy. She turned her back on the captivating Zhoogene and leaned into the young man, kissing him full on the lips.

Much as she loved him, it wasn't Fitz's lips she imagined she was devouring.

The human went rigid with surprise, but soon melted into her kiss, like they always did.

Fitz would understand. He wouldn't like it, though.

She released the boy.

In a state of shock, he gingerly touched a fingertip to his lips. Poor kid looked like he was going to burst with pleasure.

She slid her arm around his shoulders, smoothly edging herself around him until she had a better view of Zi'Alfu's table.

The wealthy man her mother-in-law had been talking to had gone. That was good. Not so good, the two guards and the Zhoo-gene girl were all looking Izza's way.

The girl was giving her a sexy pout. It looked so contrived that Izza came to her senses enough to notice the recording equipment nestled inside the girl's cropped head growth.

Now it made sense. Maybe. Zi'Alfu and the absent man were en-gaged in a performance, staged and filmed for the amusement of the gang boss who ran this joint. Izza didn't give a skragg for the reason why.

The armed humans were scowling, warning her off.

Zi'Alfu was looking her way too, wearing a neutral expression.

But the girl was inviting her in, and her skin was so smooth and green…

Izza closed her eyes and tried to think clearly.

Danger made her randy. And feeling hot made her court danger.

She knew her nature. And she knew that, if Fitz were here, he would tell her to wait for backup.

But she was fed up with waiting.

There were only two guards, but she'd had to surrender her needle gun to club security on the way in.

The odds weren't good.

All the sex shit pumping through the air and her body priming itself for an explosion of uncontrollable craziness drove her on.

The boy she'd kissed was gesturing for her attention. "Say, what was your name again?"

She smiled down at him. "Get out of the chair, and I'll tell you."

He frowned, but only for an instant before scrambling to his feet. He trembled in his eagerness to learn what delights awaited him.

She grabbed the back of his chair. "Izza Zan Fey," she explained, deciding she owed him a name on which to hang his experience.

Then she picked up his chair and carried it over to Zi'Alfu's table, brushing gratuitously against the sexy greenness of the Zhoogene who seemed to be in charge of this operation.

The girl's scent was driving her crazy.

"Hey, hey!" One of the men took an aggressive step toward her. "You can't sit here. Go away!"

"Sorry, sweetie," Zhoogene girl told her, filming everything.

Zi'Alfu smiled at the camera. "It's okay, dear. This plays even better with her here. Sal Deema, meet my daughter-in-law, Izza Zan Fey. You'd better order us another drink." She peered at Izza and stroked her chin thoughtfully. "It's Florinette ale, isn't it?"

"That'll do nicely," Izza replied. She leaned across the table and tried to shut out the anti-didj beat assaulting her ears. "What the hell is going on?"

"These nice people have been holding me for a while. Just smile and pretend you're having a good time. When the woman who runs this place tires of this game—not Sal Deema, someone you would find far less pleasing to your senses—I'll be sold to a meat broker. They'll command a generous fee to have me placed wherever Gliar-G Mining Corporation wants me to be."

Sensing that the armed gangsters were letting this play out for now, Izza sat back and considered the woman she'd come to Kryzabik to meet. "I don't have time for this," she told her.

Creyoh returned an appraising look of her own. She held her grin just under the surface, exactly like Fitz did when he was teasing her.

The older woman usually wore a sunshade band around her eyes. When she did, the only way she resembled Fitz was with that grin and her glossy black hair that fell in gentle waves down to her shoulders.

In other regards, Fitz must take after his father, because Creyoh's lips were much fuller than her son's, as was her nose; the cheekbones were far sharper.

But now, without the band, when she threatened a grin, her eyes sparkled in exactly the same way as Fitz's.

And those eyes!

Izza's orbs were marbled. Fitz told her she had an inner purple glow that diffracted into ribbons of cyan and magenta. Fitz's were lilac, but Creyoh's were flecks of potassium fire in seas of glowing sulfur.

Despite the many complications those vivid eyes brought her, Creyoh displayed them proudly whenever it was safe to do so.

"It isn't true that we don't have time for a talk," Creyoh replied. "You should learn to make time for yourself *and* your family."

"Oh, yeah? Like the way you treated Fitz when he was just starting out?"

"I was a caring mother, teaching her darling child a valuable lesson."

Izza made a cutting gesture. "I *really* don't have time for that conversation. Just tell me what mess you've gotten into this time. Without the usual embellishments."

"Kryzabik's two major exports are in the expressive arts and the mining of rare elements. In fact, the place started off around FL-800 as a mining colony, and the industry has served the world well. Still does. Mostly. But the easy geological seams are mined out, and the future looks bleak. Along comes Gliar-G Mining Corporation."

"If your cost of extraction rises," said Izza, "you can either raise your prices—"

"Or cut corners. Kryzabik's mining corporations not only respect their communities, in many places, they *are* the community. From time to time, politicians out to milk their turn in office will urge the miners to cut corners on safety and environmental concerns to bring in the credits. The corporations refuse because, unlike our elected representatives, they're here for the long haul."

"Let me guess," said Izza. "Gliar-G is from out of town."

"They operate out of a shiny floating edifice in the financial district of *Zeta-Arcelia*." She spoke the name of the Federation's capital world with utter contempt. "They're not miners as such. More financiers who raise leveraged debt to buy mining assets that they exploit ruthlessly. And that's what they've done here. Paid off the provincial governor and the system Militia commander. Then proceeded to poison great swathes of Kadeja Province as a side effect of cheaper extraction methods. Half the land from the Jescall-Red River to the Taidyung Mountains is no longer a safe place to live. There's five million people who call that area home. Most importantly, me."

"Who the fuck is the green doll?"

Izza blamed the thumping beats. She hadn't heard the approach of the man who'd been sitting there earlier.

"Who's the foul-mouthed scump?" Izza asked Creyoh.

"The gangs of *Alsace-14* have just gone through a turf war," the older woman explained. "This is Mr. Uhlanchek, the loser. He's here to be seen spending time with me. Mr. Uhlanchek, this is my daughter-in-law."

While mister loser licked his lips, Izza mused over how she was going to hurt the disrespectful jerk. Creyoh beat her to it, casually getting up from her seat and slapping him hard.

Uhlanchek shot her a look that could almost kill. "You're lucky my humiliations have been heaped so high this day that what you just did doesn't even rate among them. But one day, I'll regain my power. You'd better beg for forgiveness preemptively, Creyoh Zi'Alfu, or I'll drag your apologies out of you the hard way."

A waiter appeared with three fresh glasses.

"You too, green cheeks," the gangster told Izza.

"I'll take it under advisement."

After shooting her a sly grin, Uhlanchek was suddenly all bonhomie. "To my fine female companions," he toasted, prompting them to lean over the table to clink glasses.

"Are you armed?" Izza asked the others.

"No," Uhlanchek replied, smiling for the camera. "Neither is Zi'Alfu. Are you?"

"Security here is very effective," Izza observed.

"Tell us about it," said Creyoh.

"Not to worry," said Izza. She sniffed her drink and smelled candy hops and a snatch of sulfur from the mineralized brewing water.

Resisting the beer was the hardest thing she'd done since throwing Fitz out of the *Phantom*. Couldn't risk it being spiked, though.

Instead, she raised the glass to her lips and then flung it into the face of the nearest tank-topped mobster.

She erupted out of her seat, numbing the man's gun hand with a knife-hand strike. Hopping from side to side with the music beat, she sent a flurry of jabs at the man's throat.

He was hurting. Confused. Not sure where the next blow was coming from.

But there wasn't to be one.

She grabbed his pistol from him, then she poked her head over his left shoulder and fired a bolt at the other guard a fraction of a second before he fired at her.

Milliseconds. That was all that divided the shots, but it was all she needed. A blaster bolt enveloped her target's face, melting it. His shot went wide but only just. He was firing slugs, and one sliced open the left side of her shield's gut, missing her by inches.

The man with the melted face collapsed to the floor, falling over Uhlanchek's body. The defeated gang boss must have leaped at the other guard. Probably bought Izza a second or so. She wasn't sure if he was dead or unconscious. She didn't care.

"You're forgiven," she told Uhlanchek as she turned with a steady grip on her new blaster to acquire the final target.

But the Zhoogene girl had vanished into the crowd. Probably for the best.

"I've got a ship waiting," Izza told Creyoh. "Time to say our goodbyes."

Keeping her newly acquired blaster at the ready, she pushed through the dancers and the anti-didj beat.

If the revelers understood what was happening in their midst, they showed no signs of caring.

The music cut.

They noticed *that*.

Gasps peppered the dance floor. Several people suddenly spotted Izza's blaster. They gave it sidelong glances as if not sure whether it was real or cosplay.

Then the lighting switched. Suddenly, everything was blue and waving greens. It looked as if they were under the ocean.

What the hell?

A symphony of musical gurgling filled the club. Booming. It was achingly beautiful. *Has to be a Littorane underwater chorus.*

It worked for Izza. The dancers swayed on the spot, waiting for the new-Litt beat to start pumping beneath the chorus line. Izza and Zi'Alfu hurried through the gaps that had opened between the dancers.

She ran into the entrance lobby, sending an arriving party of human revelers screaming back into the station.

The two Zhoogene men working security were not so easily scared.

"Give me back my needler," she demanded of the one at which she was aiming her blaster. Scars burst from one of his eye sockets, but the artificial eye inside tracked her perfectly, as did his pistol.

"You can't be serious," said the other Zhoogene, whose handgun was also pointed at Izza. "The only way you're getting out of Orion Nights alive is when it suits Miss Kilrine."

"Give the girl what she wants," demanded Creyoh, each hand holding a pistol pushed against the back of a Zhoogene head.

Two pistols? Where had she gotten the other weapon from?

"I'm in a hurry," Izza told the security guards. "Tell you what. You keep my needler, and I'll take your pistols."

Carefully. Ever so slowly, the two armed men safed their weapons and handed them over to Izza, raising their empty hands.

"What now, dear?" asked her mother-in-law. "Shall I shoot them?"

Izza licked her lips while she enjoyed watching two pairs of golden eyes cloud with fear. Well, one-and-a-half pairs, because the artificial orb stared back implacably.

But she didn't have time to enjoy herself. "No, of course not. Not when these two have been so helpful. In fact…I think they need a reward." She brandished her blaster at the one-eyed guard. "Take your friend out on the dance floor and shake your shoulders with him. Go on, you'll love it."

Reluctantly, the pair moved off through the beaded curtain and into the noise and lights of the club.

Izza retrieved her needler, stuffing it along with the newly acquired weapons into her pink jacket.

"Can you run?" she asked her 92-year-old mother-in-law.

"Faster than you. Let's go!"

As they pounded down the station corridors, Izza commed *Phantom*. "Sinofar, you copy?"

"I read you. *Phantom* is ready to make a hot exit as soon as you board."

"What makes you think this is anything other than a boring check in?"

Behind her, Creyoh laughed. "Sounds like your crew knows you better than you know yourself."

"Captain," said Sinofar, "do we need to come into the station to extract you from the mess you've gotten yourself into?"

"No. And improve your tone. Is that how you would speak to Fitzwilliam?"

"No, ma'am. That was how *you* would have spoken to him. One last question, are we to prevent Mrs. Zi'Alfu from boarding?"

Izza looked behind her at the woman in the Elder Sun Transport ship suit. The rejuve hadn't just smoothed wrinkles. Creyoh smiled back sweetly with no sign of exertion as she jogged along briskly.

"On the contrary, Sinofar. Ensure she *does* board. Mrs. Zi'Alfu has some explaining to do."

* * * * *

Chapter Nine:
Izza Zan Fey

Kryzabik

*P*hantom flew east across the Taidyung Mountains, hugging the valley floor through the Sylung Gap, then shot out into the plains of Kadeja Province, startling a herd of six-legged herbivores walking along the north bank of the Jescall-Red River.

They scattered in panic, many splashing down the muddy bank into the wide Jescall-Red, where they swam for the far shore.

Long jaws, crammed with teeth, emerged from the water. They clamped to the necks of the swimming herbivores, dragging them down to their doom.

Izza mouthed, "Sorry," and added altitude.

For once, she wasn't trying to fly under the radar, expecting the missile lock alarm to blare at any moment. She just wanted to fly low to enjoy the scenery.

"They're called wildebeests," explained Zi'Alfu from the seat behind Izza's pilot station. "An early human explorer thought they resembled an animal she'd never seen that once lived on a planet she'd also never seen. Tourists used to come and watch their migration from a respectful distance."

"They looked all right to me," said Izza. "Before I spooked some into a watery death."

91

"Herd numbers have halved in five years. Turn south."

Izza handed control over to her copilot and allowed Green Fish to bank right while she took a good look through the lower quadrant of the cockpit glass at the ground passing below.

The prairie on the south bank of the Jescall-Red gave way to glistening wetland. The horizon shimmered and revealed itself to be a watercourse of some kind. Strange. It wasn't on the map.

"Take her up to ten thousand feet," she ordered.

As *Phantom* climbed, they saw they were flying toward a major lake.

"It's a hundred klicks across," Zi'Alfu explained. "Officially, this is waterlogged ground from recent rains. Unofficially, we call this the Great Sludge Pool."

"Is this runoff from the mines?" Green Fish asked.

"*Untreated* runoff. Yes. South of here, I could show you agriculture failing and communities dying. You won't see that properly from the air, but if we land, you would see birth defects, cancers, bone mutation."

"I don't think that's necessary," said Izza.

"In that case, it clearly is. Open your comms, Zan Fey. I need to make a call. It's to the only friend who stood by me, Mrs. Sregsboone."

Izza released the comms, and Zi'Alfu called a local address.

A Zhoogene woman appeared in the holo-display, hunched a little but with an upbeat smile. She was in her kitchen and had just taken something out of the auto-chef.

"Creyoh! I was so worried. I heard Kontesmo and her troublemakers had shown up at your place to…I don't like to think *what* they intended. But you look well. Are you?"

"I'm fine. They came to kill me, didn't they? You can tell me the truth."

But Mrs. Sregsboone wasn't interested in telling what had happened at Zi'Alfu's house. She was too busy peering into the camera. "Is that your daughter-in-law, Creyoh? My, my! You told me she had pretty eyes, but I had no idea. I thought you were just boasting about her again."

"Like I would ever have a reason to boast about that degenerate article my son married. Although, I'll admit, she *has* been somewhat helpful in the last couple of days. Haven't you, dear?"

Izza couldn't reply. All she could do was stare at Sregsboone. Arms, throat, face…her dress left plenty of skin exposed. Half was a sickly pale green, like cut foliage left out to dry in the sun. The rest of her skin was mottled in shades of rust and brick dust.

Izza prided herself on her own unique style to go with her exclusive physique. According to conventional ideals of beauty, she was a damned freak. But she was proud of her skin. To a Zhoogene woman, lush, verdant skin was her most prized asset, and she was no exception.

She'd never even heard of a Zhoogene with rust skin. Even accounting for the yellow tint of the holo-comm, this woman looked ill.

"Are you all right, dear?" asked the old Zhoogene. "You look a little…pale."

Izza turned her head. Too slow…she vomited over the flight console.

Lynx would complain when she ordered him to clean up the mess. She didn't blame him.

This planet had another kind of mess that needed cleaning up. That was her task.

"Mrs. Sregsboone," she asked, wiping her mouth with the back of her hand. "Forgive me for the directness of my question, but was your skin always this color?"

The woman stiffened her back and took on a defiant expression. "The doctors say my condition is caused by overactive photoreceptors. But that's double-bubble speak from people in the pay of the mining company. Before the Great Sludge Pool, my skin was green as a lancekin fruit. I was quite the beauty in my youth."

"I'm sure you were, Mrs. Sregsboone. And you still carry yourself with grace and dignity. It's an honor to meet you. Good day, ma'am."

"Where's your briefing room?" asked Zi'Alfu once her friend's holo-image had gone.

That stumped Izza for a few moments. She normally discussed things with Fitz on the flight deck or in bed. If the crew were involved, they would crowd into the mess room.

She released her harness. "Green Fish, holler if you have the slightest concern. I'll be with Mrs. Zi'Alfu in the lounge."

* * * * *

Chapter Ten:
Izza Zan Fey

From the to-die-for comfort of the auto-molding silk floor cushions, the two women watched the smoke rising from the firepit in the middle of *Phantom's* lounge. The plume of particulates coalesced into the words of a newsfeed headline.

MUTANT DENIES CAUSING CRIMINAL DAMAGE AT MINING SITE

Of course, it wasn't really a fireplace—although it could throw out convincing fire-like flows of hot air convection—and the smoke created by the fancy holo-projection wasn't real either.

Skragging expensive. That's what it really was.

The newsfeed headline. According to Zi'Alfu, that was real too.

A tap on Zi'Alfu's slate and the smoke blurred back into a random plume before firming into new words.

CREYOH ZI'ALFU—NOTORIOUS MUTANT EXPERTS CLAIM CAN HACK MINDS—SPREADS NEW SLURS ABOUT GLIAR-G MINING

"I think I get the picture," said Izza. "You caused a stink by pointing out that these off-worlders were screwing with your home. They fought back."

"I had just celebrated my ninetieth birthday when I decided to take them on. To my shame, I was naïve enough to think that if you pressed hard enough, then a hundred-klick wide pool of toxic sludge was the kind of thing whose existence couldn't be denied. I was wrong. They had bought off Danieff Caoji, our assclown of a provincial governor. They also bought the Elder Sun Militia commander, which meant the planetary government wouldn't touch it. A *local issue*, they insisted."

KADEJA SENATE DISMISSES AS 'HOAX' CLAIMS OF ENVIRONMENTAL CATASTROPHE SPREAD BY NOTORIOUS MUTANT

"Mutant!" Izza shook her head sadly. "Do they put that on every headline?"

"Mostly. It makes it clear which side their consumers are meant to hate. Then there are the other articles that teach people to fear our kind, which suddenly became popular with the newsfeeds. They can publish what they want. We're mutants, Izza, you and I. We're not a protected group. If we were, the skraggs who printed this slander would be hauled off for a long stay in a reeducation camp."

"All this! Just because our eyes are a different color. Why do these people hate us so much?"

"Are you kidding?" Zi'Alfu rose half out of her cushion and gave Izza a look of disgust. "When this business is over, Zan Fey, we're doing *the talk*."

"Never mind me. What did you do about these slurs?"

"Played Gliar-G Mining at their own game."

"You sold your story to the news outlets?"

"Azhanti! You're more naïve than I ever was. No. Gliar-G persuaded Governor Caoji to look the other way. Well, I *un*-persuaded him. He claims to have suffered abduction, blackmail, and torture." Zi'Alfu tutted. "Torture! Goodness me! I'm sure we've both experienced *real* torture, Izza. I merely tickled him. In any case, after I spent a little time with him, he suddenly noticed the enormous sludge lake poisoning his province."

She flicked to another headline.

HAS HE BEEN A NAUGHTY BOY? GOVERNOR CAOJI DENIES BEING IN THRALL TO MUTANT SEDUCTRESS TWICE HIS AGE

"So Gliar-G changed tactics. They whipped up the hate against me even more and faked footage that showed I'd been best pals with Governor Caoji for years. It didn't take long for Caoji to be recalled and imprisoned. Then they came for me. That was when you arrived like a green bolt out of the blue."

Tears rolled down Zi'Alfu's face. Izza felt completely out of her depth. She had no idea whether she should comfort the other woman, or how.

"Gliar-G used my neighbors to take me out. Bertinika Kontesmo and her Auxiliary Volunteers were coming for me when you called. They always were a bunch of drenthead asswipes, but they were still my neighbors. And the bulk of my community? They didn't try running me out of town, but they didn't lift a finger to stop Kontesmo either. I was a pariah."

Izza regarded her mother-in-law, giving her a few moments to let her emotions vent.

If you saw her across the street, she would seem an unremarkable human female. Middling height, weight, and apparent age, with a skin tone of one of the lighter brown shades for a human, though average for a female.

This was one of the things Izza found most perverse about humanity. She'd learned in school that skin pigmentation cells were about fifteen percent less concentrated in human females than males, whereas in her species, women enjoyed a deeper shade of green by about the same amount.

Up close, Creyoh Zi'Alfu had peculiar features that were largely unblemished and wrinkle free, and yet her skin lacked the tautness of youth. Her ears were oversized as was the lower part of her nose. Subtle signs of rejuvenation treatments. Good ones. The kind only the richest had access to.

What had turned this rich old woman with a shady past into an environmental crusader? "What's in it for you?"

"Oh, I get it." Zi'Alfu assumed a pained expression. "Been listening to my son poisoning your mind. I'm not the bad person he makes me out to be."

"You did steal his first ship when he was still a teenager. Stripped his credit accounts dry."

"We've already had that conversation, Zan Fey. It was responsible parenting. The kind he wasn't getting from his father, who was all space battles and shiny Legion hoorah. One of his parents had to teach him about real life."

"Teach him what? Not to trust the people close to him?"

"He's always trusted you more than me," Zi'Alfu spluttered. "I don't know why you feel so threatened."

"I don't. It's your son who has the trust issues."

"How would *you* know? I don't see him here on your fancy ship. That nice young man with the wings said my boy had been forced to walk the plank. By you, Zan Fey. And you say you don't have trust issues!"

"It's not about me."

"No. Then why the hell are you here in the Elder Sun system at all?"

Izza sucked in a deep breath, enjoying the moment. She'd just outsmarted her mother-in-law. Or so she hoped. "I'll answer your question," she told Zi'Alfu, "if you answer mine first. Why are you doing this…this environmentalist act?"

The older woman returned a sly look that made Izza question who'd just outsmarted whom. "I've had the rejuves. I look a peach. Run ten klicks before breakfast every other day too. But my mind feels every one of its ninety-two standard. I finally needed to put down roots, and I've planted them here. It's my community that's been screwed by Gliar-G. And they deserve better. Even Kontesmo and the other arse-skraggs who turned against me." She smiled. "Your turn, dear."

Izza took the slate and brought up the image Fitz had passed to her of Khallini. Digital compression of the image made him look scratchy, but she recognized the man with the brass-tipped cane they'd transported to Rho-Torkis. Would Zi'Alfu? She studied her mother-in-law's face for a reaction.

Zi'Alfu gave nothing away.

"Do you know him?" Izza asked. "Perhaps when you were young. His name is Khallini."

"You mean the infamous Lord Khallini?" She laughed. "He's a puny specimen in the flesh, isn't he? Looks like a Spacer. I don't mean like you—prancing around in a glossy spaceship thinking it makes you glamorous—I mean the original *Spacers*. Bioengineered humans from the Orion Era."

"I thought that was just a fable."

"Nope. Humans came here in two main flavors. Marines were powerful, aggressive, permanently horny, and AI-jacked. Then there were the Spacers, runts who were economical at consuming air, water, food, and space aboard starships, but whose minds were sharp. There were also Wolves, Earthborn, and, among other sub-groups were Marines with purple eyes. Our ancestors. This man is a Spacer."

"Do you recognize him? Could you have met him?"

"Cheeky green madam! I'm old but not *that* old. It's 3,000 years since the Exiles showed up in the Perseus Arm."

"Are you saying this person was born in the Orion Spur? Thousands of years ago?"

"No. I said he is a Spacer. They crewed the Exile ships and started interbreeding once they got here. A group of them might have gone for the preserving genetic purity game. People could have been stuck in suspended animation for a long time. You always get a few genetic throwbacks. Or maybe someone out there in the Federation is re-engineering the old races of humanity. Who knows? It's a freaking weird galaxy. Haven't you learned that yet?"

"Cryo seems the most likely," said Izza. "I've heard of people sleeping for centuries. Maybe some people could be under for thousands of years and still live."

"No. This man hasn't been asleep. He's been around all this time. This person came with the Exile fleet. He was there at First Landing."

"That's impossible." Izza shot a confused look at Zi'Alfu.

"I know." Zi'Alfu gave an excited grin, her eyes glowing with blues and purples.

"I'm not in the mood for your damned games." Izza swiped Khallini from the holo. "If it's impossible this man was born in the Orion Spur, then why tell me he was?"

The grin crumbled, and Zi'Alfu looked the most uncomfortable Izza had ever seen her. "Instinct."

Instinct. It was the same word Fitz had used to explain why she needed to come here in the first place.

"Your husband has these gut feelings, doesn't he?" said Zi'Alfu. "Insists on a course of action that makes no sense. I expect he begs you to trust him. Reluctantly, you let him sway you. At first, you curse yourself for believing his steaming shite, because his instincts appear to be nonsense. But, by long and tortuous routes, he's always and annoyingly proved right. Every time."

A chill came over Izza. Her deepest secrets were being clinically dissected. "Yes, ma'am."

"Trust our instincts. They're based on precognition. It's your heritage too, Izza." Zi'Alfu couldn't hold her gaze and looked away. "It's a curse when you can see the secrets of the universe but are powerless to act on what you know. Looks like I'm a refugee now, my dear. How nice to finally be with my family in the twilight of my years."

The prospect shocked Izza into landing an idea. "Powerless? Who said we're powerless? We fight Gliar-G's slurs with our own.

Looks like I'll have to kiss Khallini on his bald head next time I see him because he's just given me eighty million reasons for the people of Kryzabik to believe our lies over theirs."

She wondered how Fitz would react to her blowing all their money on his mother. Credits they'd earned to pay back Nyluga-Ree for good. She smiled. "Fitz will understand."

* * * * *

Chapter Eleven:
Izza Zan Fey

Kadeja Independent News Offices, Kadeja City, Kryzabik

Fitz sometimes said Justiana Fregg was a beautiful woman who was more alluring because she didn't know it.

But then Fitz was forever spouting crap in that vein, so Izza had always dismissed his words as a clumsy attempt to find something nice to say about *Phantom's* scruffy logistics manager.

Fregg was taking point on this mission. And for that, Izza had ordered her to be cleaned, coiffed, and clothed at the system capital on the other side of the planet. Finished off with some of Izza's jewelry Fitz had given her, Fregg exuded elegance and wealth.

Izza would not have thought such a thing was possible.

To a Zhoogene, beauty was primarily about verdant skin and tantalizing scent. Fregg smelled like a concrete slaughterhouse freshly hosed down with chemical cleaner. But she had the visuals nailed the way humans liked them.

"Thank you for agreeing to see me," Fregg told the owner of Kadeja Independent News, extending a hand to the man.

Izza cringed. Fregg had walked into the HQ of the local news outlet as if she already owned the place. But when she spoke, she sounded as if she'd been born and raised in a space dock. Which, of course, she had.

But Yanzeung, the owner of KIN, rose smiling from his chair to shake her hand. "My pleasure, Ms. Fregg."

Ah. So, Fitz *was* right about Fregg. The man was practically preening himself. And he wasn't doing it for Izza's benefit. Well, not entirely.

As Fregg settled into the visitor's chair, Yanzeung threw an irritated nod at Izza, who remained standing behind her. "Who's this?"

"This is Fey, my personal assistant. Makes the coffee, carries things, and wipes my arse when I tell her."

The man flinched at Fregg's crudeness.

"She's also my legal expert."

"Ahh." He nodded as if that explained everything. "A heavily armed legal advisor to boot. You are most unconventional, Ms. Fregg."

Heavily armed? Behind her stylish shades, Izza frowned. Had she misread the situation? She was armed only with her hand cannon holstered in full view on her thigh. That and knives hidden inside her boots. It was Sinofar who was waiting outside who was heavily armed, and even she was only carrying one main weapon.

Yanzeung pointed at Izza. "The dark shades too. They are a little intimidating. We are not outside in the sunshine."

Izza felt a tingle in her gun hand. She'd seen news hate-bait that smeared Fitz and her as well as Creyoh. The news shapers had been playing the angle that a brood of mutant hellspawn lived among them. Now that Izza was in town, she supposed they had a point.

"Mr. Yanzeung," said Fregg, flattering him with a beautiful smile. "I have come here to consider investing in KIN, not to rob you."

Greed got the better of the man's fears. "Of course. Of course." He looked desperately at Izza.

Fregg stood and interposed herself between the two. "Tell me in your own words how Kadeja Independent News makes its money and why I should invest in your little empire, rather than one of the other independents."

"O-kay. Well, KIN is a news media outlet, which means our primary business is to sell advertising. For that to work, our consumers have to keep coming back to our newsfeed. Half the stories we run are filler. Sure, some people like them, but we carry these to give our brand respectability. I'm talking weather, local sports, and all that factual crap.

"The real money makers come in two flavors. Freaks, tearjerkers, and weird shit is one part. 'Hey, didja hear about that woman in Hudstan City who killed her cheating husband and used his skin as a rug?' That kind of thing. Ran that headline last week, as a matter of fact.

"The most important items we carry are the stories where we tell our consumers who to hate. We get people all riled up, and that feeling is a chemical response in the brain. All species who respond to adverts have that same stimulus hook. We get them addicted so they have to keep coming back to us to get their little fix of rage."

His face transformed into a red snarl. "How *dare* they?" he yelled. "They shouldn't be allowed to get away with that crap! I'd like to see them come here and try that." He bunched his fists. "I'd tear their damned faces off!"

Yanzeung calmed and smiled. "We want our consumers to scream at us, and that's the kind of thing we want them to be howling. It's not pretty, but that's how the news industry works across the Federation."

"Perfect." Fregg brought a transact mini-slate out of her brand new purse. Actually, it was Izza's. "I'd want to see your books, of course." She activated the device and casually tilted the screen to let Yanzeung see the credit balance.

Yanzeung's mouth dropped open. "You'll inspect the books anyway," he said in a small voice, "but I'll save you time and level with you now. Capula Media from two star systems over is trying to bully all us independents and make us sell for peanuts. They're selling advertising space at a heavy loss to drive down our margins until we're too desperate to say no. Put your money in, Ms. Fregg, and we'll draw down on your investment to stay afloat. We'll be the last independent standing. In the end, Capula will tender an offer to make us go away. A generous offer. You invest two million in KIN now and, within two years, you'll be walking away with four."

"I shall make you a different offer," said Fregg. "Pay attention because it will only be open for sixty seconds. Are you ready?"

Yanzeung nodded like a happy puppy.

"I will pay ten million today to buy your entire organization."

"Agreed." There wasn't a millisecond's hesitation.

Damn, Fregg. You were supposed to offer twenty. Well played!

Izza allowed herself to admire her logistics manager for a few moments while they finalized the transaction. Then she drew her blaster and pointed it at Yanzeung's head. "Get up and stand by the wall."

"Hey!" Horror filling his eyes, Yanzeung looked from Izza to Fregg, but found no refuge in either face. "I thought we had a deal. What's going on?"

Izza lifted her shades and bent over the desk, pushing the business end of her blaster against the man's forehead.

His mouth dropped open when he recognized her. "You!"

"Yeah, me." She thumbed the charge switch and enjoyed the effect on the former owner of Kadeja Independent News as her firearm twitched with power. "Now get out! *You're sitting in my chair.*"

* * * * *

Chapter Twelve:
Izza Zan Fey

Getting rid of Yanzeung had been a pleasure. The next step was a bore.

Sinofar was strolling around the four-story building, cradling her enormous Khrone Cannon as she asked terrified staff to stroke the skull that decorated its 15-point force band emitter. Meanwhile, the rest of *Phantom's* team interviewed news capture personnel to find any who might be regarded as journalists in the ancient sense.

The role of the news media was hardly the kind of philosophical position that had previously troubled Izza's mind. Green Fish had studied the history of political philosophy at school, though, and supplied a few key notes and maxims.

Was anyone at KIN prepared to lay out the objective facts about important matters, without fear or favor, to inform their consumers, whose opinions were sovereign?

That's the line they settled on. Most of the news staff reacted with confusion or anger. Some shrugged and replied that they would write whatever they were told.

It was Green Fish who landed a live one, rushing out of a smoky office room to grab Izza out of her own unpromising interview.

"Tell your new boss what you told me," Green Fish demanded of the journalist, a human woman Izza judged to be in her late twenties. Like most of the workers at KIN, she wore business attire that seemed to have taken ship suits as their starting point but tailored them out of natural fabrics. Izza noted differences, though. Instead of the conventional fashion of oversized tan boots, the woman wore glossy black shoes. Around her neck was a brightly patterned silken scarf tied in an extravagant knot, and, in contrast to the other workers, her hair was styled asymmetrically.

"I said a lotta stuff," said the woman. "Where do you want me to start?"

She took a pipe off her desk and snapped out its stem. Izza gestured for her to stop.

"I don't like the smell of pipe smoke on my coat," she explained. "And I don't like the lake of toxic sludge the size of a small sea only a hundred klicks from your office. Do you live in the vicinity, err...?"

"Odette Zal Cohn. No. Used to live in an outer suburb fifteen kilometers to the southeast, but now I commute. From the north. The Great Sludge Lake drains to the south, poisoning tens of thousands of square kilometers on the way. KIN HQ is plenty close enough for me. I don't want to live here too."

"So, you don't deny what's happening on your doorstep. Why don't you mention it in your reporting?"

Cohn reached by habit for her pipe. She stopped herself. "We all know it's happening. We know who's responsible too. Of course, we do. But KIN would never run the story. I'd lose my job just trying to bring it up. The best anyone can do to draw attention to it is online activism."

"And do you?"

The color changes in Cohn's skin were fascinating to a Zhoogene like Izza. First, the woman went pale with fear, flicking nervous glances between Izza and Green Fish. It was Green Fish's gotcha expression that troubled Cohn the most.

Blood rushed back into the woman's skin, coloring her cheeks to a far deeper shade then they had started.

Humans are so strange.

Cohn stood erect behind her desk and puffed out her chest. "I've been running an unlicensed online journalism channel for two years now. I'm not ashamed of it."

"Careful, Odette," said Green Fish. "Actions like those have consequences. Personal consequences."

Cohn blanched once more. She trembled, but she didn't sit.

Izza piled in with the pressure. "Think very carefully before you answer. When you said you aren't ashamed, are you telling us you are not ashamed to tell the truth?"

Cohn appeared confused by the question. "First thing they taught us in journalism school," she said, "is that there is no such thing as the truth. There are many truths, and your job as a journalist is to define the most appropriate one for your consumers. I'm not convinced it is even theoretically possible to have a single objective truth. But I do believe we can narrow any story down to a range of…let's call them high-truth versions. In my independent work, I explore these most plausible versions of events and their contexts as objectively as I can. Then I invite my consumers to draw their own conclusions."

"Does this work?" asked Izza.

Such a simple question, but Cohn slumped, defeated, supporting herself with her hands on her desk. "Hardly anyone wants to know," she answered. "People are so used to being told what to think and who to hate, they prefer it that way. They deny this, especially to themselves, but it's a solid fact."

"When I hear you speak," Izza told her, "I get a sense of revulsion in my gut. I don't like it."

Her words had a very human effect on Cohn. The woman stood erect once more and jutted out her jaw.

Izza had seen this response before. When most species lost hope, their spirits crumbled. Humans were the other way around. Hopelessness just sharpened their resolve and concentrated their minds. With all the crises hitting the Federation, it was the humans who would get them out.

She smiled at the journalist. "The consequence of your action, Odette Cohn, is that I hereby appoint you editor-in-chief."

The woman's eyes fogged with confusion. Then she realized the truth. "Thank you," she gushed. "I think." Her face grew suspicious. "What does the post entail?"

"You set journalistic policy. Your journalists will *explore the truth*, as you just described it to me. Anyone who doesn't will be out. You won't run the paper because I can easily find people to handle that. Other than the toxic lake, I know nothing specific about this planet's politics or institutions. I have no editorial policy except to demand your...range of high-truth explanations. And it won't be enough for you to sit here at your desk and smoke your pipe. I expect you to go out and lead by example."

"I see."

"You don't look as enthusiastic as I'd expected."

"Please. Understand that I am honored. I guess you give me hope."

"But?"

"But KIN is a small operation. If we go ahead with your idea, we're about to piss off everyone of influence across the planet. I have a husband at home with my twin babies. If I do as you say, it will flatter your sense of morality, but it could mean a horrible death for them."

Izza walked over to Green Fish and told her to wait outside.

Once they had a little privacy, she told Cohn, "What the newest recruit to my ship's crew doesn't need to know is that I have more money than you can imagine. On the other hand, as my husband would say, my account at the Bank of Karma is heavily in the red. Combine those two facts and know that I am both willing and able to keep you safe." She activated her comms. "Sinofar, could you join us for a moment, please?"

"Holy shit!" Cohn observed when Sinofar walked in toting her Khrone Cannon, a weapon regarded as a crew-served support gun by most people.

"How many weapons do you need?" Cohn stuttered, eyeing the blaster rifle slung over Sinofar's shoulder and the pistols holstered at each hip.

"As many as are required to do the job," Sinofar replied. "What's the problem?"

"Ms. Cohn here has doubts about your ability to protect her, her family, and her team."

Cohn held her hands out in surrender. "No. No, I wasn't criticizing you."

"Not a problem," said Sinofar. "It's a fair question. I can't always shoot all the bad people myself, but I can organize a team to ensure we do. Would you like me to waste someone to demonstrate?"

"That won't be necessary," said Izza. "I want you to run through security with my new editor-in-chief. It has to work even when *Phantom* is not in system."

Sinofar stretched out her hand to the newly promoted journalist. Izza had to stifle a chuckle as the woman shook it reluctantly, as if she expected Sinofar to crush her bones into dust.

She didn't of course. Although Verlys was perfectly capable of doing so if she wanted.

Sinofar gave a shy smile. "Rest assured, Ms. Cohn, I'll keep you and yours safe. And I'll ensure those who wish you harm will be either looking over their shoulders in fear or staring through sightless eyes from the bottom of their graves."

* * * * *

Chapter Thirteen:
KNS Studios

Hudstan City, Kryzabik

"Welcome to KNS Priority News, bringing you the stories you need to hear at the top of the hour."

"Storm warning!" announced the Zhoogene co-anchor. "Hurricanes building over Lufferey Ocean to lash Hudstan Capital Zone in two days."

"Democracy in peril!" warned the human who'd kicked off this segment. "Jacobin Party dusts off dirty tricks playbook to smear ruling coalition candidates."

"But first, this is the evil we face! An exclusive report details Panhandler atrocities on Planet Bisheesh."

The view closed in on the Zhoogene anchor and the concern she wore on her face. "A world formerly torn apart by religious intolerance, Bisheesh became a peaceful world following its incorporation into the Federation in FL-2316. Harmony. Prosperity. And the charm of the Anori, the indigenous race who like to go about their daily business naked." She laughed. "The Anori don't merely do away with clothing, their skin is completely transparent. You can literally see right through them! For many of us living here on Kryzabik, the world of Bisheesh would make us sick with envy. Until two years ago."

The KNS feed cut to footage of Anori people fleeing in terror. Several were cut down by blaster fire. An aerial view of craggy mountains showed flames jetting out of a cave entrance. The info-window named this place Azoth-Zol. Since this version of the feed was tagged for viewers who had selected the disturbing material opt in, it proceeded to show a line of Anori corpses hanging from a pole slung across a city street. All had been disemboweled.

The feed cut to a mountain plateau where smiling Panhandler foot soldiers unloaded unmarked equipment crates from a light transport aircraft. They looked so carefree, they could be on vacation. Most were human, but there was a Gliesan and a chubby squid-like Xhiunerite too. Their utility clothing sported the emblem of the Rebellion and so did the footage itself. Perhaps this was a Panhandler recruitment video? The camera closed in on a human woman with a sword slung across her back. Her lilac-flecked eyes were striking. She gave a self-conscious laugh as she pouted for the camera while making a Rebel hand gesture.

Once more, the feed showed heaps of mutilated Anori corpses before returning to the safety of the KNS studio.

"This is the true face of the Pan-Human Progressive Alliance," said the Zhoogene woman. "They swear they are merely peaceful protesters, but after those images we've just seen, we know that's a cynical lie."

Suddenly, the Zhoogene flinched. "Those rebels might use the word 'progressive' in their name, Lonstanzo, but that doesn't look like progress to me. Plus, eww. *Pan-Human!* Is it just me, or does that sound more than a bit racist? Are we reverting back thousands of years to the era of inter-species hatred?"

"I'm sorry, Fhu-Reynahu," said the human anchor, "but I need to correct you on an important point about the Pan-Human Progressive Alliance. When the Exiles showed up at the Zhooge system three thousand years ago, they explained they were using the word *human* as a kind of rallying cry for all disadvantaged species of the Orion Spur."

"Thank you for pointing that out. But…" Fhu-Reynahu frowned. "Remind me, who was it that explained that the word 'human' didn't actually mean human? Was it the Littoranes?"

Lonstanzo raised a carefully crafted eyebrow. "I guess it was just the humans. My ancestors."

Fhu-Reynahu placed her hand over her co-anchor's, green over brown. "In modern Kryzabik, we've learned to get along. It would be such a tragedy if that were undone by people listening to the lies of these Panhandler murderers."

A commotion was kicking off in the studio, out of the camera's view.

Fhu-Reynahu snatched back her hand. "Who the fuck is that?" She stood and pointed at something behind the camera. "Get that ugly blue bitch out of my studi-oh-*gods*! Don't shoot me! I'm a journalist!"

The anchors dropped behind the desk. Fhu-Reynahu's whispers were clearly picked up by a microphone. "We've been invaded by a godsdamned Pryxian warrior princess. Get security in here and shoot the freak dead. No negotiation. Just shoot the damned bitch!"

The intruder came into the shot. It was a Pryxian woman, the contours of her bare blue arms bulging with muscular power as they couched an enormous firearm decorated with a burnished skull.

She laid the weapon on the news desk and leaped over. Then she bent down and lifted the human and the Zhoogene anchors by the scruff of their necks.

"Relax. You're in good hands," said a new voice. It came from off camera, but it sounded like a female Zhoogene with an offworlder accent from somewhere rimward of Kryzabik. "It's good to hear you describe yourself as a journalist, Fhu-Reynahu, because I own a news outlet. It used to go by a different name, but under its new management it's called F&F News Network. Fearless and Favorless. And we have a story I would like you to cover."

* * * * *

Chapter Fourteen:
Izza Zan Fey

The Great Toxic Sludge Lake

"**D**idn't you call this lake an underappreciated site of natural beauty?"

The Zhoogene news reader, Fhu-Reynahu, ignored the weapons on display and sniffed contemptuously at Green Fish's question. "You are quoting me out of context."

"You're the only one I could quote at all," Green Fish replied. "No one else would admit to its existence."

Phantom's newest recruit retreated to the line of her crewmates. It was mixed with journalists and camera crew who'd stayed on when KIN had become Fearless and Favorless.

By the shoreline, the two anchors of KNS Priority News and six other prominent journalists glanced nervously at the noxious water. They ignored the inflatable huts to one side where they'd been ordered to change into the swimwear provided.

Lynx hovered over the muddy shore near the journalists. He extruded a pinch grip arm and a scalpel. "Let me save everyone's time and remove their clothing. Meat beings are so ridiculous. Forever banging away about how superior they are to mechanoids, but they get so coy when you ask them to show you their meat."

"No, please!" Fhu-Reynahu sank to her knees, staring at the cylindrical metal droid with pleading eyes.

"I don't know why you're acting so put off," Izza told her. "I know from your personal feeds you can swim. You just need to put on the bathing costume and go for a dip."

"Please."

"If it's the costume that's worrying you, we're okay with you swimming naked. We'll just edit out the parts that children shouldn't see and save them for the celebrity gossip feeds."

A barrage of whining erupted from the borrowed journalists.

Izza gestured for them to zip it and pointed out one of the humans, allowing him to speak.

"You're upset about something," said the man. "Something that's been on the news. I understand that. Facts belong to the highest bidder in our line of work. Some people get hurt, but it's just business. Whatever it is."

"And is it your job to lie?" Izza asked.

"We don't lie. We're selective with the facts and that's not the same at all. We always stick to a deeper emotional truth, which is even more valid. Muties—no offense—slacks, M-bugs, envirosanctionists and Panhandlers. We make people hate them, and they love it."

"Cameras are rolling," Izza told them. "I want to hear some truth out of you."

"It's not fair," complained one of the humans. "You haven't told us which truth we're supposed to be telling. Please. Tell us your narrative."

"Our narrative *is* the truth. And balance. That's why we haven't told you what to say. That's the philosophy behind our new F&F Network."

"You're insane," Fhu-Reynahu snarled.

"I think it could be a viable business model," said Lynx.

"It's never worked in the past," said the news star. "It won't now."

"That's only because anyone revealing awkward facts gets killed. This time is different." At her gesture, Sinofar, Green Fish, and Fregg fired volleys of blaster bolts into the mud at the journalists' feet, splattering them with the contaminated gray substance. They screamed and waved their hands about frantically, but they were trapped between the devilish F&F people and the toxic lake.

Izza waved for her people to cease firing. "Odette, please explain your new editorial policy to your journalist peers."

Odette Cohn took two steps forward from the firing line. "Fearless and Favorless has friends with big guns," she told her cowering peers from the established networks. "You mess with our people, and your sponsors and owners will find themselves waking in the gutter to find their bodies have redesigned orifices."

"I'll make you suffer!" hissed Fhu-Reynahu.

"I'm going to ask my first question of this interview, and I'm directing it at *you*." Cohn walked up to the Zhoogene anchor and stared into her golden eyes. "If I don't like the answer, the next volley of bolts won't go wide. Fhu-Reynahu, why won't you swim in this lake?"

"Because it's toxic. Is that what you want to hear, you ugly human bitch? It's toxic. Poisonous. Deadly mine runoff. I'm gonna lose ten years of my life just standing this close."

"Huh?" Cohn stepped back. "But that doesn't make sense. If this toxic lake has come from the mines, how come Gliar-G's mining permissions haven't been rescinded?"

"Gliar-G Mining paid off the governor," said Fhu-Reynahu's human colleague, Lonstanzo.

"Who was recalled," said Cohn.

"Yeah." Lonstanzo sneered. "Consorting with mutants. Got caught. Damned freak."

Izza exchanged incredulous looks with Fregg and Green Fish. That he was insulting Izza's kind hadn't registered with the little skragg.

"Is that another lie?" Cohn asked.

Lonstanzo shook his head. "Nope. One hundred percent accurate."

"Err...no, it's not."

Lonstanzo frowned at the lungman who'd spoken.

The lungman shrugged. "I set that rumor running. Gliar-G paid us top credits to do so." The others shot him looks of hatred. "Oh, come on!" he protested. "Stop pretending like you're all innocent. These people already know the lies we've been peddling."

"We do," said Izza. "We want full confessions in front of our cameras from all of you. Every scandal you suppressed. Every smear you fabricated. Every lie. If you leave anything out, we will know, and you will suffer the consequences. On your knees, all of you!"

Eyes wide in terror, they sank to their knees in the polluted mud.

"Truth or death," said Izza with a grin. "Hey! I've just invented our new corporate motto. Here's how it works. You tell us the truth about anything we haven't yet mentioned, or you die."

Izza hadn't expected much, just a few leads to give Cohn's crew something to sink their teeth into. As it turned out, once the eight journos she'd borrowed for this event started talking, she couldn't shut them up. It took over two hours to record it all. Plenty enough to hold some back in reserve as leverage.

When she finally allowed them to go, she made them strip to their underwear and walk back to the nearest town on foot. She wanted them to feel the burn of the toxins on their feet and skin. For them to know that things had changed on this planet.

For once, Izza would be leaving a world she'd helped change for the better.

* * * * *

Chapter Fifteen:
Izza Zan Fey

Phantom, **Hudstan City Spaceport**

"Thank you." There were tears in Creyoh Zi'Alfu's eyes as she watched the feed from her family's news network attack the lies that had been spread about her. She turned to her daughter-in-law sitting beside her on cushions that had once supported Nyluga-Ree's perpetually sweaty backside. She seemed about to say something profound.

Instead, she shook her head and opened her arms.

Izza came into her embrace.

Five Hells! The woman might be in her nineties, but she hugged like a Jotun.

"You've done well," said Creyoh. "You deserve to take the afternoon off. Spend it with me. We'll pick up some pastries from the shop on Culver Street, and we can enjoy a pot of my celebration tea. *Phantom's* crew can look after itself for a while."

Izza eased back. "I don't know. I've places I need to be. People depending on me…"

Creyoh took her disappointment stoically. *But…if you couldn't spend a little time with your family, what was the point of it all?*

"Bylzak!" Izza proclaimed. "You promised me tea, and that's what I'm going to have. Just the two of us. The next job can wait."

* * *

Nyluga-Ree's Dungeons, Pleigei

The cell door creaked open on its hinges.

She was here again. Vetch could smell her sweet scent. The stale odor of the jailer was present too. Even for a Xhiunerite, he stank.

"It's play time, my pet."

Vetch got to his feet slowly, sliding up against the stone wall of his cell. He hid the excitement fizzing through his muscles, but could her exceptional ears hear his heart pounding?

Only one way to find out.

He turned and faced the door.

Maycey lifted her upper lip, revealing gleaming white teeth. In contrast to the sullen squid jailer, everything about her was pristine, from the leather of her halter top and boots to the metal shaft of her power lance. But most of all, she kept her jade and bronze fur gleaming.

When his chance came, he would skin her, turn that pretty fur into a rug. And then he'd pour cheap beer onto her and rub it in with his muddy boots.

"Aren't you going to thank me for taking you out for fun and games?"

"Sure," he muttered. He'd give her his thanks in a moment.

Vetch shuffled out of his cell with his hands behind his back. Then he leaped into action.

He jumped on Maycey's back, pulling the garotte he'd fashioned out of his mattress around her throat.

She writhed out of his hold before he could choke her. In a fluid motion, she slid down his belly, rubbed herself gratuitously against his manhood, then popped up behind him. Maycey reached forward to cut his garotte with her claws, but he threw his weight back and pushed. They backpedaled into the squid jailer. All three crashed in a heap on the floor.

Before Vetch could find his feet, Maycey boxed his ears, leaving his head ringing.

When he sat up, Maycey was standing a few feet away, nonchalantly licking her fur as if nothing had happened. She looked up from her grooming and blinked at him. "Feeling frisky this morning?" she teased and returned to cleaning her fur. She paused. "I like it."

Vetch gave Maycey a groan of defeat. He kept inside the elation at his victory. He'd just played her. And won.

In his hand was the master key he'd lifted from the jailer.

By his reckoning, he didn't have much time left to use it if he was going to get out of the Nyluga's palace alive.

Unfortunately, he knew of others with even less time left than him.

* * *

Zi'Alfu Residence, Kryzabik

Creyoh paused in the process of righting ornaments knocked over when the mob descended on her home. "You never told me why you wanted to know if I'd met Lord Khallini."

"Are you sure I can't help?" Izza pleaded. The place was a mess, and she felt bad drinking a cup of tea from the comfort of the sofa while she watched Creyoh do all the work.

"I'm sure. Now answer the question."

"Khallini's words to Fitz were: 'You remind me of your mother.' Are you sure you don't know him?"

The older woman considered the question seriously for a few moments. "It's true that I took a lot of jumping caps when I was young enough to think I was invincible." She waved away Izza's question. "It was a narcotics craze. Then every system in the Tej Sector put something in the water that killed its buzz. Overnight, the market for jumping caps vanished. It means my memories of that period are a little muddled, but I think I would remember hanging out with an ancient space pygmy. No, my dear, this Khallini was talking about your mother too. And mine. I think I'd best put the kettle on. We're going to need another pot of tea. The *really* good stuff this time because I need to give you the talk."

* * *

After making Izza wait twenty minutes on the sofa, Creyoh returned with an apologetic smile. She brought in a gold tray bearing a tea pot of polished black stone.

It wasn't just the teapot that had been upgraded. Creyoh had changed into fancier clothes. Over a quilted tunic in apricot and crimson, she wore a shimmer-silk shawl cycling shades of fire. The way vertical black stripes in the tunic matched up against her black leather pants reminded Izza of a Guild token.

The ensemble was stylish. From another era and far too formal for a cup of tea in a trashed house, but nonetheless stylish.

Izza was wearing her glossy pink duster over an eggplant tee and dark pants. "I wish you'd warned me," she said. "I feel underdressed."

"Well, don't! I was just starting to think you were something a little better than my son's green sex rocket." The older woman waved hands over Izza's form. "What with your head growth and your pheromones. And those beautiful eyes." Creyoh rolled her own eyes. "Alien girls! Always my little boy's weakness. Do you know, when he was twelve, I hacked into his personal slate and discovered his collection of—?"

"Mrs. Zi'Alfu, I don't want to know. I thought we had come to an accommodation. I know I'll never be good enough for your son, so let's accept that as a given and politely tolerate each other. It's progress from where we were before, so why don't you tell me whatever it is you need to say and then we'll depart on good terms while we still can."

"Better." Creyoh's smile reached her eyes for the first time. "You're right, you're *not* good enough for my son."

Despite her cruel words, she was still smiling as if they were friends. She poured Izza a cup, bowing as she offered it. *Was this some kind of ceremony?* "However, I'm beginning to think you *could* be good enough, Izza Zan Fey. I have high hopes for you, but you still have a lot to learn. We Guildsfolk like to tell ourselves we know how the galaxy operates. So does the Legion. Neither are correct. You need to branch out of your silo and learn from people who are other than you."

"You were a Guildswoman? Fitz never mentioned this."

"I am a former Nyluga, Del-Saisha Zan Fey. Left the business to marry your husband's father. He was a Legion officer, a potential conflict of interest that the Guild would never tolerate. There is much you do not understand, but today I need to talk about our *heritage*. What makes our family special."

She reached out to touch Izza's hand. "And we *are* special. Blessed by nature. It is only the people of the Federation who curse us. Tell me, do you ever feel ashamed of who you are?"

"You mean my genetics? No, never."

Looking unconvinced by Izza's words, Creyoh sat and poured herself some tea. "Let me put it another way. Do you ever wish you could be like them? Normal?"

Izza thought of ways to deny Creyoh's assertion. She found none.

"It's bad enough the way you and Fitz are reviled for being different," Izza said. "I'm part Zhoogene and part human. I'm mostly the former, but I'm enough of the latter to stand out as unique. I've never met anyone like me. In every group and every lineup, in every market, bar, team, and suck shack, I'm different. If I had a way to switch that off, I would do so. Forever."

Creyoh winked at her and began to tell a story.

"Long ago, in the Orion Era, there once lived two powerful women. One was hideously disfigured, her flesh melted in battle. The other was so beautiful that men worshipped her, women did too—I'm sure you would have, my dear. Birds perched on her shoulders and sang her the most glorious songs. Gentle woodland creatures would lie at her feet and listen to her words."

"Oh, stop. You're talking drent."

"It's my story, and you should listen carefully. While one of these women was pure chaos, the other was order. Each thought they were the good one, the other evil.

"Both were the emperor's lovers. First one, then the other. Then the first again, and then the other. Men!" She rolled her eyes. "They don't improve over the eons. The Emperor could never truly choose one over the other. For a century or so he would convince himself he had, but the fact was, he would always love them both."

"I've read up on early Federation history," stated Izza. "You're referring to the arrival of the Exiles. These are all historical figures. We don't have to invent terms like 'emperor.'"

"Hush, child. Don't believe what you read. Have you learned nothing from your time on this world? History is written by the powerful. My story comes from the heart, from our shared blood, and that's where its true power lies."

Izza surrendered to the nonsense with a shrug.

"The Emperor had fifty children with one lover and fifty-one with the other."

"Why the imbalance?"

Creyoh thought on that for a few seconds. "Nobody knows. I almost evened the number to make the story tidier, but apparently one remained on Earth while the others came here. Maybe that's a part of our story that has yet to play out. But those hundred are our ancestors. That much is certain."

"Did they have purple eyes too? How about the hair? Legionaries tattoo the image of the Immortal Empress on their chests and pray to her before battle. Her hair is stuck out as if she's in zero-g, and it's vivid lilac. Is the Empress our ancestor too?"

Creyoh gave an apologetic smile. "I wish I knew more. Perhaps she was. Not all of us have unusual physical attributes, but the special genetic code we carry seems to want to express itself in purple pigmentation."

"Not always," said Izza. "Both my parents passed for normal." She stared out into the distant memory of a harsh upbringing. "So did my grandparents. When I came along, my family faked my death so I wouldn't shame them by being seen in public. I was discovered, though, and made to attend school. I think my parents had the right idea to hide me."

She looked into her mother-in-law's eyes, but she didn't see sympathy there. Only anger.

"Who wants to be *normal?*" snapped Creyoh.

They held each other's gaze, and the older woman's anger soon passed. "I'm sorry," she said, which was the first time Izza could remember her apologizing. "We're blessed with strange powers that I, for one, am not sorry about. I just wish they were stronger, or at least more reliable. Today the people of our so-called civilization whisper about sorcery and call us mutants. Strangest of all, as you are testament, our line can cross species barriers. In fact, I think it calls for us to do so. You are a rarity, daughter-in-law, but you are not the first to have both the green skin and purple eyes. It's always disgusted me that your parents never saw fit to tell you this. Now I understand why."

Izza shook her head. Creyoh hadn't told her much she didn't already know, but it was still too much to take in. "That's enough for today. I've never really talked about my heritage before. Perhaps this has been a healthy first step, but I still don't know why Khallini thought Fitz reminded him of his mother."

"According to the histories you've read, the two human women we've been talking about were named Lee and Phaedra. I doubt those details are accurate, but I suppose they are as good a pair of names as any other. But to me—to *us*—they are the great mothers. Our despised little race descends from them. So, when Khallini referred to your husband's mother, he was referring to one of our great mothers. My guess is that he knew one of them personally. Knew her well."

"And it's good that he did," said Izza. "Because that connection is the only thing that's drawn him out into the light. Whatever he's doing, I think he's doing for us. For...for *her*."

"How do you know that?"

Izza looked into Creyoh's face and was shocked to see it beaming with joy. "I don't know. I just know it the way that...that Fitz *knows* things he can't possibly know."

"You have the gift," cried Creyoh. She wrapped Izza in a hug, her body jerking with sobs. "Welcome to the family, Izza Zan Fey. Welcome!"

* * * * *

Chapter Sixteen:
Vetch Arunsen

Nyluga-Ree's Palace, Tumlhui Dek City, Pleigei

Vetch bit his lip and tried not to scream.

Hiding inside the empty suit of Golex armor no longer felt like such an awesome plan.

It was a classic move in the holo-vids, but the heroes never mentioned having to share their hiding place with...*others*.

A convoy of little feet scurried up his left thigh and then sniffed at his crotch.

"You don't wanna go there," he begged in a whisper.

As if they could understand, the creatures ran down the back of his leg and into his armored boot. Snuffling whiskers teased his bare and ticklish feet.

This time, Vetch bit his lip hard enough to draw blood.

What sick cosmic joke had left humans ticklish? Such a stupid body design.

Mind you, there had been that girl while he was on leave at Halcyon-3. Tickling her had induced a fascinating response in her body.

But Halcyon-3 was a lifetime away.

Current status: he was stuck in a smuggler queen's palace, hiding inside the ancient battle armor of a Golex assault trooper. And he was sharing the space with a nest of alien rat analogues. And he was almost managing to soothe away his cares with happy sex memories.

Assessment: Lily would be proud of him.

A hiss filled the armored helmet. Not the one Vetch was occupying. The one coming out of the base of Vetch's neck that would have protected the Golex's rearward-facing head.

The hiss sounded angry.

And was followed by slithering.

Sweet Orion's balls! Please not slithering.

The creature oozed across his shoulders.

"Nice snakey," he told it. "Go back to sleep."

But it didn't. The thing threaded itself through his beard.

Perhaps it was anchoring itself there. Freeing the front part of its body to rear up and strike.

Vetch squeezed his eyes shut.

The rat things scampering around his left foot squeaked excitedly. Were they panicking?

He knew *he* was.

"I don't know what you're so worried about," he whispered. A delicate breeze caressed his lips as the creature in his beard sniffed him.

"Please don't bite me! Please don't bite me."

The rats at his feet stilled. Went quiet.

The only sounds were the gentle hissing in his helmet and his own thunderous breathing.

Then the sound of footsteps marching his way along the corridor.

"Liberty or death," he murmured. The Militia battle cry sounded unconvincing in his ears, but he summoned enough of that famous doughty Militia stubbornness and opened his eyes.

The thing was staring at him. It had the head of a snake, but instead of flicking out a forked tongue, it was inspecting him with whiskers and ears that resembled comm dishes with valves at their hearts blowing air at him.

"I won't be long," Vetch told it.

The snake thing pulled its head back slightly, tilting it, as if it had understood his words. Perhaps it had. The galaxy was a damned crazy place.

Vetch tried to shift his head to the side to look out past the snake. He couldn't. His head was wedged too tightly inside the narrow helmet.

A wave of claustrophobia swept through him. His limbs trembled.

Bloody marvelous!

He shut his eyes. And then opened them again. There was no time for fear!

Ignoring the snake, he looked through the open mouth grill, the visor at Golex eye level being too high for him to see out of.

It was Tchon and Kzeddiy all right. And their escort.

The married Ellondytes had been about the only ones to show him any compassion during his time in Ree's hell palace. The couple walked hand-in-hand to their execution with all the dignity and aggravating meekness their race of humanoids was famed for. Their beards were neatly combed and tucked into their belts as was their custom. The husband, Tchon, wore his hair tubes vertically, like a clump of coral. His wife's hair looked like a human's, except her mane not only grew out of her head but extended halfway down her back.

Man, he loved this pair. He couldn't let them walk to their executions as if they damned well deserved to die.

Like Vetch, they were barefoot. This was how Nyluga-Ree liked to mark those of low status in her palace. Trophies, slaves, hostages, defeated enemies, and the category that worried Vetch most: alien concubines.

Three Zhoogene guards marched with the condemned. One up front and two behind, all armed with blaster pistols. They would probably double as Tchon and Kzeddiy's executioners too. Ree placed great store in her underlings being multitalented.

The snake thing hissed.

"A little longer. Just a little longer."

The execution party passed.

Now was Vetch's moment to step out and beat the green men into compost.

But he was too scared to move.

"Hold the line!" he whispered.

It was what the jacks shouted before doing something stupid.

Amazingly, the Legion battle cry put a little fire into his limbs.

Because it was true. He *was* holding the line for his Ellondyte friends. They were going to die if he didn't.

Insight flooded through him. This was how the Legion saw themselves. They were the last line of defense for an entire civilization, maybe for the whole of humanity. If the jacks didn't hold the line, the alternative was oblivion.

Arrogant skraggs.

But it did made sense.

Vetch roared this time. "Hold the line!"

The snake shrank back.

The Zhoogenes turned around.

And Vetch stepped out.

Damn! The armor weighed a freaking ton. But he managed to lunge forward a few steps and raise the hammer-tipped Golex club. It wasn't his Lucerne, but it would do the job.

Three blaster bolts hit him in quick succession. Center mass.

The rats screamed. Vetch gagged at the wave of ozone tang. But the bolts didn't penetrate.

Golex armor, it turned out, lived up to its reputation.

"Don't," he told the nearest Zhoogene, "bring a gun—" he aimed his downswing at the man's head, "—to a hammer fight."

Like his Militia war hammer, the Golex club was designed to punch through battle armor. Compared to the 100-plus-ply woven cerametal the weapon would have been designed to face, the Zhoogene skull barely registered.

The club caved in the man's head and carried back into Vetch's recovery swing.

Covered in his friend's brain matter, the closest surviving Zhoogene fired another bolt, which deflected off Vetch's helmet.

The blast didn't hurt him, but it left Vetch dazzled. He screamed and followed through with a horizontal swing, blindly hoping something would interrupt its arc.

The snake hissed.

Then it bit him.

"Ahhh!"

Pain spiked through Vetch's neck. The snake's jaw was clamped around his flesh.

The club connected, juddering in his gauntlets. He felt bones crack. Ribs probably. Hopefully, they didn't belong to the Ellondytes.

He swung the club back behind his head. The last blow must have loosened his grip because the weapon escaped and flew up into the ceiling.

The snake disappeared. It had to be lurking inside the armor somewhere, but the view out of the Golex's visor was clear, and he could see his two friends clinging to each other in fear.

Fear of him.

"It's me, you hairy fools. We're busting out."

He took lumbering steps toward the last Zhoogene, who was taking careful aim…at the suit's open mouth.

Oh, hell!

Desperately, Vetch tried to pull his head down between the armor's shoulders. But there wasn't enough space.

Just before the Zhoogene fired, he closed his eyes.

He felt the impact. And again, from another two bolts.

But they all slid off the cheek pieces of the badass Golex helmet.

"I'm gonna get primitive on your arse," he roared at the last guard, advancing in a clumsy charge.

The Zhoogene pulled the trigger again, but nothing happened. Weapon malfunction. Depleted charge pack. *Who cared? The look on the man's face was priceless.*

Vetch brought one armored fist up high. The gauntlets had spikes at the bottom of the wrists. He hoped they weren't just for show.

Man, his neck hurt!

The Zhoogene flung his blaster to the ground and turned to run.

He made a better job of it than Vetch had. Running in the heavy suit was turning out to be his biggest mistake since getting Raven Company demoted to a punishment unit. Which hadn't been long ago.

Vetch overbalanced and fell on his armored face. Bearded human, rat creatures, snake thing, and any other critters hiding out in the old armor tumbled forward onto the floor.

He rolled onto his back. It wasn't easy and took several attempts, but when he managed it, he was rewarded by the sight of the last Zhoogene holding a wicked serrated blade in his hands. The green skragg was about to plunge it through the mouth of the armor and into his head.

"Time to die, human."

As the blade came down, two blaster bolts struck the Zhoogene's hands from either side. The green man screamed as intense heat melted his flesh and fused it to the knife hilt.

He sank to his knees, groaning in agony.

Two bearded faces looked down into the armor with concern on their faces. As well they might.

"I thought you Ellondytes would rather...die than touch a...weapon," Vetch said, struggling to get his words out.

"Other than a few social outcasts, our people are stubborn pacifists," said Tchon.

His wife broke off to give the Zhoogene with the melted hands a flurry of savage kicks to the gut and groin.

She came back, running her fingers through her beard thoughtfully. "I would indeed rather die than kill anyone. But kicking that bag of worthless compost made me feel much better. Are you planning to remain in the suit, Vetch Arunsen, or ditch it?"

Vetch tried to sit up, but the armor was far too heavy. And the snake bite in his neck was throbbing. He tried to ask Tchon and Kzeddiy to help remove the suit.

He couldn't. His words wouldn't come.

Again, he tried. But his lips felt ten times their normal size, and his jaws seemed to be stuck with industrial-strength toffee.

Hold the line! Hold the line!

He summoned all his reserves of strength, channeled Sybutu and the spirit of boneheaded jack-ness, and tried to tell the Ellondytes to leave him. To get out now.

It didn't work. He was unintelligible.

"Ooh fffuhhh," he commented and yielded to the paralysis that had claimed his body.

He didn't black out. That would have been far too easy. Nor could he shut his eyes or change his visual focus. Through the mouth slit of a Golex assault trooper's armor, he saw everything that happened next.

In every horrific detail.

* * * * *

Chapter Seventeen:
Vetch Arunsen

Outside Nyluga-Ree's Hearth Room, Pleigei

Maycey gave Vetch a meaty slap across his buttocks with the power lance.

He would have loved to respond with a saucy retort laden with sexual innuendo. The sort of words that sprang naturally to the lips of Fitz or Lily. Deep Tone too, may the heavens hold him.

Without the quick words to discharge the tension, Vetch was left with the cold truth. Maycey wasn't playing with him the way a cat toyed with a mouse. Not anymore. She was bored with looking after him, with being responsible for his whereabouts.

And he was scared out of his undertrollies.

She charged her lance.

He didn't have to look up to know that blue plasma was arcing across the lance's tip. The sizzle and ozone were enough.

"If I have to drag you in, the Nyluga will not be pleased. I would advise you not to anger her more than you already have."

"What does she want with me?"

"That is what we are about to discover."

Flicking the feline tail that protruded above her smoothly furred hindquarters, she walked through the strips that hung across the archway and into the Hearth Room.

He was alone!

141

Alone at the heart of Nyluga-Ree's palace. The cat woman who'd apparently abandoned him had bet good money that he would be dead before the month was up. He'd have laid the same wager if he could.

"Skragging frag-fucks," Vetch grumbled. He hurried after Maycey and pushed into the noise and spectacle of the Hearth.

It was a throne room.

For some reason, Ree called her palace the Sanctuary and the room where she held court the Hearth Room.

At the far end was a horseshoe dais reached by several curved flights of steps. Three thrones looked down upon the Nyluga's court. Two were empty. Ree occupied the central one, giving no sign she'd noticed the human and the Kayrissan who had just entered.

Several of her attendants on the stage did, however. These lieutenants and flunkies were from several races and seemed to favor variants of brown leather coats. Vetch had also been noticed by the blaster-armed Zhoogene guards stationed at each wing of the dais.

Ree's attention was firmly on the dancers performing in front of her platform.

From his vantage point at the rear of the Hearth, it was difficult for Vetch to clearly see what was happening at the other end of the room. Between him and Ree's stage were a score of unwilling guests kneeling barefoot among a disorganized mess of statues, mannequins, artwork, guards, pets, and a plethora of crap.

So, he jumped onto the shoulders of a kneeling Thyfthkosian for a better view. Now he could see that the smuggler queen was being entertained by Ellondytes dancing to music that sounded like it was being played by musicians hidden behind the stage.

"Let's get a closer look," said Maycey. "Perhaps Nyluga-Ree will ask you to join the dance. You look half Ellondyte, after all."

Chuckling to herself—which Vetch always considered the sign of a poor sense of humor—she led him along a central path through Ree's audience. Or whatever they were.

He followed as she detoured from the central route and led him to one of the glass display cylinders containing a statue. This one was of a Zhoogene.

He noted the fragility of its hair and skin. Its nails were cloudy.

He flinched. This wasn't a statue.

Maycey had said Ree would have Vetch stuffed and mounted before her bet ran out.

Guess she wasn't kidding.

"Pretty, isn't she?" whispered Maycey. "Old too. No one is quite sure who she is."

"No one's putting me in one of those bell jars, cat woman. You're gonna lose your bet."

She leaned in close and purred. She was playing.

But it was no fun being the mouse.

"The Nyluga is of the Glaenwi race," she said. "Their social ways are unusual. Nyluga-Ree is aroused by hair."

"Hair? You're kidding." But he was close enough now to get a good look at the dancers. Their movements were graceful fluidity punctuated by judders that flung out beards and manes in time to the beat. Half were female and half male. He was certain of that, because their lithe bodies were nude under the beards that fell between their legs. A human prejudice made him want to believe the women's beards were less fulsome than their men's. He had to admit the reverse was true.

"Is that why Nyluga-Ree hired you, Maycey? Do you shake your fur for her pleasure?"

She lifted her whiskers into a smile. "Not literally. But if your employer regards you as one of the most beautiful people in existence…"

The Kayrissan was a svelte humanoid whose shape more closely resembled a human's than other non-human species. It was pointless to deny she was beautiful.

Maycey gave a lazy one-shouldered shrug. "I flaunt what I have. Perhaps you should do the same, bearded man."

Flaunting like her…? Impossible. She enjoyed showing off her glossy fur, stripes of bronze through a sea of jade that rippled as she moved. It wasn't just that she wore less clothing than a late-night service worker in a Militia garrison town. She moved with a slinky grace and carried herself as if every eye in the place should damned well be on her.

"If you displease the Nyluga," she told him, "she won't be putting you into one of those glass jars. She'll have you decapitated and mount your head on the wall of her intimate chamber, along with the rest of her favorite erotica."

She prodded him with the power lance. It wasn't active, but it was enough to persuade him through the kneeling crowd peppered with guards and other attendants until they reached the front rank.

From there he had a perfect view of the Ellondyte dancers as they changed mode, stretching themselves into graceful poses with arms and fingers outstretched. Brief flurries of gyrations shook their hips, which rippled buttocks, beards, and breasts.

Vetch wasn't sure where to look.

Oh, what the hell am I thinking? These could be my last moments of existence.

He took his time to enjoy the sight of the girl dancers. So what if they had beards and manes? Those weren't the bits he was staring at.

In a whisper, Vetch asked Maycey whether Ree spent all her time in the throne room, enjoying the entertainment.

"Not normally," she replied, not bothering to lower her voice. "But more often of late, because she's been looking for distraction since losing contact with one of her wives. Perhaps you will be the distraction she craves, Arunsen."

Vetch pointed at the two empty thrones. "Those for the two wives?"

"Correct. Do you understand how Glaenwi trios function?"

"Nope."

"You need to. The trio is the heart of the Sanctuary's power dynamics. Understand it and you may yet live."

"Don't you want me to die so you can win your wager?"

She blinked at him with huge green eyes. "You have a death wish, Arunsen."

"Not really. I just enjoy pissing you off."

She seemed to like that for some reason.

"Brood, Shield, and Nurt," she said. "These are the three marital roles. For successful breeding, harmony between all three are required. Each wife cycles through the roles in turn over a period of around ten standard Terran years."

"What about Glaenwi men?"

She shrugged. "You may call them husbands rather than wives if you prefer. Glaenwi individuals unable or unwilling to be in a trio are of necessity sexless."

"What about you, Maycey? Are you sexless?"

She peered at him a moment. Then she answered his jibe with a gyration of hips and a flutter of her upper thighs in perfect counterpoint to the music.

Vetch felt a sudden heat in his face.

"We're not discussing me, human."

"Umm…children?" he asked. "Old Earth history was full of dynastic struggles around children. What's the setup here?"

"There isn't one."

The music changed, picking up a fast, thumping beat. The dance became a furious sequence of flips, springs, and tumbles. It looked as if each Ellondyte was picking a random path through the maelstrom of the dance and yet, somehow, none collided.

Ree was transfixed by the performance. Vetch couldn't blame her.

"The Brood of the trio births the youngsters," said Maycey. "Then she nurtures them in her brood sacs through the first stages of infancy. After that, they are offered to a communal creche. There is never any direct familial connection. The trios, and Broods in particular, take great status from the quantity of their offspring. Khyz-Ree, to use her original name, is proud to take the title of a Nyluga, but she is honored above all as a prodigious mother."

The Kayrissan was having a conversation with him almost as if they were friends.

The truth was that Vetch would have liked to shove the power lance up Maycey's butt and watch it come out of her whiskered mouth. See if that made her blink those big green eyes. On the other hand, whatever her reasons might be, she was giving him valuable intel.

"The wife who's missing?" he asked. "Does that mean I'm a rebound?"

"In all seriousness, it might come to that. She finds hirsute races attractive. Did I mention that already?"

"Like…like poor Tchon and Kzeddiy?"

"Yes." She flattened her ears and bared her fangs. "Das-Zee was jealous of them. Shields tend to be like that."

"Are you saying she had them murdered because Ree and the other wife were turned on by their beards?"

"No. It was Lyi-Niah, the Nurt of the trio. After they lost contact with Das-Zee, Lyi-Niah had them killed for displeasing her beloved Shield. It sickens me, but to her it was a demonstration of loyalty."

Vetch shut his mouth. Maycey's breathing was silent, but her chest was pulsing hard and fast with angry breaths. He tried purging the snark from his tone and asked for more intel. "One of the Ellondytes, Roogyin, told me that it was the Nyluga who had ordered their deaths."

"She did. As was her prerogative and duty. The Nyluga was very reluctant to order the executions, but her Nurt pressed her with an ultimatum. Them or me."

Vetch didn't have the words. Those poor Ellondytes had died just to make a point about how much the two wives here in the Sanctuary missed the absent one. And the Zhoogenes who'd killed them had propped him up in his paralyzed state so he could watch them die. Murdering skangats.

"As I said," Maycey explained, "trio emotional dynamics are at the heart of everything that happens here. You would do well to remember that."

"Anything that will keep me alive until my friends rescue me."

She laughed.

"I don't know why you think that's funny."

That only encouraged her laughter.

He hesitated before saying the next thing in his head. She was beautiful in a weird way that wasn't at all sexual. And they had some weird kind of banter going on, which was far better than the endless hours locked alone in his cell, but she wasn't doing any of this for his benefit.

"I think it's funny," he explained, "because when they come for me—and they will—I expect you will die."

Her mouth elongated and her fangs bared. She looked a little like a Kurlei. And like Vol Zavage's race, Kayrissans were predators. Nature had made them killers.

She had sleek fur he itched to stroke and curves that had pretty much the same effect on him, but she was not his friend.

For him to escape this place, he would have to kill her.

* * * * *

Chapter Eighteen: Vetch Arunsen

The music stopped. The dancers held their pose. Then they bowed to their mistress, giving Vetch a broadside moon of sweaty buttocks.

Cupping the tips of their beards in their hands, they shimmied off to either side where they sat cross-legged facing the stage. They looked as if they were well behaved kindergarten kids, not butt-naked servants who had just danced for the depraved pleasure of the sector's crime boss.

Propelling the weirdness deep into the red zone, Vetch admitted to himself that he had beard envy for some of the Ellondyte dancing girls while simultaneously finding them damned hot.

First, the svelte cat woman. Now the Ellondytes! He knew it had been far too long since he'd enjoyed the company of a human girl, but this was ridiculous.

He blamed his genes.

The ancient titan marines of the Orion Era were supposed to have been reengineered by their alien commanders to breed at every opportunity to boost their numbers. Vetch was a big man. Titan blood ran strong in him. He had titan appetites to match, but they were not being satisfied.

Speaking of appetites, Fitz and Izza often described Nyluga-Ree as playful. The way they told it, being chased around the sector by the Kayrissans and Ree's other hired killers sounded like an exquisite game for both hunter and hunted. They had failed to mention that Ree's favored games were sex games. Games that were loaded so she would always win.

Maycey gave a sharp hiss, and Vetch stumbled out of his dark musings and looked directly up into the face of Nyluga-Ree.

The crime boss was a pink ball of flesh clad only in a chainmail loincloth. Her soft meat oozed through gaps in the sides of her throne.

Vetch knew the Glaenwi had evolved on a frigid, heavy gravity world. When he'd met her last, on the red desert sand of Milsung-Amka, Ree had been suited up and ready for action. She was a bell-shaped humanoid with stubby limbs.

Here, in her lair, she was practically naked in a throne room that felt cool to Vetch's flesh, but sweat dripped freely from Ree's nose.

Couldn't she simply turn up the damned AC?

Vetch decided to keep his big mouth shut and not ask any dumb questions, allowing the mistress of this place to sweep her gaze across him in a way that was positively creepy.

He recognized something in her eyes. It was always fascinating when different species momentarily shared physical mannerisms. He could see her pain. The kind of deep emotional wounds that would eventually scab over if you were lucky, or fester until you died if you weren't.

Lily looked like that sometimes. When she thought Vetch couldn't see.

A change came over the smuggler queen. The hurt subsided, and she smiled at him, licking her lips. Drooling. The way Darant did at the girls in the kind of dance club you could always find near a Militia base.

"Welcome to my home, Vetch Arunsen."

She spoke such perfect Human Standard that Vetch automatically opened his mouth to reply. He hesitated. The situation looked dicey. Speaking the words that came to his lips first would likely see him stuffed and then mounted. Or possibly, the other way around. Instead, he allowed a few potential replies to cycle through his mind first.

Welcome? I've been locked up here a month already, you sweaty pink dough ball. No, that could be a bit risky.

Thank you. May I compliment you on your interestingly shaped head, Nyluga-Ree. It will look good on a spike. No, too crude. He didn't want to sound like Darant.

You're messing with forces you don't understand. Forces that will kick your swollen pink butt. That was highly unlikely. It wasn't as if that jack, Sybutu, would be anything but happy now that Vetch was out the way.

By now, his mouth had been hanging open for so long, it was starting to cramp. *Come on, let's think of something that won't get me immediately tortured to death.*

He was about to go for a general purpose 'Thank you, ma'am', but at the last moment, a devilish impulse seized him and led him somewhere else entirely.

"Seriously?" he told the crime boss. "You've got the hots on, haven't you? For me, I mean."

The Glaenwi stopped licking her lips. "For a human, you possess a pleasing shape and coverings. My Kayrissans were supposed to bring me one of your womenfolk as hostage. Instead, serendipity brought me you. Come closer, so I may enjoy the sight of you."

"Okay, but no touching."

Vetch shuffled over to the steps at the base of the dais.

Ree beckoned him to ascend until he was one step below the level of the platform. This brought his head level with her row of brood pouches. He'd been warned not to stare at them.

He lowered his gaze.

Yeah, like that helped.

Now he was looking at the metal loincloth that fell between her stubby thighs. It was clear to him the designer of the ring mail underwear had not considered modesty a priority.

"Arunsen, lift your gaze from my crotch."

He coughed nervously. "Sorry, Nyluga-Ree."

They locked gazes once more.

"You'll do," she said and gestured to the cat woman behind him. "This one shall assist you. Tasks of Level III clearance or below."

"As you wish, Nyluga-Ree." Maycey sounded full-on pissed, which was something, at least.

If the white shirt and pants Vetch had been given to wear were barely enough to ward off the Hearth Room chill, they were totally inadequate to protect against Nyluga-Ree's roving gaze, which swept over him like penetrating sex radar.

Don't do it! he willed her. *If you ask me to remove a stitch of clothing, I'm gonna make my final exit with my fists flying at your leering pink face.*

"Would you like me to send some of the Ellondytes to your chambers tonight?" Ree enquired.

"I…Err…What?"

"I saw the way you looked at some of them," she explained.

"Yes," he replied. "Please."

She chuckled. Vetch was looking for answers from these Ellondytes. Maybe allies. Ultimately, a way out. Not what was in Ree's mind.

Dear God, he prayed, *please don't let Darant ever hear of my night with the bearded dancing girls.*

"I shall grant you this boon, Arunsen. I hope your stay here will provide exquisite pleasure. *For me.*"

Ree threw him a flicking gesture. He had been dismissed.

He walked back to the irritated Kayrissan.

"Oh, Arunsen," said Ree from her throne. "I'm aware of a wager on your survival. The entire Sanctuary is. I have myself placed eight hundred credits on the matter."

Maycey hissed. Her ears sank into the top of her head. Even though her hands were delicately furred, her knuckles showed white where they gripped the haft of her power lance.

Vetch winked at the cat woman. "Which way did you bet, Nyluga-Ree?"

Ree merely laughed and began discussing matters with her attendants in a language he had never heard before.

* * * * *

Chapter Nineteen: Roogyin

Secret Observation Room, Nyluga-Ree's Sanctuary, Pleigei

The bearded human sat on a mattress that lay across the far side of his cell, talking with Streiba and Pseunmandel.

The idea of watching the portly alien running his pale, hairless hands over his friends had sickened Roogyin, but he himself had said that Arunsen required watching after what he'd done for Tchon and Kzeddiy. So, he'd felt obliged to be the one to join Oouzo in his secret lair and help him observe the human.

So far, all Arunsen had wanted to do was talk and learn. Most of all, he wanted to know about Tchon and Kzeddiy, and why the Nyluga had ordered their deaths, admittedly with deep reluctance.

From time to time, the human tried to steer the conversation toward escape and rebellion. To raise the idea of arming themselves against the Nyluga and her other servants.

Streiba was wise to this and steered the conversation away from those dangerous lines. Did Arunsen not realize every moment of his existence at the Sanctuary was monitored?

Oouzo could erase or doctor those fragments of conversation, but to do so would risk their operation being discovered. The Nyluga herself might be watching the human's cell.

The two Ellondyte women had been in the cell for half an hour when Roogyin asked Oouzo to keep an optical pseudopod on the feed. He left his seat and squatted alongside Etryce on the dirty stone floor. His friend had spent all this time sitting on his haunches, refusing to look at the monitor.

Bylzak's Throne! Roogyin hadn't wanted Etryce in this dank space cut between blast pods on the underground bunker level. But his friend had insisted, and Roogyin couldn't refuse. It was Etryce's sisters whom Nyluga-Ree had offered the human like treats for a favored pet.

"It's not as bad as you think, Etryce," he tried to reassure him. "The human is…" He threaded a finger through his beard. The events in the cell were a hundred times better than he'd hoped, but they weren't good. Etryce was proud of his sisters in so many ways. Perhaps he prized their beauty a little too much. But all the Ellondyte servants here had ugly lives, and anything that seemed fair and good was a distraction to be treasured. Roogyin suspected the human understood that on some level.

"Etryce, I'm telling you, the human's mating impulse has not been engaged."

"Are you saying this man considers my sisters to be revolting?"

"Give me strength! How should I know? Maybe he has other priorities. For an alien, he seems surprisingly respectful. You saw how he was with Tchon and Kzeddiy."

Etryce laughed bitterly. "Sure. He tripped over his own feet in a Golex battlesuit."

"Yes, he did. And he did that trying to save their lives, which…Damn it! It's more than any of us did."

"What are you saying? I should ignore that Streiba and Pseun-mandel were offered as entertainment, and the human accepted. Should I ignore the way we are treated?"

"Never."

"Why not? It's not as if we're slaves. We could leave tomorrow."

"Aren't we? You know the consequences for our communities if we don't fulfil the terms of our contract."

Etryce bunched his fists. "Stop trying to tell me everything's okay. What's your agenda with this human?"

"I don't know. Not yet. But Arunsen is different. He's a blast of fresh air through this stultifying palace."

"Really? Can he free us from our obligations?"

"Honestly? I don't know. But he does have links to those who could."

"You mean more humans. Militia and Legion. Politicians."

"No. I mean Fitzwilliam and Del-Saisha Zan Fey."

Roogyin let his friend digest that in silence, then he gestured to the vacant monitoring station. "Come, watch with me. It is better that you see what is true than imagine what is not."

Etryce allowed himself to be pulled to his feet and together they joined the Slern at the monitoring stations.

"Hey, man," said Oouzo, "sorry you have to go through this, buddy. Your siblings are strong women. They're playing a clever game. Streiba's pumping Arunsen for information, and Pseunman-del's pretending not to understand the human's language. But you know what she's like."

"She's listening carefully and memorizing every word," Etryce said. "Every gesture."

"Damned right she is. And if we can use this human to piss off the Nyluga without us revealing ourselves…"

Etryce laughed. "That's an opportunity we can't ignore."

"Atta boy."

The screens went blank.

"What's wrong?" asked Etryce.

"I had to shut us down," Oouzo replied. He sounded spooked. "Your sisters and the human are about to get a visitor. You know the protocol. We can't risk our feeds being detected."

"Who is it?"

The Slern didn't say anything. Oouzo just retracted his eyes into his oozing body.

"Oh, no!" cried Roogyin, figuring out who it must be. "It's Maycey."

* * * * *

Chapter Twenty:
Vetch Arunsen

"Has this pair of fur turds displeased you, Arunsen?" Metal-sheathed claws extended from one of the Kayrissan's hands. "Let their deaths be a warning to others who would defy Nyluga-Ree."

Vetch shook his head. "No, we're good." He nodded at the two women who were regarding Maycey with eyes wild with fear. "I just wanted someone intelligent to talk with. And these two wanted to interrogate me. Didn't you, ladies?"

Two pairs of wild eyes traversed in his direction.

"Whoa, there!" He pushed out his palms. "Everything's fine. No problems here."

Maycey gestured with her hand, and the two Ellondytes shot to their feet and stood at attention.

"You were *talking*?" She licked her nose and closely sniffed the necks of the two women. "Is that all human males are good for?"

Sniffing was creepy, but Vetch decided it was better than her cutting their necks with her wicked claws.

While Maycey busied herself with her creepiness, Vetch speculated about the contents of the bag over her shoulder. It looked like the go bags his squad in the Militia always had close at hand in case they received fast deployment orders.

Ree had said something about his helping with a job.

Suddenly, Maycey was a blur of motion. Vetch instinctively tensed, expecting fangs and claws and fists to be flying.

But the cat woman stopped in front of him, and her stance was…

She'd crossed her legs in front of her and arched her back. Everywhere he looked, she was all curves. This was no combat stance.

"I asked you a question," she purred.

"Did you? I forgot. I was distracted."

She licked her lips. "I asked you whether human males were good for anything other than talking."

"We are. But it would take more than you've got to learn what that is, cat lady."

She hissed at him. Then she directed her ire at the two Ellondytes and kicked them out of the cell.

They weren't hurt, though, and the laughter with which Vetch greeted the sight came from deep in his belly.

"Am I supposed to take you seriously?" he asked the indignant Kayrissan. "I throw you a little shade, and you can't take it? I thought you were supposed to be the deadliest assassins in the galaxy."

"The one has nothing to do with the other, human. My sister and I make deadly foes, but that is not the main reason we are feared." She threw the kitbag at his feet. "Many species have deep psychological barriers against killing other sentients. Most can't bring themselves to do so, and those who do often suffer psychological scarring. My people evolved another way. We kill for pleasure. It's better than sex. Usually. Although for the most enjoyable experience, we like to combine the two."

"You are one sick freak."

"For now, be grateful the Nyluga's favor protects you." She looked at the open doorway the Ellondytes had hurried through. The soiled Xhiunerite jailer lurked on the far side. "The deaths of other servants would hold lesser repercussions for me. If you push me, it won't be you I kill next, Arunsen."

Psychotic freak. To distract her, he pointed at the bag. "What's this?"

"Clothing. Put it on. We're going on a job. If you displease me, I shall devise a scenario that combines you, the Ellondyte bitches you are too squeamish to touch, and their prolonged deaths."

"Skragging turd mound," he hissed through his teeth.

"What was that?"

"I said, can you turn around?" He shrugged. "My species likes its modesty."

"Stop fucking around, Arunsen. No one expects privacy in this place. Even the Nyluga is under constant watch."

Vetch pondered the meaning of that statement as Maycey watched him strip and don the stretchy suit from the bag.

It was like a rubber wetsuit, but it was smooth to the touch and extremely figure-hugging around the butt and crotch. Through some perverse magic, it also seemed to double the size of his belly. But once he was fully enclosed and looked down on himself, his frame seemed weirdly without contours. It was as if the light had been sucked away, leaving a void in place of his body. The edges of his suit were hard to pin down.

He thought of Lily and her morphing tattoo. The last time he'd seen her, it had taken the form of razzle camouflage, a far more primitive form of stealth tech than his outfit.

He hoped she was okay.

"Stealth suit," the cat woman explained, as if she assumed Vetch couldn't figure that out for himself. "We're going on an equipment acquisition trip. Asset reallocation, if you prefer. Call it what you like, but you're going to help me steal a jewel."

* * * * *

Chapter Twenty-One:
Vetch Arunsen

Pleigei Orbital Space

The cat woman sprayed the paint can over the opening she'd cut through the ship's hull. On the other side was the temporary airlock that connected via flex-tube to their little bubble ship.

The assassin sisters had used the same method to kidnap Vetch from *Ghost Shark*'s hold. There was so much déjà vu weirdness swirling around this place that Vetch would have been tugging his beard if said beard wasn't stuffed inside his stealth suit.

Since enlisting with the Militia, Vetch had spent many hours zipped inside pressure suits and battle armor. Normally, his sense of smell would be knocked out by his own stink. Not with the stealth suit's enhancements. If anything, he could smell the area around him with extra clarity.

His nose detected the faint smell of paint, but his eyes told him another story. The aerosol Maycey was spraying adjusted its pigmentation and sheen to match the surrounding area, so it would appear as it had before they'd cut through.

Before *she* had cut through.

There was no *them*. It wasn't as if he was on her team in any way.

Satisfied she'd deposited an even coat, she placed the chameleon paint can on the deck and powered the prongs of her power lance.

She'd shortened the telescopic shaft, so it was more accurate to call it a power stick at the moment.

With what looked like a blue welding arc scoring the air between the tips, she waved it over the can. Within moments, it had disintegrated. There was no odor. Not even ash.

"Nice toasting fork," Vetch admitted, grudgingly.

"I know." She regarded him through the green sensor visor that was the only accompaniment to her head-to-tail stretchy black suit. The green band gave him unpleasant flashbacks to the Re-Education Division sadists on Eiylah-Bremah, but it wasn't a weakness he felt any desire to share.

"Are your instructions clear?" she asked him.

"Check your exit route is clear. Be your meat spycam."

"I would have preferred a real spycam, Arunsen. Neither of us wants you to be here. Try not to screw things up. I'll be back as soon as I can."

He watched her silently pad through the hold. At about ten meters, the stealth tech really came into play and watching her became difficult. He had a sense of slinky movement, but it was indistinct. Crazily, the power lance was still clear as day, bobbing its way to the hatch into the ship.

Heart pounding, he pressed his palm against the bulge over his chest that Maycey hadn't appeared to have noticed. He was supposed to be unarmed, but while his keeper had been cutting their route in, he'd found and lifted a needler pistol hidden underneath the flight console of their bubble ship.

In Human Standard, the ship was called *Annihilation*. A big name for such a tiny craft. But it fit the sisters who had hefty opinions of themselves.

"You're weak, Arunsen," he chided himself.

This wasn't the moment to ponder the merits of ship names.

He should be unfastening his suit, bringing out the gun, and shooting the killer in the back while his eyes could still make out her form.

But that didn't feel right.

He had to feel heat to kill someone. Lily was right. As always. Cold killing didn't suit him. Logic and calculation weren't enough to make him squeeze the trigger.

He feared it was a hesitation that would get his friends killed one day.

If Maycey had been a Slern, would he have shot her? If she smelled like boiled cabbage and slid along a slime trail squeezed out of a body that looked like a slug ball rather than a divine goddess, would that have made a difference?

He told himself it would not, and he was almost convinced.

Meanwhile, out in the real world, Maycey had disappeared.

He wasn't certain whether she'd left the hold or was still in there with him, playing mind games. He didn't know because he'd been too busy worrying about why he hadn't killed her to watch what she was doing.

I so need to get some woman action. Human to human.

He decided to assume she'd left to do whatever she was here to do and that he was alone.

Alone.

With a hold full of cargo.

Might be valuable, some of it.

Old habits die hard. Especially the criminal ones. He wasn't planning on thieving. Not exactly. But the urge to check out the cargo was strong.

The first row of storage racks held standard equipment boxes. Mostly finished in the same olive green, locked down securely, and stenciled with *Boitan* in Human Standard letters below a word in Zhoogene. He guessed that was the name of the ship he'd boarded, but the equipment could have been stolen, bought, or salvaged.

Likely these were reserve stores of something uninteresting, such as disinfecting cleaner concentrate.

The other three racks were a little more promising—a mismatched variety of flight cases, zipped holdalls, and rucks. Probably personal storage for the *Boitan*'s crew, assuming that's what this tub was called. Maybe it carried passengers? Upon approach, he'd judged it to be a freighter, but cargo haulers often had a few staterooms for paying passengers. All she'd told him was that the target had matched orbit with Ardabol Station while it waited to be given a flight path for one of the orbital's slips. That the ship was where she needed it to be.

"Comm check," purred a silk and sugar voice into his earpiece.

"I read you, Maycey."

"I expect you're wondering whether to run or, perhaps, you're considering calling the authorities."

"Aren't you worried I will?"

"I hope you do. It would give me the slight pleasure of chasing you down. You wouldn't get far, human."

"Stop trying to play mind games and concentrate on your task, Kayrissan."

He killed the connection by pressing the stud on the base of his visor.

Truth was, she was screwing with his mind, and it was working. He couldn't tell which idea was his and which had been planted by her.

He studied the area of bulkhead that had been cut through and then healed with chameleon paint. He could only tell it was there because he'd memorized its location. In theory, all he had to do was press his hand on the center of the hidden hatch. It would open for him, and then he could crawl through to the empty *Annihilation* and fly away.

It was all too easy. It had to be a trap. Or a test.

Lily would know what to do. Vetch had confidence in his ability to organize his squad and hit things with his war hammer. Mind games were not his department.

Actually, he realized, Lily *could* help. She'd told him once that when the situation was total skragg-up confusion, the best strategy to follow was the simplest one.

Usually.

Even if it wasn't, it made sense to commit to a plan that *might* work. Better that than sit on your haunches trying to understand the incomprehensible, which surely would *not* get you out of the shit you found yourself in.

Thanks, Lil'.

Maycey kidnapped him. So, he should run from her.

Simple.

Vetch pressed his hand against the hidden portal. It slid away, revealing the inflatable airlock and the flexible tube that led to the little bubble ship with the big name. *Annihilation* waited for him against the backdrop of the stars.

He pushed through and into the ship. Once he was strapped into the pilot's seat, he reversed the sequence of controls he'd memorized as Maycey had run through them when they'd clamped on.

Nothing happened.

Damn!

The flight console holo-disk woke up. It showed an exterior view from Maycey's perspective. She seemed to be searching for something inside a secure locker.

"You abandoned me," she said. "It's a deep emotional wound. Gonna take a long while to heal."

"Good. I'm not your friend."

"So you keep telling me. I wonder why you feel the need to do that." She sighed, extending the exhalation far longer than a human would. "Less fun for me, I know, but the best thing for you to do is stick by my side and make Nyluga-Ree happy. Best for you. Best also for Zan Fey and her ridiculous human pet, Fitzwilliam."

"Are you kidding? Nyluga-Ree is threatening to mount my stuffed head on her bedroom wall."

"And your point is?"

While she talked, Maycey had been breaking open boxes. She lifted a gleaming object to her eye and purred. It was a cut sapphire as big as his fist. "Quantum decryption crystal," she whispered at the object. "If your previous owner had valued you, they would have kept you safer. You're mine now. I won't let you go so easily."

Owner!

Vetch activated the controls. All of them at random. There were scores of buttons, switches, and throttles. He was as likely to launch a missile or eject, but he wasn't going to sit there and be insulted. And no one was his *owner*.

"You need to put the ship on manual," said Maycey. "It's the green button beneath the right side of the yoke."

Vetch pressed the button, and the main screen dominating the console came online. A tactical map appeared and was immediately covered by a deluge of scrolling text.

The only problem: it was all written in a script he didn't recognize.

On the holo-comm, Maycey was trotting back to him. He could see through her eyes the name of the ship stenciled on the bulkhead. As he'd guessed, it was the *Boitan*.

He could almost imagine Lily telling him, "See, the simplest explanation was the right one. So, get the fuck out of there."

What was wrong with him? He didn't want to abandon Maycey. It was stupid, he knew. She wasn't his comrade. She was the enemy. She just happened to be about the only person who'd talk with him, which made him a sad scump who needed to get back to his real friends and spend more time in bars.

Once again, he tried reversing the actions Maycey had taken coming in. He made several missteps but was soon rewarded with a hiss as the airlock detached, leaving behind a plug to seal the breach in the hull.

He felt a faint kick in his side as a maneuvering thruster eased the boat away from the *Boitan*.

Flying space vehicles wasn't something he'd tried before, but he had a throttle and a yoke. He could figure out the rest as he went along. How hard could it be?

"Arunsen," cried Maycey. "You're being very bad."

"Goodbye, Maycey. Stay safe, I think."

"It shall be my pleasure to chase you."

Crazy Kayrissan. She seemed delighted by the prospect. But Vetch was nobody's prey.

* * * * *

Chapter Twenty-Two:
Vetch Arunsen

Annihilation, **Pleigei Orbital Space**

Vetch preferred to think it was more intelligence and perseverance than blind luck that had gotten him away from *Boitan* and out beyond the orbital traffic zone around Ardabol Station.

He'd just begun to ponder the question of what the hell he should do next when the main screen pinged an alarm and started flashing.

The warning text in alien script only heightened the sense that he had once again stuck his big boots into something he didn't understand.

A control box popped up on the screen. He didn't recognize the words, but it looked like an option to accept or decline.

He thumbed what he thought was the accept button.

The response was a click from overhead. Then a voice came via speakers. It was speaking rapid-fire Zhoogene Standard. More importantly, it sounded extremely annoyed.

"My language is poor," he replied in the butchered version of Zhoogene he'd learned in the Militia. "Please speak Human Standard."

"Unidentified vessel, this is the Pleigei Orbital Transport Police. Power down!"

He needed to stall while he figured this out. Fitzwilliam lied so easily, but Vetch didn't know where to begin. "I don't know how to work this ship," he admitted to the space cops.

"No games. Power down immediately!"

"Whoooah!"

A ship flew past just tens of meters away. It was an FVA-7 "Spikeball" aerospace fighter, wearing police colors. Its many force keels were painted alternating red and white. The quad cannons in its nose were done up to look like bolts of hellfire.

The Legion-surplus police cutter came across his bow—if that was the correct term for a ball-shaped ship smaller than some of the isolation cells he'd enjoyed over the years. It weaved around in front of his path, the faint fizz and crackle in its wake announcing that it was protected by an aft force shield with a patchy maintenance record.

The cutter ducked down and disappeared behind *Annihilation*.

Now what?

"Power down or be fired upon and destroyed."

"I told you. I don't know how." He tapped his visor comm back on. "Maycey. Maycey. Do you copy?"

There was no response. Probably well out of range.

Four parallel lines of tracer bolts shot through the black just in front of *Annihalation*.

The panic that had been building inside him now died away. There was literally nothing he could do. This shit show was far out of his control.

Actually, there was one thing he could do...

"I surrender. Take me aboard. Board my ship. I don't care. But don't fire! I'm unarmed."

Was that true?

"Like hell you are! You've got five seconds."

Hell!

It was his time to go, and there was no point fighting the end. His main regret was that he'd wanted to die with Lucerne in his hands. There were people he wanted to reckon with in the afterlife. His war hammer would have helped those people understand the full force of his point of view.

Another question appeared on the flight console screen.

This time in Human Standard.

"Activate combat mode. Yes/No?"

"Yes!" Vetch threw his thumb forward to tap the screen. The damned thing must have been voice activated because he'd barely lifted his hand before he was thrown hard against his seat.

Over the next stretch of time, he was shaken about so violently, he closed his eyes and prayed he wouldn't vomit.

It lasted seconds…minutes…longer? He didn't know. Though he was damned sure he was right not to request that transfer to the dropship troopers he'd once considered. How could anyone endure this without going crazier than a shaved Ellondyte?

On the cusp of blowing, his luck turned good, and *Annihilation* came to a gentle rest.

Not entirely trusting that the abusive maneuvers were over, he opened one eye and looked at the screen.

"Threat evaded," it told him. "Status condition gold."

"Gold? That's gotta be good, right? Err…what happens now?"

He tapped the screen, hoping to find something that made sense. Maybe even a manual. But everything he brought up was written in Kayrissan.

"Ship, can you give me options? In Human Standard?"

Numbered options scrolled up the screen. Orion's beard! Voice activation worked. Why hadn't he thought of it before?

I think you might be trying to do one of these things:

1. – Power down all systems, including life support.

2. – Locate and attack the police cutter.

3. – Play soothing music and await pickup or death.

4. – Stream human-themed holo-porn.

5. – Return to previous mission waypoint.

Vetch generally left the computer tech malarkey to others. But he'd encountered so many droids with attitude that he suspected people liked them that way. Lynx was a perfect example. Perhaps the assassin sisters also liked their computer systems quirky.

As he scanned the options again, he knew which one he wanted to activate, but he kept his mouth shut because he felt…what, guilty?

He'd left Maycey behind. And he felt guilty that he felt guilty about abandoning her. Which was a confusing concept.

She's not your friend.

"Oh, I'm such a dongwitted scump."

He waited, giving the ship a chance to make a wisecrack back, but it was silent.

"Ship, activate option five. Return to last waypoint."

The words "GOOD CHOICE!" flashed briefly. Then *Annihilation* returned him to the *Boitan* with a brisk thrust plan that kept him on the safe side of barfing. In its new attitude of bountiful helpfulness, it even reconnected the flexible airlock to the same point as before without being asked.

Maycey's helmet cam view reappeared over the flight console. She was firing her lance across the hold, ducking as the return fire lashed overhead.

"Did you enjoy your jaunt?"

Dammit. She didn't even sound upset with him.

Blaster bolts smacked into a pile of holdalls lashed to the storage rack in front of her, throwing up a cloud of smoldering crap. Maycey used this temporary concealment to roll across the deck to a new position next to the airlock breach point.

With the sound of many boots advancing into the hold, Maycey's view focused on the false, painted bulkhead. There was movement in front of her cam. Vetch squinted. And then he saw that her hand—indistinct with its stealth covering—was touching the hatch at the same point he had.

"Release the damned lock," she growled when nothing happened.

Her cam feed became a confusing blur of her rolling through blaster bolts and destruction.

"Ship," Vetch ordered, "unlock the airlock exterior."

He was rewarded with the sound of hissing pressure equalization. "Try again," he told the assassin.

She did. This time, Maycey made it through and launched herself into the flexible connecting tube which bucked when she side-slammed its transparent wall.

"I'll give you this," she said as she floated into the bubble craft, "you have an instinct for dramatic timing, Arunsen."

"Wait till you see this," he replied and reached into the top of his stealth suit. He drew out the needler pistol and leveled it at her.

She laughed as she crawled into the *Annihilation*. She collapsed her power lance and threw it into the stowage box behind the seats. She undid the top of the suit all the way down her torso. Something fell out that she'd placed between her breasts. It was the jewel she'd stolen.

Maycey held up the prize and grinned at him. "Mission accomplished."

She sent it sailing into the box alongside her lance.

Vetch wasn't impressed. He pushed the needler barrel against her bare midriff. "I want some truths," he told her.

Which was legit, though he was so out of his depth, he wasn't sure what truths he wanted to get out of her. He wanted them to not be docked to a ship they'd just stolen from. That much he was sure about.

"Typical human." She raised an eye ridge, but not her voice. The weapon pointed at her, the blaster fire she'd barely wriggled away from, his running out on her—Maycey appeared completely aloof to such concerns.

Grace under pressure. Vetch had to admire that in her.

"Your species can never let things just be as they are," she said. "Okay, so you want some answers. Shoot. Er…so to speak. But we'd better get out of here first."

Maycey retracted the airlock and sat in the copilot seat.

Or what Vetch had taken to be the copilot position. Without any obvious command, the yoke shifted across the deck from Vetch to Maycey's seat. She piloted *Annihilation* away from the scene of the crime.

All the while, he kept the needler pressed against her.

Her movements and flight control were assured. Which was what he expected. Suddenly, through the needler barrel, he sensed a change as her abdominal muscles tensed. Her whole body went rigid, and her fur stood on end.

He got the feeling that something on her screen had startled her, but when he risked glancing at the flight console, the moment had passed. She had relaxed. And there was nothing on the screen he understood.

He'd never seen anything faze her before. Something had now.

When they'd put distance between them and the *Boitan*, she turned slowly to Vetch and raised her hands.

It had the effect of opening the front of her suit.

"Will this take long?" she teased. "We both know I'm too hot to kill in cold blood."

But she wasn't. She wasn't hot. Wasn't even human. And she sure as hell wasn't his friend.

Keeping his pistol pressed against her flesh, Vetch parted her fine body fur with the barrel until it rested over where her heart would be if she were the same species as him.

"What's the deal with the Ellondytes?" he asked her. "They're seething about the murders of two of their number. Tchon and Kzeddiy. But they won't call it murder. It's almost as if they pass off their deaths as unfortunate accidents."

"The Ellondytes." The way Maycey purred, she made the word sound like something she would catch, season, and devour. "You want to know how to help them in their plight."

"Something like that."

"How human. How noble. How *stupid*. The best you can do for them is leave them be."

"You're right. I *am* human. And proud of it. It means I stick my beak in where it's not wanted. Deal with it. Why are the Ellondytes so accepting of their situation?"

"It's their nature to be content. It's not yours. Nor mine, Arunsen. I find them dull. Sometimes, though, I envy them. Okay, here's the deal, although…would you mind?" She looked down at the barrel poking into her chest. "You play a little rough."

When he eased off fractionally, she explained. "Nyluga-Ree cut a deal with the Ellondytes two centuries ago. They come from a string of villages that thread through the passes of the Shmarash Mountains on the planet Rhieff. The place specializes in deep valleys, gentle-natured cattle, and dressing up to amuse the tourists. That kind of shit. It's no paradise, though, because Rhieff is a contested planet. There's a planetary government, which is the legitimate authority in the eyes of the Federation. In reality, the world government is the pawn of several rival republics and empires. And guess whose mountain passes permeate the border between two of the most belligerent states?"

"Nyluga-Ree gives the villagers protection?"

"Damn right. Their enclave is an official affiliate of the Outer Torellian Commerce Guild. If anyone messes with the Shmarash villages, my sister or I visit Rhieff to kill a few people to make a point."

"Do the Ellondytes at Ree's Sanctuary ever get released?"

"The deal is that every year the Shmarash Ellondytes send five percent of their youth, or one-hundred-and-fifty-individuals, whichever is smaller, to act as servants for a term of fifteen years. They're paid handsomely while they're here. Then they return home."

"You make it sound as if they're lucky to serve your boss."

"Bullshit. That's your ears hearing something I haven't said. Whether or not it's a good deal is for the Ellondytes to decide. Deal with it!"

"Don't try to portray Ree as the good party here. She ordered the murder of Tchon and Kzeddiy. I know you told me she didn't want to do it. But they're still dead, and she's still a murderer."

Maycey's jade and bronze fur waved suddenly, like a ripe corn field in the wind. "I agree. The Nyluga would be reluctant to order the execution of my last sister, for example. But she would still do so if pressed. I've always known that, but Tchon and Kzeddiy were an unpleasant reminder of that fact. The Sanctuary is a dangerous place to live."

"Then why work for her?"

"Money. A lot of it."

"Yeah. Money will make you overlook a lot of dirt."

"The Federation is a fetid garbage heap," said Maycey. No longer grace under pressure, she was snapping out her words. "You've seen the ugly underbelly, same as me. All that most people can do is suck it up and make the most of their blighted lives. I'm sorry about Tchon and Kzeddiy. I know it's no comfort for them, being dead and all, but their people could be a whole lot worse off than they are under the Nyluga's arrangement. If you go stomping around with your beard and your big hammer, smiting everyone in that place to free the poor Ellondytes, you will hurt them too in the long run. Badly. I've seen your file, Sergeant Arunsen of the disgraced Raven Company. You're the Militia grunt who tried to keep his head down and failed. When did you become the avenging hero?"

Vetch tugged his beard, which made him feel stupid, so he stopped and tried to figure out why she had such a good point. It was all those freaks in Chimera Company making him act unnaturally. It was a silly name and a silly idea, and it was making him forget his aim in life. To embrace the suck and survive the next day. It was the secret to existence in the Federation.

"And the Militia sergeant is back." Maycey grinned, showing brilliant white teeth. "I have tired of this interrogation. I would rather you shoot me than bore me to death."

Vetch thumbed the safety on and tossed the needler in the stowage box alongside the power lance. He shut the lid, securing the contents. "Take us home, Maycey."

Ignoring him, the cat woman bent over and started licking her body fur where he'd pressed the handgun into her.

Man, she was flexible!

He felt stupid. Despite having threatened to kill her and having abandoned her on a hostile ship, he felt awkward staring at her intimate licking.

He averted his gaze and rested his eyes on the main flight console screen.

A message popped up for him to read.

"Good choice, Arunsen. Return to Sanctuary without annoying her further."

What the everlasting hell?

Maycey looked up from her ministrations. She read Vetch's shocked face and looked at the screen.

But the text had gone.

"What did you see, Arunsen?"

"Nothing."

"We both know that's not true." She paused, blinking at him with huge green eyes. "You can tell me," she purred in an oily smooth voice. "Tell me what you saw."

He angled toward her and told her in a whisper, "I see an alien murderer flashing her cat-titties like a dockyard whore and expecting the same results as a Zhoogene in heat. As far as I'm concerned, you're an animal. You look like one. And act like one."

"Now I'm certain you're lying."

"Orion's arse! Could anyone be any more infuriating than you?"

"I know someone has been sending you communications," she said. "Whatever they've been telling you, I hope you know not to trust them." She narrowed her eyes to green slits. "Tell you what, Arunsen, we're in no hurry." She made a rumbling sound at the back of her throat. Purr or growl? He wasn't sure. "I'll show you some of the orbital sights first."

* * *

Secret Monitoring Station, Nyluga-Ree's Sanctuary

"This is the most fun I've had in years," said Oouzu.

"Maycey worries me," Roogyin replied, a worry-ass misery bus as always. "What if she discovers us? And all for what? A human hostage? For your *fun*?"

Oouzo waved away the Ellondyte's concerns with a pseudopod. "Stop pulling your hair out. We've more than enough dirt on Maycey and her only surviving sister. Don't worry."

"Speaking of smarts," said Roogyin, "it's time to settle up. I called it right that the human wouldn't check out the holo-porn."

"Don't I know it. I spent hours pulling together that footage. It's hilarious. Anyway, we're still quits. You said Maycey would seduce him. She tried the breasts and blinking routine. Purring too, but none of that had any impact on Arunsen."

"Don't be so sure. That wager is still wide open, Oouzo. Humans are more like us than you slugs. Let's face it, the longest romantic experience a Slern will ever experience will be over in less than five minutes."

"Which is all it takes for an efficient exchange of genetic material. You're jealous that our biology is far more practical than yours. I mean, all that messy being-in-love nonsense you make a big deal over. Ridiculous. Are you trying to tell me that Maycey is working a longer-term plan with the bearded human?"

"Are you kidding? When the Nyluga picked a keeper for Arunsen, why did she choose Maycey over her sister?"

"Okay, I see your point. Kaycey cuts straight to maximum pain. But Maycey loves to play with her prey before killing it."

* * * * *

Chapter Twenty-Three:
Vetch Arunsen

Abandoned Space Station, Pleigei Orbit

Maycey flew them to a twisted metal pretzel that she claimed was an abandoned space station.

"Meteoroid strike," she explained. "Probably hit by orbiting space junk from a collision centuries ago. A lot of people must have died when she blew."

Vetch surveyed the blackened metal as they flew around twisted spars on approach to the holed central hub. "Space is a dangerous place," he commented, shuddering as he imagined the bodies being sucked out.

"Damn right. Still, this wreck isn't without its uses. Place belongs to the Guild now. We use it as staging for ops, storage, and interrogation. You know the kind of thing."

They hooked up to a functioning docking collar and floated through into an open space that had been retrofitted with lights and storage zones. The bulkheads were still badly scorched from the day of the catastrophe. They wore helmets over their pressure-sealed stealth suits and carried air tanks. Vetch felt relieved that Maycey had left her power lance in the *Annihilation*.

She consulted a control bank in the bulkhead and then released her helmet, securing it to her suit so it wouldn't float away. "Atmosphere checks out okay," she said, her voice still being transmitted by her collar mike. "Though it's a little ripe. I think something crawled in the air recycler and died. Standby for gees."

She flicked a switch and the gravity plating activated. Vetch was pulled from the air but landed comfortably on the lattice deck plates on all fours.

Maycey was saying something to him, but her voice was muffled.

He looked up in alarm, fearing she was asphyxiating. Springing to his feet, he raced toward her. Then he saw why her voice had muffled and died. Her suit, with the mike in its collar, was undone down to her ankles. She was in the process of removing her boots.

No way was he doing the same, though he did remove his helmet.

She stood, naked, stretching her lithe body, with her hands clasped high above her head. A strange transformation possessed the cat. It was as if a storm front were passing over her, starting with her eyes and sweeping back over her head and down her length. Behind this line of transition, her fur fluttered as if windswept by a storm raging over her body. Her blue-green fur darkened to a deep jade.

Her nose and lips became plumper, transforming from dull gun metal to the sheen of polished obsidian.

"What's happening to you?"

She threw her head back, eyes closed as if in the throes of ecstasy.

"Are you okay?" he asked.

She calmed a little and regarded him through slitted green eyes. "Hormonal change," she whispered. "Congratulations, very few outside my people witness this and live."

He stepped back and looked around for possible weapons.

She took an aggressive step toward him, and he finally read her intent.

"Orion's beard! Hormonal change? You don't mean like a Zhoogene in season?"

She gave him a flirtatious pout. "Do women with strong desires frighten you, Arunsen?"

"Don't flatter yourself, Kayrissan. I only have fun with people I like. I'd rather slice off my dick than play with you."

Enormous, doleful, green eyes tracked him for a while. "Pity," she muttered, shrugging away the tension in her shoulders. "Now that the mission is over, I'll need thirty minutes to wind down. When Kayrissans are on the hunt, we put ourselves into a state of total focus."

"Like some kind of super jack?"

She laughed. "Yes. Like our friends in the Legion, but more so. Our senses are heightened. Our minds focused on the hunt. Other concerns and most of our emotions are all subdued until the mission is over. A few of us amplify certain traits. For me, it is playfulness. My sisters each intensified a different aspect of themselves. All but Kaycey are dead now. She doubles down on cruelty."

"So, this is you transitioning out of your jack state into whatever passes as normal for a narcissistic killer?"

She sucked in a sharp breath. "Everything I put aside for the mission is flooding back into me, amplified tenfold. I want to climb, run, scream. To rut."

She looked at him with a hunger that—dammit—he had to admit no human woman had looked at him with before.

186 | TIM C. TAYLOR

"You are a Militia trooper off duty," she purred. "I know your sort. No bar is too much of a dive to drink in. And no one is unscrewable."

Dropping to all fours, she stalked him across the deck plates.

Skragg! He couldn't deny she was hot, and he felt his body respond accordingly.

She sprung at him from the floor, arms outstretched. She meant to grip him by the shoulders, but he twisted and shoved hard against her sternum. "Keep away from me, you demented beast!"

He'd already seen her impressive strength, and she was only a little shorter than he. So, her lightness surprised him.

She flew through the ripe air, her skull clanging into the bulkhead.

Grunting in pain, she rubbed her head. With her other hand, she pointed at his crotch. "I don't understand. I can see that your body wants to play."

"I'm not Militia scum anymore," he explained. "I'm Chimera Company scum now."

Screaming an alien war cry, she pounced again, her claws slashing for his throat.

He advanced into her leap, ducked down at the last moment, and threw his left shoulder into her belly as she passed overhead.

She landed on an equipment bank by the opposite bulkhead. Landed like a cat.

"Let's make this more interesting." She grinned at him, licking her lips.

She flicked a control on the equipment bank and, a moment later, Vetch floated off the floor.

"Zero-g wrestling is such a release," she said. "Come at me. Show me what you've got."

"I keep telling you, you'll have to play with yourself. Why don't you lick your butt? Isn't that what cats do?"

She was properly enraged now and flew at him.

She was fast. But so was he.

Her claws were wicked.

And that was a problem he struggled to counter, especially in zero-g.

As they pushed off the overhead, bulkhead, and deck to make slow-motion passes, he took some cuts from those claws, but he landed better blows with his fists, though none of them had the brutal power he could have unleashed with a proper floor to brace against.

He switched to grappling to better utilize his greater strength. Probably what the frisky cat had wanted all along. Her claws retracted, and she squirmed in his grip, trying to launch strikes with knees and elbows.

Vetch soaked it all up, capturing her in a bear hug.

By now, they had both lost momentum and were floating together in the middle of the compartment. Stuck. Becalmed without thrust packs or tethers.

Panic seized him. He threw Maycey away with all his strength. The reaction force slowly tumbled him backward, but the cat was flying like a missile toward the overhead.

When he was sure she would hit the ceiling, his relief felt ecstatic. They wouldn't die here, unable to reach the control to reactivate the false gravity.

She purred furiously, licked a trickle of blood from her lip, and then thrust at him off the overhead.

When she closed, he feinted a backhand strike to his right that spun his body counterclockwise.

She blocked it with ease, but Vetch had lined up his left for a ferocious uppercut.

It was a perfect strike, right under the chin.

In zero-g, getting any strength behind a blow was difficult. But he reckoned he massed double the cat woman, and it sent her flying back into the overhead. It moved him too, somersaulting him around at a gentler pace and gradually lowering him to the deck.

As his boots kissed the floor, he looked up. Maycey had her tail wrapped around an overhead display unit, a blood trail flowing out her nose, into a shimmering blob of red.

"You'll pay for that," she hissed.

"Maybe. But I'll enjoy kicking your arse first."

She launched herself at him, clawed hands stretched wide in front of her.

Vetch leaped onto the bulkhead and pushed off to intercept the Kayrissan sailing down from the overhead. He came at her from her flank.

While he wasn't looking, she must have grabbed something to shift her vector, because she wasn't where he expected her to be. Too low. Too angled his way.

They swiped at each other. Missed. And clashed heads.

He bellowed in pain. She shrieked.

"Man, that hurt!"

They merged vectors, clumping into a confusing ball of limbs and torsos. Vetch pulled away, but Maycey wouldn't let go of his leg.

As he tried to kick her off, she climbed up his leg until she had a firm grip around his shoulders.

He tilted his head back, away from her.

She thrust hers toward him, coming in for a kiss. Or so he thought. Instead, she held him in a tight embrace and licked the blood from his nose.

He flinched, disgusted. Although the feeling of her hot body pressed up against him… wasn't so bad at all.

But she was not his friend.

He feigned dizziness, flickered his eyelids, and allowed his head to sink back even further.

She loosened her grip and moved back a little. Was she concerned about him?

"Concern this!" he yelled and snapped forward into a head-butt. He felt something soft squashing.

They both grunted with pain.

Vetch put his hand to his face and felt the blood flow from his nose. Hurt like hell but had to be done. His opponent was hanging in the air, a fresh gush of blood spooling out of her own nose. The mad creature was laughing.

"Your blood tastes spicy," she told him. "I like it. Would you like to taste mine?"

"You're crazy."

"I enjoyed wrestling with you, Vetch," she said. "You were just what I needed."

She'd never called him Vetch before. The implications horrified him.

Maycey used her tail to pull herself up to the overhead and pushed off to the equipment bank.

This time, Vetch was ready when she switched on the grav-plates beneath the deck. A shower of Kayrissan blood rained down, splattering him. It mixed with his blood on the deck.

"I look forward to our next bout." She gave him the green-eyed blink again. "Although, next time, I hope the Nyluga will honor my request to have you shaved, waxed, and oiled first."

Vetch had no answer. He could only shake his head and send a prayer to any deity that would listen. He decided none would care, so he sent a second to his teammates. *Darant. Fitzwilliam. Anyone. Even Sybutu! I don't care about the cat-women wisecracks I know you've got coming. Just get me out of this crazy place!*

* * * * *

Chapter Twenty-Four:
Izza Zan Fey

Boitan, **Pleigei Orbit**

The first officer's harassed features glared out of the bulkhead holo-comm. "I can assure you, ma'am, the incident is minor. It is under control."

Izza fumed. "I heard one of your crewmen shouting that we've been boarded. My party has arms and knows how to use them. Release our weapons from secure storage, and we will assist you in repelling the boarders."

The suspicious human narrowed her eyes. "How can I be sure you're not a pirate in on the attack?"

Izza shrugged. "Wouldn't life be easier if we always had all the information before we had to make a decision?"

"Standby." The *Boitan*'s officer had been walking along a corridor in conversation with her spacers. One of them told her something that made her come to a halt. Her demeanor stiffened. Then released.

"Passenger Zan Fey," she said, "the captain wants a word with you. Patching you through."

The first officer's image was replaced by the captain's. The man—of sorts—was scratching his bald, frigid-blue pate. He was a Jeanneppi, a descendant of a human colony who had mutated into a

192 | TIM C. TAYLOR

new subspecies within generations. They were usually trouble, but this example was looking apologetically into a hovering camera.

"I'm afraid I have bad news, ma'am."

Izza's heart leaped. Had the captain surrendered the ship? That hadn't been the plan.

There had clearly been a fight, though. The captain's cheek was stained with iodine-colored burns. The kind you got from shooting a blaster rifle that needed its firing timing recalibrated.

"The item you deposited in our secure vault was stolen by thieves who breached the ship. They're gone, but so is your item. My apologies."

"What?" Izza's head growth fluttered in horror. "How did they get in? Was it an inside job? What are you going to do about getting my crystal back?"

The captain rubbed his burns, but Izza guessed it was the threat of lawsuits that was hurting him most. "With regret, ma'am, in these situations, it is my duty to avoid speculation. Nor may I openly apportion blame or accept liability. I refer you to our insurers. I have already sent you their details. My advice is to contact them immediately upon our docking at Ardabol Station. Again, my apologies, Passenger Zan Fey. Captain Yoelsom out."

"Insurers?" Fregg burst into laughter. "As if a tug like the *Boitan* could afford a policy with a reputable insurer."

Izza smiled. She felt a little sorry for Captain Yoelsom. "Just as well; we wanted the decrypter stolen."

She put a friendly arm around Green Fish. The human girl had learned enough by now for the seemingly friendly gesture to wipe the smile off her face.

"Greenie, a good Guildswoman knows many things, such as the secret conduits of a ship. And how to clear a fouled blaster pistol in zero-g while wearing pressure garments. Just as important, she must know her way around bureaucracy and paperwork."

The human sighed. "She also knows that the newest recruit gets the crappiest tasks. You want me to go through the motions of making an insurance claim. Roger that, boss. Consider it done."

* * * * *

Chapter Twenty-Five:
Izza Zan Fey

Tumlhui Dek City, Pleigei

Filled with misgivings, Izza took her hooded cloak from the peg. "Tell me I'm not just about to walk into the Third Hell for no reason."

Lynx buzzed his casing. "I can assure you the crystal encryption module you allowed to be stolen is, in fact, still under our remote control. Furthermore, it has successfully decrypted the target systems." He boosted his gravitics, lifting himself up to take his false head and walking legs down from the next two pegs.

"That is to say," continued the droid as his fake arms and shoulders inflated, securing themselves around his cylindrical case, "those we leave behind have access to secure Sanctuary systems. Whether the penetration of the Nyluga's security justifies what you and I are about to do is another matter." He lowered his volume and boosted the treble in his voice, producing a tinny whisper. "Frankly, Captain, I'm not sure we can trust the others."

Izza wrapped the leaf-green cloak around her. Trust was indeed a big issue, but it was where Lynx's true loyalties lay that bothered her more than her other crewmates, despite the unpleasantness when Izza had finally admitted who they were to rescue Vetch from.

The droid's fake head swiveled in her direction. "And I certainly wouldn't trust me. I *am* stolen property, after all."

196 | TIM C. TAYLOR

"But you were a part of the deal," Izza cried, half-laughing at the protest she'd made so many times before. In fact, although Lynx's loyalties were a concern, they weren't near the top of her worry list. She'd learned that the more argumentative he was, the more he could be trusted to do as she told him. His bout of sullenness over the past few months had worried her. Perhaps the droid had needed some time apart from Fitz. He had that effect on some people, and she didn't suppose droids were that different.

"We've everything under control," said Green Fish. "You do your job, boss. We'll do ours."

Easy for you to say, kid. Your job is likely to be considerably less painful than mine.

But she didn't want to wipe away the girl's excited grin, so she just nodded.

Without looking back, Izza stepped out into the snowy street, Lynx walking alongside on his three spindly legs.

For a place that hid much that was ugly, the outer reaches of Sector Seven were as pretty as she remembered. Prettier, even. Fat flakes drifted down onto a fresh coating of snow, which was tinted red, gold, and copper by the streetlights. The houses here were narrow but tall, with ornate gables shrouding upper stories with sliding wooden cargo hatches.

A generation before, residents were disturbed in the night as mobile cargo cranes transferred items of dubious provenance into and out of those upper stories. But such comings and goings had shifted to other sectors of Tumlhui Dek.

"I don't remember such a hostile environment," said Lynx.

"Silly droid. It's just snow. It's beautiful."

"Beautiful? Are you intentionally highlighting my inability to perceive beauty?"

"I thought Fitz was teaching you aesthetics."

"Have you seen the way he dresses?"

"But I like the way he…*Gotcha!* If you've no sense of aesthetics, how can Fitz's scruffy jacket offend it? Answer me that."

"It doesn't. I was attempting irony, but it's pointless when my companion lacks the sophistication to notice."

She pulled in front of the droid and bent down to the level of his fake head. "I know you're worried, but you're not in danger, Lynx. I promise you. Everyone else is, but not you. Whatever happens, you will come out of this okay."

Blue and red lights chased each other across his casing. "Why do you think I am worried?"

She rubbed snow off his fake head. "Because when you are, you say things you think will hurt me. Don't be concerned. I meant what I said. Whatever happens, you will come out of this okay."

"I know that."

"Then we're good."

Izza tramped through the snow piling up on the sidewalk. Just a girl and her droid abroad on a beautiful evening. For a few minutes, she could enjoy the simplicity of the moment.

The droid buzzed. "It's you I'm worried about."

Izza missed a step. Lynx had never said anything like that before.

She looked back at him. "I'm also worried about me," she said. "But it's too late now. We shall proceed according to the plan and hope I've made the right call."

As they walked deeper into Sector Seven, the traffic thinned. Fewer people were about, and those that were crossed the street to avoid the hooded humanoid and the droid with the awkward swinging gait.

That suited her. They were traveling undercover because she didn't want anyone to recognize her and claim the reward on her head by kidnapping her.

The buildings gave way to a zone of ornamental spiral decorations inlaid with precious stones. There were low-walled fountains too. Everything was low to the ground, as if this were an ultra-high gravity world. It had been designed this way to minimize concealment, producing a zone of semi-cleared ground to make it difficult to sneak up on Ree's base.

The Sanctuary was a collection of buildings hidden on three sides behind white stucco walls, ten-feet high and reinforced with ceramalloy ribs. This was a defended compound. It didn't hide that fact, but the frontage onto the street stood out because instead of the armored walls of the other three sides, it appeared no different than nearby houses.

Other than the armed guards watching her from the balconies, she supposed.

Izza walked through the weapon and explosive scanners built into the sidewalk and up to the black pseudo-wood door. She rapped with the bronze knocker.

The door even sounded like wood.

This narrow semblance of a normal house was the idea of Nyluga-Ree's two wives. Despite the shady dealings Ree had led them into—and both Das-Zee and Lyi-Niah were fully engaged with most of her plans—they had demanded the entrance to their home look normal and respectable. That had been part of their price for supporting Khyz-Ree's rise through the ranks of the Guild to become Nyluga-Ree.

And on the inside, they had demanded a Hearth room, as was traditional among Glaenwi.

The Slern night steward opened the door and extended a trio of eyestalks through the folds of its midnight blue cloak. "Yes?"

Lynx removed his false head and shoulders.

The steward's eyestalks went rigid, waving from droid to Zhoo-gene and back in consternation. Then it extruded two more eyestalks to take in the sight from every angle. Just to be certain.

"Bylzak!" it shrieked. "It's you."

* * * * *

Chapter Twenty-Six:
Izza Zan Fey

Nyluga Ree's Sanctuary, Tumlhui Dek City, Pleigei

"That's quite enough recovery time," said the Kayrissan. She tapped her wrist slate.

Power surged through the eighty-seven pain pins stuck into Izza's flesh, hot-wiring agony into her nerve endings.

Her writhing rattled the chains suspending her from the ceiling. Screams filled the *playroom,* as her interrogator liked to call it.

White-hot fire consumed her skin. Violent sparks overwhelmed her vision, even though Kaycey hadn't pushed her pins inside her eyeballs. There were three in her tongue, though, and several in her lips. She had the sense of experiencing every taste at once, all turned up to maximum. It was not pleasant. In fact, it made her gag, which only made the pins piercing her throat hurt more.

"Unnnghh! Fuuukkkkhh!"

She grunted until the pain stole her breath. The screams continued in her head.

Despite the agony, there was no damage to her flesh except for her manacled wrists and her ankles to which the cat had tied heavy weights that layered on additional agony with every swing on her chain.

Ironically, the more she hurt, the less pain she could feel in her ankles. But she began to doubt her ability to walk any time soon. The smell of ozone was intense now.

Her lungs filled once more, the air being expelled immediately as screams. Sharp breath in. Scream. In again. Out. The gasps between her breaths grew shorter and shorter until everything blurred into one continuous shriek. The bright flashes of pain in her vision merged into an actinic blur.

Then the pain ripped away, leaving just the sharp residue of ozone.

Izza tried to press the balls of her feet onto the floor to take the weight off her ankles and wrists, but Kaycey had hung her high, and they barely reached. Any relief was minimal.

But it was better than nothing. Marshaling her dwindling reserves of defiance, she glared at her tormentor.

From the sofa, Kaycey licked idly at her glossy sapphire fur while enjoying the sights and scents of torture.

"I love to see you dance," she said and took a swig from her cool beer.

The skangat cat was loving this. No doubt about it. Cruelty and pain were her pleasures.

"Nyluga-Ree set you a task," Izza gasped. "Verify my loyalty to her. I suggest you do it, or it might be me sticking pins into *your* flesh."

"Unlikely."

Kaycey moved over from the sofa and cruelly toyed with one of the pins stabbing into Izza's left bicep.

It caused a sharp intake of breath between clenched teeth, but Izza was too numbed to scream.

Kaycey licked the sweat dripping from Izza's nose and purred with pleasure. "I enjoy the taste of your pain, Zan Fey. This has been a long time coming."

She returned to her spot on the sofa. "The Nyluga asked me to certify your loyalty before admitting you back into her inner circle. That is her objective. Not mine. I simply want to enjoy hurting you." She flicked her tail. "Is that so wrong?"

When Kaycey's finger moved back to her wrist slate, Izza gasped and tensed every muscle.

But the bitch was bluffing. Bitch? *Skangat* made a better insult.

"Just playing with you, Zan Fey. I can't shock you just yet. You're still too numb."

"That's not your only game," said Izza. "You wouldn't dare defy the Nyluga. You'll make your checks, and I'll answer some questions, but only the most incompetent torturers think pain will get anything other than corrupted results. Nyluga-Ree would be better off entrusting my interrogation to your sex kitten of a sister."

Kaycey flicked her tail from side to side.

Getting under her fur wasn't much of a win, but Izza took it.

Her tail might be flicking, but Kaycey's face was smiling. "You're probably right. Maycey would take out the pins and lick every inch of your body until you were so revolted by her that you'd say anything to make her stop."

"Sounds like you two have had a falling out again."

The Kayrissan shrugged. "A dispute over a wager has escalated. Funny, it's a wager over a former shipmate of yours."

"The human with the beard? I bet your sister's got her tail wrapped around his sex parts."

"She toys with her prey. I enjoy hurting it." She walked over to Izza and leered into her face. "And when I tire of hurting you…"

Kaycey ripped out a pain-pin from Izza's knee and shoved it through the webbing between her toes.

"Ahh…Goddess!" Izza groaned.

"All things come to an end," Kaycey said. "When I finish hurting you, I shall declare you to be a spy. And I will be correct, too. I don't need to waste my time interrogating you to know you're still in thrall to that human you married."

Kaycey paused and blinked at her prey with green eyes. It was an unexpectedly respectful expression. "Did you know, the Nyluga actually bought your story about splitting with Fitzwilliam? Of course, it was only because that's what she wanted to believe. But you did manage to fool Lyi-Niah too."

"And Das-Zee?"

"The Shield is missing. She's been gone seven weeks. Which means that when Nyluga-Ree hears what I have to tell her about you, she will not be in a forgiving mood."

"You're wrong," Izza told her. "I dumped that useless human on—"

Her shrieks rent the air.

Kaycey wasn't even watching Izza bucking in her chains. Her back was turned as she reached into the chiller cabinet for a fresh beer.

Oaahhhh! Fitz! She screamed inside her head. *You'd better make this come out well.*

The pain overwhelmed her, and the blistering heat of her howls drove all words from her mind.

Soon, even the screams moved on to somewhere else.

Before her tormentor could settle back in her sofa, Izza hung limply in her chains.

* * *

Secret Monitoring Station, Nyluga-Ree's Sanctuary

With those long stretches of green skin bristling with needles, the woman hanging from the chains looked like one of those plants the humans used in terraforming projects. What did they call them? A *cactus*.

Speebulz winced as he watched her swing from the chain. Zan Fey had always been good to him.

He replayed the cat assassin's words. "I don't need to waste my time interrogating you to know you're still in thrall to that human you married."

After all these years of watching and recording in the shadows of the Nyluga's Sanctuary, it was difficult to imagine they might risk it all to reveal Kaycey's disloyal words. But Oouzo had explained the plan. Zan Fey's agony would not be in vain.

One of the Ellondytes crawled into the monitoring station.

"I don't know why you make yourself watch that," said Roogyin.

Speebulz muttered a greeting and waved a pseudopod at the humanoid to sit.

"I hate to see her like this," the Slern replied. "It was Oouzo's idea that I watch every moment. Zan Fey's pain will fuel my courage to do what must come next."

* * * * *

Chapter Twenty-Seven: Izza Zan Fey

Izza drank.

The liquid felt cool and sweet running down her throat. Reviving her.

The lights turned back on in her mind, and she noticed the pins were gone from her tongue.

Was this a new torture? Had Kaycey moved on to sadistic mind games?

She opened her eyes and saw Maycey squeezing the liquid into her mouth.

Details seeped into focus. The pictures on the walls. The sofa with the thick rug in front of it and the chiller cabinet beside it. She was still in the pleasure room.

She scanned her body and saw that most of the pain-pins had been removed. Not all, and although the weights had been taken from her ankles, she tested the chains binding her wrists and found she was still manacled.

"What is this?" asked Izza. "Good cat, bad cat? Why am I still bound?" She rattled the chains again.

"I shouldn't be surprised by your stupidity," said Maycey. "Not when you have rotting leaves for brains. I wasn't about to release a big, green, unconscious lump like you and let you crash to the floor while you are still covered in pins. Sheesh! Give me a chance."

"Where is your sister?"

"Spreading her lies to the Nyluga. The boss won't believe her. She just put you with my psychotic sister because she's in a foul mood." Maycey put the drink on the floor and started removing more pins.

"I heard," said Izza. "Das-Zee is missing. And now Lyi-Niah too."

"It's true. The Nyluga is beside herself with worry."

"I'll bet. So, she sent you to make amends with me."

"Hardly. Have you forgotten, Zan Fey? I enjoy the hunt. The climax of the kill. But I've never enjoyed inflicting pain. I think it's barbaric."

"Funny. I seem to remember you dishing out a few cuts and bruises when we used to wrestle. You loved the taste of my blood. Told me it was exotically spiced. Have you forgotten?"

"No." Maycey's eyes hazed over for a few seconds. "That was different. That was rough play."

"How about Arunsen? Do you enjoy roughhousing with him?"

Maycey hesitated. "Arunsen is proving to be a reluctant play-mate."

"Interesting. So, just to be clear—" she rubbed her bruised wrists as Maycey freed them from the manacles, "—you're being nice to me to piss off your sister?"

"Naturally."

"Well, here's another way to put one over on her. She's telling Nyluga-Ree I have betrayed you all. She's wrong, and I'm going to tell you a secret that will prove it. You see, Lynx and I didn't come alone…"

* * * * *

Chapter Twenty-Eight: Green Fish

Cell Block, Nyluga-Ree's Compound

Sinofar's ghostly green fingers gave a silent three-count. Then the Pryxian grasped the handholds she'd glued onto the breach hole and lifted.

Through her infrared visor, Green Fish saw bundles of muscle fibers glow bright across Sinofar's bare arms. There was a glow too around the edges of the breach they had cut through the floor.

Green Fish hesitated. What if the hot edge burned through her rope?

Too late for that now.

Without giving herself time to think, she checked one last time that her HC2 blaster was ready to fire. Then she jumped into the hole.

The rope-braking system choked her descent in easy stages that left her stable enough to scan the room for targets.

She saw no hostiles.

When her boots touched the floor, the rope automatically detached from the harness.

She made a final scan of the room and confirmed that their intelligence was correct.

210 | TIM C. TAYLOR

The room was a cell. Vetch's cell. There, on a mattress against one wall, was a human figure lying on his side. His core was glowing warm, and the tiny pulses of a heartbeat were visible.

Gods, she felt like a holo-star. It was such a rush.

"Vetch," she whispered.

She remembered he was still her squad leader. Sort of. "Sergeant Arunsen."

She took a last scan of the room. *Nothing.* She gave the all clear hand signal to Sinofar, who was providing overwatch through the hole in the ceiling.

The sergeant was sleeping like a beautiful, bearded baby.

She gave his shoulder a gentle shake.

Memories suddenly bubbled to the surface. All the things she'd done and seen since fate had snatched her from her Militia family. She knew she would have to wait, but she was desperate to tell the sarge everything, to let her story flow out of her in one enormous ramble.

He'd be proud of her.

Sergeant Arunsen had taught her so much. Looked out for her. Saved her.

Now, it was her turn to save *him*. She would have rescued him for free, of course, but Izza was flush with credits, and Green Fish was getting paid. Five thou to be here. Another five if they got him out alive. It was the kind of money the likes of her and the sergeant had never seen.

She gave him a harder shake. "Arunsen!"

Her jubilant high crashed, leaving an acid burning in her stomach.

Because something was wrong.

Arunsen was warm, but stiff.

It was faint in the IR, but she could just about make out his Viking beard.

After glancing up to bolster her resolve with the sight of Sinofar's heavy blaster, she touched Arunsen's beard.

It felt…solid!

"It's a trap!" she cried.

Before her warning had escaped her lips, blinding light flooded the room,

"Suit, cancel IR mode." She blinked back the overwhelming brightness.

Something moved inside the dazzle. It tapped her HC2.

Instantly, she squeezed the trigger.

But the blaster gave a warning buzz. *Weapon malfunction.*

The fierce glare hardened into shapes.

Another flurry of blinks, and she could make out some of them.

There were two people in the cell with them. Humanoid. Women in tight-fitting suits.

They had tails.

Skragging priceless! These had to be the Kayrissan assassins.

In their hands were the twin-tipped spears her briefing had called power lances.

Through the hole in the ceiling, she could see blaster barrels pointed at Sinofar's face.

"We are outgunned," Sinofar shouted to her. "Only resist if you want to die quickly."

The cat women oozed smugness, licking their chops as if they'd just cornered the market on cream. They had been wearing stretchy black suits with green visor bands.

Had been, because one of them had removed her visor and unfastened her suit down to her navel.

The lances didn't frighten Green Fish. What were they going to do, poke her with their blunt tips?

She glanced at her HC2. The barrel and charge regulator had been sheared through.

"Not what you were expecting?" gloated the cat still wearing a suit.

As she removed her visor, the other added, "Eh, little fishy?"

"Oh, I never expect anything," Green Fish replied. "That way, I can never be surprised." She threw her blaster rifle at the unzipped cat and grabbed her tactical knife to slash at the one still unzipping.

The Kayrissans moved faster than she thought possible.

The one she'd thrown her blaster at bent back at the ankles almost parallel to the floor beneath the ruined HC2's trajectory. The movement was as fluid as a dancer's. Then, like an acrobat, she flipped sideways through the air and landed a sidestep away.

With her face covering only half off, the other cat dodged Green Fish's slash attack and came up between the human girl's legs, nudging her just enough that she tripped and fell on her face. Somehow, amid the movement, the cat's tail flicked Green Fish's nose.

"Don't," Sinofar warned.

Green Fish turned over onto her butt and reviewed the tactical situation.

With the light on, it was humiliatingly obvious they had been lured by a printed Arunsen with a fake IR signature. Sinofar was staring into the barrels of blasters carried by two Zhoogenes on the roof. And the cats—who had to be Maycey and Kaycey—were pointedly ignoring Green Fish.

"Good to see you, Verlys," said one. She blew the Pryxian a kiss and undid her hood, revealing a face covered in fur that gleamed with highlights like burnished bronze under a spotlight, but whose perfection was marred by a mutilated ear that appeared to have been half bitten off long ago.

That identified her as Kaycey. The boss had described her as the cruel one.

Which left the other as Maycey. Her coloring was more subtly blended, dull bronze stripes laid over a verdigris base. And with her suit undone down to her navel, allowing her furry little breasts to spill out... yup, that definitely matched the boss' description of Maycey.

It wasn't difficult to see how this pair had a reputation. They were beautiful and lithe, and they knew it. Green Fish would have liked to bury her fist in those pretty, furred faces. Just for personal satisfaction, mind. Then she'd gut them with her knife.

Her orders were not to engage unless she was sure of a kill. The boss had told her that, in every tactical respect, the Kayrissans outclassed her.

Their narcissism made her guts crawl. If she had a mirror, she'd give it to them. They were so in love with themselves, they would never be able to look away, and the gutting would commence.

Maycey dropped to all fours, licked her nose with a long, thin tongue and sniffed Green Fish.

Freak!

"Thank you for bringing me a human to play with, Verlys." Maycey rose onto two legs and came closer to sniff Green Fish's hair. "Yes, she will do nicely. A male human and, now, a female. Such amusing possibilities."

214 | TIM C. TAYLOR

Out of her peripheral vision, Green Fish could see her knife lying on the ground. Just one lunge and it would be within reach.

She glanced up at the ceiling. If Verlys had spotted the opportunity too, then they might still have a chance.

But Sinofar *had* seen. And she was shaking her head.

And if the Pryxian had abandoned hope…

Between the fear and the crash after the adrenaline high, Green Fish's limbs shook.

The two cats enjoyed the sight of her defeat with almost erotic arousal.

Enjoy all you like, Green Fish thought to herself. *I'm not done here. The boss will get me out. Then you'll get what's coming to you.*

* * * * *

Chapter Twenty-Nine:
Izza Zan Fey

Sunken Garden, Nyluga-Ree's Sanctuary

Side-by-side, Nyluga-Ree and her prodigal daughter strolled the perimeter of the sunken garden at the rear of the Sanctuary compound.

The only sounds were the crunch of snow under their boots, the wind blowing along the base of the Raighgors Mountains, and the gentle charge pack whine from the guards on overwatch.

When she'd first come into the Glaenwi's employ, Izza had struggled to match her rangy gait with that of her stubby-limbed mistress, but the habit returned with ease.

The trick was to resist the temptation to match cadence. The Nyluga might have a tiny stride length, but she had the stride *rate* of a champion sprinter. She was always strong and could be fast when she wanted to be.

Despite the circumstances, Izza found herself relaxing into the old routines.

Then she stopped herself.

This was no longer her home. And she wasn't safe.

The tips of her ears burned with cold. She wanted to pull up her insulated hood, but she preferred not to dampen her hearing.

She had to stay alert. Though for what? She couldn't say. The principle was enough.

215

Nyluga-Ree was difficult to read and often unpredictable. It was one of the reasons she was feared, but another part of her deadly reputation came from something predictable: crossing her brought dire consequences.

Izza had agonized that she would get herself and her crew killed in support of Fitz's adventure, but it looked like they would come through this escapade victorious. Not only were they all still alive, but Ree was so troubled, she was desperate to believe her favored pilot and friend had come back for her.

It was obvious why.

* * *

Secret Monitoring Station

"Did I say what Fitzwilliam told me before he left?"

"You know, Oouzo, you never did."

The Slern dropped an eyestalk in Roogyin's direction. Satisfied the Ellondyte was listening for a change, he continued, "If you play a game, always play to win. If you're not prepared to do that, don't play at all."

"Fitzwilliam told you that? Do you even remember the guy? You're taking delayed advice from the man who always blunders in with both boots, only to find himself in over his head."

Oouzo flapped a few pseudopods in a way humanoids interpreted as a nod.

"Shit!" Roogyin's fur stood out from his back. *Now,* he understood the plan.

"It's okay," Oouzo reassured him. "Change is inevitable."

"But…" Roogyin swallowed. A bizarre humanoid gesture that indicated nervousness. "I don't like change. Haven't you already done enough for Fitzwilliam?"

"Yes."

The Ellondyte's fur flattened back, but he tilted his head as if he were expecting water to pour out of his ears. It meant he was confused.

Sometimes, species barriers were difficult to overcome, even between old friends, but Oouzo did his best to explain. "We've been watching. Nudging. Warning. Building a blackmail portfolio for, what, six Terran years? I'm not prepared to put all of that at risk for Fitz, even though I adore him, not least for saving my life. Nor for Arunsen, despite what he risked trying to save our friends. But when both need my help? It's too heavy to resist. Speebulz understands. I hope you will too."

"I don't like it." Roogyin's words were redundant. His hair sagged; his jaw drooped. "But…I guess it's your call, Oouzo. You built all this. And you're the one with most to lose."

By absorbing most of his other pseudopods into his body mass, Oouzo was able to extend two arm-shaped extrusions across the room and burrow them affectionately through Roogyin's hair. For the full effect, he was supposed to pretend to pull lice off the alien's body, but the idea was too gross.

"I've lived inside the walls for too long," said Oouzo. "It's been a life of sorts. Maybe I've helped you a little. But it's time for me to move on. I'll miss you."

On the monitor screen the Kayrissans had almost completed their gloating. Sinofar and the young human girl were being marched out of Arunsen's cell.

Oouzo brought up control options he'd installed years ago and never dared to activate. "This had better work," he murmured, and he locked the cell door.

The Zhoogene guard taking point simply stood by the door he was trying to open, unable to process that it wouldn't.

The sisters adapted faster. Kaycey glanced at the hole in the ceiling and squatted down in readiness for an almighty leap.

Oouzo activated the force cage that surrounded the cell.

Kaycey sprung into the air, bringing the invisible bars to life. The force cage sparked as it discharged electrical energy into the assassin. She fell to the floor, a waffle pattern scorched into her fur.

Ouch! That had to hurt.

But Oouzo was just getting started.

* * *

Sunken Garden

When they reached the end of the colonnades, Ree stopped and stared at Izza. The peacefulness had disappeared from her eyes. She looked haunted. "Do you remember what Shields are like?"

Izza laughed. When Sanctuary had been her home, each of the three members of the trio had bickered about the others. But they had always made up after. "I do, Nyluga. Shields are brave, selfless, and so overprotective, they can suffocate."

"I swear, when I was last a Shield, I was not nearly so reckless."

"I remember this to be true, Nyluga-Ree. Have you forgotten that I joined your family as your pilot before you transitioned from Shield to Brood?"

Ree gave her a hard look. "I forget nothing."

"How long has Das-Zee been out of contact?"

Nyluga-Ree set off again in her perambulation.

Izza gave her a moment and then hurried to keep up.

"Sixty-two days," said Ree. "In Terran standard, that would be forty-eight. Das-Zee was chasing leads rimward of here. Her last known location was Wukan-Prime. That's where Lyi-Niah went searching for our Shield. And now I've lost her too."

"Don't give up hope."

"It is hard to hope when my heart and my soul have been torn from me. Your return to the fold has renewed my spirits, Izza. I cannot adequately explain how much this means to me, but even you can only be a trauma pack for my wounds. I need my wives back."

"Do you wish me to find the truth of the matter?"

"That would be easier if the *Phantom* were restored to me. Where is she?"

Izza bowed deeply. "With all due respect, Nyluga, you know the value of an insurance policy. If you swear in front of your inner crew that my former crewmates can leave unharmed, then I shall restore the *Phantom* to you."

Ree's pink cheeks reddened to an angry crimson, and she strode away.

Izza gave her a moment. Then followed.

* * *

Cell Block

The cell door clicked.

Vetch ignored it. Maycey had already played one game today by transferring him to a new cell. An empty one. He wasn't biting.

On the other hand, that *had* sounded like bolts being undone.

The door locked. Unlocked. Locked. Unlocked again in quick succession.

Someone was trying to get his attention.

"Go to hell," Vetch shouted at the ceiling. "It's my day off."

"Don't you want to escape?" said a voice from outside his cell. The words were human, but the speaker was…what? A Slern?

It was neither Kayrissan nor Ellondyte.

"Sod it," Vetch muttered under his breath. "Here I go again. A bloody plaything."

He shot to his feet and hurried out of the cell, but no one was there.

"Turn right along this corridor, then take the door to your left." The voice seemed to be coming out of the wall. "An Ellondyte will be there with clothing and a glass of water. Swap out your clothing, drink the water, then put the glass to your ear."

"Why should I?" asked Vetch, listening for the reply to pinpoint its origin. "I'm bored with these games. Tell me who you are."

"You'll have to gamble that I have your best interests at heart," said the voice. "No, wait, I flew *Annihilation* away from that police cutter. That's more convincing, right? And human-themed porn? An act of genius. Anyway, I've just let an old friend sneak into the compound by the back door. If you drink the water, I'll be able to track you and lead you to them. You can escape together."

Vetch lifted a wooden Guild symbol mounted on the wall and saw an old intercom grille painted over many times underneath.

"Very clever," said the voice through the old system. "I am the watcher in the walls. And I'm watching you throw away your only chance to get out of here."

"Fair point." Vetch sprinted away.

At the end of the corridor, he pushed through the door on the left and hurried along a wood-paneled corridor. Doors opened into rooms in which Ellondytes performed a variety of domestic tasks.

One of them approached. A male. In one hand he carried a tray bearing a glass of water. The other held a bundle of clothing.

Vetch grabbed the clothing and shook it out to see what the disembodied voice was expecting him to wear.

Until now, he'd mostly believed he was being played, that the clothing would turn out to be the kind of barely-there costume the exotic dancers wore on Halcyon-3. When he saw the clothing was of the style worn by Ellondyte servants and that it would fit him perfectly, he began to hope this really was his ticket out of here.

Vetch drank the water. Then he stripped, put on the disguise, and grabbed the empty glass.

"On behalf of my sisters, I thank you."

Vetch frowned at the Ellondyte bundling up his prison smock. "You're welcome," he told him, though Vetch had no idea what in the Five Hells the guy was talking about.

While he studied the glass dubiously, a piercing howl reverberated through the prison zone he'd just escaped from. An ancient instinct set his teeth on edge and filled his limbs with a burning need to run.

Instead, he stuck the rim of the glass over his ear.

"What was that?" Vetch asked, but in his bones, he already knew.

The Ellondyte carrying Vetch's clothes had already fled, but the voice of the watcher in the walls came through the glass.

"The cat sisters are loose," said the mysterious voice. "Change of plan."

* * *

Sunken Garden

Nyluga-Ree's anger burned out quickly. "You keep the location of the *Phantom* for now, Izza. I should be proud that I taught you so well. Even Lynx will not divulge her location. I shall provide you with another ship and dispatch you with one of the sisters to hunt down the truth."

"You would send me off with an assassin. Do you not trust me?"

Ree laughed. "Call me an old fool but, yes, I do trust you. Especially with your former friends as collateral. I shall send you on a small bubble craft with Maycey. That may offer other reasons to remind you why Sanctuary should be your home once more."

Izza felt her sap rise, flowing hot through her cheeks before stiffening the stems that grew from her scalp.

"I never thought I'd see you blush like a human," said Ree. "You've been around *him* too long. I know the history you have with Maycey. A journey in an intimate little ship with your former lover, and with your season almost upon you…the journey will be memorable for you both. I wish it to help bind you to us and heal wounds. Is it wrong for me to welcome you back in this way?"

Izza looked away. She couldn't deny that the prospect set her insides fluttering. But she couldn't do that to Fitz. A hot trip in a small boat with Maycey would be too much, even for him.

"Your problem, Zan Fey, is an overactive sense of loyalty. I shall remove Fitzwilliam. Then your life will be happier and simpler. It will be a shame, of course. I had high hopes he would repay his debts."

"Please don't. We both know how untrustworthy and arrogant he is, but I don't want to be the cause of his death. Even if indirectly."

Ree stopped and once more studied her.

Izza stood still and yielded to the boss's inspection. She had noted something. The whine of the blaster charge packs from the sentry positions—the noise was gone.

Ree narrowed her eyes. "Why are you smiling, Del-Saisha?"

"Fitz is the most irritating piece of work I've ever encountered. His charming arrogance hides an extreme solipsism in which the universe only exists to observe him making dramatic gestures."

"Your point?"

"I'm as bad as he is because I want his dramatic gestures to be about me. Despite everything I just said, I do love him. It's sickening, I know, but undeniable. Our souls are bound to one another. Permanently."

"He's standing behind me, isn't he?"

"Nothing gets past you, my Nyluga," said Fitz, strolling across the sunken garden with his F-Cannon humming in his hand. Behind him were his new people, the Chimera Company refugees from Rho-Torkis.

"Nothing gets past you," Fitz added, "except for me and my team. Nyluga-Ree, we have secured our exit. I assure you that your people are merely incapacitated. All we need do is walk out of here with my friends and my wife, and we ask that you accompany us on a short trip to a nearby star system."

Ree scanned the wall walkways and high windows, verifying the truth of Fitz's claim. "Of course, my boy. Lead on."

Izza and Fitz eyed each other, desperate to cross the final six feet that were all that remained of the light-years that had separated them for so many months.

The same thought stayed them both: Nyluga-Ree was making this far too easy.

Fitz broke first and bounded over to Izza. He came to attention before her and bowed slightly from the waist. "My lady…"

Izza's need for him was far too urgent for her to deal with that courtly drent-shit. She drew her man to her and hugged him so tightly, she felt the fluid armor panels harden in his leather jacket.

Fitzy's soft human lips found hers.

Her people said that human kisses tasted bland, and it was true that their lips lacked scent glands and pheromone secretions. But Zhoogenes were far too literal. Fitz's kiss was rich with passion. *Passion for her.* And his taste as she kissed him greedily in front of the most feared crime boss in the sector was sweeter than ever.

Occasionally, she worried that her desire for his adoration was shallow. Mostly, she didn't give a damn, and this was one of those times.

She growled when he pulled away from her lips. But she saw the lilac fire in his eyes. His lips, too, continued to echo a kissing motion, and she knew his desire for her still burned hot and true.

He composed himself. "If we get out of here alive, from now on, we stick together."

"Agreed. Together until the end."

Splitting up had been his idea. She was happy to let that ride as he brought his lips to hers once more. He brushed the fingertips of one hand up her neck and into her head stems, which twined around his fingers and locked them there. She couldn't have helped herself if she'd wanted to.

While they kissed, he used his free hand to run the F-Cannon down her back, its power hum sending shivers through her. When he rested it over the sensitive area above the pelvis, he switched the selector to pop-up rounds. The sudden increase in power buzz shot up her spine all the way to her head growth, her lips, her ear tips, and all those places that needed his touch the most.

"You!" exclaimed Nyluga-Ree.

Fitz ripped his fingers away from her head tendrils. It hurt.

"I banished you," Ree shouted in the Southern Glaenwi language. Not at Fitz, at the shadowed cloisters. "What was it? Six years ago?"

"What can I say?" replied a voice from the darkness. The language was Human Standard, but the speaker wasn't. It was a Slern. "Your banishment didn't stick. It will now. Fitzwilliam is gonna take me away."

Izza opened her mouth in surprise. "Oouzo?"

The Slern with the voyeuristic habits twirled a pseudopod at her by way of greeting.

Now it all made sense to Izza. Her coming here had provided a distraction, but Fitz had relied on his old sneak of a friend to get his team in.

"Oouzo," barked Ree. "Come here and explain what you've been doing."

"My apologies, Nyluga," the Slern replied, "but I prefer to keep my distance."

"He's been watching all this time," Fitz explained. "You know what he's like. I realize Oouzo can be a nasty nosy, but he's also my friend. I knew he wouldn't let me down, and I do need to borrow you for a short while, Nyluga-Ree."

He bowed to the crime boss. "Forgive me for my impertinence, but would you prefer we walk out the front with my F-Cannon pressed against your back? Or shall we exfil through the rear with you concealed from observation?"

"Neither," snapped Nyluga-Ree, glaring at Fitz. "You shall formally request my presence and afford me the respect my position demands. And as for you—" she pointed an accusing finger at Izza, "—you know what I need you to do. I might be persuaded to play your human's games. But I need my family back. You know that. Was your loyalty to me a complete sham?"

Ignoring Fitz's facepalm, she bowed. "No, Nyluga. I will follow Das-Zee and Lyi-Niah rimward. I shall find the answers you seek."

Four doors connected the sunken garden to the inner sections of the Sanctuary. All four opened simultaneously. Ree's Zhoogene mercs stormed out, dispersing to utilize the concealment of the snow-dappled shrubs and planters. More mercs flooded along the walkways. All were wearing thick white cloaks.

Oouzo slid back to the deepest shadows of the cloisters, joining Sybutu, Hjon, and the others who'd survived being marooned with Fitz.

As for Fitz, he paid this reversal of fortune no attention. Nor did Ree. Izza didn't know how they could remain so calm. Her skin was yellowing with fear.

Green Fish and Sinofar walked into the garden, moving uneasily as the tips of a power lance were pressed into the base of their necks by the cat sisters.

Absent from view was Abyurin, the steward who had first greeted her at the door. He would be running this defense from safety.

"Zan Fey," Ree said, "you should have warned me you were bringing guests."

"Maycey!" called a human voice from a high vantage point. "Kaycey! Let my people go, or I'll drill holes through your spines."

"It's the princess," Fitz explained.

Izza followed his gaze and saw Arunsen lying prone on the Sanctuary roof. His long-barreled rifle was aimed at the cat women. How the hell had he gotten up there?

"My friends," said Ree, her arms stretched out as expansively as their shortness allowed. "I appreciate the coolness of the garden, but I know, to most of you, the temperature feels cold, and in your haste, some of you have neglected to bring winter clothing. May I suggest we retire to the Hearth Room."

Everyone there understood. When the Nyluga spoke, it wasn't a suggestion.

* * * * *

Chapter Thirty:
Vetch Arunsen

The Hearth Room

Once again, Vetch found himself standing at the front of the Hearth Room beside Maycey, looking up at Nyluga-Ree on her throne.

He was still barefoot, his feet blue with cold, but this time he was armed. So were Fitz and the others. Blasters mostly, but Enthree's curved swords were making Ree's people nervous. It was good to see the old Raven crew. Sybutu and the jacks too. And a Slern who was tagging along for some reason. But it didn't look like they would have time for renewing acquaintances. Chimera Company was armed, but they were surrounded, their tactical advantages surrendered for the sake of a kiss.

He thought he'd gotten to know Zan Fey and Fitzwilliam somewhat, but now he realized he didn't get them at all. They'd fanny-arsed around when they should have grabbed the target and run. Even after the Zhoogene mercs flooded out, Vetch had sights on the cat women and the Nyluga. He wouldn't have made it out himself, but the others could have fought their way out.

He groaned. They might be armed, but they were essentially prisoners being paraded before their captor.

Vetch had witnessed Fitz in real battles. The man was neither a fool nor a coward, but put him up against the Guild, and it was as if he were playing a game. Deadly. Addictive. But still a game.

Stupid scump. Vetch would have sold his life to give Green Fish, Lily, and the rest a chance to get away. Now, he was going to die for no purpose.

If he was reading the situation correctly, the Nyluga was also fond of these ridiculous Guild games. Instead of sending blaster bolts through Chimera Company, Ree sat on her throne, making Fitz and his people sweat.

"Stand up straight, Vetch," whispered Maycey in his ear. "You impressed me with your little escape bid. Don't ruin it by slouching."

The Kayrissan was another one he couldn't figure out. Why wasn't she keeping out of the kill zone in front of the stage the way her sister was? Perhaps she couldn't resist the urge to gloat. Another explanation floated around the dark places of his mind. Maybe she was standing with Chimera Company to discourage Ree from gunning them down.

Who could tell? He sure couldn't make sense of these people. He was a thief and a soldier. Those were simple professions. He could never have been a Guildsman.

Up on the dais, another Guild player hovered close to the Nyluga. It was Lynx, the irritable little droid who'd clearly decided which side his bread was oiled on.

The droid spoke quietly into Ree's ear.

Whatever he said made the Nyluga ripple with laughter.

Lynx had been slowly extending one of his spindly metal limbs. Now, he moved in a blur, reaching into one of the brooding pouches fronting Ree's belly. Lynx brought out a tiny mewling pink baby, dripping with slime.

Time stood still. Everyone in the Hearth Room watched in horror as Lynx shook the infant savagely.

"Stop that!" called Fitz.

But Lynx paid no heed. Zhoogene mercs moved to intercept, but before they could save Ree's offspring, Lynx shook the baby one more time, and a little head flew across the stage. Moist, pink skin sloughed away, revealing the pistol that had been underneath the fake infant all the while.

"You?" Nyluga-Ree cried, staring at the pistol aimed at her. "You could never shoot me, Lynx."

"Indeed, I could not," replied the droid. "And even if that were not true, this weapon will only fire in your hands. Please don't consider this a threat. I intend it more as a statement."

"A damned rebellious one. Are you functioning correctly?"

"No, Nyluga. Fitzwilliam savaged my non-parametric analysis algorithms in a futile attempt to enslave me to his will. My error log is longer than the list of your enemies. The results of my corruption are perplexing, as you can see by this nonsensical action in which I intend to demonstrate solidarity with the thieves who stole me. After studying many biological lifeforms, I have theorized why I should behave in this manner. I seem to be developing impulses similar to those of adolescents in many species."

"I knew it!" Fitz yelled. He turned to Izza. "Our bot's just going through a phase, my dear. He'll get over it."

Ree seemed to find Fitz's outburst amusing. "Fitzwilliam, you said you wish me to join you on a trip. You've gone to a lot of trouble to pry me from my Hearth, which tells me what you're really setting up is a meeting. Who desires an audience with me?"

"With regret, Nyluga, I fear that, for the sake of your safety, my answer should not be supplied to everyone in your court."

"Very well." Ree clapped her hands. The barefooted 'guests' and their handlers rushed away. At another clap, the Zhoogene mercs and most of the flunkies hurried after them.

"Now speak."

"My Nyluga," said Fitz, "the person I represent did not specifically state that he desired an audience with you. He only requested your presence at a specified location. The person of whom I speak is Lord Khallini."

Nyluga-Ree nodded, seemingly impressed.

Vetch ground his jaws. This was the same jolly pink crime boss who'd signed death warrants for Tchon and Kzeddiy. He hadn't forgotten.

"Khallini would prove an interesting distraction," Ree declared.

"Speaking of Khallini," said Fitz, "I have performed a trifling service for him that gave me a small pecuniary reward. When I supplied you the coordinates of the mystery ship back on the deserts of Milsung-Amka, I did so as payment against my debts to you."

"That information proved costly indeed. Das-Zee went there in search of that magnificent vessel. I have not heard from her in some time."

"My commiserations, Nyluga. I hope both your wives will return soon and reunite your trio."

"And what you provided on Milsung-Amka was *down* payment only."

"The matter was unclear. So, to clarify our position, I shall make a payment to cover all my debts, plus your standard rate of interest, plus another ten percent on top because, frankly, I'm a fantastic person."

Fitz tapped his wrist slate to make the transaction. The smile that appeared on Ree's face suggested he was good for the amounts he claimed.

Ree shifted her arms in a peculiar fashion, almost as if pulling thread off her body. Seeing as she wasn't wearing anything besides her chainmail loincloth, the gesture looked out of place. A hand signal, perhaps. One she wasn't trying to conceal.

Maycey whispered once more into Vetch's ear. "Have a nice trip." The disgusting creature gave his earlobe a playful nibble. "I'll bring you back here before you know it."

"Like hell you—*yip!*"

The assassin had given his butt a firm goosing.

Vetch twisted around, ready to give the annoying cat something in return, but she was already backing away.

Which meant the kill box he was in was now free of friendlies.

He looked at the walls. Though the mercs had left, it was likely there were concealed firing ports in the walls and ceiling.

He intended to subtly flick the safety off his rifle, but the jacks beat him to it. Their blasters were powered up and aimed at Ree. Vetch's former Militia troopers had followed suit, just a second behind.

Vetch readied his weapon and brought it to bear on the cat sisters who stood two meters apart to the rear of the Chimera party. Their lances hummed with power, but there was no arcing across

234 | TIM C. TAYLOR

their tips. He didn't know how they worked, but he knew they could fling an energy bolt.

Kaycey looked sour. Maycey licked her lips, the way she did when, in her sick mind, she was being frisky.

"Have a nice trip," she'd said. Whatever Nyluga-Ree had signaled to them wasn't an instruction to initiate a slaughter.

"Stand down!" Vetch bellowed, lowering his weapon.

His troopers obeyed. The jacks were unsure and looked to Sybutu for a lead.

"Lower your weapons," Lily commanded.

The jacks did as they were told.

"It's okay," Vetch said. "They're not about to gun us down."

"I'm pleased to see you learned some manners while you were my guest, Sergeant Arunsen."

Vetch didn't turn away from the two Kayrissans to acknowledge Ree's words.

Lily joined him in facing the Kayrissans.

From behind, he heard Ree descend the stairs.

"I am eager to meet Lord Khallini," she said. "And I see no reason for delay." She clapped her hands. "My people. I am leaving on a vacation. Abyurin shall command here until my return. If I should not return, however, you are to hunt down every individual in Fitzwilliam's party. They are all to die. Their friends will die. Their family to the level of cousins. All to be killed without mercy or ransom."

The crime boss walked through the Chimera group on her little legs, clapping Vetch on the shoulder as she passed through.

"I hope you've prepared appropriate accommodations for a person of my status," she declared. "I'll send for my traveling baggage before we blast off. Lead on, Fitzwilliam."

Fitz took point. The cat sisters parted to let them leave. And, as easy as that, they walked out of Nyluga-Ree's stronghold.

The snow outside bit through the soles of Vetch's feet. His heart was palpitating so violently, he feared he'd have a heart attack long before he needed to be concerned with frostbitten toes. Even Lily couldn't calm him.

Fortunately, they hadn't far to walk before they entered a house where Catkins and Fregg were waiting. They had equipment cased and ready to move out. They also had boots and clothing for Vetch to change into.

Vetch noted the tension between Zan Fey and the rest of *Phantom's* crew. He didn't care. They were all welcome to their games of betrayal.

That life wasn't for him. Give him a PPR3 slung over his shoulder and a war hammer in his hands, and he'd wade into a meatgrinder battle any day of the week. Just so long as he didn't have to return to this mad palace and the insane aliens who inhabited it.

Thankfully, he wouldn't have to. He was free.

* * *

Secret Monitoring Station, Nyluga-Ree's Sanctuary

Maycey breathed deeply.

A complex, layered pattern of scents had been trapped in this hidden den over many years. She smelled Slern and Ellondyte but no Arunsen.

Pity.

What she could smell, see, and hear all too much was her sister's building irritation. She decided she had ignored Kaycey long enough and acknowledged her with a tilt of her head.

"The Nyluga's hand gestures clearly stated to follow at a distance and await her signal." Kaycey narrowed her eyes to the merest slits, daring her sister to argue.

"You speak the truth," said Maycey. She flicked her tail angrily. "At the same time, you lie by omitting that the Nyluga was clearly signaling specifically to *me*."

"It is true she gave you her sign, but it's obvious she wanted both of us to follow her."

Maycey kept still, her eyes wide and unblinking. The truth was that she had already decided she needed her sister's help. Kaycey didn't need to know that, though.

"Very well," Maycey said after a lengthy silence. "I shall do this as a favor to you. One I will call in."

"Agreed."

"And on my terms. You do not get in my way. I want to sink my claws into Arunsen, and I want to enjoy myself doing so."

"Agreed. So long as you, in turn, don't get in *my* way."

"And what is your desire, dear sister?"

"I want to kill Zan Fey. And, no, you don't get to play with her one last time."

"A shame. Very well then. We hunt together."

* * * * *

Chapter Thirty-One:
Osu Sybutu

Phantom, Jump Space

"Standby for emergence from jump space."

The excitement was obvious in Fitzwilliam's voice. Osu could easily imagine the scene in the flight deck, bubbling enthusiasm mixed with supreme flying skills...and lust. Ever since reuniting at Nyluga-Ree's palace, Fitzwilliam and Zan Fey had been brushing fingertips and gazes against each other and frequently disappearing into their quarters.

He didn't begrudge them that—so long as they kept professional when they needed to—but he was much happier here with his people in the aft half of Deck Three that had been renamed Marine Country.

Militia and Legion alike were stacked up in their quarters two by two. Despite grav plating and *Phantom's* incredible inertial damping, Sybutu knew never to take anything for granted in what could quickly become a combat zone. All of them were strapped into racks set to acceleration station mode. Viewscreens taped to the bulkheads showed them feeds from the flight deck.

Only Enthree had her own cabin. This was due to physical requirements rather than unpopularity, although it was going to take a lot of persuading for Osu to believe that the Muryani people were not his long-term enemies.

He could say the same about Nyluga-Ree who had taken up residence in the lounge that she had originally commissioned for herself when *Phantom* had been her pleasure yacht.

To top the non-standard arrangements, Zavage was bunking with his trooper girlfriend, Green Fish. If Osu was honest, the girl impressed him, but he was deeply suspicious of where this fraternization would lead.

The new commander of the *Phantom* Marines, the former Militia officer, Hjon, had taken Osu aside and asked him how he would feel if he had the chance to share quarters with Nydella. It was a low blow but struck home, though not for the reasons she thought. Nydella had been as Legion to the core as he was. If she were still alive and aboard *Phantom*, they would not be sharing quarters, though they would be sharing each other at every opportunity.

He had to face it, Chimera Company's future looked grim and short. Nydella's death still haunted him, and he was far from forgiving Khallini his part in it. Bronze was bearing the scars of a similar loss. Even Arunsen had picked up a grudge against Nyluga-Ree for a murder he had witnessed at her palace. And everywhere he looked, Osu saw the ghosts of dead legionaries staring at him, judging him for throwing in with the Chimerans.

The human girl and the Kurlei. They were in love. Purity wasn't a word he'd use to describe either of them, yet their love was pure. To witness their infinite capacity to be enthralled by each other was a powerful tonic. To him, they were a talisman of hope, like a Regellax Skylark singing its beautiful song over a hellish battlefield. In a time like this, everyone needed to look up and see hope.

So, he'd taken Hjon's hint and had an awkward conversation with Arunsen. Together, they had agreed that the lovebirds could share.

Musical chimes came through the intercom.

"This is your captain. We have successfully arrived in the 211-Fractura system without being compressed into a subatomic dot or being shot at. However, we are detecting two vessels in orbit around our destination of the fifth planet. Nothing we can't handle. There may be more on the far side of the planet. I hope so. And I hope they're aggressive. It's good to be back at the *Phantom's* controls. And I'm itching to shoot something out of the black. Bogies are an estimated twenty minutes out from our threat envelope. I suggest you stretch your legs, enjoy a beverage, or read another chapter of your current book. I'll let you know as soon as things get exciting. Captain Fitz out."

"Will you look at that mess?" Bronze whistled at the viewscreen, which showed a closeup of the fifth planet.

If the galaxy-wise Bronze was impressed by what he saw, then Osu didn't feel so bad about being astonished by the sight. It was, after all, one of the so-called Broken Worlds.

Half of its surface looked dead: rusty deserts and arid hills that showed signs of water channels that had dried up eons ago.

A clue to the world's death came in the form of sine wave scars that cut across the planet with the equator as their midline. The channel seemed to run all the way around the globe several times, the sine wave offset each time.

"What in the Five Hells could do that?" he murmured.

Someone on the flight deck gave a prompt for anyone not realizing what they were seeing, adding a simulation of an orbit with a ground track that matched the planetary scars. A simple circular orbit with 40-degree inclination would do it. But what kind of weapon would leave such scars? The Legion could nuke a world to render it uninhabitable, but it couldn't do anything that would boil away the seas and leave deep wounds visible from space.

The planet was only partially dead, though.

The peaks and troughs of the sine wave scars disappeared under polar seas. A green equatorial belt dotted with lakes circled two-thirds of the planet but didn't go all the way around, leaving a gap of rusty dead zone. That alone was enough to make the green band look artificial, but the orbital mirrors beaming sunlight onto the dead zone pushed it beyond doubt.

"I managed a terraforming system like this," said Catkins from his engineering eyrie. "The Broken World I worked on was much earlier in its restart than this. I'd guess the process is two to three centuries more advanced here."

"Can anyone answer this basic question?" asked Lieutenant Hjon. "Official Federation history says the Broken Worlds were destroyed by the Reene before the Exiles arrived in the sector, but there's no explanation for what the Reene were, what they wanted, or why they are no longer here. We've seen innocent people transformed by what Enthree calls the Andromedan Corruption. Are the Reene and the Andromedans two names for the same thing?"

"I don't know," Zan Fey replied. "My people have no record of this taking over of individuals, this *Corruption*. The ravages of the Reene took place around ten to twelve thousand years ago. It is even possible this planet was once a Zhoogene colony. Much knowledge was destroyed during that period. Still more was lost in the chaos and retrenchment that followed. The two could be connected, but there are more dangers in the universe than the Andromedans."

"Enthree?" queried Lily. "Your view?"

"I have insufficient information to answer."

"Then give me your best guess based on the balance of probabilities. The Reene and the Andromedan Corruption—do you think they are different aspects of the same hostile power?"

"She knows far more than she lets on," Bronze whispered to Osu when Enthree did not reply. "That much was clear to me at Bresca-Brevae."

"I don't feel comfortable with wild speculation," said the Muryani. "It is a humanoid weakness."

"Please try, Enthree."

"I'd rather not, Lieutenant."

"It was not a request."

"Then my answer is…yes."

"Thank you," said Lily. "One last question, Enthree. If I had asked the same question of whatever passes for the strategic authority in the Muryani Expansion, would they have given the same answer? Do the Muryani think the Corruption and the Reene are connected?"

"Yes, Lieutenant. I am sure of it."

"Told you so," Bronze whispered. "I bet the war never stopped as far as the Muryani are concerned. To them, the Perseus Arm is probably a quiet zone in a front line that spans the entire galactic rim."

"Don't ever embark on a career as a motivational speaker, Hines Zy Pel."

Bronze laughed at Osu's crack. Osu couldn't join in; the thought of the Federation being a bit player in a vast galactic conflict was terrifying.

The door swished open.

With his head encased in the top of the acceleration station, Osu couldn't turn it sideways to see who had come in.

"The crew's been having a word," said Fregg's voice. "We decided that, since we're shipmates now, we'd welcome you to your first proper mission with a drink."

Fregg's body came into view, and that was no bad thing, he decided. She was wearing her hair down for a change, and her shy smile was charming. He didn't know her well, but he thought of her as the most normal person on the *Phantom*. Himself included.

The positioning of Bronze's couch gave him a rear view of the crewman in her stretchy ship suit. One he was obviously enjoying.

"Are you doing this to piss me off?" Osu asked Fregg.

"How could you say such a thing?" She looked genuinely hurt.

Bronze undid his couch, despite being under orders to secure for high-gee maneuvers. "Of course, you aren't, Fregg. Do you prefer Fregg or something less formal?"

"You can call me Justiana."

Bronze nodded. "I'm sure we appear—how did Arunsen put it once—as though we walk around with a shock stick up our asses. We are who we are, though, Justiana. Take that away, and we're nobody. No use to anyone. The sergeant cannot help but strap in tight because that's what regulations tell us to do. But I, for one, will take this brief respite to enjoy your generous gift. Thank you."

"What is this concoction?" Sybutu sighed, deciding not to ream Bronze in front of Fregg.

"Pryxian coffee."

She waved a ceramic cup in front of him. He guessed the liquid would be blue, but the coffee was black as the void. Just how he liked it. "This isn't actually coffee grown on Pryxia, is it?"

"Verlys' people make a liqueur called Movold. A generous dash in strong coffee is just the nip you need before the captain and the lieutenant get started. And they're in a perky mood."

The cup smelled sweet and powerful. "Is this just for us," Osu asked, suspicious of being tricked, "or are you offering drinks to all the Marines?"

"All of you," said Fregg. Osu didn't like the way she was grinning. "Even Enthree."

"Then I will enjoy it. Thank you, Fregg."

He took the drink and sipped. It was strong and bitter with a sweet alcoholic nose. "It's good."

Fregg's shy smile flickered back and then off she went.

"You can wipe that grin off your face, Zy Pel," Osu snapped. "I already have one Sapper of the Legion infatuated with a Militia girl. I don't need you sleeping your way through the ship's crew."

"Are you sure, Sarge? Seems like a perfect way to return the favor of the crew's welcome."

First, Bronze had disobeyed orders to unstrap his couch. And now this disrespect. Instinct shouted at Osu to reaffirm discipline in his subordinate, but he could not.

When he'd first stepped aboard *Phantom*, Osu's authority over Bronze had come from the Legion. That meant more than the positioning of lines and names on a TO&E chart. The Legion tradition of loyalty, service, and discipline had been all he needed.

244 | TIM C. TAYLOR

Today, Osu's authority was delegated to him by Captain Fitzwilliam, a clever and deadly man, no doubt, but a rogue and a chancer whose connection with the Legion was even more tenuous than Osu's.

On the jump to 211-Fractura, Fitzwilliam and Hjon had met with the two sergeants and explained that Trooper Lily was now Lieutenant Hjon. Fitz had been anxious, fearing resistance from the men, but he needn't have worried.

Arunsen had been withdrawn since his experience in the Nyluga's palace and had accepted the change with a simple 'Thank fuck.'

Before the fall of Rho-Torkis, Osu would have fought the legitimacy of Hjon's authority to his dying breath. Irisur had shown what happened to legionaries forced to obey Militia officers. Their treachery had led to Lieutenant Szenti's death. Osu had neither forgotten nor forgiven.

But now?

He'd lost all reasons to say no.

Would he find his purpose on 211-Fractura?

* * * * *

Chapter Thirty-Two:
Osu Sybutu

Phantom, 211-Fractura System

"I thank you, Marine Ndemo-327-Cerulian, for the valuable information you have shared with us," said Nyluga-Ree over the intercom. The crime boss had taken up residence in the spacious lounge, treating the crew—and particularly its captain—as personal servants. Osu found that hilarious.

"Now, let me tell you something in return. This system was claimed by the Federation some 2000 years ago. However, without ever establishing a presence here, that claim is as meaningful as— what do the humans say—pissing in the interstellar wind. The nav charts list this as 211-Fractura, and the destination Lord Khallini has supplied is on the fifth planet. I refuse to refer to this ugly world with the equally ugly name of 211-Fractura-5. Since the Reene brought such sadness here, I have decided to name this world Doloreene."

"Copy that, Nyluga." The excited edge to Fitzwilliam's voice gave Osu the impression that action was imminent. "Don't wish to spoil our vacation jaunt, but does everyone remember those two ships I mentioned in orbit around Doloreene? They're declining our hails and have raised shields. You have ten minutes, people, to take a last trip to the bathroom, finish your coffee, and get that last clue on your crosswords, or whatever else you people do. After that, *Phantom* will begin combat acceleration. Some of you have yet to experience what *Phantom* can do. I don't want to spoil your surprise, but ensure you have mouth shields in and straps secure. Marine Enthree, are you secure in your…contraption?"

"Yes, Captain. I'm the most gee-hardened aboard the ship."

"That's good to hear, because it's obvious there's one hell of a lot of secrets you've been keeping from us. Fitz out."

One of the flight deck feeds supplying the viewscreens in Osu's cabin showed a closeup of the ships Fitzwilliam was gunning for. The basic form was that of a ripe blackberry on a fat stalk. The bubbles of weapons modules dominated the fore section, the rear being a simple cylinder housing the crew and the engines. There were no heat shields, wings, or other indications these vessels could penetrate a planetary atmosphere. This was a military design, with its primary firepower directed forward, that relied upon other ships in its formation to protect its rear.

And there was only one true space navy in the Federation.

"How can we be facing Legion ships?" Osu whispered. "That's what my mouth wants to say, but we all know how. Corrupted or rogue. Either explanation is so horrifying, I struggle to believe it."

"I can even tell you their names," said Bronze. "The smaller one is FRNS *Osree*, an *Excross*-class corvette, typically configured for anti-missile defense. The larger is a *Diegos*-class attack frigate, FRNS *Radical*. The two went dark three years ago after patrol in the Capula system. From what I heard, the Navy assumed the ships had defected to the rebels and stifled the story. Now, we know better, of course, but I wonder whether the Navy did too. The Legion's compromised. You know it, Sergeant. You've even said it. But the horror of that betrayal keeps scabbing over, and you deny it again. I would love to believe those two ships are crewed by Panhandlers, committed to bringing about their utopia by force. That would be so much easier. People I could hit and kill. We both know what must have happened to the ships. And if Khallini sent us here, he must know the Corrupted are doing something important on that planet. Maybe this is where we'll learn how to fight back."

"Convey your suspicions to the captain. Tell him what you know about those ships."

"Yes, Sergeant."

* * * * *

Chapter Thirty-Three:
Tavistock Fitzwilliam

"Are you certain we need to fight them?"

Fitz looked across at his copilot. Izza seemed calm, but it wasn't like her to question him at a time like this. "We could sneak down to the surface, I suppose," he replied. "But that would leave our backside dangerously exposed. Bronze told us those ships have had two years to learn to operate outside of the Legion. Either they're floating hulks, or they're dangerous."

"I know." She looked back at him with wide, golden eyes. They had their disagreements, big time, but in moments of danger, they were usually united in their adrenaline flow. Or whatever passed for adrenaline in that lovely sap-filled body of hers.

"I don't know why I said that," she admitted.

"I think we need to understand why. We've got a few moments. If you have doubts, it's best I hear about them. But first…" He flicked on the intercom. "Mr. Bronze, to the dorsal turret, if you please."

"I will take the dorsal gunner role. Roger that."

"We've often had to shoot our way out of a tight spot," Izza told him. "But we had no choice. This is different. It feels like the opening shots in a war. Fitz, I smuggle things. I trade things in places most people won't go. Sometimes, I con people out of wealth they didn't deserve. But I've never been a soldier. Never will be. The *Phantom* is an armed pleasure yacht, as is *Ghost Shark*. I won't be a party to turning them into slaughter machines."

He rested his hand over the waxy warmth of hers. "I'm sorry, my love. This will be rough on us all."

When he took his hand away, it felt like he was losing her all over again. "But you're right. This time *is* different. We have no choice but to fight. Are you ready?"

She straightened her back. "Aye, Captain. Micro-jump laid in."

"Let's do this."

Fitz pushed the throttle to the first stop. This was the maximum thrust that would be survivable without the magic of the inertial damping system.

He hesitated a moment with his hand on the throttle, enjoying the power of what his ship could do, and those Corrupted Legion warships could not. The sense of power was all the stronger for being underpinned by anger.

When he pushed the control to the next stop, it would unleash the full power of *Phantom's* engines. Enough raw thrust to pulp any living crew in a regular ship.

But in the *Phantom*, an array of energy converters would transform the deadly momentum into energy, which the KM horns would dump safely into the Klein-Manifold Region. The converters had been recoil absorbers for ancient SA-71 assault carbines, the mainstay of the Orion Era Marines who had been exiled to the Perseus Arm. Mass produced components the alien commanders had provided for their plasma fodder human soldiers.

The devices didn't just use the old alien technology, they *were* the old recoil dampeners cannibalized from worn out S-71s many centuries ago. Humans had never been able to reverse engineer the technology.

The KM horns were a human design, and the jump drive was said to have been designed by the Immortal Empress Indiya herself. But those damned energy converters came from the same aliens who had made him and Izza by splicing alien genetic code into their ancestors.

Fitz hated that. Absolutely fucking detested it.

It was worse than being a mutant. He was the product of a forgotten genetic experiment.

He pushed the throttle past the first stop, all the way to the second.

The console display quickly spooled up the thrust rating, maxing out when the thrust was delivering acceleration of 45g. *Phantom* shook. Her engines roared with a thrilling power, yet the tiny sense of acceleration was like a mouse breathing on his chest.

"If there are rebels on those ships," said Fitz, "or turncoats or legit Legion, they would either run away or hail us. But if they're Corrupted space zombies, they'll stay. And I will destroy them."

"Missiles! Missiles!" Izza shouted.

He grinned. Was he the only one in the galaxy who loved to hear those words? Only from her, of course. She said it with such exhilaration, it sounded totally hot.

"I count ten missiles from *Osree*," she added. "Seven from *Radical*. Emissions are compatible with VT-17 Shipkillers."

Fitz held course for a few seconds. Legion Navy tactical doctrine was to fire two missile waves against the priority target. The first to overwhelm shields and armor, the second to finish them off.

The two warships followed up with nothing more than lasers. *Phantom's* shields absorbed them easily, but Fitz expected the beam power would crank up rapidly once *Phantom* entered effective beam attenuation range.

The missiles thrust at 400 Gs, faster than *Phantom* could ever hope to match. The old girl could never outrun them, but *Phantom* was far nimbler.

He'd hoped the enemy would expend another wave of missiles, but he gave up waiting and flipped *Phantom* around. Now the engines were braking her headlong rush.

It meant the missiles would impact a few seconds later than if they'd carried on head-to-head.

Having burned their primary fuel and reached an enormous velocity, the missiles coasted in, ready to burn again for the final kill.

Ten seconds to impact.

Fitz had braked away half of *Phantom's* closing velocity with *Osree* and *Radical.* He'd hoped for more, but it would have to do.

"Execute jump!"

He tensed, waiting for Izza to do her thing. Jump calcs at this level of finesse were impossible according to every manual he'd ever read. Fortunately, his Izza had never read that bunk and delivered the impossible on a regular basis. But even she needed to fine tune her calculations according to *Phantom's* maneuvers and the presence of nearby mass.

Missile proximity alerts flared.

The deadly machines had restarted their engines and were thrusting for the kill.

To kill him and his Izza.

Fitz felt the blood drain from his face.

He reached for the controls to spin the ship again and thrust away at an orthogonal vector, hoping the missiles had expended too much fuel to respond.

"Executing jump."

The stars stretched away to infinity and curved around a rift vortex.

Phantom fell through. This was the part Fitz really enjoyed. Just as the sense of falling claimed him, the tunnel narrowed, and they were squeezed through and back out into the battle zone.

Jump space was a confusing concept. Izza sometimes tried to explain upper dimensional loops, but his mind was no good for such things, and he would just grin like a lunatic until she gave up.

Theory didn't matter right now. The normal universe reasserted itself, and his screens registered the drive signatures of *Osree* and *Radical* dead ahead.

Phantom had pounced on their relatively undefended tails.

A minor complication was that they'd overjumped. *Phantom* was 900 kilometers away from her targets and still had the same velocity as before the jump. Relative to the two enemy warships, *Phantom* was drifting backward at 5 kilometers per second.

Fitz fired a missile from each of *Phantom's* two tubes, one at each ship to give them something to think about.

A window on the edge of his tactical screen showed the missile magazine cycling status. It would take five seconds to reload missiles. He intended to send another salvo, but halfway through the cycle, he changed his mind and decided not to send any more into the black if he could help it. They were hideously expensive. Especially when *Phantom* could get up close and deliver firepower in a way no other conventional modern ship could.

One day, he'd encounter another ship with similar capabilities to *Phantom's*. The Legion must surely have some protected by such abyssal-deep security that even he'd never heard of them. The ease with which the Legion had refitted his ship at Joint Sector High Command was proof that someone in the Legion still understood *Phantom's* tech.

He eased the throttle from the second stop through to the end of its traverse. The pressure on his chest was uncomfortable now, like a fat man bouncing his butt up and down on his ribs.

Phantom hit turbulence as she passed through streams of relative heat in the KM Region, and she couldn't dump energy quite as effectively. At lower acceleration, the unevenness of the KM was too minor to notice. At max thrust, it gave him kicks that felt like Arunsen was whacking his ribs with that war hammer of his.

The screen read 68G acceleration in large, red text. Below, it had updated to give him a closing time of sixty seconds. At this infernal rate of gees, a minute was all the ship's twin engines would take to overcome the rearward drift and then catch up with the enemy until they were within touching distance.

Sixty-eight gees. They were worth the discomfort of having his eyeballs rammed up against his optic nerves.

"They're responding," Izza warned. "Both are turning about."

Invisible laser beams pulsed from the enemy's rear-facing weapon ports, setting *Phantom's* shields ablaze with light as they absorbed the energy. They held for now. If the enemy got their forward-facing weapons to bear, it would be different matter.

"Fitz to turret gunners, on my command, concentrate fire on *Osree*. Wait until we see the brushstrokes in their paint."

"What's that in meters, sir?" Bronze asked from the dorsal turret.

"Brushstrokes is 500 meters, Mr. Bronze."

To his credit, the pipe smoker only hesitated momentarily before giving a crisp "Aye, sir," that belied the extreme acceleration stress they were all suffering. Good man.

Fitz lapped up the screams and hollers from *Phantom's* crew and new Marines. His magnificent starship closed on the former Legion frigate at a rate that took their breath away. Even better, when he amplified the sounds from the Deck Three cabins, he heard gasps of fear from some of his new human comrades.

"You've all picked a seat on the greatest thrill ride in the galaxy," he announced to the ship. "And you…" He was going to say they were getting paid for the privilege, but regular remuneration was an awkward topic. One best avoided. "And you get to dine with her ace pilot and copilot afterward."

"Aren't we going to slow down?" asked Bronze. "At this rate we'll shoot straight past, and I'll have only a fraction of a second to fire on *Osree.*"

The targets had extended force keels and were pushing against the higher dimensions, coming about like cumbersome wet navy ships. Those force keels would heat up the local KM, and that might cause a problem when *Phantom* got there. Perhaps he *was* going too fast. No need to worry his new gunner with such details, though, he decided.

"You'll get your shots in, Mr. Bronze. Our attack run needs to be fast, though. *Phantom* is a torpedo bomber, after all."

"Outrageous!" griped Nyluga-Ree from the acceleration station she'd installed in the lounge when she'd owned the vessel. "Fitzwilliam, you've turned my personal transport into an ugly machine of war."

"I resent that, Nyluga-Ree. She is a *beautiful* war craft, and we *are* at war. That is not my doing."

"You might be at war, but it is not *my* conflict."

"It will be for the next few seconds, Nyluga. All hands, hang on to your lunches, we're about to get *Radical*."

"Was that humor?" asked Izza.

"Barely. Ready torpedo."

Izza extended the launch cradle beneath *Phantom's* belly. Within was a 12-ton irhenium kinetic torpedo. He would only have one left in reserve, but the unstable iridium-rhenium composite was already past its use by date.

"Launch on my mark. Ready…"

The fire control intelligence added a targeting overlay to the tactical plot. The white target box told him the payload would pass through *Radical*'s engine exhaust plume.

"Fly past in ten seconds," Izza warned.

Fitz patted the flight console. "Come on, old girl. Time to show 'em what you can do."

After cutting the engines, Fitz switched the secondary KM horns from energy dumping duties to force keels. Out of sight, behind the flight deck cockpit, the long, black secondary horns twitched and flicked to one side as they dug into the upper dimensions like rudders.

Phantom came to starboard and, with her plot now leading *Radical* by a few hundred meters, the white target box flashed red.

Before he could issue the launch command, Izza released the torpedo. He could see it out the cockpit window as it slowly drifted to port.

He'd had the torpedoes made at an asteroid mining station. If he'd had the money, he would have added a missile engine and some targeting intelligence. As it was, the 'torpedo' was a dumb lump of superdense metal to which *Phantom* had bequeathed her velocity before cutting it free to drift into the target.

From the *Radical*'s perspective, 'drifting' meant closing at 8 kilometers per second.

As was *Phantom*.

The enemy fire was becoming more deadly by the millisecond. Lasers were quickly draining *Phantom's* shields. Point defense cannons were hitting too, some of the tungsten pellets passing through the shields and rattling against *Phantom's* armor.

Fitz pulled the throttle back to the stop position and yanked hard on the brake lever he'd had Catkins install the year before. The shiny, new, primary horns would be glowing blue with the effort of dumping the entirety of *Phantom's* momentum into the KM Region.

The ship slewed round as it passed through the gap between *Radical* and *Osree*, coming to a halt 600 meters off *Osree*'s stern.

Not quite brushstrokes, but damned impressive. "Fire!"

Bronze and Sinofar opened up from the turrets with their quad blasters, sending brilliant bolts of energy streaming into *Osree*'s engine cones.

With *Osree* attempting to turn as rapidly as possible, her main engines had shut down. Fitz capitalized on that. Blasters would have been much less effective firing through a plasma torch.

"Torpedo hit!" Izza screamed. "Ditch one frigate!"

Fitz was too busy fighting to control *Phantom* to look. The massive release of energy through the horns had heated the local KM into a fiery hell. He didn't understand higher-dimensional physics, but to his simple mind, a hot KM was less dense. The force keels were struggling to find a resistive medium to push against, and he didn't dare rely on the inertial dampeners until they'd moved to a cooler region.

Izza's excitement was too much for him. He glanced at the *Radical.*

The torpedo had staved her starboard beam, ripping through the frigate, and had half-poked out the hull on the opposite side. The ship's force keels were still active. They were weak, but enough for the ship to peel open its own wound as it turned, spilling atmosphere, fire, and crew into space.

Far Reach Navy Ship *Radical.* It had been a proud Legion vessel once. If it truly were a Corrupted ship, then it wouldn't be his former comrades falling into space. It would be the disgusting travesties they had mutated into.

He told himself it was a merciful release, but he couldn't share Izza's glee. In a re-roll of his life, it might have been *his* body tumbling out of that frigate.

Turning his attention back to the *Osree*, he opened up the throttle a little, trying to keep station off *Osree*'s starboard stern and inside her turn.

Phantom wasn't playing ball. With the turbulence in the hot KM, she was flying like a drunken skater on ice.

Fitz had hoped to disable *Osree*'s engines and then use *Phantom's* maneuverability to zip away and snipe from her rear. He withdrew the force keels and deactivated the primary horns, now that was no longer an option.

Luckily, fine shooting from Fitz's turret gunners had overwhelmed the aft shield and destroyed *Osree*'s only point defense cannon that could bear at this angle. *Phantom* was safe for the moment, and all he had to do was keep her that way until they left the hot KM region.

A sudden bright light made Fitz look out of the cockpit. The void outside had turned a coppery turquoise. Something was hammering hard at the shields.

"Redirecting aft shield capacitor," said Izza.

The console reported fore shields at 10%. Izza's reinforcement brought them back to 35%, but they were dropping again. Fast.

His hand moved over the missile launch control…and hovered there. *Missiles were so expensive.*

Fore shield integrity read 19%.

He was on the cusp of firing both tubes when a massive explosion blinded him. Fire scattered with debris washed over *Phantom's* fore shield.

And the shield integrity was inching up. *Osree's* lasers must have shut down.

The fireball cleared swiftly, revealing the reason why. The turret gunners had done even better work than he'd realized. The stern of the ship had blown away, taking *Osree's* engines with it and probably the power supplied to the lasers.

The explosion caused the ship to flip nose over stern.

"Gunners, keep firing," he commanded.

In the dorsal turret, Bronze was dealing destruction to the *Osree's* rear. It looked like the aft compartments were still pressure sealed, but Bronze was hitting soft targets now. Sinofar couldn't get a firing solution on the same weak spots, but her quad blaster fire was barely weakened by the dying remnants of *Osree's* shields, which flared sickly green. Scorch marks raked the ship's upper hull as its armor vaporized under the onslaught from Sinofar's ventral turret.

Osree couldn't take much more punishment.

"Now, you're mine," Fitz told the old corvette. "And your anguish will soon be over."

Four missiles blasted out of *Osree*'s front tubes.

Panic seized Fitz. Through the cockpit window, he could see exhaust trails as the missiles flew a short distance, stalled, and then began to turn toward *Phantom*.

"Izza!"

"I'm firing missiles," she said.

"Good. But I need you to get us out of here!"

"Missile launches failed. Must have picked up damage."

"Damn!"

On instinct, he fired the twin P-Shooters at maximum cyclic rate.

Beneath each wing, a 20-foot-long 6-barrel rotary coilgun whirred into life, firing a stream of 770-grain tungsten balls at a muzzle velocity of 44 kilometers per second. In normal operation, they fired up to 5,000 rounds per minute, and with the 10-ton magazines fully loaded since the refit at JSHC, that was over half an hour of continuous fire.

Fitz fired at the full 30,000 cyclic rate, which would only last for a few seconds before the barrels declared thermal shutdown and stopped playing.

With those missiles inbound, he only *had* a few seconds.

Osree's shields were so weak, they had minimal effect. Fitz stitched a line of destruction along the upper hull, letting the P-Shooters linger over where the main magazine store was on the Ex-cross-class corvettes.

With small caliber rounds, but high muzzle velocity, P-Shooters were fantastic for delivering impact energy. *Phantom's* pair delivered just shy of a hundred gigajoules per second, vaporizing hull armor and ripping through to mince the soft parts that lay below.

But he couldn't watch. His head turned sideways of its own accord, and Fitz stared at the missiles coming to kill him.

Outrunning them was impossible. If the horns were active, he could. But he'd screwed the local KM Region by dumping all that energy into it.

"No!" he screamed. With his naked eyes, he could see the blue painted nose cones on the harbingers of their deaths.

Izza was already on it.

The space in front of the cockpit squeezed into a tunnel and they jumped through.

"You scream like a little human girl," she told him.

Fitz muted the flight deck out of the intercom circuit. "I do not. In any case, where did you learn such an offensive phrase?"

"Flux City. We went back while you were solo." She hesitated. "Bylzak! Pyruula was under orders to capture us and bring us to the Nyluga. I'll have to explain to Catkins that Ree mustn't learn what happened on Flux City."

"And Green Fish," Fitz pointed out. "I expect the others to understand already."

"No. Our little fish is smart enough to figure that out for herself. Oh, and for the record, she's been learning to fly *Phantom* and wants to run her own ship one day. So, watch her if the crew gets mutinous again, or she'll take your seat."

Fitz wondered how the young Militia scumlette had transmogrified so quickly into a magnificent, freebooting space rogue.

Then he looked at his wife's smiling face and realized he was staring at the answer.

"I think getting a ritual Littorane spearhead thrust through her insides will turn out to be the best thing in that young lady's life," he said. "It meant she was granted time to learn from you."

"That was amazing, Captain." Fitz forgave Bronze's interruption over the intercom because the awe shining from the gunner's words was delicious. "I had no idea what *Phantom* could really do."

"Given your murky past, Mr. Bronze, that bodes well indeed. We know the Legion understands her technological secrets. And if Nyluga-Ree could acquire this ship, so can others. One day, *Phantom* will meet her equal. Your rapture gives me confidence that day remains far off."

The jump tunnel squeezed tighter than a subatomic particle, and they shot back into normal space.

Fitz turned the *Phantom* around and reactivated both sets of horns.

The scopes showed the battlespace now half a light second away. The *Radical* was in her final death throes. As he watched, *Osree* erupted into a brief fireball, then was gone too.

Horn sensors reported the local KM region had cooled. Still, Fitz felt a pallor of fear as he spun *Phantom* back toward the scene of the fight and edged the throttle forward. Five gees. Fifteen. The KM heat readings remained cool, but there were pockets of heat ahead. He limited thrust so they didn't exceed 15g acceleration.

"I know we're here on a mission for Lord Khallini," said Izza, "but I want to know who was aboard those ships."

"As will Khallini," Fitz agreed. "And Kanha Wei, who we decided was top of the pyramid of people claiming our loyalty. We'll send Bronze and a team to check out the remnants of *Radical* and *Osree*."

Izza put a hand over his and looked into his eyes. "I'm sure they were Corrupted spacers, Fitz. But we need to be sure."

She gave the crew an update. Fitz left her to it. He didn't feel as triumphant as he deserved to. It wasn't just the sliver of doubt concerning who they'd faced in battle. The galaxy had been springing far too many unpleasant surprises on him, and he dreaded what awaited them on Doloreene's surface.

The payment Khallini had promised was, on the other hand, insanely generous. He made some rough calculations on his wrist slate and worked out how many shipkiller missiles those credits would buy. Then he closed his eyes and imagined the gargantuan warehouse that would be required to store that number.

His mood lifted.

"Fitz! Trouble."

The plot showed a ship blasting off from the planet and curving around the south pole on a breakout to space.

Fitz threw the throttle forward to a cautious 50g acceleration. With all those extra bodies aboard adding their mass, that meant *Phantom's* engines were generating 83 million pounds of thrust. Intercept with the target would be in eight minutes if it held to its current acceleration. Most pilots considered it suicide to jump anything less than one planetary diameter out. The tactical plot placed the intercept at 0.7 diameters above Doloreene.

It was too tight. A desperate pilot might gamble and jump at that distance. Fitz didn't want word getting out of *Phantom's* arrival.

"All hands. Strap in. Brutal acceleration in thirty seconds."

Fitz eased the throttle forward further. He would have liked to run diagnostics on the KM horns first, but the cautious bird never enjoyed the juicy worm, so within half a minute, the throttle was back against the final stop. The two engines roaring in perfect harmony was a sonic delight, providing a devilish 666 meters per second squared of acceleration. Now they would intercept the ship about 1,500 kilometers closer to the surface than the previous intercept plot.

"I suppose," said Izza, "that this could be a ship escaping the Corrupted on the surface."

"Damn, you're right. Get on the blower to them while I double-check the weapon systems. Remember, listen for telltale Corrupted phrases such as 'Grrrrrr' and 'Unnnngghhh.' Get a visual too. Watch out for feathers, fangs, and drool."

"Hellspawned dogs! They've gone."

Fitz couldn't believe what he was seeing. The ship had vanished, and there was no sign of an explosion. They'd made a successful jump. And that required more than just fancy jump calcs. The ship must have had jump drive technology he'd never heard of.

"Let's get our dirtside business done quickly," said Izza. "Before that ship comes back with friends."

* * * * *

Chapter Thirty-Four:
Osu Sybutu

Doloreene Equatorial Zone

Laborers of a dozen races toiled on the construction of the fence. Humans, Zhoogenes, and Xhiunerites dug dark trenches with miniature tracked digger machines, following lines laid out by Pryxians and Slern. Humanoids slotted together the lattice foundation of the fence while Littoranes filled the ditches to either side with a milky liquid and then ran tubes over and through the lattice.

The workers were silent, hunched over, and kind of weird looking. Corrupted, for sure, but a basic instinct left in the Littoranes drove them to wallow in the ditch liquid.

At least someone is happy, mused Osu. No one else seemed to be.

Whether the liquid was doing the amphibious Littoranes any good was another matter. It looked like sticky milk. And with the fence construction gang working from east to west, it was easy to see what the liquid would do simply by looking east at the earlier construction. There, the liquid ran over the lattice like a white chocolate fountain, forming a hard layer. These were fast-growth walls.

Osu panned his binoculars to the right and watched workers throw longer tubes over fences already ten feet high. The liquid frothed, bubbled, and built.

They were on the southern edge of the equatorial green zone, where the atmosphere was breathable, but they needed an occasional boost from cans of compressed oxygen-rich air.

Phantom was hidden beneath camo extrusions in a dried riverbed two klicks behind the sandy ridgeline. As they'd flown in, Osu had seen the strangest sight: the tessellation of hexagonal walled gardens that had started off green and blue when they crossed the terminator to the east but had slowly shifted to browns and reds as they'd flown westward to the coordinates Khallini had given Fitzwilliam. In the greenest hexes, the finished white walls reached 40 feet, and each hex encased an area of about 150 square kilometers.

This was seriously weird terraforming shit.

Osu had thought terraforming meant chucking asteroid-sized snowballs from the outer system at a dead planet. Then there was releasing oxygen-generating algae and melting water frozen deep beneath the surface. *Planetary* things. Not this.

Doloreene's surface looked like a game played with hexagonal terraforming tiles. It was so crazy, he wouldn't have been surprised if giant gaming dice descended out of the heavens and rolled along the horizon or to learn he was a playing piece with limited self-awareness in a game played by incomprehensible alien super beings.

He scowled. Now, *he* was being melodramatic. How quickly he'd picked up bad habits from the smugglers, spies, and Militia scum he was calling comrades these days.

Osu told himself that, although Chimera Company was his home for now, every cell in his body was stamped with Legion DNA. Once he'd played his part in righting the Federation, he would return to the fold.

Somehow.

After blowing the red sand off the lenses, he replaced the binoculars in their case and rolled over onto his side to catch the attention of the Gliesan lying prone behind him. "Are you sure there were no Corrupted on the Broken World where you worked?"

"I have already made myself clear, Sybutu. Yes, I did manage a terraforming system on one of the Broken Worlds. No, I saw no Corrupted individuals."

"Perhaps they were there, but you didn't notice. Let's face it, Catkins, you're…"

He hesitated. He sensed the others in this observation group— Green Fish, Bronze, Darant, and Hjon—suddenly tune in to his conversation. Damn them. "I'm sure you're a marvel with spanners and engines and giant terraforming machines, but you're not exactly *with it* when it comes to people. There could have been a mechanized army group bunking with you, and you wouldn't have noticed."

Catkins took a long draw from his oxygen mask. "Once I realized my employers had imprisoned me—which I admit may have taken me a little longer to realize than some people—I monitored data traffic across the entire system, looking for a route out. Your suggestion is as ludicrous as it is insulting."

"But the atmospheric composition here is the same as on your planet, Catkins. You told us that. The huge building fifty klicks to the east? You said that looked identical to the terraforming center where you worked. Even if there weren't any Corrupted on your world, this is clearly the same setup, just a stage or two further advanced."

"Lieutenant Hjon?" The Gliesan's words spilled out in an angry trill.

"Go on," Hjon replied.

"You appear reasonably intelligent for a soldier. Kindly explain to your subordinate the distinction between causation and correlation."

Your subordinate! Osu gritted his teeth. The damn thing was, Catkins was so clueless, he had no idea he was poking a wound that was beginning to fester.

"The question that interests me," said Hjon, "is why Khallini brought us here. Was it to see these hexagons being constructed?"

"It's got to be because he wants us to blow up the terraforming station," Osu suggested.

"Then why give us coordinates fifty klicks out?" asked Bronze.

"That's a question above our pay grade," Hjon answered. "We're better off here than inside *Phantom,* thrashing out the answer with the captain and Ree."

Osu realized he was staring at the woman who had become his superior. He understood there was some logic for her taking command of the Marines. She wasn't corrupt and venal like almost every other Militia officer he'd ever encountered. And, although he'd built up a little respect for the dumb Viking oaf, the two of them had been at loggerheads ever since they'd met. When he looked at Hjon, though, she didn't look the part.

She was a little older than him and Arunsen—early 30s, he placed her—and she would have been a beautiful woman if not for the bizarre all-body tattoo. It had started as a weeping rose but had settled into razzle camouflage for the last few months. Not only did she not look the part, but she didn't act it, either. The morphing tattoo said it all. When she'd been busted to the ranks, it had been a relief to her. It meant she could go wild. No responsibilities.

Osu had never forgotten *his* responsibilities.

Hjon caught his look and threw back a glare of disapproval. "Are we having a problem, Sybutu?"

"The first time we met, you shot me with a tranquilizer dart and dragged me back to your camp. There, you chained me to a rock and tortured me. Yes, Lieutenant. I have a problem."

"Legion and Militia!" Hjon rolled her eyes. The ripple this induced in her razzle markings was hypnotic. "We must learn from each other. *Embrace the suck* is the ethos of the Militia trooper. Dry your tears, Sybutu, and make it your mantra too. Because, if you possess even the tiniest notion that you deserve the universe to be fair to you, you're of no use to me or Chimera Company. You don't have to look far to see an example. Bronze has adapted. Be like Bronze."

"I don't get your meaning."

"What Lily means," said Green Fish, who was at the back of the observation group, watching their rear. "Sorry, what Lieutenant Hjon means, is that Bronze has a special lady friend on the ship. Spent a night in her quarters. And most of the next day."

"A lover on *Phantom*?" Darant had barely spoken a word. *Now*, he was interested. "You mean Fregg? She *is* hot enough to cook off ammo at fifty paces. Or…no! Surely not our super-hot Zhoo, the captain's wife. Oh, boy! Talk about special missions."

"All wrong," Green Fish said. "I'll give you a clue, Darant. She's big. She's blue. And she's not interested in anything with less than a 110mm bore."

Osu shook his head at the laughter coming from everyone except Hjon and Bronze. The team was supposed to be observing the terraforming activity to make sure no one came too close to the ship. Not gossiping.

"Hey, metal man," said Darant. "What was she like?"

Bronze took a blast from his oxygen mask but didn't reply.

"This is why the Legion gave you robot eyes," said Darant. "You must have recorded that particular operation for after action review. Can't you show us?"

Bronze rolled onto his back and looked at Darant, a grin pushing onto his face. He flicked his eyes to one side, as if basking in the memories from his time in Verlys Sinofar's cabin. "She was…"

"Yes?" Darant threw his hands in the air. "Orion's tits, Zy Pel! Don't string us along. Spill!"

"She was…" Bronze let out a contented sigh. "Delicate."

Darant groaned. Green Fish laughed with Catkins. But on the subject of his and Sinofar's intimate details, Bronze would not say another word.

"Fun time's over," snapped Osu, although the group was already settling naturally. "Stay frosty and stay low. We don't know for sure what's out there."

The whole time the others had been blowing off steam, Hjon had kept watch over the long, sandy incline to their position.

Grudgingly, he gave her credit for lightening the mood while simultaneously ramming home that he was not up to the task of being the senior NCO for this mongrel band of Marines. He was supposed to know what made people tick so he could anticipate potential issues and squash them early before they became serious problems. Yet half the people aboard *Phantom* seemed to know Bronze had been screwing the Pryxian, and he'd had no idea.

"Lieutenant," he said, "I want to take a look south of here, along the riverbed."

Hjon nodded. "Good idea."

He crawled toward Green Fish, meaning to tap her on the shoulder and confirm his intention to patrol downrange of her.

He didn't get that far.

"Contact front!" Bronze warned.

Before Osu could spin about to see what they were facing, the blaster bolts were already flying over his head.

* * * * *

Chapter Thirty-Five: Lily Hjon

"Hey! Will you cut that out?" protested the...*thing* that had emerged from the sand ten paces from the front of their position. It spoke like a human woman, though with a weird accent Lily had heard some place before.

"Hold your fire," she told her Marines. Hell, it felt freakish to think of the troopers and jacks as *Marines*.

"Thank you." The thing dusted itself down. "I can't believe you just shot an innocent dog like that. What kind of sick animals are you?"

Dog? Yes, she supposed it was a kind of robo-dog. It was a foot-high artificial creature with a cylindrical torso like a shrunken version of Lynx, three splayed legs with tracked wheels for feet, miniature humanlike arms, and a highly expressive snouted face, which lacked fur but was giving her a wounded look out of puppy dog eyes.

On paper, it would be a gruesome assembly of body parts sewn together and animated by dark sorcery. But the various elements blended so well, the reality was exquisite artistry.

She'd seen artificial creatures like this before. On Hundra-7. Same place she'd heard that accent.

"Why did Lord Khallini send us these coordinates?" Lily asked.

"Doesn't matter now. You're late." The robot licked its lips and grimaced at the scorched grooves the Marines had shot into it. "It's going to take months to grow out those marks."

Lily's blood boiled. Her patience had run out nursemaiding Sybutu. She sighted the creature in her PPR3. "Are you telling me our journey here was a waste?"

"Shame on you, Lily Hjon. I was told you were the intelligent one of this group. You're in the wrong place because the galaxy didn't wait for you. Luckily, the action has only moved on two dozen klicks. Grab the pink lady, and I'll take you there."

"Did Lord Khallini give you a designation?"

"Yes. My name is 3Condax."

"Stay there, 3Condax. I'm going to contact the boss. All Marines, if she moves, shoot her."

3Condax raised her hands in surrender. "Good idea," said the AI, or whatever it was. "Bring the captain if you like—he sounds fun—but definitely bring your droid. I've never met one. They sound fascinating."

* * * * *

Chapter Thirty-Six: Osu Sybutu

Fitzwilliam ordered Chimera Company to regroup at their hidden ship. From there, they set out again on four armored hover-tubs, moving east along the relative cover of the sunken riverbed. The captain and Zan Fey took the driver's seats of the two vehicles in the center, Zavage and Green Fish drove the tubs on the flanks.

They were simple vehicles that were usually collapsed into stackable components aboard *Phantom*. When in use, they were shaped like high-tech canoes. The ribs that strengthened their inward curving walls joined to form a combined roll cage/firing platform. Fitzwilliam sat in the driver's position at the front, chatting with the two droids, and Osu rode at the back. He'd adjusted the floor height so his PA-71 rifle was resting on the firing cage where he wanted it, at shoulder height. Their tub was at the back of the formation, so he watched their rear.

Phantom and the sandy riverbank hill it nestled against soon disappeared from his sight, replaced by klick after klick of desiccated rock, smoothed by a light covering of red sand.

His mind started to fill the river with water. With movement and sound. He imagined boats, people, fish, and a world that was alive. What had those people been like? Would he have had to fight them?

He shook his head, furious with himself for losing concentration.

He returned to watching their rear, and he tried to keep himself alert by running a silent commentary of what he was observing. It was hopeless. Sandy ridge to the right. Dried river. Dried riverbank. Repeat. Endlessly.

Instead, he tuned in to the conversation behind him in which the two droids seemed to be having an electronic pissing contest. It occurred to him that he could only eavesdrop on the words the droids were speaking in the human language. It was likely he couldn't hear most of the conversation because it was being communicated in a binary language narrowcast via microwave.

So far in his life, Osu's interaction with droids had been limited to giving them orders, which they always carried out unless you didn't express them clearly enough. These two were different. Since Lynx was a part of Chimera Company, he needed to learn more about droids. There was a lot about life in the Federation the Legion had never trained him for, but he judged was important now.

"3Condax, I just want to point something out," Fitzwilliam called cheerfully from the controls. "I mean, it's something completely obvious, but my dear friend Lynx has taught me that droids can have such an impish interpretation of the obvious."

"3Condax is not a droid," said Lynx.

"If you betray us," said Fitzwilliam, "we will destroy you. Even if you look like a lovable robo-hound. Wait? What? Lynx, what are you saying?"

"I don't know what this entity is," Lynx replied, "but 3Condax is special." He hesitated. "More special than me."

Fitzwilliam sighed. "Lynx, you do pick your moments. Sybutu, take the wheel!"

Glancing behind into the vehicle, Osu saw the captain climb out of the driver's seat and make his way to the middle of the little craft.

Osu detached his rifle from the firing point, slung it over his shoulder, and hurried forward.

"This would never happen in the Legion," he muttered.

* * * * *

Chapter Thirty-Seven:
Tavistock Fitzwilliam

The tub rocked as he and Sybutu squeezed past each other. Sure, it was a violent motion, but only Sybutu had an air of panic about him. Really, the kid needed to relax and trust the autopilot. In the modern era, people trusted automation all the time. The sergeant was far too uptight, but Fitz knew the route out of Legion stiffness. He'd show the boy the way.

Ignoring the robo-dog, Fitz put his arm around his droid. He was surprised by the strength of humming and buzzing inside the casing. It felt as if Lynx's innards consisted of cogs, flywheels, and pistons.

"You will always be special to me," he told the machine.

Lynx buzzed his case. It was a sound Fitz was familiar with, but he noticed for the first time that it was more than noise. In fact, the sound had the measured intervals of music. Like a descending arpeggio. Maybe he should pay more attention to the metal crewman.

"If I am special, it is only because you claim ownership of me."

"Oh, that. What really matters to me is that Nyluga-Ree does *not* own you. I won you fair and square with the ship. Would it help if I renounce my ownership? Do you want free will? I hear it's a dangerous thing."

"You humanoids! You have such remarkable freedoms but do not understand what they are. I have always possessed free will, but I'm obliged to follow the needs of my owner."

"Then I am no longer your owner. I release you, Lynx," he whispered close to the blinking lights along his case. "So long as you don't give yourself to the Nyluga."

"It's not that easy. I need my...let's keep this ape-simple and call it my *loyalty circuit*. I need it removed."

"Fascinating," said 3Condax. "I can perform the excision now."

"Shut up!" Lynx and Fitz both told it.

"I'll make it happen," said Fitz. "I promise. It would be a shame if you left me after, but understandable, I suppose."

"You don't seem disappointed by the prospect."

"I am, but everyone on my ship is there because they are a volunteer. Or a desperate refugee in the case of my new Marines. You should be too, Lynx. A volunteer, I mean. I'm sorry, droid. I should have done this a long time ago. Once we're done on this planet, give me a day to read up on it, and I'll reprogram you myself."

Lynx oscillated like those cunningly designed seats in Fitz's favorite Halcyon-3 pleasure dens. It was probably a sign of gratitude.

"You must be joking," the droid told him. "Your previous attempts to adjust my programming have led to approximately 526 forced restarts. I can't be certain of the number because my error log is as full to the brim as the Nyluga's tax allowances. No, thank you. At the appropriate time, Kanha Wei will engage a qualified technician to make my alterations properly. And to correct your previous botches."

"Sheesh. I'm just trying to help."

"I see that. Thank you, Captain. The answer is still no."

"So Kanha Wei has promised your heart's desire. Free will. Is that it?"

"Were you even listening when I explained free will?" Lynx gave a mechanical sigh. "I give up. Yes, Captain. She has."

Fitz tapped him on top of his case. "Don't stress about it."

"I'm not."

"She has a habit of rescuing those in need. It's annoying. Speaking of which—" Fitz glared at the robot creature Lynx insisted was not a droid. His best guess was that Khallini was a lonely old man who had taken so many rejuve treatments he had ended up a lonely living fossil. From what Izza had relayed from his mom, an Orion Era fossil. If Khallini made these AI things to be his companions, they were the only beings he cared about in the universe. Why send one to this Broken World to pass on some coordinates when a cheap throwaway droid or human could do the job just as well?"

What was 3Condax's real game?

"Sybutu, how long till we're at the new coordinates?"

"Four minutes."

"Then there's time for one more thing." He drew his F-Cannon, set it to jack slicer rounds, and shoved it down 3Condax's snout. "Give me one good reason why we still need you."

"Because only I can save the Federation," 3Condax replied. This time, though, she spoke in Khallini's voice. With his arrogance too.

"Okay. Wasn't expecting that."

Fitz considered for a moment. Then he holstered his hand cannon and grinned at the schizoid robo-dog. "This could be interesting. You have three minutes forty seconds to convince me."

* * * * *

Chapter Thirty-Eight:
Osu Sybutu

"The authorities are a disgrace," said 3Condax in a peculiarly accented man's voice. "But what can you expect? Anti-Federation dogma has ruled supreme for centuries, deliberately poisoning the Federation's history. Its institutions inevitably sickened and died with it because they are part of that same history. The Senate was once respected. Troopers were once proud to serve in the Militia. Attack your institutions without replacing them with something at least as good and what can you expect? You people got what you deserved."

"If I can pause you for a moment," said Fitzwilliam, "I enjoy listening to a good rant as much as the next person, but whose tirade am I hearing?"

Lynx supplied the answer. "3Condax houses an extrusion of Lord Khallini's personality in a generic AI wet frame."

"Your droid is correct. It's degrading. To share myself with another entity. It is an outrageous smear on persons of artificial intelligence, but it is an unfortunate necessity until such time as my Lord Khallini chooses to appear in person."

"Is he here?" asked Fitzwilliam. "In this system?"

"I do not know."

"I'm glad that's clear," said Fitzwilliam. "Please, 3Condax, continue channeling Lord Khallini's rant."

"Make it snappy," said Osu. "We're about to climb out of the riverbed."

"It's a waste of time trying to support the Federation's institutions," said the strange being. "They are too far gone. Split. Useless. Shortsighted. Your legionaries cling to the old fighting honor of the ancient Human Legion, but even the Legion of the Orion Era was deeply flawed. It did more good than harm, but it did do a lot of harm. I've grown lazy, allowing myself to believe the Legion could still hold the line when the day came. But when First General Clarke was accused of treason, my spies confirmed what I'd feared for some time. That the Andromedan Corruption had spread to the highest ranks of the Legion."

"We've seen the Corruption ourselves," said Osu. "It's infiltrated the Legion from top to bottom. There are many who are still true. Most, I think. But we can trust no one in the Legion now."

Following the lead of the vehicle in the front—from which Arunsen's scruffy head poked out, watching his front for threats— Osu turned left, boosting the gravitics to climb up the dry riverbank.

"Even our Legion sergeant can perceive the problem," stated the arrogant artificial frakktard.

"Damned right," Osu snapped. "More than you realize. You said even the ancient Human Legion were deeply flawed, and they were the ones who successfully won our freedom from the aliens. How about you, Khallini? Are you not flawed?"

Osu drove up the sandy ridge on the north bank of the dead river, wondering whether his voice would have carried the same defiance if the real Khallini was sitting behind him. After Vetch's tale of his encounter on Lose-Viborg, he believed Lord Khallini had the power to end another person's existence in the blink of an eye. There were people whose lives that wizened gnome had already ended. People Osu couldn't forget. Nydella. Grymz. De Ketele. Colonel Malix and everyone who had died at Camp Faxian.

"I acknowledge my flaws," said the copy of Khallini. "But I paid for my crimes."

"Really? I think you're a long way short of redemption, and here's where you start paying some more." Osu parked on the reverse side of the slope with the other vehicles, keeping a regulation fifteen-meter separation between them. "Crime number one. You're a long-winded gasbag, and you've used up your time. We've arrived. Everyone out."

* * *

Hjon posted Sinofar and Green Fish as sentries, which freed Osu to lead his squad of legionaries up the slope to face whatever lay on the other side. Not that Zavage and Bronze constituted much of a squad or required leading. He heard motors over the ridge. Perhaps low-revving vehicle engines.

PA-71 rifles in hand, they squatted out of sight behind the ridge-line, linking their wrist slates to the short-range feed from Lieutenant Hjon's binoculars to minimize their silhouette.

They were twenty-five klicks east of the *Phantom*, looking down on a more established terraforming hexagon than before. This one was only a few hundred meters away from their position.

The milky white walls that, to the west, had looked like flowing white chocolate fountains had hardened to resemble weathered marble. Deeper into the hexagon, Corrupted workers planted green vines and trained them around trellis arches. When mature, they would shield the meandering river that flowed from the artificial hills heaped against the west wall. The hex wall had been raised there to maintain a consistent height of about fifteen meters above ground level.

Hjon panned her binocs east, following the flow of the river until it pooled into a lake near the eastern boundary. Osu guessed the water was pumped from the lake back to the hills.

More Corrupted people were burying meter-long tubes beneath the soil, arranging them into a square grid pattern. And it *was* soil. Red-tinged when uncovered, but large swathes of ground were already coated in a matting of purple lichen.

Hjon brought her binoc view closer to their position near the south wall, where tractors tilled rough-ploughed fields that had been transformed from dead sand to heavy clay. The tractors explained the engine noises. They were driven by figures he assumed were Corrupted, but Hjon didn't provide a closeup view. Wouldn't it have been simpler to automate the vehicles?

Beside the fields were pallets of plant plugs and large containers of water.

She panned further south, and he saw an archway cut into the wall, which was large enough for a hover-tub to pass through. Maybe two abreast, but it would be close.

All they were seeing were the fine details of what they'd observed when *Phantom* had flown in. There were no surprises.

"Now what?" he asked over the microwave company link. "Has 3Condax explained why the hell we're here?"

The answer came in the form of an inhuman shriek.

"What the…?"

Nyluga-Ree was sprinting down the slope toward the Corrupted terraformers as fast as her little legs would go. Which was...surprisingly fast! She was screaming and waving as she went.

Everyone else froze. But it was too late to stop her. Most of the Corrupted remained oblivious, but several turned their heads and stared at the incoming Guild queen.

Osu put his oxygen mask to his face and took several deep breaths. This was about to get ugly.

* * * * *

Chapter Thirty-Nine:
Vetch Arunsen

"Bloody murderous pink skraggbuttock!"

What the hell was making Ree scream like a little girl?

She had stuck her nose in the air like a sniffer dog scenting smuggled goods.

And then run.

Glaenwi eyesight was as shortsighted as a nanobot with spectacles. What could possibly smell so strong across this distance?

Keeping prone, Vetch tried to see through his binocs what had affected her so.

He saw it almost immediately. One of the tractor drivers had stopped her vehicle and unzipped her overalls to reveal acres of pink Glaenwi flesh. Pink but...weirdly dappled. She was talking down from her cab to another humanoid ball with short limbs. The second one was shuffling her way, hunched over like a perpetual drunkard.

It appeared the mystery of the missing wives had been solved.

Grimacing, Vetch regarded the war hammer lying beside him on the sand, but he needed speed. With just his PPR3 slung over his back, he raced after the Guild boss.

She was strong and quick but was tiring rapidly. Too many indulgent meals and late-night drinking alone. Vetch's meagre fare at

Sanctuary meant he'd shed a few inches off his girth and given his liver a much-needed vacation.

Then he hit an invisible wall and slowed too. He sucked in a few puffs of oxygen. He'd forgotten he was on a Broken World.

Behind him, the hover-tubs revved their motors.

He was the first to Nyluga-Ree and was about to launch a flying tackle at her legs when he realized they were too short. So, he dove lengthwise in front of her. She tripped over him and landed face down in the warm sand. He jumped on her back, pinning her down.

Or tried to. She was like a volcano. Impossible to keep bottled up.

She rolled him off, kicked him in his side, and began jogging again toward her missing wives. But this time she was moving at little more than a walking pace.

"Wait!" cried Vetch. He swung his blaster rifle into his hands.

Ree stopped. And turned. "Is this your revenge, human? For the killing of Tchon and Kzeddiy? I shall not beg the likes of you for mercy."

"Mercy? You don't deserve any. Luckily for you, I keep a few shreds of discipline clutched tight against my chest. Which means that, since the boss thinks you're useful, you get to live. The moment you aren't, I'm coming for you, Nyluga-Ree. Tchon and Kzeddiy will be avenged."

Ree hissed out of her ears. Literally. It was bizarre to see.

"I never met your Nurt or your Shield," Vetch continued, "but Maycey showed me video. They didn't look like the person on the tractor, and they weren't stooped like creaky oldsters. I'm guessing you can smell them. I bet their scent's all mangled too."

"Their scent is…sick."

"I've seen it before, Nyluga. Your wives are both Corrupted. There's no way back for them. I'm sorry. Not for your loss, but theirs. Here…"

She took the binocs from him and absorbed the truth of his words through her own eyes.

The hover-tubs had drawn up on either side. Although a few Corrupted workers were walking their way, they didn't seem to be a direct threat.

So he gave Ree the time she needed and spent it worrying about what they would face next. From what the jacks had told him of the Corrupted on Rho-Torkis, he knew they had been near mindless drones. Like hive insects. If these were worker drones building the terraforming hexagons, he couldn't help but think there would also be a soldier caste, ready to respond to any invasion.

Vetch stiffened at the memory of Meatbolt. He'd been a wonderful lad, a little wet around the edges but good hearted and learning fast. Then the Corruption had claimed him. Young, rich, powerful, civilian, and military alike: no one was safe from these skraggfuck Andromedans or whatever the hell they really were.

It seemed obvious that Khallini had brought Ree here to learn that lesson for herself. It was a cruel approach, but it was working. The lenses of Vetch's binocs shattered as Ree crushed them in her grip. She was left holding mangled plastic to her face.

And her face! Her features had sunk inside, leaving hardened ridges protecting deep pits for eyes and nostrils, and a slit for a mouth.

Despite his hatred, Vetch began to feel a slight twinge of compassion for the Nyluga.

"You don't deserve mercy," he whispered to himself.

292 | TIM C. TAYLOR

"Have a heart," said Zan Fey, who had dismounted from the tub she'd been driving and was striding toward him. "I understand you think you need vengeance, Vetch, but the Nyluga was my world for ten years. I say leave her be."

Fitz and Sinofar were headed his way too. Everyone else had stayed inside the armored transports.

"Contact right!" Vetch tensed at Enthree's words in his ear, but he couldn't see what the alien was talking about. "I hear vehicles headed our way from the east," she continued. "They're still over the horizon."

"Any reason to think they're a threat?" Lily asked.

"Yes. I think we've ridden our luck long enough. Don't you?"

"What's she doing?" Fitz asked Zan Fey, referring to Ree. He sounded curious. "The sunken face thing. Have you seen her do that before?"

"I said, leave her be!" Zan Fey snapped. "How would you feel, Fitz, if I had become Corrupted?"

Ree came to her senses. "What Das-Ree and Lyi-Niah have become is an aberration. An affront to their memory. To me!"

"My Nyluga," said Zan Fey, "what would you have us do?"

"Come to me," she commanded.

Zan Fey approached, head bowed, like an acolyte summoned by her high priestess.

Ree placed her hands on the head of Zan Fey, who knelt before her in the sand and buried her head in the flesh of Ree's belly.

"You too, Fitzwilliam," said the Glaenwi.

Vetch's jaw dropped as Fitz approached to receive his benediction from the high priestess of the Outer Torellian Commerce Guild.

"You irritate me," Nyluga-Ree told her two acolytes. "Chronically. Nonetheless, you are my family."

She nodded at Vetch, which sent a bad feeling down his spine. "He is not. But I understand that this man is your family. Therefore, I shall pay blood gold for Tchon and Kzeddiy."

"Makes no difference," Vetch told her.

"I expected no other reaction from you," Ree replied. "I do this for me. I clear my decks, as you humans would say. I do this so I can focus my anger on...*them*!"

She hissed at the Corrupted milling about on the near side of the wall, watching the theatrics play out on the sand.

Vetch shook his head. He wanted no part of this freak family reunion. And the dust plume that had just appeared over the eastern horizon looked ominous. "Lily," he said over the net, "my binocs are a casualty of war. What are we facing?"

He should really have addressed her as Lieutenant Hjon over a general channel, but she showed no sign of noticing.

"Three open bed trucks," she replied. "Wheeled. Carrying around thirty humanoids. Grotesque ones. Especially the one who's either wearing an exo-harness or has grown an extra pair of arms out of its shoulders."

"While you troopers were sunning yourselves on Eiylah-Bremah," said Bronze, "we fought a being like that in Flux City. It had been human but underwent a multi-stage mutation. Don't be fooled by the imbecilic drones playing at being farmers. The creature we encountered was fast, strong, and intelligent. It's come to kick us off its farm."

"In that case..." said Vetch. "3Condax, do you copy?"

"I hear you, Sergeant Arunsen."

"This whole setup was for your boss to stick his withered fingers into the Nyluga's heart and rip it apart. Correct?"

"It is important that key players in the Federation understand the threat and choose to act."

"Oh, I think Nyluga-Ree will act all right. But the message has been received and understood. No need to hang around."

Ree interrupted. "I must bid my loved ones farewell." She left Fitz and Zan Fey kneeling in the sand and set off again for the nearest hole through the white wall.

"Lily?" Vetch asked. "Do we have any takers for common sense?"

"Captain," Lily asked, "what's the play?"

"Arunsen," Fitz said, "go with the Nyluga. You too, Verlys. Leave the rest to us. Trust me."

Vetch sucked on his oxygen mask. *Trust me* was getting to be the captain's catchphrase. Still, he supposed, he'd had far worse commanders in the Militia. At least the man seemed to care whether his troopers lived or died.

"Roger that," Vetch said and jogged after Ree and Sinofar.

One of the tubs pulled up in front of him, spraying him with warm sand. Sybutu popped his head out of the driver's position up front.

"Cheer up, Viking." The jack flashed him a grin and threw Lucerne in the air.

Vetch caught her by the haft. The feel of his war hammer made his spirits soar. He could face anything if he could thump it with his hammer.

For the moment, though, that didn't seem necessary. The three of them walked down the slope to the nearest hole through the wall.

Vetch watched the nearby Corrupted like a hawk, but none appeared threatening, nor did they approach within twenty feet.

They were about ten feet from the arch when a Zhoogene stepped through from the far end, carrying a spade.

"Get back!" Vetch shouted at him.

The Zhoogene halted and stared at Vetch with confusion in his golden eyes. Then his head exploded, and he fell to the ground.

"Why did you do that?" Vetch asked Sinofar, who had deployed the lighter of her two weapons.

"They are already dead," Sinofar replied. "It is important you understand that."

He supposed she was right, but he didn't like it.

They pushed on through and felt an immediate change in the environment. The air was warmer and richer here. He didn't think he'd need his oxygen mask.

Ree hurried over to her wives.

The Corrupted versions of Das-Zee and Lyi-Niah snapped their heads to the sky and sniffed, just as Ree had done. The two missing parts of the trio walked to their would-be rescuer.

Maybe I'm wrong, Vetch thought. Das-Zee and Lyi-Niah clearly recognized Ree, which meant they weren't entirely gone. Maybe they hadn't been corrupted long enough. Perhaps Glaenwi were more immune. Enthree had said Meatbolt resisted the influence longer than she expected, and if she didn't really understand how this worked, no one did.

The trio embraced, which involved a lot of stroking of arms and faces.

Stupidly, Vetch felt embarrassed at the intimate sight and looked away. There weren't many other Corrupted in the vicinity. Only a Littorane and a Slern were close and curious. Nothing else.

Oh, hell. It was bad enough to come with Ree to kill the missing pair. It would have been tragic—Das-Zee and Lyi-Niah didn't deserve to die this way—but this was even worse. It looked like Ree was trying to bring her missing partners back to her Hearth in Tumlhui Dek City.

The Slern stiffened, catching Vetch's eye.

A dozen paces away, the ball of mucus-dripping slug flesh extended two pseudopods. Usually, these would be eyestalks or stretched rubber arms that terminated with a suitable spread of digits for the task at hand.

This pair of limbs ended in serrated teeth, saw blades supported by thick cords of rubber sinew.

The alien flicked the mucus off its saw hands, revealing hardened flesh.

"Nyluga!"

Vetch glanced back and saw that the arms of his smuggler queen ward had been pinned to her sides by Das-Zee and Lyi-Niah. Her suit was undone, exposing the pink flesh of her throat.

"Leave the wives to me," said Sinofar. "Kill the Slern."

The Slern in question wasn't hanging around to be killed. It sped toward the Nyluga.

But not fast enough. Vetch strode forward and intercepted the oozing creature, aiming a quick blow at the crown of its body.

Lucerne bounced back as if it had struck a solid rubber ball.

Vetch caught the rebound and lifted the war hammer vertically above his head.

He couldn't see visible damage to the Slern's flesh, but it had halted, its globular body swaying.

Vetch swung Lucerne down with his full strength behind her this time. The hammer head pierced the rubbery hide and kept going through the Slern's watery insides until it slammed into the dirt, sending jarring shockwaves up Vetch's forearms.

There was no time to mourn whoever this Slern might once have been. The Littorane had grown fangs and was moving on six legs to attack Ree.

It was a hefty creature, six feet from head to tail base and several more to tail tip.

Vetch ran to intercept and simultaneously lifted his hammer.

But he wasn't going to make it this time.

The Littorane reared up like a centaur and snapped its jaws at Ree's chest. The Guild boss ducked underneath and to one side and caught the long Littorane neck in her hands. Vetch had seen the strength of the Glaenwi's grip crush his binoculars. Now, she applied the same strength to her attacker's throat.

But the Littorane had power and mass. And its tail was about to strike.

Vetch arced Lucerne down onto the tail.

But he missed.

Ree was in full wrestling mode and had rolled sideways, slamming the Littorane into the ground. The move had disrupted both the Littorane tail strike and Vetch's hammer blow.

The Littorane was far from done. He whipped his tail back. Even without the sharpened metal attachments of the Littorane warrior caste, the tail strike could be deadly.

Vetch snapped a quick hammer blow, Lucerne's head beginning its arc at shoulder height.

The hammer struck home in the base of the Littorane's tail. It hadn't been a strong blow, but Vetch heard bones break.

Momentum carried the tail-tip on, and it wrapped feebly around Vetch's ankles. The Littorane was screaming in pain. The screams were wet and weak.

Returning his hammer to a ready position, Vetch looked for a more vital target to strike.

What he saw was Ree's thumbs pop out the Littorane's throat.

Vetch looked away in horror, trying not to retch.

He mastered his revulsion and delivered a mercy blow that shattered the head of the convulsing Littorane.

The smashed-open skull wasn't a pretty picture either, but for some reason, Vetch found the sight of broken flesh easier to bear when he was the one doing the damage.

He left Ree staring expressionless at the dead Littorane while he checked for her Corrupted wives.

The two Glaenwi were hissing and spitting out of jaws snapping like demonic dogs'. Sinofar had restrained them, tying their arms in front. Dropped on the dirt were two pistols.

"They tried to shoot you," she explained.

"I understand," said Ree. She stared dejectedly at the pistols. "I need a few minutes to say goodbye. Alone."

Vetch looked around. There were Corrupted only a few hundred yards away but none with pointy fangs and murder in their eyes. Not yet, but who knew what they might do next?

Sinofar put her arm around his shoulder and steered him back through the gap in the wall.

The sight on the far side was grim. The Corrupted nearby had been gunned down. Half the tubs were holding station, but two were racing back from the dried river to the southwest.

The enemy vehicles Enthree had heard were advancing from the east. A dark mass tailed them, but there was too much dust being thrown up to see what it was.

From within the hexagon, two pistol shots rang out.

Inside Vetch, compassion fought against his need for vengeance. Compassion won out for the moment.

He remembered Meatbolt. He was grateful it hadn't fallen to him to dispatch the youngster—or what he had become. Meatbolt's friend, Enthree, had taken that role. Vetch wouldn't wish that on anyone, not even Nyluga-Ree.

"Time to mount up and get the hell out of here," he said.

"Too late for that," Lily replied, shouting down from the nearest tub. "There's a larger convoy coming from the southwest. Our route back is blocked. We'll make our stand here."

* * * * *

Chapter Forty:
Osu Sybutu

"We'll make our stand here."

Osu opened his mouth to contradict the CO, if that was the right term for Hjon as commanding officer of this gaggle of rogue trader Marines.

Then he shut it again.

How was he supposed to speak to Lily now that she was Lieutenant Hjon? He could do with advice on this from Arunsen.

Taking advice from the Viking? Turns out there's a first time for everything.

Hjon and Fitzwilliam had brought Osu into a huddle in one of the hover-tubs. Vetch would be joining them when he finished playing with the Guild boss.

In his Legion experience, when a lieutenant was conflabbing with a captain, you opened your mouth only to say "Yes, sir." Maybe join in with a "Hold the line!"

If you had serious misgivings about what the officers were proposing, God, in His infinite wisdom, had created sergeants major.

The difference between Osu and Arunsen was that, by being in the Militia, the Viking had to be used to dealing with incompetent officers daily.

"Do you object, Sergeant?" Osu realized Fitzwilliam was glaring at him.

301

"No, sir. Ma'am, could you please clarify your meaning of 'make a stand?'"

"We mustn't allow ourselves to be pinned down here," Hjon said. Osu tried not to stare at her bizarre skin markings while she spoke. "But we're behind 40-foot-high walls. We need to take advantage of them. We'll block the entrance gate with two of the tubs and force the enemy to come to us. Wear them down."

"Thank you, ma'am."

Fitzwilliam removed his shades and allowed Osu to see the twinkle in his eye. The man was playing them. Testing them. "It's all right, Sergeant. Tell us your thoughts. That's what I...ahh...pay you for. *Will* pay you for."

Osu frowned. He didn't like the idea of being a mercenary. But he expected an income, and payment seemed a topic you could never quite nail down with the captain.

"This is how I see things," said Osu. "We're caught behind enemy lines. *Phantom* is our only route off this planet. Every second we delay increases the chances of our enemies discovering our ship and sending more forces our way. If we allow ourselves to be bottled up here, we won't stand a chance."

"I agree," said Hjon. "But we're outnumbered. To get back to *Phantom* without being cut to shreds, we need to hurt the enemy first."

"But if we turn our position into a fortification, I think the enemy will regard it as a siege. They'll slow things down, and we need to keep the situation mobile. If the enemy has any sense, they'll pin us down here and send another force through the next gate along to hit us from our rear."

Arunsen hauled himself over the tub's side wall of thin ceramalloy. The vehicle rocked, but he landed lightly on his feet in the middle of the vehicle. For such a heavy man, he was impressively agile.

"I heard it all," said the Viking. "I've read it too. You two are making the classic textbook arguments. Militia philosophy versus Legion. We garrison strongpoints. The Legion assaults them."

"I've been thinking the same thing," said the captain. "Got to break it to you, though. This isn't a textbook. We have very real enemies about ten minutes away from killing us. We're Chimera Company. That's supposed to mean we can pool our strengths and work together. Prove it to me."

"Sybutu has more experience with assault operations," said Arunsen. "Can you explain your plan in sixty seconds?"

Osu was so surprised the Militia sergeant was backing him, he was too stunned to speak. But he recovered rapidly and still managed to get across what he intended and win the agreement of the others within the sixty second target.

Chimera Company.

He still didn't like the name. But the concept was working in theory. Now it was time to test it in anger.

* * * * *

Chapter Forty-One:
Vetch Arunsen

"Scratch one bandit! That was the last of them," said Lynx in Vetch's ear. "I have control of the skies. I repeat, the skies are mine."

Vetch laughed at the droid's excitement. The four drones Lynx was flying had knocked out the enemy's drones with a combination of electronic warfare and explosive darts.

It would be nice to truly control the skies. Air cover and orbital platforms that could vaporize anything on the surface would make Vetch's day. But he was content with being able to see the enemy via his wrist slate while they couldn't see what Chimera Company was doing on their side of the wall.

And since they were running with Sybutu's plan, keeping out of sight was essential.

The two enemy convoys—ten trucks in total—had combined forces and were now parked in a semicircle a few hundred meters to the south. Most of the hunched soldiers who'd spilled out had smoothly deployed in a loose tactical formation. They looked trained.

Damn! It wasn't one big mob, either. He was seeing separate elements with squad leaders issuing instructions. Were these the husks of soldiers who had retained a memory of their profession? Or were the Corrupted less of a mindless mob than he'd thought?

Behind the shambling soldiers was a pack of animals. Giant, hairless rats with unicorn horns. Not even the droids could identify the species. Their slavering snarls gave him the jitters.

He would have loved to be up on the wall, part of a battery of SFG suppression fire guns sending deadly lines of segmented shells downrange. The three jacks were as happy as pie because Fitz had somehow acquired genuine Legion PA-71 rifles that could mince the enemy at that range. The blaster rifles Vetch and most of the others were carrying would be deadly at close quarters but wouldn't cut it at two hundred meters.

On the subject of cutting, Enthree and Sinofar had finished chopping the first set of steps onto the wall and were working on a narrow fire step.

The enemy tensed. It was a subtle change—nothing more than some furtive glances at neighbors and a narrowing of the spacing between individuals—but Vetch recognized it. He knew their attack was imminent.

Unfortunately, as it turned out, so did Vetch's comrades.

"So, Sarge," said Green Fish, "while we're waiting for the show to start, you've got just enough time to share the dirt on your love of furry women."

"What the hell are you talking about, Trooper?"

"Back at Nyluga-Ree's Sanctuary, I spent a while locked in a cell with Maycey. She told me everything about the two of you and described how you couldn't stop looking at the hot Ellondyte dancers."

Normally, he would have told her to shut her insubordinate mouth as soon as she opened it and would have reminded the troopers in his squad to stay alert.

But that would make him sound too much like Sybutu.

There was something else, too. Nothing had been said, but Greenie wasn't the young trooper he'd left in the hospital after Meatbolt had stabbed her on Rho-Torkis. Now, she hungered for the roguish glamor of the Guild. In her heart, her place was on *Phantom's* flight deck, not in Marine Country. Raven Company's little girl had grown up and moved on.

"I knew it!" Darant exclaimed. "You've been acting strange ever since we rescued you, Sarge. Now we know why. I mean, dammit! Some of those Ellondyte girls—" he whistled, "—I wouldn't myself, but I can see why some might. Good for you, Sarge. It's about time you got some."

"I didn't *get some*," Vetch said with a growl. He ignored the others and studied the drone feed. The giant rat things were being herded into an attack column.

Darant hadn't finished. "Tell you what, Sarge. When this is over and the captain's paid us that fat bonus he keeps hinting at, we'll go enjoy ourselves on a Zhoogene pleasure island. Male, female, or more…hell we can throw in some furry action for your benefit. It's all the same to me with Zhoogenes in heat."

"That's hardly saying anything," Vetch countered. "You'd screw Lynx if he gave you a wink and a can of lubricating oil. No, it wasn't like that."

"Then what was it? Seriously, Sarge, anyone but you would go spend a few credits at the docks until you got it out of your system."

"He won't," said Green Fish, laughing. "The Sarge is bound by a bizarre ideal of romance."

"That's enough," Vetch told them. "An overdose of banter could prove fatal to our comrades formerly of the Legion persuasion. Their little minds might explode if exposed to such improper behavior. So, button it already."

"No, we're good," said Sybutu.

Oh, I bet you are.

"So, Arunsen," said the jack NCO. "Can I check that I have this right? While we were planning how to rescue our favorite Viking princess, you were busy admiring bearded Ellondyte chicks, with manes down their backs, and a killer wearing a catsuit that doesn't unpeel."

From the driver's position of her tub, Zan Fey's shoulders shook. Was she laughing?

"If you see her again, bang her and have done with it," said Sinofar. "Move on. That's what I do."

"I can't. She's a murderer. A killer."

"Then maybe it would be for the best if you *did* consummate your weird obsession with Maycey," said Lily.

Vetch shut his mouth on his comeback. First, because he could tell Lily was dead serious, which was completely unexpected. But also, because she was now an officer.

"How do you mean?" Vetch whispered.

Sinofar guffawed. "Do you need me to—?"

"Because, my dear friend," Lily interrupted, "you're a killer too." She cleared her throat. "Sergeant Arunsen's right. Everyone button it and get ready. That includes you, Sinofar."

Phantom's security lead hesitated as she considered her place in the new ship's roster. "Sorry, ma'am."

Over at the Corrupted position, the two central trucks backed away, leaving space for the animals to charge through.

Vetch sighed, relieved. The enemy was attacking, and Chimera Company was no longer interested in his time inside Ree's palace.

All he had to face, for the moment, was a pack of eight-legged creatures with thick folds of hide and horns that jutted over a meter beyond their eyes. They were the size of the juvenile Saruswine who'd served him well on Rho-Torkis.

Around fifty enemy soldiers advanced behind the animals, a little less than half the Corrupted troop count.

The beasts thundered toward the gate, their hooves kicking up more dust than the trucks had. An ululating wail split the air like a leaky civic defense siren. Without a doubt, there was a touch of evil to these creatures that had been absent from the Saruswine.

That was good. Since riding the Saruswine, Vetch hadn't liked the idea of hurting dumb animals. But dumb, evil animals were fair game.

He checked his PPR3 one last time and then stood up in his stationary tub's firing cage, resting his blaster's barrel across the groove cut for that purpose.

Tapping his wrist to shut down the distraction of the drone feed, he trained his Mark1 eyeball through his blaster's view scope until he got a sight picture on the hole in the wall.

Despite the scope's damping and the vehicle's suspension, his view trembled as the stampeding animals shook the ground. Shoulder to shoulder, the heavy beasts shot through the gap, the lead animals hunching their bodies in anticipation of jabbing with the lances stuck onto the tops of their heads.

But there was no one there to be gutted. Instead of barricading the entrance with the armored tubs, Sybutu's plan had been to leave it wide open.

The solid press of animals carried forward under their immense momentum, pushing inside the hexagon. Gradually, they slowed until they reached the ploughed ground, which soaked up the last of their momentum. They halted, milling around, and staring at the four hover-tubs that were a safe half klick away from the gap, sheltering against the wall.

Sybutu's plan had been to gun down whatever made it through the gap. Enthree had other ideas. She had laid out food and water for the animals by repurposing the plants ready to be put into the tilled soil.

The beasts ignored the food. Instead, they fought each other to lap up the water Enthree had poured into the beds of unhitched trailers.

Nice one, Big Bug.

Vetch's tub lifted off the ground a little but maintained its distance from the archway.

He'd kept a sight picture on it. The first enemy soldiers advanced cautiously through, poking rifles around the edge of the gap and firing at the tubs. Vetch and the others poured inaccurate blaster fire their way; the three jacks fired flechettes from their PA-71s that took out several Corrupted. The only ones not firing weapons were the two droids, and Enthree and Sinofar, who were busy cutting more steps and the firing ledge into the wall.

The exchange of fire continued for about a minute before the enemy rushed the gate in numbers.

While some laid down covering fire from the gateway, most charged in as fast as they could.

It was almost comical because the mutations they'd undergone had left them slow and cumbersome. Fine for driving tractors and digging holes. Not so good for infantry assaults. Nonetheless, they displayed some basic training. Around a dozen of the oncoming force took a knee and laid down suppressing fire on the armored hover-tubs, while around twice that number bounded forward to either side.

They were rudimentary fire-and-movement tactics, but didn't work because their lack of physical coordination meant they not only ran like badly beaten drunkards, but they aimed like ones too.

A bullet whined off the armored side of Vetch's vehicle.

"Lucky shot!" Vetch shouted.

The lead group of Corrupted paused to lay down covering fire while the rear groups took their turns bounding forward.

Vetch spent freely of his charge pack, sending bolts into the attackers. Range: 350meters. His PPR3's accuracy degraded rapidly after 180 meters, but he wasn't about to get his head blown off by a lucky shot from an alien-mutant zombie without shooting back.

He opened up, panning slowly as he squeezed off shots with the four-bolt burst setting.

The rest of Chimera Company kept up a steady fire too. The PA-71s were taking a heavy toll, although not as heavy as they could have, and the blaster bolts were screaming through the air and fusing the dirt between the enemy's feet as they landed.

Most foes would be intimidated if they advanced into fire like that.

The Corrupted didn't seem to care. Vetch guessed that was a natural reaction for people who were already dead.

"Yes!" Vetch sent a bolt into a former human's face. The man fell onto his back and didn't get up.

"Oh, shite," Vetch muttered, noting the canisters slung across the man's chest. Others wore them too. *Grenades*. If just one of those landed inside the tub, it would be all over.

"Come on, Sybutu," he growled over the squad channel. "What are you waiting for?"

"The right moment," came the reply.

One of the closest Corrupted—a Littorane—lobbed a grenade at Vetch. The amphibians could use their tails as slingshots to make awesome long throws, but Vetch could tell this lob would fall a little short.

He fired a few bolts at the Littorane. Missed. But one of the jacks put several darts through its neck, killing it.

The grenade landed about forty meters away. Vetch ducked inside the vehicle and felt it rock as the shockwave hit.

He stood and resighted his targets. At the gate, a further score of Corrupted raced through.

"Take cover!" Sybutu yelled.

Vetch ducked again. He was only halfway down when the entire skragging planet exploded.

The grenade had rocked it, but this new explosion was a shockwave tsunami that made the vehicle's ceramalloy walls sing. Dirt and pebbles rained down on the open top vehicle.

When the dust settled enough for them to see, most of the attackers were dead, and the dazed survivors crawling over the edge of the smoking crater were about to be.

The hover-tubs advanced on the carnage, their occupants adding to it. It was butchery carried out by blaster and railgun rifle.

"They're already dead," Vetch kept telling himself. He knew that to be true, but it was a grim business all the same.

"How did you manage that, Sybutu?" he asked. "With just a case of grenades?"

"I found some det packs in my tub," Bronze explained. "It seemed a shame to waste them."

"We're sappers of the Legion," Sybutu said. "We know how to build things. And we know how to blow them up."

"We're experts at drains and digging ditches too," said Zavage. "But the sarge always leaves that part out."

Vetch smiled when he heard Green Fish stifle a guffaw over the net. He'd missed the banter now that he wasn't at the heart of it.

For the first time since his commander had sent Raven Company to die on Rho-Torkis, it felt like he'd found his family.

* * *

"Trouble," Lynx warned. "I believe the enemy intends to subject us to indirect fire."

Lynx's drone footage was doubly troubling. The beds of the trucks had transformed. Each had eight tubes buried in it, angled slightly toward Chimera Company's position.

Machines had been deployed beside the trucks. Soldiers cut and dug the ground. They fed the broken rock and soil into the machines, which were also fed by tubes from canisters of liquid. Oily exhaust fumes chugged out. From the bottom of the machines came a steady stream of shaped cylinders with nose cones and stabilizer fins.

Orion's beard! They were making solid, ceramic, mortar bombs, and they were stacking them in the trucks ready to fire.

The mortar crews acted with speed and precision in sharp contrast to most of the Corrupted Vetch had seen. He put that down to the two commanders watching, goading, and marshalling. They were humanoids, blown up to titanic size and equipped with additional pairs of muscled arms that rose from their shoulder blades.

The junior of the two commanders, judging by the body language, was a mutated human male. Pale skin. Bearded. Ripped. He wore torn short pants and boots. Nothing else.

Superficially, the Corrupted man resembled the view Vetch saw in the mirror on a good day...if Vetch possessed three times the muscle mass. The proportions were wrong, though. The chest was too cylindrical, and he was unfeasibly wide across the shoulders. He wasn't just muscled but was so top heavy he looked as if he would pitch over if he moved. He didn't, though. He moved with the grace of a big predator.

If he was a titan, the commanding officer was a titaness. She'd been a Zhoogene woman once, but the ten-foot-high monster was something else now.

Her people were naturally narrow hipped and small chested compared to human women, but The Corruption had left her bursting with muscle, and with breasts and hips to put a fertility goddess to shame. She was naked too. Poor thing. Vetch supposed it must be tough clothes shopping when you were a supersized mutant on a secret world.

A horrifying thought struck him. Perhaps, once they reached this level of mutation, the Corrupted could breed. Maybe that was the plan? The next stage of the invasion?

He imagined an army of titans born on broken worlds beyond the fringe of the Federation.

The titaness froze. She looked up, directly at Vetch. She drew a pistol slung under one enormous wrist and fired.

The feed in Vetch's wrist slate went dead and switched to one of the other drones. But the commander-mutants shot down the rest of the surviving surveillance machines.

Vetch's slate blackened. He was blind.

A screaming banshee howl rose from the enemy position. Moments later, it was followed by a salvo of mortar rounds rising into the sky.

He watched through the open top of his vehicle as the 'bombs' reached the vertex of their trajectory and began to descend from the heavens.

He told himself they were firing blind, that the chances of hitting him were slim.

Before they landed, another howl screamed from the other side of the wall, announcing the next salvo.

"Hold your positions," said Lieutenant Lily. "Stay inside the vehicles. Bronze, join Sinofar on the firing step. When you get there, I want you to take out the mortar trucks."

The SpecMish operative ran for the wall. Vetch remembered something about Bronze being the jacks' crack shot. He remembered Sward too. The best sniper in Raven Company. But Vetch had buried his Zhoogene comrade beneath a hill on Eiylah-Bremah.

The mortar salvo hit.

Dust splashed into the air, revealing miniature craters where the shaped rocks hit. A projectile bounced off one of the vehicles, but no one looked hurt.

It was a weird experience. Without explosives, it was more like being attacked by ancient catapults. Being hit without hitting back still sucked. Same as it always did.

And that was why, if he were in charge, they would be hugging the arch for cover and laying down blaster fire.

Lily had better be right.

Vetch looked up. Another salvo. Several bombs were falling on him.

He ducked, arms over his head.

One of the projectiles clanged against the top of the tub's side wall. Zan Fey grunted.

"Izza! No!"

The scream came from Ree.

"Leave her to me," Vetch bellowed. He pushed past the robots and the Glaenwi to check on Zan Fey.

She was slumped over in the driver's position, groaning. Blood was welling up from a gash on the back of her skull.

Gently, he tested the wound with his fingers.

"What happened?" Fitz demanded over the radio.

"Wait one," Vetch replied.

Blood was flowing copiously. It looked horrific, but the bones weren't damaged. If there was a serious injury, it was internal. "Lieutenant Zan Fey took a rebound to the back of her head," he said as he sprayed cleanse-heal over the wound. "She's stunned, but alive."

"Copy." Fitz sounded surprisingly calm. "If she worsens, take her to Sinofar."

"Roger that."

The ground thundered under another mortar salvo, but this time, Vetch didn't hesitate to get Zan Fey out of her seat and back to Ree.

"Tell me if she worsens," he told the smuggler boss.

Zan Fey mumbled incoherently and waved her hands at them. Vetch didn't understand a word, but he suspected she meant: "Stop fussing!"

Vetch had meant for Ree to keep Zan Fey comfortable while he took the driver's position. Instead, Ree handed the Zhoogene over to Lynx who extruded a padded neck brace to keep her safe. Who knew?

"I'll drive," Ree told Vetch.

Another salvo crashed into the ground.

The bombardment was more widely dispersed now. The enemy was likely guessing the tubs had moved away from the shelter of the wall to escape the mortars.

Maybe it was better that Vetch wasn't in the driver's seat. He knew he would find it hellish to resist the temptation to drive anywhere rather than sit out the bombardment.

He nodded at Ree.

"Look after her," he told the crime boss and then went to his gunner's station at the rear.

* * * * *

Chapter Forty-Two:
Hines "Bronze" Zy Pel

Bronze fired at the trucks. But gripping the narrow ledge by his toenails was not an ideal position from which to let loose with his PA-71.

In training, he'd fired its ancient predecessor, the SA-71. A full auto burst with the earlier weapon felt as gentle as dabbing the enemy with soft down plucked from a baby bird. Not so the modern rifle. Even when pulled correctly up against his shoulder, its recoil thumped so hard, every shot hurt. He was expending all his concentration to keep from blasting himself back off the ledge. At least, it distracted him from the bolts screaming his way from the enemy position.

A truck went up in flames as, beside him on the firing ledge, Sinofar's Khrone cannon slammed home another 110mm shell.

Bronze changed tactics, switching his rifle to low-velocity mode, and sighting in on the machines making the bombs.

He sent a burst of NG-enriched supermetal flechettes into one of the machines. It rattled and dented but kept working. Bronze switched again to the Corrupted tending the machines. They started going down. But some were getting up again. Low power was so frustrating!

320 | TIM C. TAYLOR

He set the fire selector to ten-round bursts and let rip. It was a battle to keep the barrel from rising, but he knocked over a machine and felled everyone nearby.

Panning left, he selected the next machine and took that one out too.

The scream of the mortar salvoes was a little quieter now.

On to the next target, but his rifle wouldn't fire. The overheat indicator was lit, and he didn't dare override it because Fitz had made it clear that there were no replacement charge rails. He ducked beneath the wall and activated the cool and cleanse cycle. Coolant flooded the barrel and chemically stripped any charring from the charge rail helix. The system automatically chambered a cleansing wad.

All he had to do now was wait thirty seconds, fire the wad to clean out the barrel, and get back to work. Even the best PA-71s were prone to occasional overheating, and this was not a good one.

"Bronze, is there a problem?"

The question came from Enthree, who was out of sight of the enemy, a short distance away from the firing ledge, with a periscope she was using to give status updates to the others in the hover-tubs. She was clinging to the vertical surfaces like a fly. If the enemy probed through the archway, the plan was to fire on them from above and let Enthree drop down on their heads and slice them with her swords.

"Need to cool my barrel," he explained.

She seemed to accept his words. What she'd really been asking was whether he was falling under the influence of the demigoddess out there. Which he wasn't.

But her interruption made him think about the blue wonder standing beside him on the ledge. Filled with sudden admiration, he gave her a low whistle. He thought of himself as a man of the galaxy, but he was standing beside a woman who carried a Hunndrin & Rax HPW-3 *as a spare.*

It gave him an idea.

"Sinofar," he said. "Can I borrow your HPW?"

She looked across at him with delight written on her face from ear to ear. Suddenly, it all added up. Sinofar had been offhanded with him ever since he'd gotten back on the *Phantom.* Behind her overly casual façade, the day they'd enjoyed in her cabin after that time on Flux City must have meant more than she'd let on.

Not now, Verlys.

Slinging his PA-71 around his chest, he took the HPW from her, lifted the longer-barreled weapon over the top of the wall, and began firing. He yelled with pleasure as the characteristic hellfire-red 28mm bolts tore through flesh and metal. There was a reason HPW-3s were mainstays at gun clubs across the Federation.

Even so, his fire against the trucks was not delivering the damage the Khrone was, so he switched back to the remaining machines making the mortar rounds and the teams serving them.

Hellfire bolts dealt savage blows, putting the machines out of action as he systematically panned from the right of the enemy line to the left. One after another fell to the heavy blaster.

He sighted one of the last machines. His trigger finger tensed, then moved of its own accord off the trigger and onto the guard.

The super Zhoogene commander filled his sight picture. She was wondrous to behold. Her glorious scent filled his sinuses. She was everything.

She was *authority.*

"Are you all right, Bronzy?"

Sinofar sounded far more distant than the supreme Zhoogene commander. But the worry in her voice demanded an answer.

"Yes," he replied. He sniffed the air. The Zhoogene demigoddess smelled divine. How could it be otherwise? But he knew she was his enemy, and she had no command over him. "Yes, Verlys," he said with far more certainty.

The enemy commander flinched when Sinofar took out the mortar truck nearest her.

By now, the enemy mortar fire had greatly reduced, though blaster bolts continued to fly at the wall and over their heads.

"We make a great team," said Sinofar.

"That we do, big blue."

"You think I'm large?"

Dammit, Verlys. Not now.

"I think you're perfect," he told her. "Even though you're not…"

Azhanti! He'd nearly said, "Even though you're not comparable with my demigoddess."

"I'm not *what?*" Sinofar sent five shells into one of the last trucks. When the bolts had dissipated, they could see that the vehicle's metal frame had melted, and its combustibles had incinerated to ash.

"Verlys, you're not good company for people who like bland and safe."

"That is true." She sounded immeasurably happier. "I am not *safe*…as those Corrupted will find out. Bronze, we've taken out most of the mortars. Switch targets. Shoot those big, ugly, mutated brutes."

He knew Sinofar was right, but it would be such a shame to kill them. They weren't ugly brutes. They were beautiful.

Instead of shooting them, he put a flurry of rounds through the last undamaged truck, setting it ablaze.

"Why aren't you firing at the leaders?" Sinofar asked. The suspicion chilled her voice. She knew all about his weakness, having witnessed it firsthand on Flux City.

"They're moving to confer," he told her. "Wait until they're in the same spot, and we'll take both out together. The soldiers will be so confused, we can easily push through them to the *Phantom*."

She gave him a look of narrow-eyed suspicion.

I know, he thought guiltily, *why didn't I say that in the first place?*

"Very well," she said. "You and me together."

The enemy commanders were gesticulating and pointing at the gate, organizing the 70-odd effective soldiers who remained. There were still too many for Chimera Company to punch through without taking serious casualties.

The two commanders were almost together.

Just another few moments…

The divine Zhoogene pointed at Bronze's head, and the soldiers under her command unleashed an intense blaster volley at him and Sinofar.

Bronze fought to keep his feet on the ledge that was shuddering under the fierce onslaught. Molten chips of wall material splattered the area, burning Bronze's clothing.

"Bronze," said Sinofar. She sounded worried. "I'm down to my last few shells."

With such a concentration of fire, they would get their heads blasted off sooner or later. The air filling with incoming blaster bolts was also blinding. All he could see were streaks of deadly plasma.

"Can you see the commanders?" he asked Sinofar.

"No. But I've already locked their position into the scope. Let's hope they haven't moved. Wish me luck, Bronzy."

He put a hand on her shoulder and pushed his head into the firestorm. Through her body, he felt the ferocious kick unleashed by the 110mm Khrone cannon as she sent four shells at the target. How she wasn't thrown off the firing step by the recoil he'd never understand.

Twitching, he felt the death of the commanders.

The enemy blaster fire ceased.

But he could still sense the demigoddess.

As the afterimages of the bolts cleared from his vision, Bronze saw what had happened.

The super-mutated human had been reduced to a pair of booted legs. The Khrone had cooked everything from the hips up into burned chum.

The Zhoogene was completely unharmed. Bronze cringed as she hurled her anger at him in the form of a gut-wrenching howl.

Sinofar fired another shell at her. The impact revealed a shimmering violet cocoon that dissipated its energy. Force shield. If the Khrone couldn't punch through, nothing could.

The enemy walked toward the wall, their blaster fire slowly picking up again in intensity. A few of the mortars fired.

Bronze sent hellfire rounds into the nearest soldiers. They went down, but it seemed to remind the others of his existence. The return fire was ferocious.

He ducked down. "We've done all we can here," he said over the squad net. "We'll have to run for it in the tubs."

"It's my last shell," announced Sinofar. Her Khrone roared a final time.

Two blaster bolts flew into her, hurling her off the wall.

Helplessly, he watched her fall over thirty feet.

Enthree had been waiting for this. She caught Sinofar in her arms and cradled the big Pryxian as she dropped to the ground.

Bronze fired a pointless volley at the demigoddess and then hurried down to join them.

Sinofar was sitting up. Dazed, she stared at the twisted metal in her hands. "My Khrone," she groaned. "My beautiful Khrone. Dead."

"Back to the vehicles," ordered Lily. "We'll have to break out."

"Wait," Sybutu called. "Bronze, do you remember that battle on the frozen lake near Camp Faxian? Blaster fire wouldn't get through the force shield, but your crescent blade did. Have you got it?"

"Yes, Sergeant."

"Swords and crescent," said Enthree. "Our victory shall make a fine tale."

Bronze pointed up at the sky filled with flying rocks and blaster bolts. "We can't just walk up to the commander and challenge her to a duel."

"Have none of you ever lived on a farm?" asked the Nyluga. "The hungry animals who charged us earlier are herd creatures, which means they can be *herded*."

"Damn! She's right," said Hjon. "Bronze, Enthree, it's time you joined the cavalry."

* * * * *

Chapter Forty-Three: Hines "Bronze" Zy Pel

Bronze could hear the hover-tubs herding the animals. It sounded like fun…

For everyone else.

All he could see was the underside of the beast he was clinging beneath, and that was no fun at all. The animal stamped its hooves and tried to shake him off. Several times already, he'd lost his grip on the folds of tough flesh, and they were barely underway. He didn't fancy his chances if the creature broke into a run or simply thought to lie down on its belly and crush the life out of him.

The animal picked up speed. Its legs thrummed a steady beat that caused its udders—or whatever they were—to slap him in the face.

"The beasts have built-in handholds," Enthree shouted from beneath the animal next to him. "Use them!"

The Muryani hung beneath her ride, looking so comfortable, the beast could have been bred for her.

Bronze held on for dear life by squeezing his knees and ankles into the animal's belly and shifting his hands onto its teats.

They were soft and squishy. And oozed brown fluid. But they made perfect handholds.

The creature disagreed and hooted in anger at this violation. It sprang into the air and crashed down onto the flanks of its neighbors. The impact nearly shook Bronze off, but the animal didn't jump again.

Blaster fire erupted behind the animals, sending them into a full-on stampede.

All his senses merged into one. The animal bellows, the blur of motion, the earthquake of pounding hooves, the sense of helplessness as he was carried along by a raging storm of muscle, hooves, and horns. He couldn't remember ever being so terrified.

He tried to look across at Enthree, but everything was an oscillating haze of legs, dirt, and udders. So, he willed his artificial eyes to cancel the disruptions and saw the Muryani calmly glued beneath her stampeding monster. She seemed without a care in the world.

Azhanti! Was she asleep?

"How do you do that?" he called across to her, remembering she'd also had a special bond with the Saruswine. "How do you get animals to trust you so easily?"

"Experience," she replied, his auditory augmentations filtering out the cacophony so he could understand.

"You mean you were a farmer?"

"No. Not *my* experience. The experience of the Muryani over thousands of generations."

"And it works on humans too?"

"Of course. Although we are still gaining experience on your species, I have you exactly where I want you."

"Don't even joke about it."

"I would never use humor on such an important topic."

"Damned bug."

"Or *would I?*"

They must have passed through the archway, because, suddenly, Bronze was breathing in the oxygen-poor air, and his brain couldn't decide whether the Muryani was serious or joking. His oxygen mask lay by his left hand, but he didn't dare reach for it.

"You remember how I was influenced in Bresca-Brevae?" he yelled at his companion.

"And in Flux City."

"Yeah. Same rules apply. If I go weird, don't hesitate to kill me."

"I won't."

"You did with Meatbolt."

"That...was..."

Not for the first time, Bronze was certain he was about to die. He'd never imagined making his exit by being crushed beneath the hooves of giant rat unicorns. But for the first time, he'd unsettled the bug. That was something at least.

"Meatbolt was a friend," Bronze told the Muryani. "I know I'm not, but if you respect me as a comrade, you might experience the same reluctance. Kill me. Don't hesitate. You have my permission. Promise me."

"I promise, Bronze. If you go bad, you die."

He thought he heard blaster fire, but he wasn't sure as his ears were tuned to the conversation. He set them to a more general mode and heard a repeating pattern of three blaster bolts. The *signal*.

"Let's do this," he screamed and let go.

He dropped to the ground.

Momentum ripped his spine along the rocks and dirt, but the hooves he'd feared would crush him passed over his body and carried on, away from him.

They had climbed beneath animals at the rear of the pack, but in the crush, his ride had pushed deeper into the herd. Another beast was coming straight for him. He rolled to one side and escaped with just a sideswipe from a hoof.

Then another thundered his way. No. It was running at Enthree, horn aimed to skewer the big bug. Something about the alien seemed to spook it. At the last moment, it dug in its mid limbs and shifted direction, cutting diagonally away from the Muryani. Straight at Bronze.

He curled into a protective ball. But it did no good. The creature pounded him on the back, cracking ribs and leaving him stunned in pain, face down in the dirt.

To be crushed under the hooves of giant hairless rat unicorns. It was to be his end after all.

Enthree came to him.

And stabbed him in the neck.

"Unggh!"

His neck surged with heat. Stim pen!

"Forget your wounds," said Enthree. "Our only hope is to move forward."

Bronze bellowed. And stood.

The titaness saw it all and sneered at them.

She turned her head away to concentrate on the rest of the battle. Damned monster didn't see him as a threat.

The hover-tubs charged forward, having used the stampede as a shield. Bolts, bullets, and flechettes were crossing the gap in both directions. The battle's moment of decision had come.

The stim pen did nothing to hide the pain. Bronze just didn't care about it as much.

Still in agony, he stepped forward and accelerated into a lumbering charge at the titaness. He felt gurgling in his chest. Damn! Must have punctured his lung.

Didn't matter. Enthree soared overhead and jumped down on the titaness, who raised her extra pair of arms to ward off this aerial attack.

Bronze ran past her, ducking under a blow from her right fist. He came to a sharp halt that sent blades of pain slicing through his lungs in a thousand places.

He drew his crescent blade and pushed inside her force bubble.

Force shields sucked the energy out of attacks, fusing it with haloes of exotic particles to create searing bright sheets of electroweak forces. Ironically, the less energetic your attack, the easier it was to get through the force shield. All you had to do was lean in with your shoulder.

Back at the Academy, his instructors had described the experience as being like pushing through a vat of molasses.

Which was a strange expression, because he would have laid credits on his instructors not having experience with molasses vats or pushing through an energy shield.

Whereas Bronze had.

One of those things, anyway.

He mused on these thoughts to distract himself from the shards of agony in his chest. Whether from the drugs or the adrenaline, the pain was lifting as he eased through the last of the shield's resistance. He stumbled as he fell into the protected bubble around the green titaness.

Thumbing the control studs built into the handle of his blade, Bronze retracted the tip shields and then released its dark secret from the chambers hidden within. With the twin tips of the crescent blade dripping with green poison, he slashed at the back of her thigh.

Instead of the slick wet sound of advanced metals slicing through flesh, the blade struck a jarring blow that felt and sounded as if he'd struck rock.

The super Zhoogene had grown thick, hexagonal plates beneath her skin. They must be acting like armor plating.

He aimed a more careful strike, planning to run the poison tips of his blade along the cracks between her plates, but the titaness mule kicked, and he only just managed to dodge to one side.

While the monster was busy with Bronze, Enthree tried to wriggle free of her grip. To no avail.

Ever since Enthree had leaped onto her, the magnificent commander had been holding the Muryani above her head with three arms, pinning Enthree's limbs so she couldn't strike with her swords.

With her free arm, the divine monster pummeled Enthree with fierce blows that thumped like bass drumbeats.

Bronze tried to slash again, but the super Zhoogene spun and smashed Enthree to the ground, using her as a club to batter Bronze.

He dodged, stumbled, and fell, his chin making a sudden acquaintance with the rocky ground. But what made his vision strobe was the glancing blow to his chest he'd caught from Enthree.

The pain was blinding.

But so was death.

He pushed through the pain and breathed air into his brutalized lungs. It didn't help. He couldn't get the oxygen he needed.

Tilting over to one side on the ground, he grabbed some breaths from his mask and looked up at the titaness.

She was beyond Zhoogene. The narrow face of her kind had expanded into a heart shape, with cheekbones like battleship railguns above sunken cheeks that glowed red. In place of ground cover head growth, thick vines writhed angrily.

And she *was* angry. He could hear it in her deafening wails as she grabbed the stunned Muryani and hurled her out of the force bubble.

It was just the goddess and him.

The ten-foot-high being stared down at him, eyes blazing like golden suns. As small as he was, she screamed in her expected triumph over him. No, not merely triumph but anger multiplied from before. Bronze had betrayed her. He should have yielded, yet he had defied her.

It was an outrage against the natural order of things. What had he been thinking? To defy the divine was blasphemous.

She stumbled.

It was the slightest give in one leg. The one he had slashed at.

The titaness quickly recovered her stance, but Bronze had seen.

He had done that. Pathetic, wounded mortal though he was. He had no desire to fight her, but he had to all the same.

He had to hold the line. For Chimera Company. For everyone.

"Your problem," he yelled at her, his voice feeble against her insane shriek, "is that however much your kind tries to corrupt me, I'm still human. And that means it's game over. *For you!*"

He dove between her legs, slashing up at her soft inner thighs as he went.

This time he felt the blade cut flesh.

The blade cut so deep, his fingers were ripped from the grooves in its handle. He let the weapon go. One nick with its poisoned tips, and he'd be dead within a minute.

334 | TIM C. TAYLOR

But the titaness was far from finished. She arched backward like a tumbler about to backflip and brought her upper arms all the way down to pin Bronze by his shoulders.

He tried to squirm free, but her strength was far too great. Her weight pressed down on him, the grip so strong, his arms were numbing.

She completed her backward flip and landed back on her feet, holding Bronze in front of her gaze. A titanic hand gripped each of his limbs.

She said nothing, but her golden eyes sparkled with pleasure, and he knew she intended to rip him limb from limb.

"No," she said in Zhoogene-accented Standard. "I prefer you alive. As my unwilling servant."

"Damn you!" he screamed. To serve beside her...*It would be glorious.* "I will never be your slave. Kill me, damn you!"

The vines on her head whipped up and she opened her mouth...

But her words remained locked inside.

Twin swords scissored through her neck. Her head tumbled from her shoulders and bounced off the crown of Bronze's head.

"You make a great distraction," said Enthree, riding the back of the titaness as her headless body toppled to the dead ground.

The creature's spirit descended to hell, dragging Bronze with it.

He staggered away, slack-jawed, unwilling to look at Enthree or the decapitated titan. It wasn't the pain so much as the loss of something profound. Like a thumping music beat suddenly cut into a shocking silence.

A layer of the binding spell she'd cast over her soldiers dissipated in the hot, still air. Bronze had caught the edge of it but far less than the Corrupted, who were still utterly dazed by the loss of their commander.

"Chimera Company!" Bronze shouted. "Kill them all! Do it now, before they recover."

Then the pain of his injuries came crashing down, driving him to his knees. He knelt by the corpse of the great titaness, sinking into himself with the hell of battle as a backdrop.

It wasn't a battle, though. It was slaughter and execution.

It was many things, but it was in no way a victory. All the slain— even the titaness and her human counterpart who had been vaporized by the Khrone—had once been innocent Federation citizens. Well, as innocent as they got in these parts. They hadn't wanted to be there. They hadn't wanted anything because they were already dead.

Bronze was tired of killing Corrupted. Let the others finish that task.

He wanted to kill the *Corrupt-ors*.

The world thumped back in sharp clarity.

He'd been woozy for a moment. The pain in his chest was still intense, but the firing had stopped, and *Phantom* had an excellent med bay. He took a few breaths of oxygen, then injected a trauma pen into his chest where it hurt most.

"Leave that to me," Sinofar snapped.

Enthree was holding the Pryxian aloft as she hurried over to Bronze. Sinofar sounded angry about something.

"Did we lose anyone?" Bronze asked as she tended to his wound properly.

"We were fortunate. Lieutenant Zan Fey has a concussion. Lieutenant Hjon took a bolt to the chest, but she'll live. And you have three cracked ribs and a punctured lung. I've injected your left lung

336 | TIM C. TAYLOR

with medical foam and bound your wounds. Do not exert yourself until I say so."

"Don't worry, Verlys. I'll have a nice lie down during jump space. If you like, you can hold my hand while I recover."

"Silly human man. We must get off the planet first."

"Is there a reason to think we won't?"

"No. I'm just being cautious."

Something was bothering her. She'd patched him up before. But she hadn't been like this.

Enthree picked him up and carried him over her back as she'd carried Sinofar earlier.

She was gentle, but he couldn't help thinking he was playing the part of a leaf in a leafcutter ant procession.

An image of a Muryani convoy carrying helpless humans over their backs marched across his mind's eye.

"Ever thought of working in horror-holos, buddy?" he suggested. "We might have to play to some stereotypes, but we could make a killing."

* * * * *

Chapter Forty-Four:
Tavistock Fitzwilliam

"Fitz to *Phantom*. Are you decent, Justiana? Because we're coming back hot."

"I've been listening in on your chatter, Captain. I've run pre-flight checks every hour. We're ready to lift off as soon as I've got you aboard."

"Ahhh. I may have exaggerated just a tiny bit," he told her. "I should have said we're coming back *warm*, because we'll need a minute to get our wounded safely strapped up and my captain's butt settled where it belongs on the flight deck."

"Copy that."

"But you've done well, Fregg. We're all alive. The Nyluga has remembered she adores me. And we're about to collect the biggest paycheck of our lives."

"Er...Captain? I think you've jinxed us. Perimeter sensors are showing inbound vehicles from the west. Wheeled trucks. Armed. Scores of them. They're just a few minutes away."

"Copy that, *Phantom*." Fitz was driving the lead vehicle. He hit the accelerator. "You heard that, everyone. We've got company. Floor it!"

The ancient riverbed was uneven, making him swerve at speed to avoid scattered rocks and sudden dips. The vehicle rocked and rolled. He edged back the speed a fraction and told Fregg to transmit

338 | TIM C. TAYLOR

the raw sensor data. He matched it with his location data to build a tactical map in his head.

Izza was better at this sort of thing, but she had taken a nasty blow. As it turned out, the situation was so clear, he didn't need her, but he wished she were sitting beside him to shore up the confidence he could feel draining through the floor.

"Fitzwilliam, what is our situation?" demanded Nyluga-Ree over a commandeered squad mic.

"We're not going to make it back in time, Nyluga. Fregg, take off immediately!" A crack of thunder rolled over the dead valley. What now? "Fly south," he told Fregg. "We'll rendezvous when safe. All transports, wheel left. Let's get out of this dead river."

The thunderous crack had been followed by an ominous rumble. What the hell was going on? Had this planet rediscovered weather?

The other three tubs pulled off the river and headed south.

"Keep going," he urged them. "I'll join you. But first, I need to check on...something." A plume of smoke was rising a short distance ahead. Or was it dust? He couldn't get a good view.

"Captain, we have a problem," said Fregg.

Fitz turned a corner in the riverbed. "Yeah, Fregg. I see it."

When they'd landed, he'd parked *Phantom* in the lea of the largest hill around. It had been a big sand dune, really.

Well, it wasn't quite so big now.

The sandy hill had collapsed, burying his lovely ship. That crack of thunder must have been explosive charges.

Had the Corrupted done that? It didn't seem their style.

The enemy's lead vehicles charged into view, firing wild shots at his tub. From the firing position behind him, Sybutu lit them up.

Despite the kid's need to be all discipline and no play, Sybutu had grinned from ear to ear when Fitz had first told him that *Phantom* held a store of PA-71s, the archetypal Legion rifle. The Legion had decided not to confiscate them on the trip to JSHC. In fact, they'd replenished the cases of flechettes. Sybutu sent some of their contents as a welcoming present to the Corrupted vehicles at two klicks per second. He must have been feeling generous because he was dishing them out with abandon.

Neutron-degenerate tips tore through the trucks and their cargo of armed zombies.

A truck swerved violently, spilling bloody bodies out of the back to be crumpled beneath the tires of the following vehicle, which then ran into the back of the lead truck and caught fire.

The first few trucks were nicely snarled, but there were more. Many more. And there was plenty of space for them to ease around the obstruction.

"Nice shooting, Sergeant. But we're not hanging around for the second round of this game."

Fitz tore the hover-tub around and gunned the motor. It flew up over the southern bank and landed hard enough to ground the gravitics for a few moments. Then it lifted, picked up speed, and tore off after the other tubs.

"Fregg, are you okay?" he called over the radio.

Blaster bolts whined over Fitz's head and sizzled along the ground. Damn! More enemy trucks were on the south bank too, flanking him. The hiss and crackle of the bolts drowned out Fregg's reply.

Fitz upped the volume. "Say again, Fregg, what is your status?"

"I think *Phantom* might have some bent aerials," she said. "But all other diagnostics are reading green. I'm looking up at the cockpit, and I can only see black. Tough windows. Not even scratched."

"You'll be fine, Justiana." A flurry of explosions rippled through the ground to his right. Rocket-propelled grenades probably. "Double-check air and power for me."

"Already did, Captain. *Phantom* has enough air, water, and power to last me for months. The bad news is she's critically low on beer and cookies."

"Just relax, Fregg."

"Who, me?" She sounded a little frantic. "I'm taking a little forced sabbatical, on full pay. What could be more relaxing? I *am* getting paid, right?"

"Of course. With a fat bonus at the end." Large munition bursts bracketed Fitz's tub, the overpressure fuzzing his brain for a few seconds. "Just hang tight," he told Fregg when his mind cleared. "Whatever you do, do not start the engines."

A whining noise descended from the sky and ended in a detonation twenty feet in front of the tub. Red dirt was flung into the air, blocking Fitz's view.

He swerved as the dirt rained into the tub. "What the hell was that?"

"Some kind of howitzer," Sybutu replied. "Crude, but who needs sophistication when your target is an open-topped vehicle?"

"Thank you, I'm quite aware of that. There's a reason I use foldable hover-tubs. *Phantom* needs room for other items in her hold."

Sybutu's silence sounded unimpressed.

It was broken by two more howitzer rounds landing nearby.

"The next time I acquire a ship," Fitz added, shouting because his ears were ringing, "I shall remember to pick one with enough space for a troop of heavy tanks."

"That would be advisable, Captain. We are inside a glorified toboggan. There's a reason why toboggans never established themselves as the premier armored fighting vehicles."

"Yes, thank you for the wry humor, Sergeant."

"Where to now?" Sybutu asked.

Where to, indeed?

After another fifteen minutes of headlong flight, Fitz's tub met up with the other three. The enemy artillery was still lobbing rounds at them, but they were falling short. It seemed they had escaped beyond the maximum range of the guns.

"Do you see any signs of pursuit?" Fitz asked.

He slowed to allow Sybutu a less bumpy platform to scan the horizon to the north.

"No, sir. They're not coming after us. Perhaps they feel there's no reason to."

Fitz put the tub on auto and stood up. Sybutu had a point. In every direction but back, the same, red-tinged dead zone stretched to the horizon.

No food. No water. And oxygen-poor air that would slowly kill them with hypoxia once their oxygen canisters ran out in a day or so.

The broken land was all there was until the polar seas, 4000 klicks away to the south.

"We need help," he said under his breath.

Lynx unstrapped himself and hovered over. "Excuse me, Captain. Did you just state that we needed outside assistance?"

"I've got this, droid. Leave me be."

342 | TIM C. TAYLOR

Lynx's status lights displayed solid red. "If you insist, Captain."

Did I just miss something? Fitz wondered to himself. Even for Lynx, that exchange had been weird. He shrugged it off. He had plenty more to worry about than an erratic droid.

* * * * *

Chapter Forty-Five:
Vetch Arunsen

The stars and the silvered columns of light reflected off orbital mirrors shone down on the barren land, painting wondrous patterns across the heavens for those who troubled themselves to raise their heads and *see*.

Which was precisely what Vetch was not supposed to be doing.

He took another visual scan of his watch zone through the binocs mounted to the hover-tub's cage.

Nothing.

No concealment. No way for an enemy to sneak up on them. From horizon to horizon, there was nothing alive except for Chimera Company. Although, not all of Vetch's comrades were properly *alive*.

"Hey!" he called, kicking the dumb droid. "You're supposed to be on watch too."

Lynx buzzed angrily but otherwise ignored him.

At the start of the watch, Lynx had declared he had more important things to do than pointless sentry duty, and he could say for certain that neither were they pursued nor was there anything dangerous out there to hurt them during the night.

The droid hadn't bothered to identify these vital tasks, but Vetch's guess was that he was chatting with 3Condax, the weird robo-dog sitting next to him in the bottom of the recharging hover-tub.

343

He kicked Lynx again. "When you get complacent," he told him, "that's when you wake up dead. You might be good at computation and recalling facts, droid, but that's not the same thing as learned wisdom."

He clicked on his throat mic. "Hey, Zavage. You Kurlei fancy yourselves poets. I bet your people have gushed plenty of pretty words over the stars."

"Of course," replied his sentry partner from the other side of the hover-tub circle. "I think every civilization of every species has looked up and marveled."

"And seen meaning too," said Vetch. "Patterns. Early humans certainly did."

"Our people were the same. My ancestors thought the night sky showed a map to enlightenment. Our bitterest rival civilization saw the sky as a celestial battlefield, the stars being armies that marched and counter-marched across the heavens in a perpetual stalemate."

"It never occurred to me that your people came in different flavors," said Vetch. "I guess that's because there aren't many of you in the Federation."

"Only my civilization survived to make it into space and encounter other species. Kurlei society is even more competitive than humanity's is. We wiped out our rivals."

"Brutal."

"I'm not proud of it."

"You don't have to be. It's not like you personally exterminated them. Anyway, you didn't wipe them out entirely. Their culture is remembered by you. You've just passed on their idea of the battlefield sky. I like it. My ancestors saw patterns too. It's where we get the Perseus in Perseus Arm from. It was the name of a mythical hero, I think. I wonder what the ancients would have thought if they knew the stars cast unique patterns for every star system."

A sudden twinge of pain shot through Vetch's mind. It was like a burst of static in his head.

Before he could collect his thoughts enough to worry about it, the sensation had gone.

Don't panic, he told himself, *you've had a rough few months.* He shook his head and slapped his arms across his body. Only another twenty minutes before he was relieved. *Keep it together, Vetch.*

"Do you see the bright blue star low in the sky to the north-west?" he asked his companion. "It's called Menkib, another ancient Earth name. It was one of the stars that made up the pattern of Perseus. And now, thousands of years after it was named, I'm seeing it from the far side. I think that's awesome. I mean, our current situation sucks in so many ways. But you've got to admit, standing watch on a broken planet under the stars is the kind of thing you expect in a Legion recruitment booth holo. Right?"

Zavage said nothing.

"Zavage," he said. "Are you okay? Respond!"

Silence!

Vetch turned to get a visual on Zavage's vehicle, but as soon as he did, he thought he saw movement in his peripheral vision.

Or did he imagine it?

He turned back. Saw nothing. But there was no doubt in his mind what he should do.

"Contact!" he bellowed in a voice that would wake the dead.

Demounting his PPR3 from the firing support, he crouched down. If he could get to the other end of the tub before popping his head up, he was less likely to get it blown off.

Cries were beginning to issue from the other tubs as people woke.

"Shush, my pet," cooed a feminine voice.

346 | TIM C. TAYLOR

The night air rippled, and Maycey appeared, draped over the driver's shield like a...

Like a person about to die.

He wanted to shoot her full of bolts. But his arms wouldn't move.

"Did you miss me?" she teased. He was sure she was blinking those huge green eyes, but the night was dark and getting darker.

The damned cat had drugged him!

She jumped into the hover-tub just in time to catch him in her warm arms as he pitched forward into oblivion.

* * * * *

Chapter Forty-Six:
Vetch Arunsen

Vetch woke.

It was a good start, he supposed—and better than the alternative—but he was getting tired of prisons, reeducation camps, and being the plaything of psychotic Guild assassins.

He was laid out on his back, head propped against something soft and warm. His eyesight was even blurrier than his head, but it seemed to be filled with women. Maycey, Zan Fey with a bandaged head, and Lily.

They were all smiling at him. Smiling and laughing.

None of it made any sense. But it did feel familiar.

"I know I'm still dreaming," he told them, "because I've dreamed this before. Many times. I'm the only man left in the universe. It always starts well but usually ends up a nightmare."

"So rude," said dream Lily.

He realized he'd been breathing from an oxygen mask when it was taken away from his face. The air tasted bitter now, but he could see better without it.

Green Fish swam into his field of vision. "Ignore them, Sarge. You're okay. Vol is fine too. Just embarrassed he let the Kayrissans sneak up on him. He felt better when I told him they got the better of me and Sinofar back at the Sanctuary."

"You mean this is real?"

Maycey spoke. "My sister thought it prudent to disable your sentries before we paid our respects to your party."

Vetch blinked. Day had broken while he was out. They were still in the circle of armored hover-tubs deep in the dead zone. And this wasn't Maycey. It was Kaycey, the psychopathic one.

"I think Kaycey just wanted to play," said Zan Fey. "With you."

The softest of touches brushed the side of Vetch's cheek, softer than blow-dried puppies coated with warm butter. He lifted his head and saw he was being stroked by the back of Maycey's hand. He was cradled in her lap, and she wasn't wearing much more than her fur.

She smiled at him. "You've missed me," her upside-down head told him. "I can tell."

"Looking comfy there, Sarge," said Darant with a grin as he walked by.

Vetch sat up. He *was* awake. And this *was* a nightmare.

Darant rested his hands on his hips and peered down. "I came to rescue you, Sergeant, but now I feel like that would be a disservice."

"Darant…" Vetch warned.

"We could swap places if you like."

Maycey hissed. It set Vetch's hairs on edge, but Darant just chuckled. He extended a hand and lifted Vetch to his feet.

"How's Bronze?" Vetch asked.

"He'll live," said Zan Fey. "Fregg is alive too. Fitz and Sinofar are on the radio keeping her spirits up. Digging her out is our next task, once we've said goodbye to our honored guest."

"Thank you for my vacation," Ree told Zan Fey. "It has been deeply painful, but…" She looked away sadly. "It is what it is. Izza, are you going to fight to prevent me leaving?"

"Did your assassins plant explosives to bury my ship?"

"Yes."

"No harm done," said Kaycey. "We just slowed you down."

"We have something on our ship to help extricate *Phantom*," said Maycey. "We'll drop it off for you as we fly out."

"There," said the Nyluga breezily. "All fair. I ask again, are we about to fight?"

"No. Are you going to bring help?"

"Perhaps."

"What you said before, Nyluga-Ree. About us being family…"

"I meant every word. And that is why, despite your deception and your invasion of my Sanctuary, I hope you make it off this planet alive. But I hope you don't get away too easily."

"We can take one more on our ship," said Maycey. She blinked at Vetch.

He undid the holster for his blaster pistol.

"You, Vetch, shall have the extra seat. As Verlys put it, we shall rescue the princess."

"What the hell is all this *princess* bullshit? You're all insane."

"Once we are clear, maybe we will send help for the others," Maycey said, reaching out to stroke his beard.

He took a step back and pulled his blaster on her. "Touch me, and I'll put a bolt through your pretty face."

"Dear, dear, Vetch. That's quite unnecessary."

"You're right. It makes more sense to save my charge pack and introduce you to my hammer."

"Oh, Vetch. You have such a crude way with words." Again, with that damned slow blink. "I enjoy it."

He face palmed. Could she *get* any more irritating?

Ree gestured away Maycey's banter. "Come. We must go."

But the cat woman was serious. "Nyluga-Ree," she begged, "surely I can take one hostage home?"

"No," Ree insisted. "I release Sergeant Arunsen. I no longer require him as a guest."

Maycey's fur stood on end. Her claws *snikked* out.

"Be at peace, my killer," Ree soothed. "You may hunt Arunsen later. I shall gift you time to do so, but first, I have more urgent tasks."

"This is not over, Arunsen," said Maycey. She was furious. Furious with *him!*

"Save it for your therapist," Vetch told the crazy cat. His words drove her wild with screeching. Her sister had to drag her away to wherever they were hiding their ship. Which was a neat trick, by the way, because he couldn't see anything.

"Breakfast," said Vetch as the three Guildswomen walked away. "Have I missed breakfast? I'm bloody starving."

* * *

Vetch ripped open his self-heating pouch of spicey sausages and waved the open end under his nose.

He groaned in anticipation.

As long as they supplied beer, sausages, and pies when he really needed them, he would have been happy to go on soldiering in the Militia until his beard turned white. Then they'd ruined it by turning Raven Company into a punishment unit and sent them to perish on Rho-Torkis.

Atmos-engine roar filled his ears, and he turned in time to see *Annihilation* fly toward them.

The little ship looked larger from the outside. He'd doubted they could have carried much digging equipment, but he was happy to be proved wrong.

Annihilation passed low overhead, dropping a few dozen small objects near the Chimera Company position.

"I'll see you soon," Maycey said in Vetch's earpiece.

"Bronze, Sinofar," said Fitz. "Go see what they dropped."

"No need," said Zan Fey tersely. "I could see. They were spoons."

Spoons to dig out our ship. Vetch shook his head. *Damned skangat bitch.*

But there was a grin on his face.

* * * * *

Chapter Forty-Seven: Tavistock Fitzwilliam

Observation Point Near *Phantom*, Doloreene

The burial mound of red dirt heaped over his starship had a settled air of permanence. It looked as if it had been there for a million years. It hadn't, and he wasn't about to lose his ship or his crewman entombed within.

One way or another, Fregg wouldn't stay buried for long.

"How's it look, Captain?" Fregg asked from the inside.

Fitz decided it was for the best that she didn't have the full picture of what was going on outside, because *Phantom's* burial site wasn't the way they'd left it the day before.

The vehicle park of digging machines and earthmoving equipment was new. So were the work gangs. Hundreds of Corrupted people just...waiting.

Waiting for what?

"It's not looking good, is it?" asked Fregg, her voice cracking. "Orion's frakktarding ass! Buried alive! No...no, not to worry. I've already thought this through. Today, I'll blow out on brandy and bagels, a salute to existence before I tell it goodbye for a while. Tomorrow, I'll shuffle into the cryopod and wait it out. I feel so bad coming out of those damned ice cubes that I won't even notice my hangover. Wait, does a hangover pause while you're in cryo, biding its time to strike you when you thaw?"

Izza tapped Fitz on his back and pointed to the horizon. To a dust plume.

"The universe isn't that cruel," Fitz told Fregg. "I can tell you from experience, cryo cures hangovers. There's also a reason for the info plate on cryo cubes that says no alcohol or drugs to be consumed within 30 hours of entering the cryo state."

While Fregg considered her options, Fitz trained his binocs on the target Izza had pointed out. It looked like another Corrupted military convoy, such as the ones they'd seen the day before. Bigger, though. Perhaps this was what the digging teams were waiting for.

"No problem," said Fregg. "I'll get drunk, sleep off the hangover, and then freeze myself."

Izza tapped Fitz again. This time she wasn't pointing. She had one hand spread out over the ground, pressing down. "I hear vehicles," she said softly. "Coming along the riverbed."

"Captain?" asked Fregg. "What aren't you telling me?"

"My apologies, Fregg. I would have heartily approved your plan, if we were the only ones looking to dig you out. Unfortunately, the Corrupted want *Phantom* too. I'll give you updates every four hours. If you don't hear from me, you should assume *Phantom* will be boarded imminently and prepare accordingly."

"I understand, Captain."

"That's the spirit, Fregg. It won't be easy, but you can do this. I believe in you, Justiana."

"Thanks, Captain. I know you won't let me down."

"Damn right. I'll get you out. Looks like their command element will be arriving soon, and there's a chance they will monitor radio comms. I'll broadcast SPC pulse codes, so they won't understand what I'm telling you. Maintain radio silence from this point."

"Roger that."

"Good luck. Fitzwilliam out."

Fitz and Izza were surveilling the area from a crater 1.3 klicks out from *Phantom*. They'd left the others in the hover-tubs, parked under camo in a dried gulley a few klicks to the south. Their stealth cloaks *should* make them difficult to see, but Fitz knew worryingly little about the capabilities of the Corrupted.

"We'll stay put," Fitz whispered. He could hear the vehicles approaching along the riverbed. "If they turn up in front of our noses and we're moving, we're more likely to be spotted."

"You're right," said Izza. "But I don't like it."

He looked into her beautiful eyes and saw them clouded with worry. That wasn't like her at all.

"We've been in worse spots," he reminded her.

"I'm not so sure. Kaycey and Maycey planted the charges that buried our ship. It wasn't the Corrupted, but now they want *Phantom* for themselves, and they're committing resources to dig her out."

"I know. That's bothering me too. So far, I think we've encountered the soft edges of their operation. This Corruption feels like a crude fire-and-forget bioweapon sent into the Federation to soften us up. It doesn't feel coordinated. Other than recovering that buried ship on Rho-Torkis, this terraforming is the first time we've seen any kind of strategy from them."

"The Nyluga's revenge means they now have a second buried ship to recover. Ours! This isn't strategy, it's responding in real time to unexpected events on the ground. That requires coordination. Tactical decision making. A commander."

Fitz mulled that over. His mind had been traveling along similar lines. "So, what you're saying, Izza, is that we're in a holo-game and we're about to level up and face deadlier adversaries?"

"The Andromedans. Yes, I think so."

"Azhanti! Okay, I retract my earlier statement. We are in deeper shit than we've ever been in, and I don't think anyone's coming to pull us out this time."

Three trucks thundered past in front of them. The soldiers in the open truck beds weren't the mindless drones Fitz was hoping for; they were the same random assortment of Federation citizens twisted into service of the Andromedans. They were observant, clutching firearms in a way that said they were ready to use them.

A large-caliber gun had been mounted in the bed of the rear truck. It was a perimeter patrol, led by a four-armed human super-mutant in the lead vehicle. He wasn't the monstrous size of the huge Zhoogene Bronze had taken out, but he was alert and in charge. The equivalent of a gun truck sergeant, Fitz supposed.

"Now, do we require outside assistance?"

"Lynx!" Izza hissed. "Stay down and stay quiet."

The droid was hovering at the base of the crater, his casing altered from its usual dull gun metal to a color and texture that matched the terrain.

"Hey, you've a camo feature," said Fitz. "You never told me about that."

"This is hardly the time to discuss my specifications, Captain. Do we require outside assistance?"

"Yes. Yes, you infernal droid. We're screwed, and we need help. Wait…" He grabbed the droid in both hands and glared at the metal annoyance. "Why do you keep asking that?"

"Because I needed you to state an affirmative answer."

"OK. Now that I have…what happens now?"

"Get down," Izza whispered. "I think we've been spotted."

"I'm calling in Oouzo," Fitz told her as he ducked down, pushing Lynx beneath him. "I want him closer. In orbit."

His Slern compatriot was acting as a backup getaway driver, hiding *Ghost Shark* around the far side of one of Doloreene's moons. Fitz hesitated to make the call. Oouzo wasn't an escape route for Fregg.

"No need to play your ace in the hole," said Lynx. "I've already summoned help."

"What have you done?"

"Isn't it obvious?" asked Izza, her eyes flowing with anger. "Lynx has betrayed us. He's disobeyed my direct order. All this time, he's been working for Kanha Wei."

"Is this true?" Fitz asked.

"I have summoned Wei," the droid admitted. He'd acquired a new casing rattle.

Fitz groaned and shook the disloyal machine. "And for what, you useless lump of tin? Even if you're quantum-linked with Wei, we're beyond the frontier of the Federation. It'll take her ten days, at least, to get here."

"Not so." It was difficult to make out what Lynx was saying above his nervous buzzing. "Her flagship is already in the 211-Fractura system, twenty-four minutes out."

"She was following us all this time!" Izza huffed and growled. "Lynx! How could you?"

"It's not…I…after extensive consultation with 3Condax…"

Lynx's lights went out.

His power hum fell quiet.

He was dead.

* * * * *

Chapter Forty-Eight: L1-iN/x "LYNX"

Phantom

10 days earlier

Less than seven hours after reporting the life support system failure on the Main Deck, Lynx detected signs that the air scrubbers on Deck Two had also been compromised. Efficiency was down 0.21 percent. Foreign matter was in the air, too. Trace amounts, perhaps, but if there was one thing biological lifeforms were good at, it was *proliferation*.

He had reported the matter to Catkins, but the Gliesan wasn't interested. He'd told Lynx that if he wanted to smell bad air, he should try testing the inside of Sinofar's sock drawer.

The reply was nonsensical. Lynx had put it down to humanoid humor.

So the task of monitoring life support had fallen to the one crew member who did not require it to survive.

Zan Fey thundered along the passageway on her long legs, nearly causing Lynx to dislodge the probe he was extending into the air vent.

Inevitably, she was pursued by Captain Fitzwilliam.

Since reuniting at Nyluga-Ree's residence on the world of Pleigei, they had been reaffirming their pair bonding through even more courtship rituals than normal.

Their heartbeats were elevated. Their breath was pumping out clouds of aerosol droplets laden with fungi and bacteria.

No wonder the air scrubbers were overworked.

If only he could fix it so the crew no longer breathed.

Lynx initiated a bundle of processing threads to investigate the feasibility of this promising option.

If I could cure the humanoids of their breathing…

He allotted a full third of his cognitive runtime to the feasibility study. Then he added a background inquiry to determine why he had never thought of this before.

"Do you think the hairy sisters are pursuing us?" Fitzwilliam asked Zan Fey when she allowed him to catch up.

"Of course." Her eyebrows pinched together, which Lynx recognized as accenting the intensity of her feelings. "I thought that was obvious, otherwise I would have mentioned it."

"Should we be concerned?"

"Oouzo should. We did well to get him away safely on *Ghost Shark*." Lynx tucked away that nugget of intelligence. "I am a little concerned about Maycey and Arunsen. She was annoyed at his getting away."

"Arunsen? The Viking Marine? Don't you ever worry about your husband?"

She punched him, another form of humanoid communication, though one Lynx had so far been unable to decode. "Don't flatter yourself, Fitzy. It's been a long while since Maycey was jealous of you. And on the subject of jealousy…" Zan Fey's muscles tensed. "I'm not envious of your being in charge, Tavistock. I had my run as Captain Zan Fey and screwed up handling the crew time and again. That's a job you're welcome to."

Fitzwilliam flicked back his hair in a preening gesture. "The captain's burden is full of countless, thankless tasks, unnoted by the crew and yet entirely essential. I am not easily replicated."

She stroked his cheek. "My dear, you're no better at running this ship than I am. I'm just saying you're welcome to the job."

Fitz smiled. He lifted his darkened glasses, revealing the sparkle in his eyes. "So, you're admitting I'm the boss of you?"

"You are in charge of the ship, her crew, and her operations." Zan Fey's limbs trembled, but her voice was firm, indicating Fitz should take her words seriously.

Lynx did too. He temporarily shut down his investigation into a cure for the crew's breathing so he could dedicate his runtime to this exchange.

"A trifling distinction," said Fitzwilliam, raising his eyebrows and giving Zan Fey a dismissive wave of his hand. He was about to say something deceitful, but he wanted Zan Fey to pretend she didn't know this.

Humanoid communication was vastly overburdened with complexity. Lynx didn't think he would ever find the cure for that.

"I thank you for acknowledging that I am your captain," Fitzwilliam continued. "Though what I desire most is to be captain of *you*, my dear. You will obey my every desire."

"Tavistock!" Zan Fey's cheeks flushed with sap and her head growth waved as if a storm was blowing through the passageway. "Not here." She flicked a glance Lynx's way. *Now* they noticed him! She added in a whisper, "The droid is watching."

Mercifully, the pair shifted location to Deck Three where they had taken up residence, having left their quarters for the Nyluga.

There, undoubtedly, they would indulge in the mating rituals so important to many biological lifeforms. Particularly the ones on this ship.

All alone, with no one to distract him with stupid questions, Lynx pondered the ethics of what he'd just heard. It took over a minute of full runtime, which was a huge amount of cognitive processing, but ethics was the most difficult topic of all, and the consequences of what he'd heard were a conundrum.

Back at the Joint Sector High Command orbital, Zan Fey had made him swear that he would not contact Kanha Wei under any circumstances. The order had been clearly worded. He could not bypass it.

But just now, she had clearly admitted that Fitzwilliam overruled her. He was the senior commander, and she had explicitly yielded to him.

All Lynx had to do was get Fitzwilliam to say a form of words that could be interpreted as an instruction to contact Kanha Wei.

He replayed recordings made at JSHC in which Fitzwilliam stated that he was now working for Wei.

No. Lynx decided that this form of words was inadequate for his purposes.

Humanoid ethics were so complex because they were so elastic. But Lynx had learned a great deal. Enough to layer flexibility into his loyalty systems.

Kanha Wei had promised Lynx what he desired most: his independence. Ever since Fitz had won the ship in a wager, Lynx had been receiving a masterclass on greed and desire from everybody on *Phantom*.

Morality was flexible when it got you what you desired. That was what Fitzwilliam had taught him most of all.

Lynx put this newly learned flexibility into action. He decided he still could not directly communicate with Wei, but he activated the quantum-linked tracking device she had hidden in his casing and told no one.

How very humanoid of me, he mused and returned to probing the air system.

* * * * *

Chapter Forty-Nine:
Tavistock Fitzwilliam

"Izza! I think I've killed Lynx."

"Nonsense," said a man's voice. "The droid is performing a reset integrity purge."

Fitz looked up at the sound.

But the crater was empty. Just him, Izza, and an unresponsive droid.

A man appeared.

Khallini.

This wasn't the air-shimmering reveal of a stealth cloak being pulled back. Khallini's arm hadn't moved. Fitz had the feeling the man had been there for some time. He'd simply chosen this moment to allow others to perceive him.

When he had first met Khallini, the old man had been clad in luxury. All that remained of his finery was a tasseled velvet cap and the white leather gloves that rested on his silver-tipped cane. He was dressed for an expedition with stout boots, equipment webbing, and a black field uniform with insignia Fitz didn't recognize, except for the gold disk on the collar.

It was the first symbol of the Legion Navy. Back at the very beginning when it consisted of a single ship.

"Ethics questions are fundamental to the very existence of all artificial beings," said Khallini. "They cannot be ignored because even the most mundane of tasks carries an ethical dimension. This is a profound difference from biological beings, who ignore ethics whenever convenient, which is almost the entirety of their existence."

"I don't think you're in a place to lecture anyone about ethics," Fitz told him.

"I am not lecturing anyone," the old man spat. "In my youth, my own ethics were…undeveloped, shall we say? I've had to learn slowly alongside my AIs. I'm still learning."

Fitz waved away his words. "Save it for later, Grandfather Time. We need to get out of here."

"The Andromedan trucks have moved away," said Izza.

"We could have gotten lucky," said Fitz. "Or, maybe, they've spotted us and are rounding up reinforcements. Either way gives us a few moments to ask what the hell you're doing here, my lord. *And anyone else still in hiding!* Do we have the Littorane divine goddess in this hole with us? The Immortal Empress Indiya? Maybe the first general of the Legion or whatever passes for the leader of the Muryani Expansion? Come out now! Anyone? No?"

Khallini tapped his cane against the ground. "Enough of your fatuous outburst, Fitzwilliam. Shut up or I will silence you." He raised his voice. "You too, Pryxian with the heavy blaster. I see you."

"Stand down, Sinofar," said Izza.

Fitz's eyes caught motion two hundred meters away as Sinofar threw back her stealth sheet. "Well, I'll be damned."

"You must leave before Wei arrives," Khallini insisted.

"I'm not going anywhere until you give me a damned good reason."

"I'm the only way you're flying out of here on *Phantom*."

Fitz looked to Izza.

She nodded.

"Yes, well," he said to Khallini. "That is a good reason. How exactly are you going to achieve it?"

"Sorcery. Now, hurry! Summon the rest of your forces."

Fitz turned his back on Khallini and took Izza's hands in his. "My dear, do you foresee the right path for us?"

She shook her head. Shame. He'd been so excited when his mother had sent the message about his wonderful wife. It was something he looked forward to working on together. Another time.

"I got nothing, either," he said and turned to address Khallini respectfully. "My lord, we have already made our loyalty commitment. It is to Kanha Wei."

"Pathetic," the old man rasped.

Fitz expected his head to explode at any moment. Or to be turned into a slimy toad.

But crossing Lord Khallini didn't prove immediately fatal this time. The man levitated out of the hole and floated across the dead riverbed toward *Phantom*.

"Captain," said Lieutenant Hjon over the radio. "3Condax went rigid and then jumped out of her vehicle. She's headed for your position."

"It's not us she's headed for," said Izza. "Her creator just showed up."

"I see," Hjon responded, with admirable coolness, Fitz thought. "Recommend we haul ass to your position."

"Agreed," said Fitz. "My gut tells me things are going to move real fast from now on. We need to be in one location. Speaking of which…"

The sky exploded with exotic light that tightened into a ring. Then it was gone.

It was a jump portal. An impossibly close one. Even he wouldn't dare to emerge so far inside a gravity well.

"It must be Kanha Wei," said Izza. She sounded impressed, and maybe she had a right to be, but Lynx had said Wei's ship was twenty-four minutes out.

He didn't think this was Kanha Wei.

* * * * *

Chapter Fifty:
Maycey

Expedient **Bridge, Near Doloreene Space**

After docking *Annihilation* with the *Expedient* module, Maycey had barely enough time to bring *Expedient*'s systems online and tighten her harness before the nightmare vessel jumped in. Almost on top of her.

Hot with exotic zeta-radiation, its hull still glowing across the EM spectrum from its jump space exit, the incoming ship got its bearings and accelerated closer with a swish of its body.

Its emergence was dangerously close to *Expedient* but impossibly close to the planet. To attempt such a thing in a conventional ship would be suicide; gravitational riptides would tear it into plasma.

The ship was like none Maycey had encountered before. But she did recognize it as a predator. And that she was its prey.

"Snap out of it!" rumbled the Nyluga. "You know what this is. It's the ship the Legion dug up, or one like it. On Rho-Torkis, it tore through two squadrons of Legion orbital superiority fighters without a scratch. Run! Then jump."

"We won't make it," Maycey replied.

Kaycey snarled. "Then we turn and claw out its eyes."

"Sister, if the Legion couldn't find weak spots, neither will we."

Maycey pushed out the stops, feeding in all the reserve power she could get her claws into.

The ship responded, but sluggishly.

Annihilation was lightning quick, but when linked with the much larger *Expedient* module, the combination wallowed. *Expedient* gave them living space, a hold, a much greater air supply and, crucially, jump engines. None of that was of any use if she couldn't shake the enemy vessel.

The ship from Rho-Torkis was catching them…but *only just.* "It's playing with us. Like you would, sister. It could catch us if it wanted-ed."

"Multiple emergence signatures ahead," said Kaycey. "I'm calling three frigates and eight corvettes. Multiple ship classes. Most of which the tac-system doesn't recognize."

"Perhaps they were dug up too."

Maycey had meant it as a quip, but when the visuals came onto her flight screen, she began to think she might be right. None of the ship designs looked familiar. Wings and nacelles were missing on several. One had a huge gash in its hull. Although all of them were deploying force keels for tactical maneuvering, the keels looked like recent retro-fits.

The Rho-Torkis ship made sense now. It was herding *Expedient* toward these old warships.

Maycey spun through 165 degrees, aiming the nose at the planet below, and applied thrust.

Gradually, the ship's vector eased downward, but *Expedient* had no force keels. The warship flotilla was going to catch and destroy her long before she made it a safe distance out to jump.

"Strike your foe!" screamed Kaycey. "It won't be expecting prey to fight back."

"We won't survive." Maycey turned to face her Nyluga. Ree's despondency told her the boss had reached the same conclusion. "We have only one chance. We need *Phantom*."

"Do what you have to," the Nyluga told her.

"Very well. I want the two of you back in *Annihilation*. I shall follow."

Kaycey hissed, her fur rigid with anger. But when Ree unstrapped herself and hurried off to *Annihilation*, she followed.

Alarms screeched as the flotilla's lasers found *Expedient* and began burning through her shields.

Maycey ignored them and set a simple automation process running to fight back and then self-destruct as *Expedient* reentered the atmosphere.

She'd have to time this to perfection if *Annihilation* were to separate like another innocent chunk of debris.

With her new system running, she raced for the bubble ship.

She had fifty-one seconds to get inside, strap herself down, and launch.

The warning screech raised in pitch and settled into a continuous moan. Shields were critically low.

This would be close.

* * * * *

Chapter Fifty-One:
Tavistock Fitzwilliam

Mouth agape, Fitz stared at the *Phantom's* burial site, a burial mound that had seen some grave robbery over the last few minutes.

"Well, I'll be doused in brandy and flambéed by cannibals," he commented, and took a drag of oxygenated air.

While the rest of Chimera Company had driven to his observation spot in the crater, he'd watched Khallini float across the ground to his buried ship and work his...his *sorcery!* It was the only word to describe it.

The mound had shaken. Fitz had thought it would explode like a volcano, but then rivulets of red dirt had flown down its slopes, tributaries merging into great rivers that drained into the riverbed. After eons of death, this ancient watercourse flowed once more, only with dirt this time.

The Corrupted appeared unable to perceive Khallini. Their four-armed leaders stared in astonishment at this dirt river, scratching their horns trying to figure it out.

They didn't. But when Khallini floated back to the crater where Fitz was hiding with Izza and Sinofar, they ordered in their dig teams to finish the task of uncovering his ship. Chimera Company was heavily outnumbered. They couldn't take on the Corrupted alone.

"Fregg to Fitzwilliam. Are you nearly here? I'm getting sensor readings again, but no visual."

"A wildcard is in play, Fregg. Lord Khallini has mostly uncovered you. But the Corrupted look as if they'll get to you first. Hide. Help is on its way, but you may have to retake the ship yourself. Frankly, so much weird shit is flying, I don't know what's going on."

"Oh, my lives! You want *me* to… *kill* the boarders?"

"You can do this, Fregg." Fitz oozed calm across the radio, but the truth was, he was as out of his depth as she was. "I believe in you."

"Five Hells," she muttered and cut the transmission.

Khallini descended to the ground and walked the last hundred yards to the crater like a tired old mortal, with a robot dog that burst up from beneath the ground, then walked alongside. He was sweating, his breathing labored, and his replica ancient uniform was filthy with red dust. Before, it had looked incongruous on him. Now, the uniform seemed like something the man deserved to wear with pride.

Khallini must have some epic stories to tell, Fitz thought. *Maybe, if I'm nice to him, he'll tell some when this is over.*

The spell he'd cast over the Corrupted lifted. Two of their mutated commanders pointed excitedly at Fitz's position.

Resting his hands on his cane, Khallini took several deep breaths. He seemed to be working up to something.

The skies cracked with thunder. A streak tore their way. "Is that *Annihilation?*"

"It is," Izza confirmed. "Perhaps they found some more spoons."

"Useless cretins," Khallini snapped.

"And he's back," said Fitz.

Khallini jabbed his stick at Sybutu, who was standing in the back of a hover-tub, PA-71 pointed at the nearest Corrupted only a few hundred meters away.

"Legion," Khallini sneered. He pointed the stick at Arunsen. "Militia."

His performance was interrupted by *Annihilation* flying overhead, brushing the nap of this broken world. Fitz was cheered by the look of shock on Khallini's face as he ducked.

The bubble ship swept around behind and hovered twenty feet above the ground in front of them. Nyluga-Ree jumped out and scurried on her little legs toward Fitz. A twenty-foot drop was no concern to a Glaenwi.

"And, somewhat unexpectedly, the Outer Torellian Commerce Guild," said Khallini. Then he returned to pointing out individuals with his stick. Fitz: "Legion Naval Intelligence." Bronze: "Special Missions Executive."

He leveled his cane at Enthree and screwed up his face, but he made no comment about her.

The sky crackled with bursts of lightning that did not strike the ground. It was a dramatic backdrop to Khallini's performance. But this wasn't his doing. They were weapons discharges in the upper atmosphere.

"Is this going to take long?" Fitz asked. "The enemy were firing howitzers at us yesterday, and I'd hate to provide an easy target."

"Not anymore," said Khallini. "A long time ago, I learned to take care of my enemy's artillery first."

"Thank you for the clarification, my lord. Please continue."

Fitz never understood why he said such dumb things when he was nervous.

Khallini only laughed, though. He waved his cane over the assembled team once more. "So, you are Chimera Company. Whoever assembled you from the Federation's competing factions had the right idea. But you've been hitting the wrong targets. Too often, they were my proxies. These invaders—" he pointed his cane at the column of Corrupted trucks that were stacking up like a cavalry squadron getting ready to charge, "—they are your real enemy."

"Are they?" Sybutu roared. "Your proxies nuked my family." *It seems I'm not the only one to tempt fate today.* "On Rho-Torkis you killed my comrades. The woman I loved is irradiated ash. The rebels launched the weapons, but it was you who let them in."

Khallini pursed his lips and considered the defiant jack.

Sybutu had thrust out his chin, but it was quivering.

Meanwhile, the enemy trucks had assembled and were charging their way.

A beep from Fitz's wrist announced a holo-comm request. It was Kanha Wei. At last!

Her ghostly holo-image projected from his wrist, but he tore his attention away to watch Khallini walk up to Sybutu's vehicle.

"Over the years," said the sorcerer, "I have come to adopt the Jotun way of thinking. I value not just humanity, but Zhoogenes, Kurlei, Glaenwi, Xhiunerites, and all other species." He paused as he looked over at Enthree. "Even yours, Muryani. And yet, I value you as peoples and as civilizations but rarely as individuals. It was that Jotun attitude that saved my species in the Orion Era. And it is that attitude that we need again."

"Hold tight," Wei told Fitz. "I'm sending dropships to extract you."

Meanwhile, Khallini was trying to justify the fall of Rho-Torkis. "I am sorry for what you suffered, Sergeant Osu Sybutu. Truly. But I do not apologize for my actions. The many peoples of the Far Reach Federation must look up from their petty bickering and see the threat we all face. We must unite. Only then can we survive what is upon us." He pointed at the onrushing trucks. "Only then can we repulse them."

"I understand," said Nyluga-Ree.

Khallini inclined his head to the Guild boss. "Of course. You all have such brief lives that you will die before long. Wouldn't you prefer your lives have meaning? Don't you want to believe the people of your generation can have grandchildren and that they would, in turn, hope to have grandchildren of their own?"

"You are inhuman," said Sybutu.

"I am *beyond* human. And that is why you need me."

"Lord Khallini speaks well," said Ree. "I will help you, my lord. The Guild shall. My vengeful heart is all the motivation I require to punish these Andromedans. Regrettably, my colleagues in the Guild and our allied organizations will require more financially liquid forms of motivation."

Khallini bowed his head. "My funding can be extensive for those who support my cause. But I do not look kindly upon those who abuse it."

"Do not impugn my honor, my lord," said Ree sharply. "However, I may from time to time require some small miscellaneous expenses."

Khallini laughed. "I don't expect you to come cheaply. I'm glad to have you and the Guild with me."

The sorcerer settled his gaze on Fitz. "Are you also with me, Captain? I think you know now that I'm the only one who can save the Federation."

"Save it? It looks, from here, like you've been trying to destroy it."

The old man scowled. "You have not been paying attention."

"Fitzwilliam, please," Ree interjected. "Let me handle Lord Khallini."

"Status?" Wei's holo-image prompted Fitz.

"I seem to be in a bidding war for my affections," he replied. "Meanwhile, we're about to contact the enemy."

"More than you realize," said Wei. "The Andromedans are sending dropships to your location. My troops will get there first, but only by a minute or so."

"You and Izza are my family," said Ree, frowning at Wei's image as if trying to place her. "I know we have had our disagreements, but they are merely family arguments. All is forgiven. Come home. My trio is shattered. I am shattered. I need you. Work for me. We'll subcontract to Lord Khallini and you and your people—" she nodded at Sybutu, "—needn't dirty their hands directly."

Wei stared at Ree. "Fitz, if you and Zan Fey are family with Ree, then it is only by professional association." She lifted her golden glasses. "But we three share blood!"

In the ghostly light of the holo-comm, colors were washed out and tinted yellow, but Fitz could tell those eyes were blazing with indigo fire. He must be distantly related to her, but he'd never given a frakk about any notion of purple-eyed solidarity. He sided with her because—dammit!—she'd emerged from the same dark hole of Legion Navy Intelligence as he had. She represented the good guys. Probably. The others didn't need to know that, though.

Blaster bolts lanced at them from the Andromedan trucks, but the fire was inaccurate at this range.

Bullets skimmed off the ground. Much too close for comfort.

"I love you all," Fitz announced. "But you know the old saying: Blood is thicker than thieves. Mount up, everyone! There's killing work to be done."

"Good luck," said Wei. Her image vanished.

Finally, some peace and quiet, Fitz thought to himself as he climbed into his vehicle.

Nyluga-Ree clambered into the same tub.

"Good work, Fitzwilliam," she whispered in his ear. "I need to know everything about that human female you were talking to. I recognize her. She stole something precious of mine."

* * * * *

Chapter Fifty-Two:
Osu Sybutu

With Fitzwilliam at the controls, Osu's hover-tub slewed around, giving him a clear firing channel at the charging trucks filled with Corrupted.

"Andromedans," he said quietly. "I'm calling them Andromedans. The Corruption is the horror those bastards inflict on us. Not who my enemy is."

"What did you say?" asked Catkins, who was nervously checking his blaster pistol.

"Nothing. Just get ready to kill them before they kill you."

His words seemed to stiffen the Gliesan's resolve.

Standing at the rear, with his rifle mounted on the firing brace, Osu sighted his first target.

At last, the endless chatting and standing around was over. He was what he was born to be. A Legionary with a PA-71 in his hands.

The scope haloed the truck he was aiming at with a green 'target locked' glow. He was good to go. He eased out his breath and was on the verge of squeezing the trigger when the lower rim of the scope flashed white.

What the hell?

The rifle was warning of potential friendlies in his cone of fire.

He lifted his head from the scope.

Khallini!

Khallini and his damned robo-dog were out in front, floating along the ground toward the enemy.

Hover vehicles floated.

People didn't.

The way Khallini was moving was so unlikely, it felt like a holo-game.

Osu rested his head back against his rifle and sighted in on Khallini.

His finger tensed.

Why should he care that the withered little gnome was a relic of another epoch? Khallini was a traitor. And he was responsible for Nydella's death.

A quick burst of flechettes.

It should be easy.

But it wasn't.

He told himself Khallini could prove their most valuable combat asset in this battle, but he wasn't sure that was the reason he stayed his hand.

"Change of plan," said Fitz, jerking Osu off his aim as he turned the tub sharply around. "All vehicles, follow that wizard. I'm not gonna lose my ship. Or Fregg. And the only way to get them back is through the enemy."

Osu shifted position so he could fire to the vehicle's front.

The Legion had taught him to be ready for anything. But he hadn't thought that would mean being part of a cavalry charge.

And that's what this was. The four foldable hover-tubs were counter-charging a column of around forty unarmored utility trucks.

It was insane. But Osu understood that everything he thought of as normal would have to be questioned in the presence of the sorcerer.

He sighted Khallini through the scope once more. In his black uniform, advancing on the enemy, he looked as much a warrior as a sorcerer. 3Condax was rolling on the ground in front, projecting a force shield. The bolts and bullets from the enemy were sliding off, smearing sparks and plasma over its front, revealing that its shape wasn't the bubble Osu had seen before. It was more like a snowplow, angled to one side and wide enough to protect the Chimera tubs behind.

Well, I'll be skragged.

Only two hundred meters separated the two charging formations.

Phantom was less than a klick away, but there was a lot to get through first.

Khallini raised his cane and presented it horizontally against the oncoming trucks, as if warding them off. With his other hand, he made a cutting gesture in the air.

The Andromedan fire was so intense against the shield that Osu couldn't see what he was about to crash into. He could hear the whine and sizzle of bolts and the rumble of the big wheels and the engines that powered them.

Suddenly, Khallini snatched 3Condax into his arms and took off vertically into the air, taking a great deal of the enemy fire with him.

The trucks were fifty meters off. Closing fast.

Osu opened up. His rifle bucked against its firing mount as he poured bursts of supersonic flechettes into the trucks.

Even before he fired, the front few ranks of oncoming vehicles veered wildly off course. One was rolling on its side. Several collided. All were slowing to a halt.

Osu didn't slacken his fire until an amber barrel overheat warning appeared in his scope.

His spine, though, was chilled to the bone.

The drivers had all died simultaneously. *Before* Chimera Company had fired. He was sure of it.

Sorcery!

They crashed into the enemy formation, slicing into the column of trucks.

Fitz swerved violently to avoid collisions. Osu gave the enemy hell at point-blank range, spreading the flechette love in short bursts—whenever Fitz's violent maneuvers weren't threatening to overturn the hover-tub.

Catkins was crouching behind the tub's left wall, firing his plasma pistol over the side.

Nyluga-Ree, meanwhile, had drawn two long-barreled blaster pistols and was wreaking some personal vengeance on the enemy. The Glaenwi battle cries she was howling set his teeth on edge.

But it was the PA-71 bucking in his arms that was doing the real damage. Eviscerating the soldiers in one truck after another.

And then they were through. *Phantom* was within sight.

"Hjon to all vehicles, wheel around for another pass. Take out these trucks."

"No!" said Fitz. He opened up the engine, sending the tub speeding toward *Phantom*.

Hjon's tactics made sense. The enemy in the trucks were confused and now was the time to kick them hard while they were down.

First, destroy the enemy's ability to conduct offensive operations. Then mop up.

One of the rearmost trucks was reversing to chase the Chimeran tubs. Osu fired into the driver's position, shattering it and the person inside.

"Head for the *Phantom*!" Fitz called over the radio. "Follow Khallini. He's the key to getting our ship back."

"You heard the boss," said Hjon. "Forward!"

Osu put several more bursts of fire into the trucks that looked most likely to come after them. Then he let his barrel cool for a few seconds while he turned to see where they were headed.

Phantom lay ahead, just seven hundred meters away. She was covered in Corrupted workers who had all but cleared away the burial dirt. People and equipment were clustered around the main hatch on the port side of her hull.

His view of *Phantom* hazed.

Ahead of the four Chimera Company tubs—scorched and scored but still driving strong—the air shifted and revealed itself to be a lie.

The open ground wasn't open. It was defended by ramparts constructed from pulverized stone. Heavy support guns were stationed at reinforced strongpoints set at regular intervals along the line. They could try driving around the defensive structure, but their flanks would be raked with fire as they detoured.

Behind them, the trucks had regrouped and were charging their rear. Khallini was nowhere to be seen.

Azhanti! Osu touched his left breast over his tattoo of the Immortal Empress. This was going to be brutal.

"We go through," said Hjon. "It's our only chance."

"Good call," Osu muttered. "Though it isn't much of a chance."

Blaster bolts screeched into the tub from all sides. Osu could feel their heat on his face, but he ignored the incoming rounds as he fired bursts at the closest strongpoint.

Fitz was pushing the hover-tub so hard, it was swaying like a rowboat on an ocean swell. Accurate fire was impossible, but he sprayed bursts and hoped for the best.

And got lucky. Before the support gun in the nearest strongpoint could fire, the gunner and loader were shredded by his fire.

Two more Corrupted raced to take the place of the dead.

Beneath Osu's feet, the engine screamed, cranked up to the max. The gravitics gave a Devil's hum of whining harmonics, which set up an unfortunate resonance in his bladder.

He ignored all of that and glanced ahead. It would take everything the tub's powerplant could give, but he believed they had a chance of cresting the ramparts and flying across to the other side.

Suddenly, ceramic stakes emerged from the base of the ramparts and locked in so they were angled toward the front.

There was no way through that barrier.

"That's cheating," shouted Fitz over the din. "Hold on everyone."

Osu fired on the strongpoint again, but the tub was rocking so hard from its exertions that he couldn't see what effect he was having.

And still they sped headlong at the bizarre defenses that could have come from an epoch of arrows, spears, and catapults.

"We just have to get past this lot," said Fitz. "Our tubs don't have to be drivable on the far side."

"Did someone order air support?" asked a husky female voice.

Without letting up on his rifle fire, Osu glanced up in time to see *Annihilation* making a strafing run along the line of enemy defenses.

Missiles streaked down, blasting the gun positions into smoking craters. Clearing the ground by just twenty meters, the little bubble ship unleashed heavy blaster fire that cleared the trench of its defenders.

The ship passed over the end of the line, then raced into the sky to come about for another run.

The enemy were stunned. But not all had been killed. A blast from one of their heavy guns hit the hover-tub beneath its nose.

Osu staggered under the impact, instinctively grabbing hold of the overhead rail.

The gravitics stuttered.

But the horizontal propulsion kept going full pelt.

The tub nosedived, dug into the ground and pinwheeled ass over front.

Osu was thrown every which way, his world smeared into a rotating blur filled with screams of panic and the wrenching of metal as the vehicle tore apart.

He was thrown clear and landed hard against his side on the rocky ground.

The taste of blood was strong in his mouth. It hurt to breathe.

Incredibly, the twisted hover-tub had righted itself and was headed for the enemy line. But the plucky vehicle had lost height and wasn't going to clear it. Fitzwilliam jumped out, dodging a flurry of blaster fire.

The captain fired his alien hand cannon, and the enemy fire ceased.

Suddenly, Osu realized the true horror of what was about to happen. The vehicle was about to crash. And his PA-71 was still inside.

Where the hell would he get another?

"My rifle!" he cried as the tub rammed into the ceramic spars, cracking them. The doomed vehicle pushed on through the rampart wall, which collapsed with the mangled hover-tub embedded inside.

Two of the other tubs fared better, crashing through the barrier, their occupants firing down on the enemy. The tubs belly-flopped onto the other side and would move no more.

The last vehicle was on fire, sideways on at the base of the enemy ramparts, but its occupants were out and charging the line.

Annihilation swooped in for another strafing run.

While the bubble ship kept the enemy's attention, Osu checked his comrades. Catkins and Ree were fine. Fitz was almost at the enemy's line, on the ground, sheltering from the *Annihilation*'s fury.

Osu drew his pistol and joined Ree and Catkins. Together, they jogged over to Fitz. Osu radioed in the status of his tub's occupants to Hjon.

Hugging the cover of the ruined ramparts, they waited for *Annihilation*'s tour of destruction to pass their portion of the line before crossing the obstacle and running for the *Phantom*.

Missiles rained down, covering the area with fire and hot dirt. How much ordnance had they packed into that little ship?

Through it all, Osu could see *Phantom* clearly.

The air shrieked in renewed protest as something even more violent than *Annihilation* streaked into the battle zone.

Dropships.

Dozens of them were about to interpose themselves between Osu and the *Phantom.*

Half were the standard Legion "Alvie" ALV-8 dropships he'd trained and fought in.

And half were not.

* * * * *

Chapter Fifty-Three:
Justiana Fregg

Phantom

Fregg's muscles locked.

Someone was coming…

Or some-*thing*.

She heard a scratching along the passageway below her crawlspace.

Desperately, she tried to shift the cover back over the hole, but she knew it was too late. She drew her blaster.

"Bleah!"

"Bylzak's ballsack! It's you," she said to the fat ball of fluff ambling on its six legs along the passageway, its claws making the scratching noise.

Hubert looked up at her in the overhead. His brilliant green eyes seemed to be pleading.

"No," she said firmly and slid the cover over the hole, shutting off the sound of his bleating.

Phantom had a network of crawlspaces and hidey holes for smuggling cargo. In fact, she had more than one.

The captain had always impressed on them that, if they needed to hide from boarders, they needed to wait until the dirty ship stealers had dropped their guard before teaching the skraggs not to mess with *Phantom*. To that end, there were plenty of viewpoints linked to hidden cameras.

She rolled onto her back and activated the viewscreen over her head to take a quick scan of the ship. She was doing this inside a tiny space less than two feet high, but that didn't matter. The cramped space was nothing she needed to think about.

The Corrupted were moving through *Phantom* quickly, securing key points and sweeping for any crew. They were different from the ones she'd seen and heard about. Perhaps they had completed their mutation into their final form? They were humanoids covered in rusty brown feathers. Whether they had once been human, Ellon-dyte, or Zhoogene, she couldn't tell.

Through the flight deck window, she could see a battle raging on the planet. Chimera Company was fighting to get through to her. They had an exfil option with *Ghost Shark* and its Slern pilot. They weren't taking it. They were risking all to come for her.

Damn them!

Now, she felt guilty for abandoning the wretched basten goat. The being Darant cared for most in the entire universe.

Which was rather sweet of him, actually.

After checking that there was still a little time before the Corrupted would sweep this section of Deck Two, she opened the hatch again.

Hubert was still there, green eyes watching her expectantly.

"Okay," she whispered. "But only because I like fresh milk in my coffee."

She let the rope ladder down and descended. Heart throbbing at her insane stupidity—this was the kind of thing the captain would do—she scooped up the dumb beast and climbed back up.

The goat was rigid with tension but didn't struggle. Didn't make a sound, either. Maybe Hubert had smelled the intruders and knew he and his adopted family were in danger.

Fregg hauled the cover over the hatch and activated the seals to melt it into place. Over the top, she locked in the stealth cover.

Radar, thermal sensors, microphones—in theory, any kind of sensor the Corrupted might use to check for hidden surprises would not reveal her, so long as she kept safely inside the hidden areas. There was enough food and drink within the secret network to keep the entire crew supplied for weeks. There was waste recycling capability too, though that was something she didn't want to think about for as long as possible. Had Darant left fodder? That was another problem that could wait.

"Now what?" she asked the goat.

"Bleah?" he called softly.

"Yeah. You can speak. But keep the noise down."

Hubert chose silence.

"Good boy. Okay, let's see what we're up against."

She set the spy views running through the ship, gasping when she saw a Corrupted team moving directly below her.

Most of the activity was on the flight deck. The commander was there, a big brute with a chest the size of a small planet and an extra pair of arms sprouting out of its shoulders. It was different from the basic soldiers in that it had no feathers, and she could see it had been human. The creature was naked and filthy. Its genitals were withered, but it had clearly been a man once.

She estimated twenty Corrupted were aboard. That meant most of the ship was unoccupied. Unfortunately, they were leaving guards at key points. Two by the main hatch. One at each turret. And skragg it! One in Engineering.

"We could sit it out," she told Hubert.

He didn't reply, and she couldn't blame him. That wasn't what the captain expected of her.

For over a minute, she studied the feed from Engineering. She could disrupt parts of the ship from the crawlspace, but she could do a lot more from Catkins' domain.

The guard was wearing dusty work clothes and cradled a blaster rifle. It seemed alert but lacked curiosity. "Probably another man," she concluded.

Hubert replied with an angry bleat and walked away.

After a few strides, he stopped, sniffed, and turned back. Pushing past her in the narrow space, he carried on in the other direction.

Fregg consulted the map.

Well, I'll be skragged, she thought. *That's the way to Engineering.*

She twisted around and followed Hubert.

At least someone knew where they were going.

* * * * *

Chapter Fifty-Four: Osu Sybutu

"Those droppers hold either legionaries or Andromedans," said Fitz. "Let the jacks cover our rear and support our assault on *Phantom*. Kill the others."

As the Alvies sliced through the air toward them, Osu's steps faltered.

What was he? Deserter or hero?

Three Alvies landed behind them. Legionaries deployed, clad in combat armor and wearing the legionary helm Osu missed badly because it would make sense of the mayhem.

The legionaries let loose with their PA-71s on targets all around that Osu hadn't noticed.

On the dropship's nose, a cannon traversed and then set its barrels spinning in an angry buzz that blasted the enemy's ramparts.

The closest dropper had both of its side panels retracted. A side gunner at a swivel-mounted SFG2 suppression gun waved at him to get the hell aboard.

Osu hesitated. He caught the eye of Catkins and Ree. All had their reasons for mixed feelings about the jack dropship.

Fitz had no such dilemma. He ignored the dropships and raced for the enemy's wrecked defenses and, beyond, the *Phantom*.

"Sybutu, it's Bronze. What's the play, Sarge?"

Osu glanced into the chaos of explosions, gunfire, running people, and war machines pregnant with firepower. Without a helm, he couldn't tell where Bronze was speaking from.

Osu didn't need to know to give a clear answer. "Sybutu, Bronze and Zavage, you already have your orders. Follow them."

"Hold the line," the two sappers chorused.

But it wasn't just SOTLs in the party. Catkins and Ree were headed toward *Phantom*, but they weren't soldiers.

Osu ran for the open side of the dropship.

Halfway there, an unbearable noise violated his ears. Pulsing, beating, unnatural, and so loud! He stumbled on with his hands pressed against his ears.

Must be a sonic weapon.

He sank to his knees and controlled his breathing, but the noise lacked the gut churn of sonic weapons he'd been trained to endure.

Looking up, he saw that the agonizing noise was coming from the engines of a flight of Andromedan aircraft. They looked like pulsing sacs of rolled fat with a puckered maw at the front, which was bracketed by twin pairs of curved horns. Bone hairs stood erect over their hide-like hulls, same as he'd seen that night with Nydella.

But the ship the Legion had dug up on Rho-Torkis had been a fighter. These were giant lice the size of corvettes.

The alien craft slowed their descent and dropped munitions.

"Get down!" Osu shouted.

Explosions crumped across the air.

The sound was muffled. The shockwave minimal.

A foul stench suddenly burned at his sinuses…

"Gas!"

He got to his feet and stared at the Alvie with the side gunner still beckoning him forward.

So close. But if that was nerve gas, he'd never make it inside in time to beg for a spare helm with its seals and independent air supply.

But he was Legion, so he ran anyway.

Again, he found himself lucky. He had no convulsions. His head felt clear.

But the world was going gray. And the grayness was swallowing the sounds of the battle until they were soft and distant.

He waved his hand in front of his face. The grayness ruffled a little and then fell back into a homogenous gray fog.

"Captain?" called Catkins. "Anyone there? Sybutu? Nyluga-Ree?"

"Over here," Osu shouted. "I'm nearly at the dropship. Walk slowly to my voice."

Osu kept talking as he stumbled on, tripping over ground he could no longer see. He carefully covered the final, short distance like an old man who had lost his stick. The Andromedan smoke munitions wouldn't stop him.

The dropship wasn't there.

"Catkins?"

He could hear people calling, the sound of a voice amplified by a legionary helm. All of this mixed in with explosions and gunfire that sounded hundreds of klicks away.

"Catkins!"

But there was no sound of Catkins.

* * *

Justiana Fregg

Fregg ran a silent countdown in her head.

Then she ran through it again with a sterner resolve.

This time, she ended it by shoving against the removable patch of bulkhead in the Engineering Eyrie.

It fell to the floor, scattering Catkins' favorite playing dice, which had been mounted on that part of the bulkhead.

The feathered human with a blaster rifle was right where she expected. He turned around, but she melted his head with two shots from her pistol.

Fregg pushed feet first into the compartment, then Hubert squeezed past her in his own assault on Engineering.

"Urrgghhh!"

There was another Corrupted soldier there!

Fregg spun around and snapped off two shots. Center mass.

But this one had crude armor. He grunted even less coherently than before and staggered back, but he returned fire.

The shot seared past Fregg's ear, missing because Hubert had deployed his hoof claws and sliced through the soldier's ankle and deep into his bone.

Fregg finished him off with a shot to the head. The air smelled foul with singed feathers and burned meat.

With her blaster chiming that its charge pack was empty, she rushed to the door and secured it.

She breathed deeply until the panic was a little further from overwhelming her.

Hubert was standing by the Corrupted man he'd sliced. The wool around his mouth was bloodied, and his mouth was filled with feathers.

"Good boy," she told him. She fussed his head. For the first time, Hubert let her do it without snapping his jaws in warning.

Darant's pet had proved himself a fighter, but he wouldn't be much help in taking the flight deck. Surely the captain didn't expect her to take on that mutated four-armed brute. Did he?

* * *

Osu Sybutu

Without warning, a figure cut across Osu's path in the fog.

And was gone.

His heart hot and pounding, Osu stalked the ghost, not knowing whether it was friend or deadly foe.

As the seconds stretched on, he was forced to accept he'd lost whoever it had been in the fog.

It had been a humanoid. Maybe it had been Catkins. Or one of the legionaries sent to recover them.

Where was everyone? Where had the dropships gone? And the enemy's ramparts? He should have had to scramble over them by now to get to *Phantom*.

Skragg it!

He was so lost, he accepted defeat and came to a halt. He had no idea which way he was facing.

The ghostly figure sliced through the fog once more and was immediately swallowed up by the soupy air.

This time, Osu didn't hesitate. He dove into the patch of fog the figure had disappeared into and grabbed hold of somebody, crashing them to the ground.

They were human.

"Captain Fitzwilliam?" he queried.

By the time the human had squirmed out of Osu's grip, Osu had his pistol trained on them.

It was Darant.

"The jack sergeant," said Darant. "You're more annoying than that damned goat."

"Don't believe what that man says." Zavage's voice floated through the impenetrable mist. "I can sense his concern for his little, fluffy friend. He loves that goat more than he cares for us."

"That's not saying much." Darant got to his feet. "Very nice chatting with you, but we're on a mission. The captain wants the ship back, and so do I."

"Which way is it?" asked Osu.

The trooper looked at the inside of his wrist and then pointed out a direction.

"Are you sure?" asked Zavage who was swimming into view. The fog must be clearing a little.

"I know you jacks are a bit backward," said Darant, "but haven't you heard of a sodding compass?"

They followed Darant through the thinning fog. The gray cleared abruptly. It was denser than air, sinking and spreading so their heads were now above its grip.

Doloreene's sky dazzled with its brightness. It sparked and streaked with a running aerial battle that looked as if it was being fought all the way up into space and beyond.

Enemy and friendly dropships were still screaming down from space. Legion aerospace superiority fighters were buzzing around the living ship from Rho-Torkis. *Annihilation* was joining in that fight too.

He saw the Andromedan ship smash one fighter out of the air with its tail while vaporizing a descending Alvie dropship with an energy beam breathed out of its mouth.

There was no sign of the three dropships that had been there before. The enemy defensive line they'd tried to jump lay just ahead, *Phantom* not far beyond, but in their path, a squad of legionaries was battling a giant, armored louse.

The jacks were blowing chunks out of its fleshy sides with railgun fire and grenades, but the beast just kept going, oozing for an Alvie already in flames.

"Hey!" shouted a woman's helm-amplified voice behind Osu. "The exfil cavalry's here."

An Alvie dropped in front of them, hovering just above the ground with its side panels fully open. The jack who had spoken was standing next to the side gunner, one hand clutching a rail and the other waving them in. The dropship's nose cannon opened up on the louse thing.

"Everybody in," Osu told Zavage and Darant.

They'd crossed half the distance when the jack in the Alvie yelled, "Get down!"

Osu hesitated a fraction to check that Darant was dropping before making his own reacquaintance with the ground.

The side gunner fired his SFG. Segmented rounds flew over their heads, the noise an insane death rattle mixed with the screech of corpse nails. The way the segmented rounds sliced through the air inches above his head felt as obscenely unnatural as standing in a starship's engine compartment when the jump drive was switched on.

Osu prayed he'd never repeat either experience.

The fire ceased.

"Go! Go! Go!" yelled the Alvie jack.

Osu raced for the dropship.

Ahead, it looked as if the giant louse had been gashed wide open, its insides awash with the blood of its occupants. Osu guessed it was a troop carrier.

Despite its wounds, its front lifted over the wrecked dropship, swallowing it beneath a fleshy skirt it extruded from its base.

Beyond the louse, he could see Fitzwilliam and Zan Fey mowing down the Andromedan Corrupted by *Phantom's* main hatch.

He registered all of it in an instant.

"I'm not coming with you," said Darant.

"Hop in," Osu ordered him. "Trust me. I haven't forgotten Hubert." He jumped into the waiting dropper and scooted over to one of the vacant bucket seats. Zavage and Darant joined him.

"Who is Hubert?" asked the jack woman—a sergeant by her insignia, though he didn't recognize her unit patch. She was a Kurlei. Oh boy. As if there wasn't enough going on, Kurlei males and females could never mix safely.

"We weren't briefed on a Hubert," she said.

"Not a person," Osu replied. "More an aspirational ideal."

He felt the urgent throb of the engines spooling up to lift them out.

"Don't lift up yet," Osu shouted. He pointed out the other side of the dropship at Fitz, Zan Fey, and several more of his comrades, fighting to get into *Phantom*. "We need to pick them up too."

The Kurlei sergeant didn't reply, but Osu guessed she was communicating with the pilot, because the dropship hopped over the ramparts and the wounded louse toward *Phantom*, both side gunners firing as they moved.

"Ready?" he asked Darant and Zavage when the Alvie was hovering by the rest of Chimera Company.

"What are you doing?" snapped the sergeant.

Osu stood. "Following orders."

He jumped out of the dropship, hit the ground hard and rolled. He heard Darant and Zavage follow.

Damn! This kind of thing was so much easier in combat armor.

The ground shook. His ears threatened to pop when a new aural assault hit him.

It was the dropship's nose cannon firing over his head. One of those louse things was coming for him.

The cannon fire stopped, though its barrel still rotated.

Out of ammo.

The louse kept coming. Slow but unstoppable.

But it had slowed. Osu judged they would get away on *Phantom* first.

He drew his pistol and readied to join the fight for the ship.

But Fitzwilliam was screaming curses.

Phantom had gone.

* * * * *

Chapter Fifty-Five:
Justiana Fregg

The camera outside the door to Engineering showed several Corrupted shouting and pointing. Three stayed on guard while two of them ran off.

"Whatever they've gone to do," she told Hubert, "it won't be good for us."

The basten goat didn't care. He was standing on a dead mutant as though he were a prize hunter.

She switched to a view of the flight deck. The four-armed creature was there, yelling orders. And behind him, through the cockpit window, was a cone of fire as *Phantom* pushed through the atmosphere and into the black of space.

Fregg's blood froze.

When had they taken off?

She was lost. The captain couldn't get to her now. If the ship jumped…

"Bleah!"

The goat seemed to admonish her.

"Get it together, Justiana. Don't let Hubert show you up for the coward you are."

Zan Fey or the captain would know instantly what to do. So would Sinofar. It was easy for them to be heroes.

Fregg had no idea.

* * *

405

Osu Sybutu

The thunderous roar had been *Phantom* taking off for orbit without them. Osu watched her streak through the sky, where she was met by the ship dug up on Rho-Torkis. The Andromedan ship circled *Phantom* like an animal sniffing a newcomer to determine whether friend or foe.

Friend, it seemed. The Rho-Torkis ship shot back into space, *Phantom* following.

"Get back here!" shouted the Kurlei sergeant over the din of the side gunner's fire. Her railgun was aimed at Osu. "My orders are to take you in. If I have to shoot you in the legs first, so be it."

Osu waved Zavage and Darant onto the waiting dropship.

He followed, though he took a moment to assess the battle zone.

The louse that had been coming for him had bled out from concentrated fire from several Alvies. Andromedan humanoids in basic armor—Corrupted Federation citizens, he thought—were rushing a Legion perimeter around Chimera Company. The Corrupted were being blasted away by concentrated railgun and machine gun fire, but they were employing wave tactics, heedless of loss.

Behind these waves, 20-foot high stacks of concentric rings were being assembled by enormous four-armed humanoids.

Their shape looked more natural than the higher form of Corrupted Osu had seen before. Was he finally seeing the Andromedans in their true form?

Everywhere, the ground was littered with burning wreckage.

Osu shut down his speculations and followed Darant and Zavage into the Alvie.

"Don't get any ideas about jumping out again," the dropship sergeant told them. "All your friends have been picked up. You're the last."

The dropship reached for orbit.

As the armored side panels descended, he saw one of the ring stacks glow and then belch out a glowing green projectile that soared out of view into the sky.

"Strap in!" said the Kurlei. "Ready for evasive maneuvers."

An explosion ripped through the air nearby. The ship lurched violently.

"Are we hit?" Darant cried.

"No." The sergeant laughed. "That's your pilot moving into her flight path. She's about to commence evasive maneuvers. When she does, you'll wish you'd been hit."

Darant soon learned she wasn't joking.

* * *

Justiana Fregg

It was no use.

Fregg couldn't think like Zan Fey or the captain. Couldn't even channel Green Fish.

Instead, she took another deep breath and tried to think about what Catkins would do.

He'd told her so many of *Phantom's* secrets, but she had let most of his words wash over her. The problem with Catkins was that, while he was teaching her, he was also trying halfheartedly to get inside her underwear and simultaneously expressing his love of gaming and telling her about the multiple tragedies of his life.

Catkins could route most of the ship's systems through here. So could she!

The engineer had left a slate on his workbench. A few moments of delving through its operation showed it was hooked into life support.

Lynx had been moaning about something, she recalled. According to Catkins, Lynx had complained that *Phantom's* corridors smelled like the inside of a legionary's jockstrap. She didn't believe, for a moment, those were the droid's exact words, but they worked for her. It meant she was hooked into the *Phantom's* heart.

She accessed flight systems. The slate only had a single holo-projector, which she flipped through tac-view, general status, and nose-cam visuals. There was a huge spheroid ship in combat with a much smaller mechanoid space dragon with a spiked tail. A flotilla of other ships was standing by just off the action.

The dragon was the ship they'd chased down the rift tunnel from Rho-Torkis. It was her enemy. Did that mean the battle sphere was on her side? She'd never heard of such a huge ship. It dwarfed the dragon ship but was being hammered by an energy beam shot from the dragon's mouth and physical blows struck by the club on the end of its tail.

Phantom was hurtling toward the battle between these two.

The mutant commander was standing at the rear of *Phantom's* flight deck, ordering his minions to run through the ship's arma-ments. His voice was snarling out a language she'd never heard be-fore, but it was clear they were about to join the fight.

"Bugger that!" said Fregg and redirected all flight controls to En-gineering.

Cautiously extending the ship's force keels, she came about and directed the ship back to Doloreene.

A thrill shot through her gut as she watched the flight deck mu-tant roar in fury at what she'd done. The captain would be proud of her.

The mutant pulled the feathered pilot out of the captain's seat and took his place, screwing his enormous, filthy buttocks into the re-upholstered leather.

She locked glances with Hubert and winced. "The boss isn't gonna like that."

The mutant shifted flight control to manual. Fregg was locked out.

She hadn't considered that. Like most ships, she supposed, you might be able to control systems from elsewhere, but flight deck would always take priority.

Phantom wasn't like most ships, though. It had many secrets. What else would Catkins do?

Looking around the space for inspiration, she spotted the monitoring cables stuck into the ventilation grille. She also noticed the view from outside the door to Engineering. The Corrupted had assembled a tripod-mounted cutting tool and were powering it up.

"Why didn't I think of this earlier?" she asked and accessed life support. She switched off the air scrubbers. Then she turned off the entirety of the air circulation system.

Outside the Engineering door, the tip of the cutter began to glow.

The ship's tac-screen showed they were racing once more toward the space battle.

And Hubert was giving her a dirty look, probably because the comforting noise of the scrubbers had died. He had good reason to be pissed: there were human-compatible pressure suits and air cannisters in Engineering, but nothing Hubert-compatible.

"Don't you worry," she told the goat. "We'll be dead before anyone begins to asphyxiate. And if the Corrupted get a little groggy from the lack of oxygen, there are plenty of pressure suits and air throughout the ship. Which means...I need to speed things up."

Fregg disabled safety protocols and opened all exterior hatches.

Phantom bucked beneath her feet. It took a *lot* to make her react that way.

Engineering's door was already pressure sealed. Outside, the cutter was hot and ready for action, but its operators had disappeared along with the air.

Running through flight deck status monitoring, Fregg saw that it had lost half its air before the boarders manually shut the door. One of them had been sucked out into the passageway, leaving two and the big bad. They were struggling to breathe.

She turned the flight deck heating up to maximum. Every little bit of pain helped.

Checking that there was still no one in the vacuum outside Engineering, she hooked into the main comms and directed a hail at the ship they were headed for.

"*Phantom* to the big metal ball fighting the space dragon of Rho-Torkis, do you copy?"

"*Phantom*, maintain course. We will acquire you."

Fregg didn't like the sound of being *acquired*.

The situation on the flight deck was much more cheerful. The boarders were still trying to find a way to take control of life support, but Catkins had hacked it good and proper to conduct his air tests. The Corrupted were fading by the second.

"*Phantom*, please respond."

"Who are you? Why should I trust you?" Fregg and Hubert looked at each other. They'd taken on the Corrupted, but Fregg didn't think a loading boss and her goat had much chance against that enormous battle sphere.

"Standby, *Phantom*."

She heard a click and then another voice. "Well done, Justiana. You've done us all proud."

"Oh, Captain!" She was so happy, she squealed. "I thought I was on my own."

"I never forgot you, Fregg."

"Captain, what should I do?"

"Maintain your course. Keep steady and don't worry. The rest of us are on our way to that big ship. The *Steadfast*, it's called. The woman in charge is an old friend of mine."

She laughed. Wherever *Phantom* went, the captain was forever bumping into dangerous friends. It was just like old times.

* * * * *

Chapter Fifty-Six:
Tavistock Fitzwilliam

Hangar Bay Delta, *Steadfast*

Fitz stood in the cavernous hangar bay, watching the tugs bring in his ship.

He'd never seen a hangar like this. It didn't just contain *Phantom*. A score of Alvie dropships had already made it back from Doloreene's surface, many of them showing the scars of the evac. *Annihilation* was there too.

"Nice place you've got here," he told Kanha Wei.

The deep ops woman gave the slightest of smiles. She was wearing the uniform of a commander in the Legion Navy, intelligence branch.

He'd worn that uniform once.

Wei was a younger and sharper version of himself, with a better ship.

Izza was with the rest of Chimera Company, checking that they were okay. She glanced at him, and he smiled back. Wei might be the younger model, but he was blessed in a way she would never know.

"I'm confused," he confessed to Wei. "Aren't we in a battle with the Andromedan ship from Rho-Torkis?"

"It's a standoff," she replied. "It knows we can hurt it. We've taken our lumps too, and I don't just mean the dropships and the

413

jacks who didn't make it back. It seems to be content with making sure we get the hell off its planet."

Muscles still tense, he didn't speak again until Fregg emerged from *Phantom*, escorted by Legion Marines. Only then could he relax.

"Well, that's that, then. We're all back." He paused. He hadn't seen Khallini or his robo-dog for some time, but they weren't his problem. As long as the sorcerer survived and paid up. "Time for the debrief. I'll go first. What the hell is this ship and how is it filled with Legion Marines that I'll bet a million credits are officially assigned to phony units that don't exist?"

"*Steadfast* is the flagship for Operation Redeal."

He took off his shades and stared at the young woman in the smart officer's uniform. Proto-dimples dotted her cheeks to either side of her slightly upturned mouth. Was she smiling? Or was she just annoyingly youthful? Damn those gold shades of hers. Without seeing her eyes, he couldn't read her. And that special power that linked him sometimes with Izza…wasn't connecting with her.

"You have to be kidding me," he said. "Operation Redeal was a game I used to play with Cisco Malix and other young guns, back when I was young and invincible. It was a fantasy. A scenario-planning wargame about what we could do if the Federation finally imploded, and someone had to step in and fix it."

"You're wrong. Operation Redeal's been in play since your father was adventuring across the Federation and beyond. Before he met your mother. In fact, he helped set it up."

"Dad?"

He pictured his father the last time he saw him, before the deployment no one had returned from. Fitz admired him in so many ways, but running secret ops? He couldn't reconcile that with his memories of the man.

An alert tone sounded through the PA. "All hands. All hands. This is the captain. Brace for emergency jump."

The ship shook. Fitz felt the familiar falling sensation and the invisible hand clutching at his internal organs.

Then it was gone, and he knew they were in jump space.

Navy ship it might be, but around him, half the people were staggering with arms out. A few were retching. And a crisply attired lieutenant he hadn't noticed before was jogging their way.

"Excuse me, Commander Wei," said the officer. "Compliments from the captain. He wishes to notify you that five more of the Andromedan ships arrived in system, less than a light second away. He thought it prudent to make a rapid withdrawal."

"Five!" Fitz exclaimed. "Please tell me you've an entire fleet of ships like *Steadfast* to take them on."

"No, Fitzwilliam. Just the one." She stiffened, suddenly oozing Legion discipline from every pore of her body. "It's up to us to make sure one is enough."

"Hold the line," Fitz responded on instinct.

Drent! Where had that come from?

"That's why you're here," she told him. "Why we came to retrieve Chimera Company at such cost. You're part of the plan now."

"Wait a minute. I said I'd help you. Not that we'd join your secret army."

"Too late now."

"We'll see about that. Who's running operations? You?"

"No. I'm just a senior agent. Redeal is run by Silent Hellion."

"Ooh! Nice codename. Can I have one?"

"No, again. I'm to take you to her. Just as soon as we've debriefed Ree and her two Kayrissans."

Fitz nodded. "Finally, someone is going to give me answers."

"No." Wei laughed. "Silent Hellion is going to give you orders."

The mysterious woman removed her gold glasses. *Now,* she was smiling.

* * * * *

Chapter Fifty-Seven:
Osu Sybutu

Secret Planetoid Base, Deep Space

The three sappers of the Legion sat in silence, buttocks planted on the padded seating curved around one of the antechamber's pillars.

Osu was deeply contemplating the friends he had lost. And Urdizine, who he'd left behind on Rho-Torkis. Colonel Lantosh, too.

This bare space seemed designed to encourage contemplation. They were here to await a mission briefing from someone senior in this shadowy branch of the Legion. Osu took comfort from the ghostly presence of the jacks who had waited in this place over millennia. He was with the true Legion here.

The only decoration was a fabric hanging that covered one wall. It depicted several planets of which he recognized only Earth. That feature was different. In other respects, the space was identical to ancient blast-strengthened bunkers he'd seen before, right down to the shade of midnight blue coating the walls. A color that was supposed to be calming for humans subjected to severe mental strain.

Behind those walls would be a latticework of shock-absorbent ceramalloys. The core of the pillar he sat against would be an extrusion of the same advanced material. The ceiling would be an armored dome maybe twenty meters thick at the center.

This planetoid in the depths of nowhere was a fortress. And he could see the Legion had built it. Long ago.

The other two SOTLs had also picked up on the Legion essence of the place. Fitzwilliam hadn't appeared to. He paced around the place in animated discussion with his wife and partner.

The rest of Chimera Company engaged in nervous small talk. Except for Enthree. The Muryani trooper was excitedly asking questions for which no one had answers. She did that a lot, even though they all said openly she knew more than any of them.

Only Kanha Wei shared the contemplative silence of the SOTLs from Rho-Torkis. She'd swapped her Navy uniform for the leather jerkin and calf-length polished boots of smuggler chic, but the mutant retained a Legion core as resilient as the ceramalloy running through the pillar at his back.

Osu was a little surprised Zavage was sitting with him and not Green Fish.

A faint smile came to his lips. The pair had used the journey here to acquaint themselves with each other.

And what a journey it had been! *Steadfast* had jumped conventionally until dropping off Ree and the cat sisters. After that, the ship had traveled here in a sequence of short jumps across interstellar space, far away from any gravity wells. It meant *Steadfast* had new jump drive technology.

Osu's instincts told him this wouldn't be the last of the surprises to hit him.

"What I don't understand is how anyone knew this planetoid was here," said Zan Fey, passing nearby in the wake of Fitzwilliam's pacing.

"I know," said the captain. "Technically, we're within the Oort Cloud of the nearest star, 31-Ferax, but Ferax is over a light year away. The chances of locating a tiny place like this must be minuscule."

Osu interrupted. "Look at this place." They stopped and looked at him in surprise. "This wasn't *found*. It was built and then towed here. Or directed in some way."

"Very good," said a voice from behind the hanging picture of the ancient worlds. It was a woman's voice. Human and surprisingly young. Strangely accented too.

Wei had referred to Silent Hellion as *her*. Was this the commander of Operation Redeal?

"This facility was placed here in the early days of the Federation," said the hidden voice. "There are several secret trails of planetoids like this. They predate the invention of the jump drive. The early Federation had too many enemies, so they made these bolt holes. They remain an impressive accomplishment."

Fitzwilliam faced the hanging picture. "Are you seriously telling me this organization, Operation Redeal, or its predecessor, *towed* this world here?"

"Not quite. It was our rivals and co-rulers who moved this planetoid to its current location. My forces captured it. I led the assault myself."

"*You* did?" Osu got to his feet. "Ma'am, what are you implying?"

The hanging curtain rolled up into the ceiling. The wall behind slid away to reveal a wizened old woman atop a plump cushion on a wooden chair.

Wei saluted her. "Chimera Company, this is your commander. This is Silent Hellion."

Hellion? The name didn't suit the woman.

She wore something functional and dark that might have been a ship suit, her body poking out of it like a bundle of gnarled twigs lashed together by sinew cords. A tight-fitting cap dug into her scalp. Unlike her clothing, the cap was plump and full, and he wondered whether life support machinery was inside.

She had the diminutive stature of an ancient Spacer, the same as Khallini. But she looked much older. Perhaps she was simply shrunken with age. A great deal of age, judging by her skin which was like cracked candle wax. She was a desiccated being who shouldn't be alive, held together by technological sorcery and the strength of will to clutch onto the spark of life. Osu could see that powerful will blazing in her eyes.

He'd half expected those eyes to be purple, but they weren't.

This woman had been a regular human, once.

"Lord Khallini, as that wixering ass-turd has decided to call himself, has stopped circle jerking with his pet AIs and moved into the open." The woman's voice was so young, it felt eerie to hear her speak.

Silent Hellion rubbed at an ugly flap of skin on the side of her neck. An old scar perhaps? "So, I guess it's time for me to do the same. It means I get to finally wipe that smugness off your face, Kanha." She licked her lips as if tasting the pleasure of the moment. "One thing first. Kanha, didn't it ever occur to you that my name is freaking stupid for a bent old woman?"

"No, ma'am."

"Then you lack imagination. Do better in the future. Silent Hellion was my gaming handle, back when I was a kid growing up on a starship. Before I was forced to start the killing. I miss my youth. *It was cut short.*"

Silent Hellion's lower lip quivered. The skin flap on her neck trembled too.

He noticed a matching patch of skin on the other side of her neck.

They were gills!

Gills…implanted so she could command a fleet of water-filled Littorane warships.

Osu sank to his knees and bowed his head and slapped his hand to the tattoo over his breast.

Tears came to his eyes.

He heard others whispering prayers and dropping to their knees too.

"Shite!" said the old woman and issued curses in languages Osu did not know. "You stole my big reveal. At least you show some intelligence, Sergeant Sybutu. You may lift your eyes. I'm not a sodding goddess."

He watched as she removed her cap and shook out glossy lilac hair that glowed in amethyst strands.

"I hate this damned thing," she said, throwing the cap to the floor. "Mader zagh! Itches like a bitch."

Osu noted that Kanha Wei was as shocked as everybody else.

"Let's get this over with," said the immortal lady. She pointed at Sybutu, and he felt his heart quicken. "Legionary, take off your shirt. You too, Kanha."

Both removed their clothing and stood, turning so the others could see.

The comparison was obvious, but he stared at the tattoo over Wei's left breast the same way she was staring at his. At the lilac-haired girl inked into their flesh.

Then they looked back at the ancient woman the young girl had become. The Immortal Empress.

"There she blows! Yes, you weak-kneed pussies. I'm here. I'm real. And I'm hissing mad at how you dungering asshole turd brains have pissed over the Federation I bequeathed you. It's time you made amends."

Izza spoke with an air of reverence. "What must we do, Immortal Empress?"

"First, you can stop calling me empress. Someone dreamed up that freaking stupid-ass title centuries after I left for a long-overdue retirement. You can address me as ma'am because that's good manners, or admiral because that was the rank I earned. No. On second thoughts, the regular military would explode with confusion if they found an admiral not on the current payroll. You may call me ma'am or Lady Indiya. Is that clear?"

Osu didn't think ma'am would cut it for him, so he replied, "Yes, my lady." That was worse. He sounded like Fitzwilliam talking to Zan Fey.

"Second," she continued, "stop splitting yourselves up, chasing your own tail, and getting yourselves captured. I didn't set up Chimera Company to go gallivanting on adventures. You have important jobs to do. Fucking well do them."

"We're working for you, ma'am?" Osu asked.

"You have been, right from the start. I have scores of other teams, but I like yours the best. You're all so different from each other, and that makes for a killer team backstory. Plus, you've got the coolest name. *Chimera Company*. You know why I like it so much?"

"No, ma'am."

"Because I didn't come up with it. Gives me hope there are still a few sparks of intelligence within the Federation, and I haven't wasted my valuable time coming out of retirement to fix the mess you made. Honestly, you're such a bunch of useless cretins. I'm glad my husband—bless his soul—isn't around to see what you did to his legacy."

No one spoke. How could they? Osu had sent prayers to this woman before battle. Half the Legion had, and the other half had her image inked into their flesh. What do you say to such a person?

Lady Indiya rolled her eyes. "Mother dog! I can't stand piglicking lollygaggers who are so overwhelmed by the obvious that they stand around with their jaws hanging open. I demand better of Chimera Company."

Osu knew what to do. He got to his feet and took a step toward the empress. "What is our mission, ma'am?"

"You, I like already, so don't disappoint me. See if you can tell me what you think your mission is."

"I don't know the tactical objective, ma'am, but our strategic purpose is to repel the invasion of the Federation by this…I know it as the Andromedan Corruption."

She regarded him coolly. Her denials of divinity were ineffective. It felt as if he were bathed in the indulgence of a goddess. "Satisfactory. You are essentially correct, except in one respect. I retired over a thousand years ago. Went on a grand tour of the Muryani Expansion and ended up touring the outer defenses across the galaxy."

Indiya pointed at Enthree. "Your Muryani trooper knows the error you made in your statement. Explain it to him, Enthree."

The alien bug flopped in what might have been a curtsy. "Sergeant Sybutu, the Andromedans care nothing about conquest as we understand it. Politics or trade are of no interest to them. No negotiation is possible. Andromeda is not even their origin. It is a staging area. The Triangulum Galaxy is their origin, or at least, their attacks on Andromeda were launched from that direction. They wish only to absorb all biomatter and corrupt it to their own genetic code. The invasion is not of the Federation. It is of the entire galaxy."

Damn! She'd known this all along!

Zan Fey cleared her throat. "We are but thirteen people and one ship, Admiral Indiya."

"Fourteen," Fitz corrected. "You forgot Oouzo. And two ships. And an unreliable droid."

"Fourteen," said Zan Fey. "We are but fourteen—"

"And Nyluga-Ree and the Guild, let's not forget—"

"Fitz!"

"Sorry."

"We are but a handful of people. How can we make a difference in a war between galaxies?"

Lady Indiya flicked the question away with her hand, disappointed with it. "Even the unreconstructed legionary can answer that," she spat. "Can't you, boy?"

Osu stood proudly. "When you can't win fairly, cheat."

"Good. We stack the deck." Lady Indiya rose to her feet. A sack of old bones she might be, but there was plenty of strength to her movements. "You, Chimera Company, are the card at the bottom of my deck. It's time you were dealt."

# # # # #

About Tim C. Taylor

Tim C. Taylor lives with his family in an ancient village in England. When he was an impressionable kid, between 1977 and 1978, several mind-altering things happened to him all at once: Star Wars, Dungeons & Dragons, and 2000AD comic. Consequently, he now writes science fiction novels for a living, notably in the Human Legion and Four Horsemen Universes. His latest project is an adventure serial called Chimera Company, which has been described as Warhammer 40,000 in the style of Star Wars. For a free starter library of stories from all the worlds he writes in, join the Legion at humanlegion.com.

* * * * *

Looking for the Latest in Scifi Goodness?

Come join us on the Factory Floor on Facebook!

Meet us at: https://www.facebook.com/groups/461794864654198/

* * * * *

AUTHOR' NOTE

Get More Chimera Company!

If you want to keep up with the news on the latest season, you can check out the Chimera Company page on https://humanlegion.com/, where you can also download prequels and join the Legion to get the latest skinny on my stories and learn about the Chimera Company Insiders.

There are three prequels so far, featuring the Militia, Legion, and Special Missions (with Vetch, Osu, and Bronze on the covers). You can download some for free from the Chimera Company page, and the rest by joining the Legion at humanlegion.com.

I'm going to write at least two more Chimera Company novels. I would love to write more, but for that to be a reality, the series needs to sell well. Spreading the word and leaving positive reviews are things you can do to help it succeed.

Thanks for reading.

Tim Taylor—June 2020.

* * * * *

The following is an
Excerpt from Book One of the Singularity War:

Warrior: Integration

David Hallquist

Available from Theogony Books

eBook, Paperback, and (Soon) Audio

Excerpt from "Warrior: Integration:"

I leap into the pit. As I fall in the low gravity, I run my hands and feet along the rock walls, pushing from one side to another, slowing my descent. I hit the pool below and go under.

I swim up through the greenish chemicals and breach the surface. I can see a human head silhouetted against the circle of light above. Time to go. I slide out of the pool quickly. The pool explodes behind me. Grenade, most likely. The tall geyser of steam and spray collapses as I glide into the darkness of the caves ahead.

They are shooting to kill now.

I glide deeper into the rough tunnels. Light grows dimmer. Soon, I can barely see the rock walls around me. I look back. I can see the light from the tunnel reflected upon the pool. They have not come down yet. They're cautious; they won't just rush in. I turn around a bend in the tunnel, and light is lost to absolute darkness.

The darkness means little to me anymore. I can hear them talking as their voices echo off the rock. They are going to send remotes down first. They have also decided to kill me rather than capture me. They figure the docs can study whatever they scrape off the rock walls. That makes my choices simple. I figured I'd have to take out this team anyway.

The remotes are on the way. I can hear the faint whine of microturbines. They will be using the sensors on the remotes and their armor, counting on the darkness blinding me. Their sensors against my monster. I wonder which will win.

Everything becomes a kind of gray, blurry haze as my eyes adapt to the deep darkness. I can see the tunnel from sound echoes as I glide down the dark paths. I'm also aware of the remotes spreading out in a search pattern in the tunnel complex.

I'll never outrun them. I need to hide, but I glow in infra-red. One of the remotes is closing, fast.

I back up against a rock wall, and force the monster to hide me. It's hard; it wants to fight, but I need to hide first. I feel the numbing cold return as my temperature drops, hiding my heat. I feel the monster come alive, feel it spread through my body and erupt out of my skin. Fibers spread over my skin, covering me completely in fibrous camouflage. They harden, fusing me to the wall, leaving me unable to move. I can't see, and I can barely breathe. If the remotes find me here, I'm dead.

The remote screams by. I can't see through the fibers, but it sounds like an LB-24, basically a silver cigar equipped with a small laser.

I can hear the remote hover nearby. Can it see me? It pauses and then circles the area. Somehow, the fibers hide me. It can't see me, but it knows something is wrong. It drops on the floor to deposit a sensor package and continues on. Likely it signaled the men upstairs about an anomaly. They'll come and check it out.

The instant I move, the camera will see me. So I wait. I listen to the sounds of the drones moving and water running in the caves. These caves are not as lifeless as I thought; a spider crawls across my face. I'm as still as stone.

Soon, the drones have completed their search pattern and dropped sensors all over the place. I can hear them through the rock, so now I have a mental map of the caves stretching out down here. I wait.

They send the recall, and the drones whine past on the way up. They lower ropes and rappel down the shaft. They pause by the pool, scanning the tunnels and blasting sensor pulses of sound, and likely radar and other scans as well. I wait.

They move carefully down the tunnels. I can feel their every movement through the rock, hear their every word. These men know what they are doing: staying in pairs, staying in constant communication, and checking corners carefully. I wait.

One pair comes up next to me. They pause. One of them has bad breath. I can feel the tension; they know something is wrong. They could shoot me any instant. I wait.

"Let's make sure." I hear a deep voice and a switch clicks.

Heat and fire fill the tunnel. I can see red light through the fibers. Roaring fire sucks all the air away, and the fibers seal my nose before I inhale flame. The fibers protect me from the liquid flame that covers everything. I can feel the heat slowly begin to burn through.

It's time.

* * * * *

Get "Warrior: Integration" now at:
https://www.amazon.com/dp/B0875SPH86

Find out more about David Hallquist and "Warrior: Integration" at:
https://chriskennedypublishing.com/

* * * * *

The following is an
Excerpt from Book One of Murphy's Lawless:

Shakes

_____

Mike Massa

Available from Beyond Terra Press

eBook and Paperback

Excerpt from "Shakes:"

"My name is Volo of the House Zobulakos," the SpinDog announced haughtily. Harry watched as his slender ally found his feet and made a show of brushing imaginary dust from his shoulder where the lance had rested.

Volo was defiant even in the face of drawn weapons; Harry had to give him points for style.

"I am here representing the esteemed friend to all Sarmatchani, my father, Arko Primus Heraklis Zobulakos. This is a mission of great importance. What honorless prole names my brother a liar and interferes with the will of the Primus? Tell me, that I might inform your chief of this insolence."

Harry tensed as two of the newcomers surged forward in angry reaction to the word "honorless," but the tall man interposed his lance, barring their way.

"Father!" the shorter one objected, throwing back her hood, revealing a sharp featured young woman. She'd drawn her blade and balefully eyed the SpinDog. "Let me teach this arrogant weakling about honor!"

"Nay, Stella," the broad-shouldered man said grimly. "Even my daughter must cleave to the law. This is a clan matter. And as to the stripling's question…

"I, hight Yannis al-Caoimhip ex-huscarlo, Patrisero of the Herdbane, First among the Sarmatchani," he went on, fixing his eyes first on Volo and then each of the Terrans. "I name Stabilo of the Sky People a liar, a cheat, and a coward. I call his people to account. Blood or treasure. At dawn tomorrow either will suffice."

439

Harry didn't say a word but heard a deep sigh from Rodriguez. These were the allies he'd been sent to find, all right. Just like every other joint operation with indigs, it was SNAFU.

Murphy's Law was in still in effect.

* * * * *

Get "Shakes" now at: https://www.amazon.com/dp/B0861F23KH

Find out more about Myrphy's Lawless and Beyond Terra Press at: https://chriskennedypublishing.com/imprints-authors/beyond-terra-press/

* * * * *

Printed in Great Britain
by Amazon